Wartime Friends

Margaret Dickinson

Wartime Friends

MACMILLAN

First published 2022 by Macmillan
an imprint of Pan Macmillan
The Smithson, 6 Briset Street, London EC1M 5NR
EU representative: Macmillan Publishers Ireland Ltd, 1st Floor,
The Liffey Trust Centre, 117–126 Sheriff Street Upper,
Dublin 1, D01 YC43
Associated companies throughout the world
www.panmacmillan.com

ISBN 978-1-5290-7791-9

1 3 5 7 9 8 6 4 2

A CIP catalogue record for this book is available from the British Library.

Typeset in Sabon by Palimpsest Book Production Ltd, Falkirk, Stirlingshire
Printed and bound by CPI Group (UK) Ltd, Croydon, CR0 4YY

Visit **www.panmacmillan.com** to read more about all our books
and to buy them. You will also find features, author interviews and
news of any author events, and you can sign up for e-newsletters
so that you're always first to hear about our new releases.

For all my family and friends for their love, encouragement and help throughout the years

ACKNOWLEDGEMENTS

Even though this is, as always, a work of fiction, I do a great deal of research to try to get the background details as correct as possible. I am always very grateful to everyone who kindly shares their knowledge and expertise with me, and throughout all the years I have been writing, the library services have been unstinting in their support by obtaining unusual – and sometimes out-of-print – books and often actually researching on my behalf. This year I am particularly grateful to the staff of the Lincolnshire and Leicestershire Library Services.

I also wish to thank Peronel Craddock at Bletchley Park Trust; Kathy Phillips, chairman of the Loughborough Library Local Studies Volunteer Group; Lynnette Webster for information on Gibraltar Point, Skegness; Barry Watson for guidance on F. W. Woolworth & Co. Ltd.; and all the staff at Beaumanor Hall in Leicestershire when I visited to carry out research there.

There are many other sources of information, most notably for this novel: *England Needs You: The Story of Beaumanor Y station, World War Two* by Joan

Nicholls (Joan Nicholls, 2000); *Skeggy! The Story of an East Coast Town* by Winston Kime (Seashell Books, 1969); and *The Story of Gibraltar Point* by Barrie Wilkinson (Lincolnshire Wildlife Trust, 2018). My love and grateful thanks to Helen Lawton and Pauline Griggs for reading and commenting on the early drafts, and as always to my fabulous agent Darley Anderson and his team, to my lovely editor Trisha Jackson, and to all the wonderful team at Pan Macmillan.

One

Lincolnshire, October 1938

Carolyn cycled along the narrow coast road towards Gibraltar Point. The bicycle wobbled precariously as the wind from the sea buffeted her. Just over the sandhills to her left were salt marshes, dunes and eventually the beach and the North Sea. She held on to the handlebars tightly, ignoring the gusts blowing up the skirt of her maroon uniform. She smiled to herself. At least on this lonely road and at just gone six o'clock in the evening there was no one to see her immodesty. The town was quieter now after the busy summer months; the holidaymakers had all gone and the residents had their town to themselves once more.

'We've got the best of both worlds,' Carolyn would always say defensively if anyone dared to criticize her home town. 'Bustling with life and people enjoying themselves in the summer, and peace and quiet in the winter.'

It was over two miles to cycle home from her job at the Woolworth store in the centre of the seaside town of Skegness, but she loved hearing the sound of the sea and breathing in the fresh, salty air. It was not quite as far as she'd had to cycle to attend the town's grammar school. The school had begun life as the Magdalen College School in Wainfleet, but had transferred to a new building in Skegness in 1933. Carolyn had transferred with it, staying on until she was eighteen to take her Higher Matriculation Certificate, which she'd passed with flying colours. She'd been so proud to wear the green and gold school uniform and even prouder when her younger brother, Tom, had followed her there. He still pedalled the three miles or so to school and back every day, his satchel heavy on his back.

Carolyn Holmes was tall and slim with dark brown hair falling in soft curls and waves to her shoulders, brown eyes that sparkled with mischief and smooth skin that was lightly tanned from the sun and the wind on her cycle rides. She was enjoying her job although she hadn't expected to do so. She'd wanted to go to a good secretarial college to learn shorthand and typing as her ambition was to work in an office. It was still her dream, but her mother had insisted that she find employment as soon as she left school.

'Staying on until you're eighteen, indeed. It's ridiculous. What good is higher education for a girl who is only going to get married, run a home and bear children? I left school when I was twelve and was working in service by the time I was thirteen, but your father insisted that you should stay on so – for once – I gave way to him.' Her mother, Lilian, had sniffed disapprovingly. 'You could've been bringing money into the home for the past four years at least, to say nothing of helping me about the house and looking after your grandad.'

Carolyn had held her tongue. It did her no good at all to argue with her mother. She always tried to help with the housework and nearly every day, either before or after work, she cycled to the large farmhouse where her grandfather, Frank Atkinson, still lived, but on his own now since the death of his wife three years earlier. Carolyn took the meals which her mother cooked for him, brought washing home for Lilian to launder every Monday morning and returned it, washed and ironed, later in the week. On Sunday mornings, before attending church with the whole family, she cleaned Frank's kitchen, living room and bedroom and scrubbed the wooden seat of the outside privy. On her half-day off from work, she either blackleaded the range in Frank's kitchen or polished the copper pans hanging in a shining row in his scullery. But there was no point in reminding Lilian of these facts. The only answer Carolyn was likely to get was: 'And so you should'.

Now, she took the right-hand turn to the farm instead of going straight on to her home, which stood at the side of the road, yet still on Frank Atkinson's land. It was what was known as a tied cottage. It belonged to the farm and was usually occupied by the family of one of the farm's workers. As indeed, in a way, it still was. Her mother, Lilian, still helped out on the farm at busy times. Carolyn's father, Eddie, worked for his own father, Norman Holmes, who was the local carpenter and wheelwright. His home and workshop were on the main road leading south out of Skegness towards Boston, but they were within easy reach through the rough tracks across the fields. Frank's farm was a large one and stretched from the coast road inland to the main road. He employed three farmhands; his own son, Harold, Harold's son, Adam, and Peter Carter. Peter also lived in a tied cottage on the northern edge of the farm with his widowed mother, Phyllis. She worked in Frank's dairy and also helped in the farmhouse too. There was an uneasy alliance between Lilian and Phyllis. Lilian suspected that Phyllis was 'after' Frank and his money, but what held the two women together was their mutual desire to see Peter and Carolyn marry.

As she neared the farmyard gate, Carolyn could see her uncle, Harold, and her cousin, Adam, locking up the barns, which signalled the end of their working day. Harold had built himself a house at the north end of the farmland, midway between the coast road and the main road, with lanes leading to both.

'Nah then, lass,' was his greeting as he clicked the last padlock into place. 'How's work gone today?'

'All right, Uncle Harold, thanks.' She nodded to Adam, who gave her a cheery wave as he went towards the hen house to secure it from prowling foxes.

'Not what you want to be doin', though, is it?' Harold was tall and broad and always dressed in workaday clothes, except for church on Sunday, when he donned his one and only smart lounge suit. He had an abundance of dark hair for a man approaching his forties with not a strand of grey to be seen, though it was usually covered by his cap.

Carolyn laughed merrily, her eyes dancing. 'I

wouldn't want anyone to think that I consider such work's beneath me, cos it isn't. I like the job and the other folk who work there. They're a great bunch.' She sighed. 'But for some reason I don't quite understand myself, I always fancied working in an office. I went into a solicitor's in town once and the girls working there, tapping away on their typewriters, just looked so – so . . .'

'Ladylike?' her uncle volunteered.

Carolyn threw back her head and roared with laughter. 'Ladylike? Me? You need your eyesight testing, Uncle Harold.'

Harold chuckled. Her uncle was rather a solemn man, but Carolyn always seemed to get him to smile. 'You've grown into a pretty lass, Carolyn. Don't ever let anyone tell you different. Now, me an' Adam had best be getting home, else yar aunt Eve'll have a ducky fit. Tea's always on the table at half past six an' she dun't like us being late. Ta-ra, love.'

Carolyn's aunt's 'ducky fits' were legendary though in truth they didn't frighten any of the family; they were used to them and just waited until they'd blown themselves out, rather like one sat out a thunderstorm. Carolyn loved her Aunty Eve dearly. Despite her fiery temper, Eve was good-hearted and generous. She would help anyone. Carolyn had to admit that she would always rather confide in Aunty Eve than in her own mother. Of medium height and slim with a lovely figure, Eve always dressed smartly, wearing a hint of make-up and a pale pink lipstick even when working around the house and the farm, her short, red hair tamed into neat sausage curls. Her one treat of the week was to go into town for the day every Wednesday to have lunch with a couple of her friends and then go to the cinema. Lilian frequently sniffed her disapproval. 'She'd do better to stay at home and look after her family instead of gallivanting. She'll find she hasn't time to go gadding about once Harold takes over the farm and she has to move into the big house.'

Lilian was bitter about the fact that Harold, even though he was two years younger than she was, would inherit the farm eventually. She would only be left the cottage and a few acres around it where she and her family lived now. Lilian totally ignored the fact that as her husband was an only child he would undoubtedly take over his parents' house and their business too. It was the perceived unfairness that she resented.

Carolyn leaned her bicycle against the wall of the farmhouse and entered by the back door. She stepped into the washhouse and then into the scullery on the left and from there into the kitchen.

'Hello, Grandad,' she greeted the old man sitting beside the roaring fire in the grate of the range. Even though he was small in stature, he was still wiry and strong for his age. His grey, almost white hair was parted in the centre and smoothed back. He was dressed as always in black corduroy trousers, striped shirt and black waistcoat – his working clothes. It was almost a uniform for farmers and their workers; Harold, Adam and Peter always wore similar attire. Only on Sundays did Frank, like the others, change into his one good suit to attend church. He had removed his heavy boots and was toasting his toes in front of the fire, his feet resting on the fender. He glanced up and gave Carolyn a wide grin. Apart from the time when his wife had died, Frank Atkinson was rarely seen without a smile on his wrinkled face and it was always a positive beam when his granddaughter came to visit.

'Want me to set the table for your tea, Grandad?'

'Aye, lass. That'd be nice. There's a meat pie warming in the oven that yar mam brought over this morning.'

While Carolyn busied herself setting a place for him at the table, they chatted.

'How's work going?' he asked.

'All right. They're nice people to work with and I enjoy meeting the customers.' She bit her lip to stop herself saying any more.

'But it's not what you wanted, love, is it?' he said softly, repeating exactly what her uncle had said only moments earlier. 'You should have gone to that secretarial college in London you told me about. I offered to pay for it, you know, if it'd been needed.'

Carolyn's eyes widened. This was news. Tears sprang to her eyes at his kindness. 'That was lovely of you, Grandad.' She forced a smile. Trust her mother not to tell her that such an offer had been made.

'Don't give up hope. Mebbe one day, eh? Keep the Faith.'

Carolyn grimaced. 'Not if Mam and Mrs Carter get their way.'

'Don't you listen to them two old biddies, lass.

You carve your own future. If you don't want to marry young Peter, then don't. He's a nice enough lad, a hard worker, and I'm very fond of him, but I wouldn't want you to marry anyone just to please yar mam.' He gave a wheezy laugh. 'But don't you tell 'er I said so, else there'll be no more meat pies for me tea.'

Her visit ended on a laugh, but as Carolyn cycled home she was still thinking about her grandfather's words. Although nothing had ever been voiced, she was pretty sure that her father agreed with the old man. She remembered the arguments there'd been between her parents over her staying on at school into the sixth form. Eddie, a quiet, placid man most of the time and thought by some to be hen-pecked, would stand up to his strong-minded wife when the occasion demanded. He had won that particular round, but he had lost the dispute over the secretarial college. Carolyn lifted her face to the breeze and a small smile played on her mouth. Heartened by Frank's words, she had hope for the future now. Her future.

Two

When she arrived home, Carolyn found her brother Tom struggling to get a large, oblong box through the back door.

'That looks heavy. Let me give you a hand.' She took one end and together they carried it inside.

'Where do you want it?'

'In the front room, please, Caro.'

'Radio parts, is it?' Carolyn guessed.

'It's a wireless set. Mr Fox got it for me.' George Fox was Tom's science teacher. He was helping the boy to build a radio transmitting and receiving set. Tom was fast becoming a keen amateur wireless enthusiast. 'He reckons I'll have a much wider scope with this one to listen in to transmissions in the North Sea, ships and that. Maybe as far as the countries across the water.'

'What? Like Holland?'

Tom nodded as they manoeuvred the cumbersome box into position on Lilian's dining table, now set beneath the window to accommodate Tom's wireless equipment. 'Maybe even Germany and Denmark.'

They stood back and looked down at it. 'Thanks, Caro.'

'Well? Go on. Open it.'

Together they unpacked the box, carefully setting

the oblong-shaped instrument with its strange dials and switches on the table.

'Is this a new one?'

'New to me, but it's not brand new – they cost a fortune – but it is a later model than the one I've been using.'

'D'you know what to do with it all?'

'Not yet.' Tom grinned. 'But I will. Mr Fox said he'll come out here on Saturday morning and show me how to connect it up and get it working. That's if Mam doesn't mind.'

Carolyn gave an unladylike snort of laughter. 'Mam doesn't mind anything her blue-eyed boy wants to do. You should know that.'

Tom straightened up and frowned before saying hesitantly, 'I admit she does spoil me. Does it – does it – upset you?'

Carolyn laughed. 'Heavens, no. I'm as daft as a brush with you myself. You can twist me round your little finger.' Then her smile faded as she added, 'But with Mam, I think it's a mother-and-son thing. Just mind it doesn't get worse as you grow up. Mother love is wonderful, but smother love is something completely different.'

Tom glanced at her from behind his round spectacles, his mousy-coloured hair falling over his forehead in an untidy flop. He grinned, his hazel eyes twinkling. 'No, I won't let it get out of hand, but at the moment . . .' He winked broadly and she pretended to be shocked.

'You young rascal. You're leading her on, aren't you, and getting just what you want?'

'Am I very dreadful?'

'Course not.' She leaned towards him as she whispered, 'I'd do exactly the same, if I could, but it doesn't work for me.' She sighed. 'I can't seem to get what I want.'

'I wish I could help.' He was pensive for a moment before saying slowly, 'Couldn't you teach yourself typewriting and Pitman's shorthand?'

Carolyn pulled a face. 'I might manage to learn shorthand from books, but I'd need a typewriter.'

'I reckon Dad – or Grandad – would get you one. Might only be second-hand, but it'd do, wouldn't it?'

'Of course. Anything would do to learn on, just so long as it works.'

Tom rubbed his nose; it was a habit he had when he was thinking. 'Mr Fox's wife is a secretary. She might know of someone who would teach you. I'll ask him on Saturday, because you'll be at work then, won't you?'

Carolyn nodded. Her half-day off each week was on a Thursday, the town's early-closing day. On Saturdays she had to work all day for it was one of the store's busiest days of the week, but she couldn't help a little thrill of hope running through her. It was worth Tom asking his teacher, even if it came to nothing.

On the Saturday morning, Lilian made a great fuss of Tom's teacher when he arrived on his bicycle.

'Do come in, Mr Fox. Would you like a cup of tea? It's a cold ride out here all the way from town.'

'That would be most acceptable, Mrs Holmes. Thank you,' George said as he took off his overcoat and removed his bicycle clips. In his mid-forties, he was slim in build, round-shouldered and not very tall. He was almost completely bald, with just wisps of hair growing above each ear. He wore thick, horn-rimmed spectacles, behind which his blue eyes were bright and sharp. George Fox missed nothing that was going on, as many a miscreant in his class had found to their cost. But he was a kindly man and, for all those pupils who behaved and worked hard, he couldn't do enough.

'Let me take your coat,' Lilian said. 'Do go through to the front room. Tom's waiting for you. There's a nice fire in there. I'll bring the tea in to you.'

Teacher and pupil greeted each other and then sat down in front of all the mysterious paraphernalia that Tom and Carolyn had set out. George's eyes gleamed. 'This all looks wonderful, Tom. I think you've got everything you need now.' They worked side by side, Tom following George's instructions as they set up the wireless. They were interrupted only by Lilian, who brought in a tray of tea and biscuits. She hovered a moment wanting to engage George in conversation, but both he and her son were so engrossed that she left the room quietly. She sighed. Mr Fox wouldn't even notice his surroundings: the front parlour, which she was so proud of; the china cabinet with its delicate bone china tea service, which was never used because it was so precious; the bookcase with its pristine volumes of the classics – Dickens, Thackery, Austen, Shakespeare and the poets, Wordsworth,

Keats and Tennyson. She'd never read any of them but she liked to possess them and to show them off. Neither would Mr Fox notice the watercolours that adorned the walls, for he only had eyes for Tom's wireless. It had, if she were being totally honest, been a wrench to let Tom have his equipment under the front-room window – to give up her best room. But then, it was for her son and his future.

'There,' George Fox said half an hour after the door had closed behind Lilian. 'I think we're ready. Turn her on, Tom.'

'Why do you call it "her"?'

George laughed. 'Men always seem to call their machinery "her". Goodness knows why, unless it's because they spend a lot of time with them and lavish considerable attention on them.' He grinned. 'As I expect you will be doing with this little beauty.'

As the wireless came to life with crackles and spits, George murmured, 'You will have to learn Morse code, you know, to take real advantage of this.' He pointed to the telegraph key. 'But you're all set up now.'

'How would I go about learning it?'

'If you come home with me after school one afternoon a week for a while, I'll start you off. It's not easy, but like anything, practice makes perfect. You can start by communicating with me from here. That way, I'll know how you're progressing. We'll agree a time each evening to get in touch.'

Tom knew that George Fox was a dedicated radio ham and had been for several years. A bedroom in his home was given over to his hobby.

'That's very good of you, Mr Fox.'

George shrugged. 'Any learning is never wasted, Tom.' At school, boys were called by their surnames, but here, in his own home, the teacher was thoughtful enough to use the boy's Christian name. 'And a knowledge of Morse code might come in useful,' he added mildly.

Tom nodded. He was not deceived. Their school was go-ahead and forward thinking. The older pupils were kept well informed about the political situation and what was happening in the world. Tom was one of them. He and his peers were fully aware of the unrest in Europe, of the rise in power of Adolf Hitler in Germany and of Benito Mussolini in Italy and also about the Spanish Civil War that had been going on for two years.

'There is something else I would like to ask you.' Tom was a little hesitant. He didn't want to be seen as trying to take advantage of the man's good nature. 'It's just advice really.'

'Fire away.'

'It's about my sister, actually.'

'Carolyn? Yes, I remember her. I taught her for a year.' George Fox had taught briefly at the Magdalen College School before transferring to the newly built school in Skegness too. 'She dropped science after that to concentrate on the arts, languages and such. Go on.'

Even though they were alone in the room with the door firmly closed, Tom lowered his voice. 'She wants to learn shorthand and typing so that she can find work in an office. It's what she'd really like to do.

The shorthand she might be able to teach herself, but the typing's a bit more difficult. She's been reading about it and says there's a way of touch typing where you don't have to look at the keys – but she doesn't know how to go about it, or whether she'd need someone to teach her.'

'Yes, I do know quite a lot about it, as it happens.' George smiled. 'My wife is an expert touch typist. She went to the Queen's Secretarial College in London. An excellent establishment. I'm sure your sister would get in there or somewhere similar if . . .'

He paused when he saw Tom shaking his head. 'That's what she wanted to do when she left school this summer. She wanted to go to that very same college you've just mentioned, but Mother wouldn't let her.' Tom flushed a little, as if he felt he was being disloyal to their mother, as he added, 'She – she thinks a good education is wasted on a girl – that they're only going to get married.'

George's eyes flashed momentarily with anger. It was an argument he'd heard so often and not one he subscribed to. He paused for a moment and pursed his mouth. He needed to rephrase the retort that had automatically come to his lips. With a calculated mildness he was not feeling, he murmured, ' "A woman's place is in the home", eh?'

'Something like that.'

It was a saying that never failed to enrage George. So many bright young women had never been given the chance they so richly deserved. 'As I said, education is never wasted, not even' – he smiled impishly for a moment – 'on girls.'

15

He paused and then went on, more seriously now, 'People have short memories, you know, Tom. They are forgetting – probably in a lot of cases, conveniently – how women rallied to the cause during the Great War. They left hearth and home and took on the jobs that the men, rushing to be heroes, had left behind. They did everything from driving ambulances and trams, working on the buses and railways, to teaching. Where do you think our schools and the present generation of young people would be now if it hadn't been for women stepping up?'

'Yes, we've been learning a little bit about it in history with Miss Collinson, though she doesn't dwell a lot on the war. Perhaps it's too recent. She probably thinks some of us might have lost someone.'

'As indeed did she,' George murmured. He paused and then added, 'I'm sure I can trust you, Tom, to keep a confidence.'

Tom nodded solemnly.

'She lost her fiancé on the Somme in 1916. I don't think she will ever get over it.'

'I'm very sorry to hear that.' Tom paused and then added, 'She's a nice lady. My dad didn't have to go. He works for his own father, who has the wheelwright and joinery business on Wainfleet Road, and it was considered heavily related to agriculture. But I think he almost wishes he had gone. White feathers, and all that.'

'Was he given one?' George's tone was sharp.

'I don't know. I've never asked him. It's not a subject we ever talk about. The war, I mean. And Peter Carter's father was killed on the Somme, I think.'

'Yes, I remember Peter from school too. Bright lad, if I remember correctly, though he didn't stay on after the statutory school leaving age, did he?' George was thoughtful for a moment before saying, 'Teaching was a reserved occupation during the war, but I was handed a white feather by a woman in the street. I was so mortified that I went straight to the nearest recruiting station and signed up. It was a foolish thing to do, but I was only young then, newly qualified and not hardened to taking criticism for not being in uniform.'

'Was it very bad?'

George was silent for a long moment. 'We don't talk about it, Tom, none of us do because we can't bear to. All I'll say is that it was indescribable hell. I was very lucky to come back with hardly a scratch, but I did have what they call shellshock for a while.' He smiled sadly. 'I suppose in one way I was very lucky. I was drafted into what is now known as the Royal Corps of Signals, hence my continuing interest in communications.'

'Some of my classmates lost their fathers, uncles and even grandfathers,' Tom said. 'Peacock lost his own dad, his dad's dad and his dad's brother. His poor grandmother has worn black ever since, he says. Isn't it awful to lose a husband and two sons?'

'Indeed it is. There was a family in Lincoln where a mother lost five of her eight sons. They all served in the war, but only three returned and one of those suffered life-changing injuries, so I was told.' After a long silence between them, George went on quietly, 'So you see, Tom, if another war does come and you are trained – or even partially so – in operating a wireless and you have a knowledge of Morse code too, you might be very useful in a non-combatant role. I wouldn't want you or any of our boys' – he referred to all the pupils of the school where he taught as 'our boys' – 'to become just cannon fodder. So, I will help you all I can and I will speak to my wife about your sister too, because if there is to be another war – and I'm sad to say it is looking increasingly likely – then this time, I think, girls and women will be conscripted. If she, too, has a useful skill at her fingertips – quite literally . . .' He smiled at Tom. '. . . she would undoubtedly find a valuable position in one of the services.'

'That's if Mam would let her.'

'I don't think,' George said drily, 'that your mother would have any say in the matter if Carolyn were to be conscripted.'

Three

By the following Monday evening, Tom had news for Carolyn, but it wasn't until the family had eaten and she had helped Lilian clear away and wash up, that she had time to sneak into the front room to speak to her brother alone.

In a whisper, Tom told her, 'Mrs Fox is willing to teach you touch typing, but she says you'll need a typewriter at home to practise on. I shall be going to Mr Fox's after school one day a week. Perhaps we could go on the same day. He's going to teach me Morse code. I thought I'd ask him if a Thursday was convenient. That's your half-day. You could go then, couldn't you, and we could meet up there?'

Carolyn's eyes lit up. 'That's so lovely of her. How much will she charge me?'

Tom blinked. 'Oh, I never thought about that and he never said. He doesn't charge me, so . . .'

Carolyn frowned. 'I wouldn't expect her to do it for nothing.' She was thoughtful for a moment, then she sighed. 'It's very tempting. It's what I want, but I don't think Mam will agree to me having a type-writer anyway.'

Tom chuckled. 'Go and talk to Grandad Atkinson. He supported your plan to go to college, didn't he?'

Carolyn eyed him and a slow smile curved her generous mouth. 'You're a rogue, Tom Holmes. D'you know that?'

Tom just grinned, flicked back his hair and shrugged.

After attending church on the Sunday morning, Carolyn cycled to the farm carefully transporting a dinner in her bicycle basket. She was both nervous and excited at the same time about what she was going to ask her grandfather.

'You're a good lass,' Frank said, as he sat down to eat the meal she had warmed in the range oven and laid before him. She sat down opposite him as he ate, eager to speak to him, yet not wanting to interrupt his meal. When he'd scraped the last of the custard from the bowl of apple crumble, he sat back with a satisfied sigh. 'A little nap in me chair by the range wouldn't go amiss now, afore I have to get back to me work.'

'You work too hard, Grandad. Let the others do it.'

He chuckled. 'Aye, I could. Yar uncle is quite capable of running things with Peter to help him and even young Adam. They're all willing workers, but old habits die hard. I like to give them a day off on a Sunday, but animals still need to be fed. I like to feel I can still be useful and, besides' – his face clouded for a moment – 'since yar granny went, the house is a lonely place, so I like to get outside as much as I can. Still, let's not dwell on things we can't change, eh?' He paused and looked at her thoughtfully. 'Now,

20

if I'm not mistaken, there's summat you want to say to me. I can see it in your face. Out with it then, lass.'

Carolyn took a deep breath. 'Tom has found out that his science teacher's wife, Mrs Fox, is a trained touch typist and she'd be willing to teach me.' She rushed on telling him all that Tom had suggested before Frank could answer.

Frank was thoughtful for a few moments before saying. 'D'you know how much she'd charge you?'

Carolyn shook her head.

'If you can't manage it out of your own wages, then let me know. I'll make a contribution.'

'I can't let you do that, Grandad.'

'Of course you can.' He chuckled. 'It'll be a lot cheaper than paying for you to go to that fancy secretarial college, though I'd've been willing to do that if only your mam had let you.'

'That's the one that Mrs Fox went to.'

'Is it really? She should be good, then? Does she work?' He chuckled and his old eyes twinkled. 'Outside the home, I mean.'

'Part-time, in an office somewhere, I think. Mornings only, so Tom said, but she's sent word that she's willing for me to go to her on a Thursday afternoon on my half-day off.' She bit her lip, hesitating to say more.

Frank eyed her shrewdly, his mind working quickly. Then he guessed what was troubling her. Mildly, he said, 'You'll be needing a typewriter, won't you? You'll need to practise a lot, I'm thinking, to get to the speeds an employer would be looking for.'

Frank had spent his whole life on his family's farm, rarely venturing to the 'bright lights', but he was well read and very knowledgeable. What he didn't know, he soon found out. And wisdom had come with his advancing years.

'I – I suppose so.'

'I'll keep a watch out for one when I go to market each week. Don't worry, lass. I'll sort that out for you.'

The following week, Frank arrived at his daughter's house in his farm truck on the way home from the market. It was not an unusual occurrence. He often called to have dinner with his daughter and son-in-law after the early morning auctions. Eddie cycled home for his midday meal on three days each week. On the other working days, he had his dinner with his own parents. It was an arrangement that suited them all. Eddie knew his mother still liked to feed him now and again. But he always made sure to cycle home on market day when he was able to enjoy a natter with his father-in-law.

As the three of them sat down around the table, Frank said conversationally, 'I sold three beasts this morning, Eddie. Got a good price for 'em an' all, so I've treated my granddaughter to something I know she wants. I expect she's told you all about it.'

He hid his smile. He knew very well that Carolyn would have said nothing to both her parents yet; she might have confided in her father, but he doubted even that at this stage.

'Something she wants?' Lilian frowned. 'What are you talking about, Dad?' Before he could answer, she clapped her hands and her frown turned into a wide beam. 'Oh, has Peter proposed? Is she planning a wedding?'

'Good Lord, no,' Frank's tone was sharp. 'Whatever gave you that idea?'

'Because it's high time there was a definite under-standing between them.' Her mouth tightened. 'I bet it's not him holding things up. It'll be her with her airs and graces, reckoning she's too good for a farm labourer. She'll lose that lad, if she's not careful, and then I'll be mad.'

'She's only eighteen, Lilian,' Eddie put in and earned himself a glare from his wife that would have halted a charging bull.

As Lilian opened her mouth, Frank spoke again, trying to draw the expected tongue-lashing away from Eddie. He was very fond of his quiet son-in-law and didn't want to cause trouble between them. 'As I was saying,' he went on mildly, but quite firmly, 'Carolyn wants to learn to touch type and she's found someone who is willing to teach her.'

'Who?' Lilian snapped.

'Mrs Fox. Wife of Tom's science teacher.'

Now Lilian was flummoxed. The last person in the world she wanted to offend was the man who was helping Tom so much with his hobby and no doubt with his schoolwork too. It was important for a boy to have the best education he could get. Lilian had aspirations for Tom that the rest of the family didn't yet know about.

When she'd first found out that Adam was to inherit the farm eventually, she had been very bitter.

'What about our Tom?' she had railed to Eddie in private. 'He should have a share of the farm.'

The only response Eddie had been able to give was to say mildly, 'We must follow your father's wishes, Lilian. Besides, I'm my parents' only child. Perhaps your father had that in mind. No doubt the business will come to me and I can leave it to Tom.' Beneath his breath so that Lilian didn't hear, he'd murmured, 'If he wants it.'

Lilian had sniffed. 'Knowing them, they'll leave a stipulation that you're to divide it between Tom and Carolyn.'

'Would that be so bad?'

'She'll have a husband to care for her. It's Tom who'll need a livelihood.'

But as the years had passed, Lilian had changed her mind. Adam could have the farm, she'd decided. Her Tom was better than that. He was going places. University, if she had anything to do with it. But for that, she needed to keep on the right side of his teachers.

'How – how did that come about?' she asked Frank now.

'I really have no idea,' her father said blandly.

Lilian was thinking quickly. The girl couldn't have talked to Mr Fox herself on Saturday morning; she'd been at work. So . . . ? No, surely Tom hadn't had anything to do with this.

'She'll need a typewriter to practise on at home,' Frank went on, blithely ignoring the conflicting emotions flitting across Lilian's face. 'So I kept me eye open and I was lucky enough to find one today at the market. And a proper typist's chair to go with it. As I understand it, you have to have a proper chair so that you don't get back trouble.'

More clutter in my best parlour, Lilian thought morosely. *She'll have back trouble when I've finished with her. Backside trouble, because I'll tan it for her.*

Little more was said as they ate the pork chops which Lilian had cooked, followed by stewed rhubarb and custard. Lilian was fuming, as both men knew, but they carried on eating calmly. When they'd finished, Lilian crashed the plates together as she cleared them away.

'Perhaps you'd give me a hand with Carolyn's things, Eddie, will you, and then I can give you a lift back to the workshop? We can stick your bike in the back of the truck.'

They carried the typewriter and chair into the front room and set the machine on a small table on the opposite side to where Tom had his wireless laid out.

'I hope I haven't caused you any bother, Eddie,' Frank said in a low voice, 'but I reckon that lass should have her chance.' He nodded towards the radio equipment. 'Nowt seems too good for young Tom. This lot must have cost you a pretty penny.'

'Mr Fox got a lot of it for him, and no, it weren't cheap, but I look at it this way: if we are edging towards another war, having a skill like this might keep him out of the fighting.'

Frank nodded slowly. 'Yes, you're right and I don't blame you. But just think, Eddie, if we do go to war again, young women will be expected to do their bit an' all. Even more than they did last time. They might even be conscripted and, if they are, our Carolyn is already old enough to be called up. To be honest with you, I don't have a lot of faith in the prime minister's piece of paper that they're making such a song and dance about.'

At the very end of the previous month the newspapers had been full of Mr Chamberlain's visit to Munich to meet with Hitler, Mussolini and others. Under the agreement, reached after almost twelve hours of conference, the Sudeten region of Czechoslovakia, where many German-speaking people lived, would be handed over to Germany.

'It's an appeasement, just to keep Hitler quiet,' Frank went on, 'but for how long, Eddie? You answer me that. Hitler will never be satisfied until he's trampled across Europe again. To my mind, he's determined to finish what the Kaiser couldn't. And you know as well as I do what that'll mean. So, let's you and me band together to keep that lass safely behind a desk and yet still serving her country, if we can.'

Eddie Holmes, at just forty-two years old, was broad and stocky in build, but with the slight sign of a middle-aged paunch just beginning to show as a result of all the satisfying meals his wife cooked. His sandy-coloured hair was thinning now, but he always wore a cap when out of the house and a trilby on Sundays to attend church. He liked a peaceful life and gave in most of the time to his wife's demands, but he wished now that he had taken a firmer line over Carolyn's wish to go to college. At the time, he'd believed what Lilian had said; that Carolyn and Peter were fond of each other and likely to marry.

But he was beginning to realize that perhaps he'd been wrong about that. So now he was keen to take his father-in-law's advice and help Carolyn achieve her ambition.

He would do anything to help keep his lovely daughter out of the dangers that another war would bring.

Four

'Just what do you think you've been up to, you little madam?'

Lilian was waiting for Carolyn as she stepped through the back door at just gone half-past six that evening. Carolyn blinked. Her mother was in one of her tempers and it was obvious that she was the cause of it in some way. But she had no idea what she'd done.

'Sorry, Mam, I don't—'

'Don't play the innocent with me. You've been wheedling your way round your grandad to get you a typewriter.'

Now Carolyn felt the colour flood her face. 'I didn't ask him, Mam. He offered.'

'Same difference. I expect you went whining to him that I spoil Tom, did you?'

Now Carolyn lifted her head and met her mother's hostile eyes. 'No, Mam, I did not. Whatever you do for Tom always has my backing.'

'I don't believe you. You're jealous of your brother. Always have been.'

'No, I'm not. He deserves everything you can do for him. I just don't understand why you can't let me do what I'd like to do.'

'Because you're a girl.'

Carolyn sighed. It was the old argument. It was never going to change. 'Mam, why can't I just do this one thing? I'll keep working at Woolworth, I promise.'

Lilian shrugged, flapped her hand towards her daughter and then turned away. 'Oh, do what you like, then. But to my mind, you'd be better off learning how to cook and sew and keep house. Anything else is a waste of time – and money.'

With her mother's agreement, albeit a grudging one, Carolyn took off her coat and scarf and went into the front room to find Tom. Just inside the door, she stopped and her mouth formed a round 'oh'.

Tom was grinning at her. 'Evidently, Grandad brought them at dinner time on his way home from the market.'

Carolyn closed the door behind her and moved across the room to put her hand on the chair and touch the typewriter. It was a black Imperial and even though it was second-hand, it had obviously been well looked after. 'No wonder Mam's mad.'

Tom chuckled. 'Yes, she was a bit short with me when I got in from school. I expect she guesses I've had something to do with finding someone to teach you. Anyway, I told her that Mr Fox is willing for *me* to go to his house after school on a Thursday to help me learn Morse code. What I *didn't* tell her' – his grin widened – 'is that you're going to go the same day and we can cycle home together.'

'That's perfect. Thanks, Tom. I hope Mam's not going to be funny with you, though.'

The boy, who was fast becoming a young man, shrugged. 'I've got broad shoulders. Or rather, I soon will have.'

'Has anything been said about what they'll charge us?'

Tom shook his head. 'I don't think it'll be much – if anything.'

The arrangement worked perfectly and though Lilian grumbled now and then about Carolyn not helping her about the house on her half-day off, she couldn't really stop it happening when she was so keen for Tom to do whatever he wanted. She didn't even have to pay for either of them; Mr and Mrs Fox insisted they were happy to teach the two willing pupils for nothing.

At home, the brother and sister worked together in the front room through the winter months. They hardly noticed the cold wind blowing in from the North Sea as they cycled to and from the town. They were both so engrossed in their hobbies. Carolyn's tapping on the typewriter keyboard didn't disturb Tom when he had his headphones on and the crackling and bleeping from his wireless didn't bother Carolyn, who concentrated hard on everything Mrs Fox had told her to do, even covering up her hands with a tea towel so that she couldn't look at the keys. Instead, she looked only at the sets of letters Mrs Fox had written out for her and kept to a steady rhythm – F, G, J, H – over and over again until she could type them perfectly without even taking a sneaky peek. Then she checked her typing on the sheet of paper for accuracy afterwards. Slowly but surely, she grew in confidence, gradually adding more and more letters on either side and on each row and finally the figures and symbols, until she could type everything on the keyboard without even glancing at it. Then, still keeping to an even tempo, as she practised more and more, her speed gradually increased. At the same time, Tom was progressing with learning Morse code.

'You know, I wouldn't mind learning that, Tom. Once you've mastered it, you could teach me, couldn't you?'

'I don't see why not.' He grinned up at her, his eyes crinkling behind his glasses and his hair flopping forward. 'Perhaps you could show me what Mrs Fox has taught you.'

Carolyn laughed. 'Of course I will, if you want, but I reckon Mam has something much better in mind for you than working in an office – unless, of course, you're the head honcho.'

As well as learning typing, Carolyn was also studying books on Pitman's shorthand, getting Tom to read simple passages out to her so that she could practise it. By the spring of the following year, Carolyn's speeds were improving steadily and she was also learning Morse code with her brother's help. They had even disappeared into the front room to pursue their interests on Christmas Day, after returning from the customary celebratory dinner at the farm. Frank, thoughtful as ever, had given Carolyn two reams of typing paper as her gift.

'Mrs Fox knows I'm learning shorthand in my own time and she has said she will check my progress with that too,' Carolyn told Tom happily when outside the front-room window the snow had disappeared and spring daffodils were poking their heads through the ground.

'You'll soon be able to apply for a job as a shorthand typist,' Tom said proudly.

Carolyn glanced at him and then looked away, but the pink tinge of colour creeping up her face made him add, 'You already have, haven't you? Do tell. I won't say anything. Scout's honour.'

Carolyn giggled. 'You're not a scout.'

Tom wrinkled his forehead as if that fact had escaped his notice. 'Oh no, I'm not, am I? But never mind, you know what I mean.'

Carolyn lowered her voice. 'There's a vacancy occurred in the office at work . . .'

'At Woolworth?'

Carolyn nodded. 'So I've applied for it. It's not as a typist, though. It's to help with the office paperwork, but I thought if I could get into the office there, it would be a good reference if I want to apply somewhere else in time.'

'Good for you.'

'Miss Simpson is going to talk to me. She's the one who takes on all the girls and women while the manager interviews the men for the stockroom. But, even if I don't get it, I won't lose my present job. She's already assured me of that.'

'That is good news.' Tom paused. 'Are you telling Mam?'

Carolyn shook her head. 'Not yet. If I get the post, then I will. I've told Grandad, though. He's thrilled.'

One bright morning in April, Carolyn made her way to the general office. Miss Simpson had already told her that she wouldn't need to spend long interviewing her formally because she already knew her well. In Miss Simpson's eyes, Carolyn Holmes was a girl who was conscientious, always willing to do whatever was asked of her and who never railed against the strict, but fair, regime of the company. She kept whatever counter she was assigned to well-stocked and tidy and every item correctly priced. She also knew that Carolyn had a quick mind, could do mental arithmetic quickly and accurately – even without the aid of a ready reckoner – and she always looked smart in the company's maroon uniform. At the end of their talk, the woman smiled kindly at her. 'Well, Miss Holmes, I am happy to offer you the post, starting on the first of May, and there will be a small rise in your wages to two pounds a week.'

Carolyn's face flushed with delight. 'Oh thank you, Miss Simpson.'

'Because you've so recently worked on the shop floor and know the stock well, I'm putting you on checking invoices and you will be working in the main office with the two other girls. Do you know them already?'

Carolyn nodded. 'Joan Ingall and Mary Brown.'

'That's right. I said I was interviewing you and they both seemed pleased, so I think the three of you will get on well together. In fact,' her eyes twinkled, 'they both said it would be nice to have someone they already know joining them rather than a stranger.'

Miss Simpson had the reputation of being a tartar, but Carolyn had never seen that side of her. Perhaps that was because she had never needed to be hauled up in front of either Miss Simpson or the manager to be reprimanded.

Carolyn almost floated down the stairs and took her position behind the counter selling children's clothing and toys, her head still in the clouds.

'You've been a long time,' the girl who worked with her remarked. 'Yar not in trouble, are ya?'

Carolyn shook her head. She knew she mustn't say anything to anyone at work yet, so she'd already formulated a plan if she should be questioned by her workmates. Luckily, Miss Simpson was in charge of the first-aid cupboard.

'I needed a couple of aspirin, that's all.'

Jill nodded sympathetically. 'Poor you. I get migraine sometimes. It's the very devil, isn't it?'

Carolyn bit her lip at the white lie as she nodded. 'I'll be fine in about half an hour. Right, looks like we've got customers. You go up that end. I'll serve these two little boys.'

With that, the girl moved away to the other end of the counter and Carolyn forced herself to concentrate on her work; it wouldn't do for the supervisor to have cause to complain about her now.

But she could hardly wait to cycle home and tell her grandfather, father and Tom. She knew they'd be pleased. She wasn't sure what her mother's reaction would be, but she could make a shrewd guess.

Five

'You've done what?'

'I applied for a job in the office at Woolworth and got it,' Carolyn repeated patiently, but she couldn't stop her heart beating a little faster and her fingers trembling. 'I start on the first of May. We do the same hours as the girls in the shop – five and a half days a week with a half-day on early-closing day.' She knew she was gabbling, but it was the only way to forestall her mother's reaction and, by the look on Lilian's face, Carolyn wasn't going to like what she was about to hear. And she didn't.

'You've lied to me.' Lilian jabbed her finger towards her daughter. 'You've deceived me. You never said this typing nonsense was to get another job. Why can't you ever be satisfied? Your place, my girl' – now she prodded Carolyn in the chest – 'is keeping house for your husband and, God willing, a family.'

'And if I get married, Mam, then that's what I'll be happy to do, but—'

'There's no "if" about it. You've a nice young man with his tongue hanging out to go out with you, but Miss High an' Mighty thinks herself too good for the likes of Peter Carter. Even his mother calls you a stuck-up little cow.'

'So why is she so keen for me to marry her son if that's what she thinks of me?' Carolyn shot back, for once unable to keep the ready retort in check. 'And besides, for your information, Peter has never asked me to go out with him.'

'He's shy, that's why. He needs a bit of encouragement.'

'Oh, so now you're telling me to throw myself at him, are you?'

The argument was becoming heated and if Eddie hadn't arrived home at that moment, neither of them knew what it might have escalated into. As it was, Lilian turned towards Eddie as he entered the kitchen. 'Will you talk some sense into your daughter?'

Eddie blinked. 'Oh dear, what have you been up to now, love?' He tried to make his tone stern, but Carolyn could sense he was struggling to hide his laughter.

'She's only given up her job to chase after one in an *office*, that's all.' Lilian's tone was scathing. She made it sound as if Carolyn had gone to work on the streets.

'I haven't given anything up, Dad. There was a vacancy in the office at work. I applied for it and I got it.'

'Still at Woolworth, then?'

Carolyn nodded.

'So . . .' He glanced between them, perplexed. 'What's the problem? It sounds as if it's a better job.'

'It is. I get a bit more pay and I'm not standing on my feet all day.'

As if Carolyn hadn't even spoken, Lilian said,

'She's been deceitful. I didn't realize all this typing nonsense was for her to get another job. I thought it was just a hobby. She'll be wanting to learn Morse code next.' Carolyn bit her lip and tried to stop the colour flooding her face. Tom was already teaching her and he'd said she was coming along quite nicely with it. Even Mr Fox had said as much.

'I won't be using my shorthand and typing very much. It's to help with the paperwork in the office,' Carolyn tried to explain, but her mother hadn't finished her rant yet.

'She should be satisfied with the nice job she's got until she gets married.'

Now Eddie raised his eyebrows. 'Married? This is the first I've heard of it. Somebody asked you, have they, love?'

Carolyn shook her head. 'No, but Mam and Mrs Carter seem about ready to book the church and organize a reception.'

'You and young Peter? Are you walking out together?'

'No.'

'Then why on earth . . . ?'

Lilian clicked her tongue against her teeth in exasperation. 'You know very well he's sweet on her. Always has been. And she could do a lot worse than Peter Carter.'

'And perhaps she could do a lot better,' Eddie said mildly.

'Oh really? A working man not good enough for her? Well . . .' Lilian glared at her husband. 'It had to be good enough for me, didn't it?'

Eddie turned away, but not before Carolyn had seen the bleak, hurt look on his face.

Carolyn started her new position at F. W. Woolworth on Monday, 1 May. As she walked out of the church near the centre of the town on the last Sunday morning of the month, she caught up with Peter.

'Hello, there. Haven't seen you for a while. Are you all right?'

'Oh . . .' For a moment, he turned startled eyes towards her, almost as if he hadn't expected to see her there, even though they both attended Matins almost every week.

'Caro! I was just thinking about you.'

Carolyn's heart dropped. Oh dear! She saw Peter glance behind him, a little nervously, she thought. She didn't need to look round; she knew Lilian and Peter's mother, Phyllis, were walking together. Softly, he said, 'Could we go for a walk this afternoon? Down to the Point, maybe?'

Peter was tall and slim, but his build belied his strength; working on the farm he was certainly no weakling. Though his expression at the moment was serious, when he smiled his face lit up and his laughter was infectious.

Keeping her tone light, Carolyn said, 'That'd be nice. Call for me about two. All right?'

As she fell back to wait for her grandfather to drive her mother and herself home in his truck – Eddie and Tom cycled to church, rain or shine – she couldn't fail to notice the same beaming smile on the faces of both her mother and Mrs Carter.

Considering they were not related, Lilian and Phyllis Carter were remarkably similar in both looks and character. They were both slim with greying hair drawn back from their faces. Both dressed drably in browns and blacks and both had pinched, dissatisfied faces. On most weekdays, they were always to be found in pinnies, only donning their better clothes to go into town to shop or on Sundays to attend church. Neither ever wore make-up. In fact, they were disparaging of Eve Atkinson, calling her 'fast'.

'I don't know what she saw in our Harold,' Lilian had often confided to Phyllis. 'Nor he in her. Anyone less likely to make a good farmer's wife, I've yet to meet.' As it had turned out, however, Lilian had been wrong; Eve was a very good farmer's wife, a wonderful mother and family member. She was never afraid to put on an overall or a smock – even wellingtons – and pitch in to help with whatever needed doing. She'd been known to put her arm right inside a cow to help with a difficult birthing; something even Lilian had never done.

Lilian and Phyllis were not exactly friends – they tolerated one another – but they were united in their goal to see their children joined in marriage.

'What did he say? Did he ask you out?' Lilian couldn't contain her curiosity as they climbed into the bench seat in the front of Frank's truck.

'We're going for a walk this afternoon,' Carolyn said shortly and avoided her mother's penetrating gaze.

'Then mind you wear something pretty.'

Carolyn tried to suppress her laughter, but it

escaped as an undignified snort which she managed to turn into a cough.

'Mind you wear summat warm, lass,' was Frank's only advice. 'It can be cold at the Point, even at this time of the year.'

It was her grandfather's advice she took; she loved the Point, where the land and the sea seemed to meet the sky. It was wild and lonely and desolate, with seagulls wheeling and diving overhead, their cries filling the air, but it was not the warmest place Peter could have picked for a proposal, if that was what this was. She fervently hoped not, but there was only one way to find out.

They walked side by side, the wind almost blowing them along.

'It'll be tough going back,' Peter said. 'Head wind then. Maybe we shouldn't . . .'

'No, I'm fine, honestly. Just what I need to blow the cobwebs away. Come on, I'll race you to the Hump.'

They walked and ran the last half-mile to the small hill in the road that led them directly to the marsh area, but over the final few yards Peter beat her easily and turned to face her, a huge grin on his face. 'You're getting soft in that office job of yours already. Sitting at a desk all day. And you've only been there a month.'

Playfully, Carolyn punched his shoulder gently. 'Don't *you* start.'

'Actually, I want you to know that I'm really proud of you for learning other skills to get a better job. I think it's great.'

Carolyn's eyes widened. 'Really?'

'Yes, really. How's it going? Are you enjoying it?'

'I'm loving it,' Carolyn said. 'But actually, at the moment, I don't use my shorthand and typing. Not there anyway.'

The two had been friends from childhood and Peter knew almost as much about her as she knew herself. They had cycled to and from school together. Played together and worked on the farm together, especially at 'tattie picking' time. And often, they had been each other's confidant.

'It's a stepping stone for you, though, isn't it?' Peter guessed accurately. 'Your next job – in an office of your choice – will need that sort of expertise. I'm so pleased for you. I just wish I'd been able to stay on and take my school certificates, but – well, you know the reason I couldn't.'

She knew only too well. Peter had been obliged to leave school as soon as he was old enough to find work to help support his widowed mother. Frank had been pleased to give him work on his farm.

Gently, Carolyn asked, 'I know you couldn't, but just supposing you could have stayed on at school, what would you like to have done?'

'Gone to university,' Peter answered without a moment's hesitation, but then he added with a wry grin, 'that's if I'd been clever enough.'

'I'm so sorry you didn't get the chance you deserve.'

Peter shrugged, but he couldn't hide the disappointment in his eyes. 'Don't get me wrong, Caro. I love working for your grandfather. He's a grand boss.

And I do like the outdoor life and I love where we live, even if it is a bit remote.'

'But it's not what you would have chosen to do.'

'It's just that, sometimes, I wish I'd seen a bit more of the world. But please don't tell anyone what I've said, will you?'

'Of course not.' Carolyn laughed. 'We've always shared each other's secrets and I have certainly never told another soul anything you've confided in me.'

'Me neither,' he said smiling.

They walked on in silence, reaching the very edge of the Point and then walking even further along what the locals called the Spit, a promontory of land jutting right out into the sea.

At the very end, with the cold North Sea lapping around three sides of them, Peter sought her hand and held it. 'Caro, I . . .'

'Please, Peter, don't say it. I don't want to hurt you. I love you dearly as a *friend*, but nothing more. I – I'm so sorry . . .'

She felt his hand tighten around hers and then he said, 'Oh, thank the Lord for that.' He threw back his head and laughed aloud, the sound carried away on the wind. 'Oh Caro, my dearest, dearest friend, you don't know how happy I am to hear you say that.' Then he looked down at her, his fair hair unruly in the wind, his hazel eyes full of affection and his weather-tanned face creased in smiles. 'I have agonized over this for weeks – months even. How stupid I've been not to have spoken to you about it before now. Do you truly mean it?'

Carolyn was laughing and crying at the same time.

Relief flooded through her. 'Oh Peter. We've both been foolish letting our mothers put such ideas into our heads.' Then her laughter died. 'What are we going to do about them? They'll be so dreadfully hurt and disappointed.'

'I don't think we need to say anything to anyone just yet. I still want to see you as a friend, so they won't notice anything different because there won't be.' He paused and his voice took on a serious tone, 'Caro, you do know there's a war coming, don't you?'

Startled, she turned to face him and looked up into his eyes. 'What?'

He sighed. 'Don't your parents ever talk about it?'

She shook her head.

'Don't you hear it spoken about at work?'

Now her voice was husky with fear as she said, 'No. No one's said a word.'

'And you don't read the newspapers?'

Again she shook her head. 'Mother won't have one in the house. She says they're all lies anyway.'

'But the radio? You have a wireless, surely?'

'Tom has.'

'Does he listen to the news?'

'I – I don't know. I don't think so. I've never asked him. It's not really that sort of wireless.'

'And your grandfather or even the Foxes? Haven't any of them said anything?'

'No, they haven't.' Now Carolyn felt angry. She suspected that she had been kept in the dark deliberately about national and international affairs and now she felt foolish and naive.

'I think, Peter,' she said slowly, as they turned away from the end of the Spit and began to walk back the way they had come, 'you'd better tell me everything you know.'

Six

'Start at the beginning,' Carolyn encouraged him.

Peter ran his hand through his hair. 'Trouble is, there are different views on where the beginning really is. Your grandad thinks that the Great War never really decided anything. That we've just had a twenty-year truce.'

'You've talked about it to Grandad?'

'Oh yes. He's a grand chap to talk to. He has such a balanced, common-sense view about – well, about everything.'

'He wasn't *in* the war, though, was he?'

'No, but your Uncle Harold was. Mind you, like all of 'em, he won't talk about it.'

'He went at seventeen, just for the last year of the war,' Carolyn said. 'I do know he volunteered, even though he had no need to. He wouldn't have been called up either, being in agriculture. Mam says it nearly broke Granny's heart.'

'He came back, though, didn't he, and without a scratch? He was lucky.'

'Very, but I sometimes wonder if that's why he's a bit quiet and solemn. Maybe there are things he can't talk about and yet he can't forget them either.' She paused and then added, 'Tom knows a bit more than I do about what's going on now. I think they have discussions about it in class at school. He was saying that our prime minister went to Germany last September and signed a peace agreement with them. What's the name of the chap in charge there now? In Germany?'

Peter blinked, amazed that Carolyn should be quite so ignorant of what was going on outside the confines of her own little world. He thought that, by now, she would at least have heard talk at work.

'Adolf Hitler.'

'And who is he?'

'The chancellor of Germany.'

'Oh yes, now I do remember learning about that when I was still at school. They don't have a king or an emperor anymore, do they?'

'No. They had the Kaiser but when he lost the Great War, he abdicated and went into exile in the Netherlands. I think he's still alive but now Hitler has assumed control. The only person who really stood between him and complete power for a time was the president, Hindenburg, but in January 1933, Hindenburg, by then an old man, actually appointed Hitler as chancellor in an effort to prevent a civil war between Hitler's National Socialists and the Communists. When Hindenburg died eighteen months later, Hitler abolished the role of president, proclaimed himself führer and Reich chancellor and appointed himself supreme commander of the armed forces, demanding an unconditional oath of obedience – not to the position, but to himself personally. And so, that way, he obtained absolute power. He's a dictator, Carolyn, and they're dangerous.'

'They've got one in Italy, haven't they? I do know that much.'

'Yes. Mussolini. He gained overall power in 1925 and then began flexing his muscles in 1935 by invading Abyssinia.'

'So is Hitler sort of copying him, d'you think?'

Peter smiled. At least Carolyn's grasp of the situation was sharp now that she was being told what was happening.

'More than likely. He's certainly learning a thing or two from him. Hitler's a strange man really. Not much to look at, but he seems to wield some sort of fascination. His speeches arouse such a fervent response in the crowds that they all stand and give the Fascist salute, chanting *"Sieg heil"*.'

'What does that mean?'

Peter smiled wryly. 'I didn't know, so I looked it up. It means "Hail victory". It's become the chant of Hitler's Nazis, usually accompanied by a straight, right-arm salute. Either that or *"Heil* Hitler".'

'And who are the Nazis?'

'The full name is The National Socialist German Workers' Party. He's rearming Germany and is also fostering racism, particularly against the Jews. He wants to build a master race of pure Aryan blood, as he calls it, and he's banned German-Jewish marriages.'

'That sounds evil to me.'

'It is, Caro. In thirty-six, Hitler reoccupied the Rhineland, contrary to the terms of the Versailles agreement, but he proposed a new treaty for twenty-five years' peace. There have been rumblings the last couple of years, but Britain's been preoccupied at home with the jobless marches, the death of the King and then the abdication, which no one saw coming. Behind the scenes, though, the RAF was quietly aiming to treble its strength, so I think there were a few who still saw Hitler as a threat even back then. A couple of years ago he started to call for more living space for the German people. Now, how do you get that?'

Carolyn stared at him as she whispered hoarsely, 'By taking it from neighbouring countries.'

'Exactly. In March last year, he marched into Austria, welcomed, it has to be said, by much of the population, who seemed delighted to be incorporated into the German Reich. I read somewhere that at that time Austria was a very poor nation and they thought that being a province of Germany would bring them prosperity. Not so universally popular, however, was the handing-over of the Sudeten region of Czechoslovakia in the Munich Agreement, which was seen as a way to prevent another war in Europe.'

'That was what Mr Chamberlain's famous piece of paper was about, wasn't it? I did hear someone at work talking about that and saying that there wouldn't be a war because the prime minister had got – now what did they call it?'

'"Peace for our time".'

'That was it, yes.'

'But it wasn't, Caro. It was anything but. Hitler

wasn't going to stop there. Six months later, in March this year, he broke that agreement, overran the rest of the country and marched into Prague. But this time there was no welcome for him as there had been in Austria and even, to some extent, in the Sudetenland. We seemed to wake up then and our prime minister has now pledged to defend Poland should it be attacked. Hitler and Mussolini are a dangerous pair, Caro. Only this last week they signed what they call a "Pact of Steel".'

'Ah. I can guess what that means and it doesn't sound good for the rest of mainland Europe, or even for us.'

'Exactly.'

They walked in silence for a while before Peter said, 'Our government is now quietly preparing for war. Air-raid shelters are being set up, especially in London, and plans for the evacuation of children are being made.'

They came to the Hump again and stood on top of it. They turned to face the path they had just walked. To their left was marshland and beyond that the beach. To their right, the river flowed towards the sea. Boats moored on the banks bobbed as the tide rose and then were stranded on the mudbanks when the water ebbed. Birds wheeled overhead, their cries the only sound above the wind and the waves.

'I love this place,' Carolyn murmured. Then she shook herself and turned her attention back to what Peter had been telling her.

'How do you know all that?'

'I read the papers and – like I said – I've been

talking to your grandad. D'you know what he said to me?'

Carolyn shook her head.

' "Everyone will think he's going to come across the Channel at the narrowest point," Mr Frank said, "and perhaps he will, but I know what *I*'d do if I was Herr Hitler and I wanted to invade England." '

'What did he say?' Carolyn whispered.

'Your grandad said he'd land on our East coast, where the land is flat and the population sparse. No cliffs to scale, very little in the way of defences while all our troops would be concentrating on defending the South Coast.'

'He – he means here?'

'Precisely.' Peter waved his arm, encompassing the inlets from the sea leading to the river. 'At high tide, he'd have no problem.' And then he gestured to the flat farmlands behind them. 'And just think of his troops swarming inland with no one to stop them.'

'Oh Peter, don't.'

'Caro,' Peter said softly, but there was a determination in his tone now. 'If war does come, I shall volunteer.'

Her eyes widened. 'Must you? I mean, won't they have reserved occupations like they did last time? Being a farm worker, you could get an exemption.'

'I want to go, Caro. I want to see a bit of the world. I can't just stay here all my life. I – I feel like I'm stagnating.' Swiftly, he added, 'Oh, don't get me wrong. Your grandad is wonderful to work for, but – I suppose I've just got itchy feet and this would be a chance to do something worthwhile.'

'Helping to feed the nation is worthwhile, Peter.'
His only answer was to kick a stone and watch it
roll down the slope, so she asked gently, 'What does
your mother say?'

'I haven't told her yet,' he muttered.

Carolyn said no more but she could imagine Mrs
Carter's reaction; she would throw what the Holmes
family called 'a ducky fit'.

Lilian was hovering near the back door when Carolyn
let herself in.

'Well?'

Carolyn blinked, pretending to be mystified.
'Well . . . What?'

'What happened? Did he propose? Are you walking
out together officially now?'

'We're not walking out, Mam, officially or otherwise. We're just very good friends. Always have been
and, I hope, we always will be.'

Lilian opened her mouth, but Carolyn cut her off.
'Where's Tom? I need to talk to him.'

Lilian sighed. For once, she seemed to realize she
was beaten. At least for the moment, but she'd have
plenty to say to Phyllis Carter the next time she saw
her, which was likely to be the following morning.
She'd go to the farm a little earlier than usual and
catch Phyllis before she left.

For now, all she said was, 'He's where he usually
is. In the front room playing with his wireless set.'

Carolyn pursed her mouth grimly. If what Peter
had been telling her was true, Tom's 'playing' might
soon become a whole lot more serious. She opened

the door to the sound of bleeps and whistles as Tom leaned towards his radio, turning the tuning knob carefully until the dit-dit-dah-dah of Morse code sounded clear. Then he pulled a large writing pad towards him and began to write. Carolyn reached for a pad and pencil of her own, sat down beside him and began to jot down letters. She was not as quick as Tom – not yet, she told herself – and what appeared on her paper was a jumble of meaningless letters. Tom, however, was writing recognizable words.

After a while he stopped scribbling and sat back.

'What are you picking up?' Carolyn asked him.

'Just fishing boats at the moment.'

'At the moment,' Carolyn whispered and brother and sister stared at each other. 'Tom, tell me what you know about the possibility of war coming. Peter's been explaining it to me, but I felt so ignorant. I know nothing. Do you discuss it at school?'

'Not in class, no. I think the teachers are wary of saying too much in case parents are keeping their kids in the dark.'

'As ours are,' Carolyn said wryly.

'But I talk about it to Mr Fox. This' – he waved his hand towards his radio equipment – 'is what it's all about, Caro. If there is a war, I should be able to listen in to German traffic in the North Sea. It could be very useful. Mr Fox plans to do the same.'

'But – who would you tell?'

'Mr Fox is going to make some discreet enquiries.'

'So, tell me everything you know.'

For the next hour they talked quietly, Tom

repeating much of what she'd already heard, but also filling in the gaps which Peter had left. It seemed her young brother knew an awful lot more about what was going on outside their small community than even Peter did.

'And then, of course,' Tom ended soberly, 'there are the Nuremberg rallies where Germany shows off its military strength. It's coming, Caro. There's going to be another war and we're going to be in the thick of it.'

Seven

On the last day of May, as Carolyn cycled home from work, she turned up the rutted lane leading to the farm. Frank was just finishing his tea.

'Grandad, why has no one told me that we're heading towards another war?'

Frank laid down his knife and fork across an empty plate and sighed. 'Because, lass, they want to keep you safely at home. I think we've all got the feeling that you'd want to rush off to "do your bit".'

Carolyn smiled wryly. 'I can understand that, because yes, I would and – I do.'

'Aye, I was afraid of that,' he murmured, then cleared his throat. 'Then, lass, you'd better come and sit with me by the fire and tell me what you have in mind.'

The fire in the range was kept going winter and summer for it heated the water in the back boiler, the oven for cooking and the hob for boiling kettles and pans. They sat on either side of the pegged rug which covered the hearth. He settled back in his Windsor chair, packed his pipe and waited patiently for her to begin.

'At this precise moment, I don't really know, but I suppose the women's branch of one of the services.

Surely I'd be able to put my new-found skills to good use.' She leaned forward and lowered her voice, even though there was no one else to hear. 'Don't you dare say a word to Mam, but Tom's been teaching me Morse code too.'

He chuckled. 'So, me and young Tom are going to share the blame, are we?'

She blinked at him and then, as realization of his meaning dawned, she said swiftly, 'No one will be to blame, Grandad, except me. I'd have done it anyway – learned to touch type, I mean – with or without your help.'

Frank gazed at his granddaughter's determined chin and pride flooded through him. 'What about you and young Peter?' he asked slowly. 'I heard your mam and Phyllis Carter going at it hammer and tongs on Monday morning in the kitchen. I think they thought I'd gone out so they didn't bother to keep their voices down. Such an argument, there was, about who was to blame for you and Peter not being engaged by now.'

'Peter and I went for a long walk together on Sunday to one of our favourite places. Right to the Point – to the end of the Spit, actually. We've sorted everything out between us. We're fond of each other – the very best of friends – but we don't want to walk out together and we certainly don't want to get married.' She grinned impishly. 'Not to each other, at any rate.'

'So, what are you going to tell your mamas?'

'Exactly as we have been doing. If we are asked straight out, then we tell the truth. Mam asked me on Sunday if we were walking out and if Peter had proposed, and I told her that we're just good friends. But they won't listen and they won't let it go.' Her face sobered. 'To be honest, Grandad, I think that very soon we'll all have something far bigger to worry about.'

'And you want to be part of it, do you, lass? Well, if you're asking for my advice, I'd look at the ATS.'

Carolyn frowned. 'What does that stand for?'

'The Auxiliary Territorial Service. It's the women's branch of the British Army. It was only formed last September.'

'How do you know all this, Grandad?'

The old man chuckled. 'Because I keep me eyes and me ears open. I read the newspaper . . .'

'You take a newspaper?'

Frank nodded. 'Every day. And I listen to me wireless. Just because we live out in the sticks doesn't mean we can't keep abreast of what's going on in the rest of the world.'

'So, why don't we see a newspaper? I know Mam's never wanted one before, but I'd've thought that now, with so much going on . . .'

'I've offered for your mam to take it home for Eddie to read – even if the news would be a day late by the time he got it – but she won't have none of it. Says she doesn't want such rubbish in the house. I rather suspect, lass, that she wants to keep you and Tom in what she thinks is blissful ignorance. Can't blame her, I suppose,' he mused and, as if it explained everything, added, 'She's a mother.'

'I won't do anything until war is actually declared,

but if it is . . .' Carolyn left the words hanging in the air between them. Frank merely nodded. He was saddened to think that the huge losses on both sides which his own age group had suffered in the Great War had not been enough to protect the next generation of fine young men and women from another conflict.

From that day onwards, Carolyn brought home a newspaper most days. Sometimes, one was left lying about at work and, ensuring no one still wanted it, she put it in her bag.

'I see you're interested in keeping abreast of what's happening,' Miss Simpson said to her one day.

'Yes, I am. I hope no one minds me taking them home. My mother won't allow a newspaper in the house so I have to be careful.' She smiled lopsidedly, feeling a little stupid at having to reveal such a thing. 'I even have to bring it back to work a day or so later to dispose of it. I daren't get rid of it at home. Tom, my brother, likes to see them too, but I understand my father reads a newspaper at work.'

'Where does he work?'

'For his father. He's Holmes the carpenter and wheelwright on the Boston road.'

'Ah yes, I know where you mean.'

There was silence between them. They were sitting together – just the two of them – in the staffroom, set aside for the workers to have their morning and afternoon tea breaks in. Miss Simpson cupped her hands round her mug as if warming them.

'So, what is your feeling about the news? Do you think there's going to be another war?'

Carolyn sighed. 'Sadly, I think it sounds very much like it.'

There was a long silence between them before Miss Simpson said quietly, 'Carolyn, your skills will be very valuable in the war effort. If the time comes when you feel you would like to volunteer, please be assured that I would not stand in your way. In fact, I would give you a glowing reference.'

'Thank you, Miss Simpson.' She hesitated a moment before confiding, 'Please don't say anything to anyone else, but I am learning another skill that might be useful. My brother is teaching me to read and transcribe Morse code.'

Her superior stared at her. 'Oh my goodness! Really?' A slow smile spread across her mouth. 'Then, my dear, the armed forces will be falling over themselves to sign you up.'

'I thought it was high time you had one of these.' Frank struggled in through the back door of his daughter's cottage carrying an oblong shape.

'What is it?'

'A wireless.'

'I don't want it. Don't you think we've got enough whistling and crackling in the house with Tom's equipment?'

Calmly, Frank placed the set on the table and began to clear a space in the centre of the sideboard.

'Look, Dad, it's kind of you, but I don't want it in the house.'

'Nonsense, Lilian. You'll enjoy all the variety

programmes.' He cast an arch glance at her. 'And you can keep up with what's happening in the world.'

Lilian pursed her mouth grimly. 'That's exactly what I *don't* want to do.'

'So, you all want to live in ignorance, do you?' Now there was a firm edge to Frank's tone. 'Lilian, you can't protect your children for ever. There's a war coming. You have to face it and you have to let them face it too because they're the ones who are going to have to deal with it.'

Lilian turned white and reached for the edge of the table with a trembling hand. She sat down suddenly. 'What d'you mean?'

'Get the kettle on, love. You an' me need to have a little chat.'

He sat down in a chair beside the hearth, pulled his pipe from his pocket and began to pack it with tobacco. With a resigned sigh, Lilian did as her father bade her.

'Now,' he began, when she had given him a cup of tea and a biscuit and sat down opposite him. 'You're my daughter, Lilian, and I love you very much. I even stood by when you had your bit of trouble even though your mother – God rest her soul – would have turned you out.'

Lilian flushed a bright red and hung her head.

'But I care deeply for my grandchildren too. All three of 'em. Adam's a good lad and he's doing well working for me. He'll make a good farmer one day. He's clever in a *practical* way but he's not the brightest button in the box when it comes to academic work.

Now, Lilian love, your two are bright, very bright, and they deserve to have a chance.'

Lilian lifted her head. 'To be shot and killed in a war, you mean?'

'No, I don't mean that at all.' His tone hardened. 'And it's very unfair of you to even think it.'

'Sorry,' Lilian muttered.

'It's the exact opposite, if you'll hear me out. I want them both to have skills that will keep them *out* of the front line. It's doubtful they'd send a girl to the fighting, but they might well send women into danger areas this time round. And as for Tom, well, if this war lasts as long as the last one, he'll be eighteen before it ends and he'd be called up and sent anywhere they—'

'Oh it won't last that long. In fact, I don't think there'll be one. Surely, they won't be daft enough to let it all happen again?'

Frank didn't answer but continued to puff at his pipe. Then he prodded the stem of his pipe towards her. 'If you'd only listen to the news or read the papers, you'd know it's getting very serious. This feller Hitler is very bitter and resentful about the Versailles Treaty signed at the end of the Great War. He felt his country was treated very shabbily. The Allies were not magnanimous in victory. Even I have to admit that. They extracted revenge and now he, in turn, wants vengeance. Since he came to power he has built up the morale of the German people. He has given them their pride back. That would all be fine and praiseworthy if it stopped there, but it doesn't. His dominance over every aspect of German life – even over the country's armed forces – has gone to his head. And if the rumours that are filtering out of the country about how he is treating some of the unfortunate people who don't fit his idea of a "perfect race" are to be believed, then the situation is appalling. Now, he's calling for more living space and that can only mean one thing – that he is going to invade other countries, especially neighbouring ones.'

'But Tom? What about Tom?'

'That's why I've been encouraging him and helping him to become proficient in wireless operations. I can't promise he wouldn't get sent abroad, but they wouldn't put a gun in his hands. They'd give him a wireless and a Morse code machine – I think it's called a telegraph key – that's what Tom told me anyway. They'd likely tuck him away somewhere safe to intercept enemy messages.'

Lilian's eyes widened. 'Is that what he's doing here? Planning to listen in to messages from shipping in the North Sea?'

Frank smiled. 'Now you're thinking sensibly, Lilian love.'

'So he'd be able to stay here? Even when he's eighteen, would he?'

'That I couldn't tell you. It all depends.'

'On what?'

Frank smiled slowly. 'On how useful he can make himself to the authorities until then. Let's hope the war is over long before he's old enough to be called up.'

Lilian nodded as plans began to form in her mind

to keep her boy safe for however long the conflict might last. But there was still the problem of her daughter.

'What about Carolyn? It's been my wish for her to marry Peter. And it's what Phyllis wants too.'

'If they love each other and choose to marry, all well and good, but don't force them into it. It wouldn't make for a happy marriage, now would it?'

'It would keep them both safe. Peter wouldn't have to go because he's a farm worker and surely they won't call up married women.'

Frank raised his eyebrows. 'So you do take an interest in what's going on?'

Lilian wriggled her shoulders. 'It's what Phyllis told me.'

'Ah.' He was silent for a moment, then he jabbed his pipe towards her again, emphasizing his point. 'If things got really serious, Lilian, they might easily call up women without children, so you see, that's why I want Carolyn to have a skill that will keep her office-bound. Her shorthand and typing should do that.' He bit back the words about his grand-daughter learning Morse too. He wouldn't break his promise to her. Even in one of the services, the skills she'd already acquired should be enough for her to be drafted into some kind of clerical job.

'So,' he said after a long pause. 'Are you going to keep the wireless?'

Lilian sighed. 'Yes, all right. I suppose I can't bury my head in the sand for ever.'

'It's best you know the truth, love. This war is going to affect all of us, even more than last time and that was bad enough. But listen to the entertainment programmes too, Lilian, just now and again to take your mind off the news, which I think is going to be a bit depressing. There are some very good music programmes. Have a listen to those.'

Eight

It was around the little wireless set which Frank had given them that Lilian and her family gathered at six o'clock on the evening of 3 September to hear the King reiterate the solemn words spoken by the prime minister earlier in the day. When the sound of his voice faded away, Eddie switched off the set.

'So,' he said quietly, 'that's it, then. We're at war again and with the same enemy.'

'Why do they hate us so much?' Lilian whispered.

'I don't think they do. Not the ordinary German people – folk like ourselves – but they do seem to get these power-drunk fanatics in charge, who want to lead them into war. It's sad, because I think a lot of the ordinary German people won't want it.'

'So why don't they refuse?'

'Hitler and his cohorts have such a grip on everything that if anyone dares to raise a voice against them they – um – disappear.'

'Oh my,' was all Lilian said.

'Are we having an evacuee, Mam?' Carolyn asked.

Now armed with the wireless and a daily paper from Frank, although it was a day old by the time they read it, the whole family now followed the news avidly. So, they knew all about the evacuation of children from London and the big cities that had started even before the prime minister's announcement that war had actually begun.

'Your dad and I have discussed it but we think we live too far out in the wilds for it to be practical, though I think your Aunty Eve is thinking about it.'

'They live nearer the town. It wouldn't be so bad for the kiddies there. I hear the ones we're likely to get are from Grimsby.'

'It's still a bit lonely even at Harold's place,' Lilian said. 'They'd need other children to play with. You can't suddenly plunge a city kid into the country amongst complete strangers.'

'You might have to if their lives are in danger where they live. What about Peter's mother? Will she take any? They've plenty of room in their cottage.'

Lilian snorted with laughter. 'Phyllis? Take in other folks' kids? You've got to be joking, Carolyn.'

But Carolyn wasn't joking. 'She might not have the choice, Mam.'

As it turned out, the Holmes and Atkinson families were not asked to have evacuees. Nor was Phyllis Carter. The local billeting officer thought that as none of their homes had young children, there were no friends for the newcomers to make. Transport to the town schools – especially for the very young ones – would be difficult to arrange too.

'I told you so,' Lilian said triumphantly. 'The war'll hardly touch us out here.'

But in that she was wrong. During the first few

weeks and months of the war there were quite a few events that affected the families.

Eddie insisted on following government directives to the letter. 'We've already got our issue of gas masks. You mustn't go anywhere without them. So, you just remember that, Tom. Not even to school. You must take it everywhere with you. And we must build an Anderson shelter out the back. We wouldn't have time to get to the communal shelters they're building in town. I'm helping my dad with theirs and me and Harold are building one for your dad, Lilian. Harold's building his own at home. Adam will help him do that. Tom, I'll need your help here. First, we'll have to dig a deep hole – a *very* deep hole – for the corrugated iron shelter to fit into. It'll take us about a week to do that alone, I reckon.'

'What do we do with all the earth?'

'Pile it on top and around the sides for extra protection and then we plant veggies on top to help camouflage the fact that it's a shelter and to make good use of the space too.' Eddie went on: 'Inside we'll need bunk beds for the four of us. Dad and I are going to make some and then we'll put an advert in the paper to say that we're making wooden bunk beds to fit Anderson shelters.'

'We'll need to keep blankets and pillows handy so we can take them with us if there is an air raid,' Lilian said, now realizing her husband was serious. 'No good leaving them in there all the time. They'd get damp.'

'I'll put a spirit stove in there so we can at least

make a cup of tea – and some candles and matches as well,' Eddie said.

'And I'll make sure I always have some tea and fresh milk ready.' Lilian glanced at her husband. 'But have you realized, Eddie, we might not hear the town sirens right out here?'

'But we'll hear the planes, love. Even the enemy can't creep in silently. And all of you,' he glanced around at his family, 'keep a bundle of warm clothing ready. It'll get very cold in the shelter, especially in winter.'

Lilian sighed. She would go along with what Eddie was saying. She knew he was only trying to keep his family safe, but she couldn't stop herself murmuring, 'I still don't understand why we need a shelter,' as she eyed the gas mask with distaste and turned up her nose at the strong rubbery smell. 'They're hardly going to bomb us, Eddie.'

'You never know. If what my dad said is right, we're going to have a lot of army personnel in the area. He's heard that Butlin's has been requisitioned by the Admiralty as a training centre. And we'll probably get RAF personnel here too, eventually.' Eddie laughed. 'There's plenty of room for square bashing on the sea front. And all the hotels will be ideal as billets.'

'That's true,' Carolyn agreed. 'It's unlikely we'll be getting holidaymakers next year – and maybe not for a while after that.'

The family was silent for a moment, realizing the dreadful loss to the town's economy that the absence of summer visitors would cause.

'Your dad's workshop is a veritable gossip shop. Him and your mother seem to hear all the news first.'

Eddie laughed. 'You're right there, Lilian. We get all and sundry popping in for this and that. And my mam comes hurrying out to invite them to take a cup of tea with her if they're waiting for some small job to be done. She's the one with her ear to the ground.'

At supper that evening, as the family sat around the table, Tom said gloomily, 'I don't think we can go to the Point anymore.' Like it was for Carolyn, it was one of Tom's favourite places to go with his friends, or, more often than not, on his own to watch the birds with the pair of field glasses his grandad had given him the previous Christmas. 'There seems to be a lot of activity there now. Me and a mate from school went out there on our bicycles – like we always have. We got as far as the Hump but there was a barbed-wire fence strung between two moveable posts and two sentries on duty. They were dressed in uniform. They told us to clear off.'

'I think the army have moved in very quickly,' Eddie said, 'and are building anti-tank defences. Dad thinks an emergency battery is being set up there by the coastal defence.'

'Is that a branch of the army?' Carolyn asked.

'I think so. The artillery, I would imagine.'

'It's an ideal spot, I have to admit.'

'There's definitely something going on,' Lilian said. 'I've seen all sorts of army-type vehicles heading to the Point this last week and most of them only seem to be going one way. So, you keep away from there, Tom. I don't want you getting into trouble.'

'Some of the girls at work were saying that huge rolls of barbed wire are being put all along the beach, blocking all the entrances and leaving only a narrow gap so that the lifeboat can be launched,' Carolyn put in. 'And they've heard that at least part of the beach – if not all of it – is going to be mined.'

'In that case, you stay away from the Point and the beach as well, Tom,' Lilian said swiftly and then she sighed. 'We won't recognize Skegness soon.' She shook herself and became more businesslike again. 'Right, Carolyn, when we've done the washing-up, I'll need some help with these blackout panels and curtains. And you'd better put sticking tape across all the windows if your dad is so sure we're going to get bombed.' Suddenly she smiled. 'I bet there's one thing the rest of you haven't thought about.'

'What's that, love?' Eddie asked.

'If the army are moving in down there, there's a good chance we might get our road from town tarmacked.'

The other three stared at her and then Eddie murmured, 'You could very well be right.'

'It'd make cycling a lot easier for us, Tom,' Carolyn said, as she rose to clear away the empty plates and take them into the scullery. 'Maybe not quite so many punctures, eh?'

The whole country was following government regulations and advice. Any available areas were dug up and planted with vegetables and farmers had to follow new regulations. Smallholders made use of every inch of their land. Eddie constructed a small hut and a pen at the far end of the land that belonged to the cottage.

'What's that for?' Lilian demanded.

'Three goats.'

'Goats! What on earth do we want with goats?'

'Extra milk supplies.'

'And who, might I ask,' Lilian began, folding her arms across her chest with a belligerent air, 'is going to milk them?' But before anyone could speak, she answered her own question. 'As if I didn't know.'

'I'll do it when I can, Mam,' Tom offered. 'I think it's a great idea.'

'Oh you do, do you? Well, you'll just have to be careful what you leave lying about. They eat anything and everything. We had some on the farm years ago and they got out of their pen one day and pulled all me mam's washing off the line and chewed me dad's wool vest and long johns. So,' she added, wagging her finger at her husband, 'you mind you make that enclosure good and strong.' Still muttering to herself she went back into the house while Eddie and Tom exchanged a grin.

The first few months of the war came to be known later as the 'Phoney War', because not much seemed to be happening.

'You mark my words,' Lilian said, more in hope than with conviction, 'it'll all be over by Christmas.'

'That's what they said last time,' Eddie reminded her gently, 'but it didn't happen, did it?'

Lilian's only reply was to wriggle her shoulders.

By October, 158,000 men of the British Expeditionary Force and 25,000 vehicles had been landed in France in a build-up to bolster the French defence.

'What on earth have they done that for?' Lilian demanded. 'Hitler hasn't even invaded France.'

'Not yet,' Eddie said ominously.

Nine

Christmas came and the war was not over, though a great many of the evacuee children had gone home because there was nothing happening. There was little change in the Holmes family's ritual. They all gathered in Frank's farmhouse for dinner as they always had, which was cooked and served by Lilian with a little help from Eve, who, ever since Frank's wife's death, had made the traditional pudding and a cake. As had been the custom for a number of years, they were joined by Eddie's parents, Norman and Dorothy Holmes, and Phyllis and Peter Carter.

'We'll be luckier than most,' Frank said, as he sat at the head of the table to carve the huge goose. 'Living on a farm, we won't suffer the deprivations some townsfolk will. Mind you, be warned, I shall stick rigidly to the regulations. There'll be no law-breaking on my farm, but you must all' – he glanced around the large table set out in the dining room for this special occasion – 'let me know what you need and I'll do my best.'

'I'll have to dig out my mother's old recipes,' Dorothy said. Eddie's mother – known as Granny Holmes – was like a round little barrel with fair curly hair that framed her plump cheeks and ready smile.

She belonged to one or two women's clubs and was already making enquiries as to how she could help with the war effort.

'I shall certainly join the WVS,' she said.

'Is there a branch here?' Eve asked.

Dorothy's eyes twinkled. 'Oh yes. A friend of mine organized enrolments in a cafe on the seafront way back in October. They've got over a hundred volunteers now, but they'd still be glad of more.'

'Count me in,' Eve said, as she passed around the roast potatoes.

Lilian had strategically placed Peter and Carolyn next to each other, but Peter was strangely quiet. As the meal ended with mince pies and cheese, Peter leaned back. 'I couldn't eat another crumb. That was magnificent as always. Thank you, everyone.'

'You're most welcome, lad, and I'm glad you've enjoyed it. There's no knowing what it might be like next year. Now,' Frank rose from the table, 'if no one minds, I'm going to have my forty winks in front of the range.'

Peter leaned towards Carolyn. 'Come for a walk after you've helped with the clearing up. I'm going to check on the animals. I want your grandad and Mr Harold to have a day off.'

Carolyn smiled at him. 'That's nice of you. I'll—'

Whatever she had been going to say was interrupted by Lilian. 'You two go. There're plenty of us to manage the washing-up.'

'And I'll see to the animals,' Adam volunteered, grinning at Peter. 'I've nowt else to do, seeing as how I haven't got a pretty young lady to take out walking.'

Adam was tall and gangly with bright red hair and a face covered in freckles. His brown eyes were warm and friendly and mischievous and his perpetual grin seemed to stretch from ear to ear. He had worked on his grandfather's farm since leaving school and had been promised that one day it would be his. Lilian was no longer resentful that the farm would not be left equally between Frank's grandsons; her Tom would go to university. But the country was now at war and no one knew what the future held. No one could make any plans and be sure that they would be fulfilled.

Carolyn and Peter, wrapped up well against the winter's east wind blowing in from the North Sea, set out to walk a circuit of Frank's fields.

'We'll give the Point a miss today. It'll be perishing there.'

'I doubt we'd be allowed anywhere near it now. I miss seeing the sea, but I can't bear to see all the defences ruining the landscape, even though I know they're necessary. I can still hear the sea, but it's not the same as being able to watch the waves rolling in. There's something so soothing about the permanence of the ocean. Whatever's happening, it just carries on as it always has and as it always will.'

Peter chuckled. 'Except when it gets a bit rough and we have huge rollers crashing onto the shore and threatening to flood our land.'

'It's still magnificent even then.'

They walked in silence for a while before Peter, as if he couldn't hold it in any longer, burst out,

'Caro, you remember we talked about me volunteering?'

She turned startled eyes towards him. 'I thought maybe you'd changed your mind. Grandad told me you and he were getting your heads together about applying for an exemption.'

'Well, yes, we have applied, but I'm not sure it's what I really want. I don't feel comfortable about it.'

'You're an agricultural worker. What you do here is far more important than being shot at.'

Peter flinched. 'Rationally, yes, you're right. But I can't help how I *feel*. I – I suppose I must take after my father in that respect. He didn't *have* to go.'

'Whatever will your mother say?'

Peter shuddered. 'Don't. I don't even want to think about that.'

'You're all she's got, Peter,' Carolyn reminded him gently.

'I know,' he said gloomily. 'I don't want to upset her, but . . .'

'Has anyone said anything to you to make you feel like this?'

'Not – much. I've stopped going to the pub in town though. All the lads I meet there are talking about joining up. No one's actually said anything directly to me, but there's a sort of atmosphere. I feel I'm the odd one out.'

'Whatever you decide, Peter, please promise me one thing?'

'I will if I can.'

'That you won't go because someone shames you

into it. Hands you a white feather or something daft like that. If it's your own choice to go, then that's different.'

Peter squeezed her elbow. 'You're such a good mate, Caro, and you're absolutely right. If I do volunteer, it must be for the right reasons, not just because I'm caught up in a wave of patriotic fervour like people were last time. I think we'd better go back to the farm; our mothers will no doubt have us engaged by now. We've been out together for over an hour.'

Though Carolyn smiled at his attempt at humour as they turned back towards the farmhouse, their conversation had left her feeling very unsettled. Peter's mother was not Carolyn's favourite person in the world, but in that moment she felt a twinge of pity for her.

Although there was fierce fighting between the Russians and the Finns, not much happened during the first three months of the new year of 1940 on the home front, apart from the rationing which affected everyone. Bacon, butter and sugar were the very first items to be rationed in January.

'How on earth am I supposed to feed a family of four on these meagre amounts?' Lilian complained.

'Good job Dad got the goats, then,' Tom said grinning, unable to resist teasing his mother. 'At least we won't go short of milk. I presume you can make butter and cheese from goat's milk.'

'You can,' Lilian said, still looking down at the offending ration books. 'But it doesn't taste the same.'

By March, meat had been added to the list.

'Have you heard?' Tom said to Carolyn, 'Cousin Adam is quite the entrepreneur.'

She gaped at him. 'How?'

'He's got himself an air gun and goes out shooting rabbits on Grandad's farm. And then he takes them to a butcher in town. Doing a roaring trade, so he said.'

Carolyn laughed. 'Good for him. Grandad's always been plagued by rabbits. He'll be pleased to see their numbers reduced.'

'And to be feeding folk into the bargain.'

In April, however, things began to 'hot up', as Frank put it, when Hitler invaded Denmark and Norway. Then in May, two momentous events occurred on the same day: Winston Churchill became prime minister and Hitler invaded France, Belgium, Luxembourg and the Netherlands.

'Poor feller,' Frank said, jabbing at Churchill's photograph in the newspaper. 'Talk about being thrown in at the deep end.'

'He's a bit old to be prime minister, isn't he?' Carolyn, visiting the farm after work, remarked.

'Don't you believe it. He's got the vim and vigour of a man half his age and he's been proved right. He's been warning us all for years that this was going to happen. No, he's the man for the job and no mistake.'

As she cycled home the following evening, Carolyn mulled over her grandfather's words. Tonight, she hardly noticed the small shops along Drummond Road closing up at the end of the day; the houses and guest houses with their windows criss-crossed with sticky tape to prevent flying glass in the event of a bombing raid, and blackout curtains ready to be drawn when the lights needed to go on. She glanced briefly at the rear of the grandest hotel in the town, the Seacroft Hotel, which faced out over the beach and the sea. Now there were none of its visitors' classy cars parked there. The whole town was ominously quiet, missing the influx of the first summer visitors. She wondered if there would be any at all this year. How the town would miss its holidaymakers. She pedalled on, not even daring to glance at the golf course on her left. She'd heard that concrete blocks had been built on its fairways as a precaution against a tank invasion. It was a sight she didn't want to see. As the houses petered out and she was cycling along the uneven lane, her thoughts turned back to her grandfather. She smiled to herself. Frank was only four or five years older than the new prime minister. Of course he was going to defend his capability.

Frank's words were prophetic; only a few weeks later, at the end of May and into the first days of June, came the catastrophe of Dunkirk, which, with his fine oratory, Churchill used to fire the will of the British people to fight on and never surrender.

The news of the evacuation from the shores of France had made Peter feel even more unsettled. Towards the end of July, the first bombs fell on the Seacroft golf course only a mile or so away from where they lived. Soon afterwards, Peter joined the local branch of the newly formed Home Guard, which had very recently changed its name from the Local

Defence Volunteers. But it was still not enough to assuage his conscience.

By harvest time, he still hadn't made up his mind.

'Oh Carolyn,' he said to her as they worked side by side stooking the corn in Frank's fields on her half-day off from work. She had stopped going to Mrs Fox for typing lessons on Thursday afternoons. The kindly lady had said, 'There's not much more I can teach you. All you need now is practice, practice, practice to get your speeds up. And get Tom to keep giving you dictation for your shorthand.'

'I still don't know what to do,' Peter went on. 'I do so want to join up but it's leaving Mam and also leaving your grandad in the lurch.' He grinned sheep-ishly. 'Good farmhands are hard to find at the moment. I don't want to sound as if I'm blowing my own trumpet, but I've worked for Mr Frank a long time, ever since I was a young lad still at school, and I know his ways.'

Carolyn laughed, the sound carrying across the flat sunlit fields. 'No need to be bashful, Peter. He thinks the world of you and he'd be sorry to see you go, but you must do what your conscience tells you. I wouldn't want you to regret it for the rest of your life. Why don't you leave it another few months? See how the war progresses.'

'It's not going to go so well now, is it? Not after Dunkirk, and I expect you've heard what's happening in the skies over the South of England now, haven't you?'

'I was talking to Grandad about it only the other night. He says we're putting all our faith in the RAF now. Goering wants his Luftwaffe to command the skies before Hitler can invade us and there're only our boys in blue to stop that happening.'

Peter nodded and sighed. 'That's about it, yes.'

'Well, it would take a while for you to train as a pilot if you joined now. It might all be over – one way or the other – by the time you were ready.'

Peter shook his head. 'The RAF wouldn't be my choice anyway. If I do go, I shall enlist in the army, like my dad did.'

'Oh dear,' Carolyn murmured, 'your mother wouldn't be happy about that.'

Peter's jaw hardened. 'She's not going to be happy whatever service I join. I've just got to come to terms with that.'

They worked for a little longer until Peter stood up and arched his aching back. 'I've decided. I think you've got a point. I'll leave it for now, see what happens over the next few months, and maybe enlist at the beginning of next year. And winter would be a good time to leave the farm. Mr Frank would be able to get extra help organized before the spring.'

'That sounds like a good idea.'

'Not a word to anyone though. Especially not to my mother.'

'Of course not.'

Ten

It became a regular occurrence for Peter and Carolyn to meet after church on Sundays to go for a walk and discuss any war news they had read or heard during the week. They were no longer able to visit the Point, but there were plenty of footpaths around the edge of Frank's farm for them to walk.

'I wish we could go to the beach,' Carolyn sighed. 'I do miss the sea.'

'We could cycle to the central beach in town. Why don't you come to church on your bicycle next week and we'll do that when we leave?'

Carolyn hesitated for a moment. 'I'm not sure I want to see the seafront as it is now. No children building sandcastles, having donkey rides or splashing in the shallows.'

'No admittance to the pier,' Peter added. 'I heard they've not only closed it, but they've also removed parts of the decking to hinder an invasion attempt. But we could still see the sea, Caro. Whatever happens, it'll always be there.'

'Yes, you're right. We'll do it. Mam doesn't get the Sunday dinner on the table until about three o'clock, so we'd have plenty of time.'

'Wouldn't she want you to help her?'

Carolyn chuckled. 'Not if I'm out with you.'

Peter smiled but sighed at the same time. 'Oh dear. She's still barking up the wrong tree just like my mother, is she?'

' 'Fraid so.'

Over the next few weeks, Carolyn and Peter spent most of their Sunday afternoons together walking around the farm or cycling to the central beach.

'Doesn't it look awful? All that barbed wire and only a narrow pathway for them to get the lifeboat through.'

'Someone was telling me that the beach is mined in places,' Peter said.

'That's what I heard too. And just look at all the seafront gardens.' She glanced to the right and then to the left. 'All planted with vegetables now instead of lovely flowers.'

'But we've got to "Dig for Victory", Caro, like they're asking us to do, although it'll probably be years before we get everything back to how it used to be and before all the holidaymakers return.' Peter's face was bleak as he added, 'If they ever do.'

They turned once again to the subject that was always uppermost in both their minds.

'I'm going to leave it until the New Year, Caro,' he said. 'I really don't want to upset Mum just before the festivities.' He grinned ruefully. 'At least I've decided that much.'

'Good idea,' Carolyn agreed.

The second Christmas of the war was noticeably different from the first. Previously, it seemed that little had changed, but now rationing was in full swing and people were saving every penny.

But the Holmes and Atkinson families spent the time together at Frank's farm; that, at least, was normal.

'We're luckier than most,' Frank reminded them. 'At least we've got a goose again this year.'

'You might find the pudding tastes a little different,' Eve said. 'I've used a recipe that's got carrot in it.'

'And the crackers are homemade,' Carolyn laughed. 'Courtesy of Tom and me. He's written the jokes.'

'Oh dear.' Lilian smiled. 'I hope they're not too rude, Tom.'

'Would I, Mother?'

Frank chuckled. 'Of course he would and quite right too. What's the good of having a young boy in the family if we can't have a rude joke now and again.' He winked at his grandson. 'I bet I could tell you a few, Tom.'

Tom grinned back. 'I bet you could, Grandad.'

Everyone around the huge farmhouse table laughed.

As the meal ended, Peter said, 'I fancy a trip to the cinema one day soon. Anyone up for it?'

'I wouldn't mind—' Tom began but his mother, sitting next to him, nudged him with a sharp elbow.

'What? What have I said?'

'Maybe Peter would like to take Carolyn,' she said archly.

'Of course, but there's no earthly reason why Tom shouldn't come as well. I'll keep an eye on what's coming up and let you both know.' Peter stood up.

'And now, Mrs Holmes, Carolyn and I will do the washing-up while all you ladies, who prepared this splendid meal, take a well-earned rest in front of the fire in Mr Frank's sitting room. I know there's a good one going in there, because I lit it myself. Tom, you can give us a hand.'

'Oh I don't think that's a good idea, Peter,' Lilian said swiftly. 'You and Carolyn can manage, can't you? Tom has a habit of dropping things and I wouldn't want all my late mother's precious dinner service to end up in pieces on the floor.' Carolyn and Peter dared not look at each other; if they had done, they'd both have burst out laughing.

'Not exactly subtle, is she?' Peter said as Carolyn washed the dishes and he dried them. 'And did you see our mothers' faces? They both looked like a couple of cats that had got the cream.'

Carolyn was trying to stifle her laughter. 'You know, we're awful. We really shouldn't lead them on in the way we are doing. All these walks together and now we're going to the cinema.'

Peter chuckled. 'We're doing nothing that two good friends wouldn't do, Caro. We've both told them quite plainly in the past that we're not walking out together. It's their fault if they're not listening.' He paused and then asked seriously, 'You haven't changed your mind, have you?'

'Definitely not. Have you?'

'No, I haven't. I do love you, Caro, but only as a dear friend. My *best* friend.'

As they finished the washing-up and hung the tea towels up to dry, Tom came into the kitchen. 'Mam says do you mind making everyone a cup of tea? And if you use Grandad's everyday cups and saucers, I'm allowed to help carry them through to the sitting room.'

'Pop the kettle on the hob then, Tom.'

'So when are we going to the cinema, then?' he asked.

'Probably in the first week or so of January,' Peter suggested. 'Would that be OK?'

'Suits me. Just pick a good film, that's all.' Tom grinned at them. 'None of this mushy stuff.'

'I tell you what,' Peter said, 'if you can get a Saturday afternoon off work, Caro, we'll take Tom out to tea in the cafe opposite and then go to the cinema. How would that be?'

'Great,' Tom said before Carolyn could answer. 'It's a date.'

The proposed outing took place on a snowy Saturday in January. Carolyn managed to wangle the afternoon off and Peter borrowed Frank's truck to take them into the town where they ordered tea in a cafe opposite the cinema. The late afternoon was gloomy, the sky still heavy with snow. The three of them were chatting and laughing together when they heard the low drone of a single aircraft coming closer and closer from the west towards the sea.

'I don't like the sound of this. Let's—' Peter began, but before he had finished speaking, they heard the sound of a bomb falling and then another, each time closer and closer.

'Under the table,' Peter said and then he shouted to everyone in the cafe. 'Everyone, under the tables!'

Carolyn, Tom and Peter dived under the small table they were sitting at, fearing it offered little protection. Glass from breaking windows flew everywhere and the air was filled with noise as the plane flew directly over them and then headed out to sea. As the sound of the aircraft died away, the screams and cries of the people in the cafe now filled the air.

'I reckon that was a Junkers Eighty-Eight,' Tom said, as he emerged cautiously from beneath the table.

'Come on,' Peter said. 'We'd better see what we can do. Are you both all right?' he asked as all three of them surfaced from their hiding place. 'No injuries?'

'No, I don't think so,' Carolyn said, as she glanced through the space left by the shattered window. 'Peter, look. Across the road. The cinema's been hit.'

'Oh no. There'll be kiddies there at the matinee. Come on, we'll go over.'

For the next two hours, they helped mothers and children to safety. 'That was a close shave,' Carolyn said as at last the final few made their way home. Miraculously, no one had been injured though there were still quite a few little ones crying bitterly from fear and shock.

'I wonder if anyone's been killed,' Tom murmured. 'It'll be a miracle if there weren't any casualties at all.'

'Come on, let's get you both home,' Peter said. 'I'm afraid our visit to the cinema is off for the time being.'

Later in the week, when a report appeared in the

local newspaper, they found out that there had been three fatalities; a sailor in a cafe further along the street and the proprietor of the very cafe they had been in had been hit by flying glass. A local businessman, working in his office, which had received a direct hit, died a few days later.

When they met the following day after church, Peter and Carolyn regarded each other solemnly.

'That wasn't the first bomb to fall in our area,' Carolyn said. 'And, sadly, I don't think it'll be the last.'

'We had a lucky escape, Caro,' he said softly and squeezed her arm. 'But it's done one thing for me. It's made up my mind. I am not going to sit around while Hitler thinks he can come over here and bomb poor little mites on an outing to the cinema. I'm going to join up. But not a word to a soul. Do you promise?'

'Of course I do.'

'Lilian. *Lilian!*'

The frantic banging on the back door startled Lilian just as she was lifting a hot chicken, leek and potato pie out of the oven. The pie wobbled dangerously but she managed to put it safely onto the table before she muttered under her breath, 'Whoever is making all that noise?' Then, with a leap of her heart, she realized it was Phyllis. 'Oh my!' she said aloud. 'Is something wrong with Dad and she's come to fetch me?'

She hurried to open the door. 'What is it? What's happened?'

'He's gone. Oh Lilian, he's gone.'

Now Lilian's heart hammered. She put her hand to her chest and leaned weakly against the door jamb.

'Oh no. When – when did it happen? Have you called the doctor?'

Phyllis gaped at her. 'Wha—?'

'Come in a minute, Phyllis, while I get my hat and coat. I'll come back with you straight away. Oh dear! Whatever had he been doing? Where did you find him? Was he still in bed? Did it happen in the night? Does Harold know?'

Phyllis blinked, trying to make sense of Lilian's rapid-fire questions. Then the proverbial penny dropped. 'It's not yar dad. It's Peter. My Peter. He's gone.'

Lilian stopped her bustling and stared at Phyllis. 'What – what d'you mean – gone?'

'He's gone to join up. To volunteer. And it's all your Carolyn's fault.'

'How can that be?'

'Because if she'd only agreed to marry him, he wouldn't have gone off.'

Lilian's face turned white. She turned and left Phyllis standing on the doorstep while she went back into her kitchen and sat down heavily. Phyllis closed the back door and followed her into the kitchen. She did not sit down. Instead, she stood over Lilian accusingly, her arms akimbo. 'He would've stayed here,' she continued, 'and been safely employed on the farm if only they'd got married. Am I to lose my son – my only son, my only *child* – to another bloody war? Isn't it enough that I lost my husband in the last one?'

88

Lilian dropped her head into her hands and did not answer. She recognized that life had not been easy for Phyllis. Losing her husband in the Great War, and having to bring their son up on her own, had been hard. But, just sometimes, Lilian felt that Phyllis's bitter resentment at how life had treated her was extreme. Countless other women had lost loved ones and, sadly, would do so again in this conflict. Although they would undoubtedly grieve for the rest of their lives, they hadn't allowed their loss to overwhelm them. But Phyllis still railed against how the world had treated her and her anxiety over Peter had become fanatical. Lilian had the uncomfortable feeling that the woman would stop at nothing to keep her son safely by her side.

She raised her head and moved stiffly to put the kettle on the hob.

'Look, Lilian, I know I shouldn't be bellowing at you, but you'd better warn your Carolyn that when I catch up with her, I'll wring her bloody neck.'

The two women sat with a cup of tea for over an hour, talking over what they saw as their mutual problem.

'I've been getting an earful from my dad,' Lilian confided. 'He says we – we shouldn't push them together. That it wouldn't make for a happy marriage.'

Phyllis sniffed. 'What would he know about it? Men don't know anything about such things. It's us women who have to lead them by the nose until we can wheedle a proposal out of 'em.' She glanced slyly at Lilian, causing her to blush, but the latter lifted her head defiantly. How she wished Phyllis Carter knew nothing of her past.

Lilian listened regularly to the wireless now and she even brought home day-old newspapers from her father's farm. The first time she'd brought one into the house, she'd flung it on the table after the family had finished their evening meal. 'Here, you'd better all read this, seeing as you're so keen to know what's going on.'

Now she said to Phyllis, 'I've read about full conscription of men. It's law now – has been since the war started – so wouldn't Peter have had to go anyway?'

Phyllis shook her head. 'Agriculture is a reserved occupation. He – or your dad on his behalf – could have applied for an exemption, if they haven't already. I know it's been talked about. And he would've done, if your Carolyn had agreed to marry him.'

'I'll have a word with her when she gets home tonight,' Lilian promised.

She didn't notice the gleam in the other woman's eyes. Phyllis said nothing, but her mind was made up. She'd speak to Carolyn first herself.

Eleven

That same afternoon Phyllis walked into the town and entered the Woolworth store. She went around all the counters, but she couldn't see Carolyn. She frowned. Had the girl seen her come in and was she hiding? She approached one of the assistants.

'Excuse me, miss. Do you know Carolyn Holmes?'

'Yes, I do.'

'What counter is she on? I can't see her.'

The blond-haired girl smiled. 'She doesn't work out here anymore. She works in the office. Got a posh job now, she has.' She pointed towards a glass window at the rear of the building, raised a little above the level of the shop floor. 'Go up them steps and knock on the door, duck. I'm sure they'll let you have a word with her.'

This was not quite what Phyllis had imagined. She'd wanted to have it out with Carolyn in the main body of the shop. She'd wanted to shame her in front of her work colleagues. She could see people moving about behind the window, but only a few. She'd wanted the whole shop – staff and customers alike – to hear what she had to say. Even so, she decided it was worth a try. Maybe the manager was in there. Maybe he would sack her. That would serve the little madam right.

She tapped on the door and waited for someone to open it. 'Could I have a word with Carolyn, please? I have some bad news for her.'

Phyllis guessed that the woman with short-cropped brown hair and wearing spectacles was about her own age. She glanced down at her left hand. No wedding ring. No doubt she was one of those unfortunate women who'd been left on the shelf by the dreadful loss of young men of her generation. She was frowning at Phyllis. 'We don't normally let our staff be interrupted at work, but if you have bad news, then perhaps we can make an exception.'

She held the door open and Phyllis took a step to stand on the threshold, so that the woman would not be able to close the door. Phyllis saw Carolyn glance towards her and her eyes widen as her superior beckoned her forward. Carolyn got up from her desk and came towards them. 'Whatever's wrong—?' she began, but Phyllis cut her short.

'You're what's wrong, you little madam,' Phyllis began in a loud voice and then she felt her arm grabbed and she was pulled into the room by the woman who'd opened the door. The door shut behind her. Unfazed, Phyllis went on in as loud a voice as she could muster. 'Peter's gone to war, all because of you, you selfish little cow.'

She saw a man behind a desk in the far corner of the room rise to his feet, but she went on with her tirade. 'If you hadn't been so high an' mighty and refused his proposal, he'd have stayed at home working on the farm. And that would have been quite acceptable. He wouldn't have been branded a coward because farm workers are exempted. But he's gone to be shot, just because of you.'

'Madam . . .' The man, who Phyllis assumed must be the manager, was standing in front of her. He was tall and slim with smooth dark hair. He was dressed smartly and spoke in a low voice that nevertheless held authority. 'Please come and sit down. Miss Brown, make the lady a cup of tea, will you?'

'Yes, Mr Williamson,' Mary got up at once and scuttled to do his bidding while he led Phyllis to a chair and pushed her gently into it.

'Now, tell us quietly and calmly what the matter is.' The manager was fully aware of Carolyn standing white-faced and wide-eyed, clinging on to the corner of a desk for support. Even with a quick glance, he could see that she was trembling.

'Calm, you say?' In contrast to the man's voice, Phyllis's was shrill. 'How can a mother be calm when her only child has gone off to be killed? And all because of *her*.'

Mary set a strong cup of tea down on the desk nearest to Phyllis and then stepped quickly away, though Miss Simpson came to stand at the manager's elbow. She didn't speak but he knew she was silently offering her help. Mr Williamson straightened up. 'Perhaps you would prefer to speak to Miss Simpson. She is in charge of the welfare of all the women and girls who work here. She is perhaps better suited to understand.'

Before Phyllis could answer, he had stepped back and ushered Miss Simpson forward, as if introducing her. 'I'll be downstairs if you need me, Miss Simpson.'

'Now, my dear,' Miss Simpson pulled up a chair and sat down in front of Phyllis, 'what is all this about?'

'My Peter wants to marry Carolyn, but she's refused him.' Her lip curled disdainfully. 'Not good enough for her, I suppose.'

Miss Simpson glanced over her shoulder. 'Is this true, Miss Holmes?'

'No, Miss Simpson.' Carolyn's voice was a hoarse whisper. 'Peter and I are just good friends. Really good friends – the best. But – but not romantically.'

'You're a bloody little liar, Carolyn Holmes—'

'Please, madam, moderate your language.' Miss Simpson's tone was firm; it was a tone that made all the young girls in the store quake, but it had no effect on Phyllis. 'Has your son actually proposed to Carolyn? Did he tell you that?'

For the first time, Phyllis looked a little uncertain. 'He – he didn't actually say so, but it's what me and Carolyn's mother have always wanted.' She nodded towards Carolyn. 'They both know that.'

'But,' Miss Simpson said quietly, 'do *they* want it?'

Phyllis drew herself up. 'My boy will do as I say.'

Miss Simpson raised her eyebrows. 'Really? From what you say, he's gone to join up without your say-so. Or at least without you being able to stop him.'

Her mouth was tight as Phyllis muttered, 'I didn't have the chance to argue with him. He – he went in the middle of the night and left me a note on the table. I didn't find it until I got up this morning.'

'And what is your side of this story, Miss Holmes?' Miss Simpson asked.

Emboldened, Carolyn moved a little closer but she was aware that the other two girls in the office were 'all ears'. She ran her tongue around her dry lips and said haltingly, 'Me and Peter went for a walk a while ago now – before the war started. Out to the Point. It's – it's one of our favourite places. We had a long talk and both of us agreed that, though we're very fond of each other, we're not in love with each other. We don't want to get married.'

'I don't believe you,' Phyllis spat. 'You're lying. Besides, what do you know about being in love? You ask your mother what "being in love" means. Was she in love with your father when he got her pregnant with you and there had to be a shotgun wedding?'

Now the colour drained completely from Carolyn's face and she began to sway. Mary rushed forward and pushed a chair behind her before she fell. Carolyn collapsed into it but did not pass out completely. Instead, she stared at Phyllis with horrified eyes, but the older woman only smirked grimly, 'Aye, that's a dirty little secret you knew nothing about, isn't it?'

Realizing she was going to get no further here, Phyllis stood up. 'Well, I've said what I came to say. I expect you'll get the sack now from your posh job. But I couldn't care tuppence about you. I only care about my boy. I'd hoped you'd help me get him back home, but I can see I'm wasting me time.'

She flounced out of the office without a backwards glance leaving an awkward silence in her wake. After a few moments, Mary set a freshly made mug of tea at Carolyn's elbow. 'Drink this, love. I've put plenty of sugar in it. You've had a nasty shock from that old biddy. If you ask me, you've had a lucky escape not marrying into that family.'

Carolyn put her cold, shaking hands around the warm mug and drank gratefully. She took a swift glance at Miss Simpson's face and then looked away. The woman, who had been so kind to her, was frowning worriedly. She could guess what her superior was thinking; the gossip would spread like wildfire through the store. Everyone would be looking at her and whispering behind their hands. Then they would go home and tell their families. Soon, the whole of Skegness would know.

It was highly likely that they would dismiss her; they didn't like scenes amongst the staff and especially those caused by an outsider. Even if she wasn't dismissed, she would have to give in her notice. She couldn't stay here. She would have to give up the job she loved.

Carolyn felt she couldn't share the unpleasant scene with anyone in her family. There was no one in whom she could confide now that Peter had gone. If what Phyllis had said about her mother and father was true, she certainly couldn't speak to either of them, nor could she talk to her grandfather. No doubt the memories would be painful for him too. And she certainly wouldn't burden her young brother with such a secret. She wondered how many other people knew, but living in such a small, outlying community that was not really part of the town, perhaps it had not been so very many at the time and now, years later, they wouldn't speak of it. Phyllis, in her rage against Carolyn, had blurted it out in spite. She'd wanted to hurt the girl for what she had considered a slight against her son and for being the cause of Peter volunteering. Well, she'd certainly managed that.

As she cycled home, Carolyn made up her mind; she too would volunteer. Despite her new-found skills not being used at her current employment, with Tom's help she had kept up her shorthand and typing speeds at home and she was becoming more proficient at reading and transcribing Morse. She wasn't sure if there was a combined recruiting centre in Skegness, but she didn't really want to sign up in her home town anyway. Someone would be sure to see her. Until she knew that she had been accepted by one of the services, she wanted to keep the matter to herself. She sighed as she turned up the lane towards the farmhouse. She felt guilty that she was not going to confide in her grandfather, but for the moment it must be her secret. *Another* secret. She plastered a smile on her face as she entered the back door and went into the kitchen. Frank was still sitting at the table finishing his evening meal.

Without greeting her formally, he said, 'I'll say this for your mam, she makes a good meat and potato pie. Her pastry is even better than your grandma's used to be. And that's saying summat.' He sat back in his chair with a satisfied smile.

'I'll make you a drink and wash up for you, Grandad,' Carolyn said.

While she busied herself, Frank sat in the chair by the fire, puffed at his pipe and said casually, 'Phyllis didn't come in this morning to the dairy. Do you know why that might be?' Frank actually suspected what the reason was; Peter had left him a note telling him that he was leaving home very early to sign up. He apologized to his employer but ended by saying: *I just have to do this, Mr Frank. I hope you understand.* But Frank wondered how much – if anything – his granddaughter knew.

Carolyn drew in a sharp breath. She hated telling lies to anyone, even little white ones. Neatly, she avoided answering him directly by saying, 'Mam might know, but I haven't been home yet.'

This at least was the truth and though she held her breath for a moment, Frank didn't pursue the matter any further, except to say casually, 'Mebbe she had one of her migraines.'

As she cycled the rest of the way home, Carolyn was now anxious that her mother might ask awkward questions. But Lilian was strangely subdued and, once she had given Carolyn her tea, she sat by the fireside with her head bent over a pile of mending on her lap. Carolyn cleared away her own tea things and then, with a sigh of relief, went into the front room. After spending half an hour practising her type-writing, she sat beside Tom, put on a set of headphones and transcribed the messages coming over the airwaves.

'You're getting nearly as good as me,' Tom said, grinning as, just before ten o'clock, he switched off the wireless and removed his headphones.

'Do you think you're starting to get useful messages? I mean, do you think you ought to tell someone in authority?'

'I've been wondering the very same thing, Caro. I'll talk it over with Mr Fox. I think some of the messages are in plain language. Some are in Morse in English, but there are a few in French and also German.'

'You don't speak German.'

'No, I don't, but I know enough snippets to recognize the language. A lot are now coming through in code, so I have no idea what language they're in.'

'Mm,' Carolyn said thoughtfully. 'I think it's high time you told someone.'

'I think you're right. I'll talk to Mr Fox tomorrow. He'll know what I ought to do.'

Twelve

Before Frank could say anything to her about her absence the previous day, Phyllis said, 'I'm so sorry about yesterday, Mr Frank. I had urgent business to attend to. Peter's gone off to join up.'

'Ah, so he's done it, has he?'

Phyllis stared at him. 'You – you knew?'

'Not exactly. I found a note from him yesterday morning telling me he was leaving and apologizing for it being such short notice. I guessed that's why you didn't come in.'

'I – I hope I didn't let you down with the dairy work.'

'No. Adam and me did it between us. No harm done.'

That's what he thinks, Phyllis thought morosely. *There'll be plenty of harm done if my Peter gets killed. I'll see Frank's precious granddaughter in hell.* But there was no point in complaining to the old man. He would side with Carolyn and Phyllis might lose her job. She couldn't afford for that to happen now, especially with Peter gone. She wondered if Frank would sack her anyway when he heard about what she had done the previous afternoon.

Oh well, she thought, as she went towards the

dairy to start her morning's work, *no doubt I'll know soon enough. I don't regret it for a minute.* But, to her surprise, time went by and nothing was said.

The following few days at work were uncomfortable for Carolyn. As she had feared, there was a lot of whispering amongst the shop assistants, which stopped the moment she approached. The worst moment was when Mr Williamson took her into the corner of the office 'for a quiet word'.

'Would you like to tell me what all that commotion was about the other day, Miss Holmes?' he asked.

Carolyn sighed. 'Mrs Carter's son, Peter, and I are good friends, but it is the wish of both our mothers that we should marry. We are very fond of each other but not – like that.'

'So – he's gone off to join up, has he?'

Carolyn nodded.

Mr Williamson frowned. 'But I don't see why she is blaming you for that. He'd have been called up very soon anyway.'

'It's unlikely he would have been conscripted. He's a farm worker.'

'Ah, I see.' Now the manager began to understand. He sighed. 'But I really can't have scenes in the store like we had last week.'

'I know. I'm so sorry about it.' She bit her lip, wondering if she dared to confide in him. 'May I take you into my confidence?'

'Of course.'

'I would like to take the whole day off tomorrow

instead of my usual half-day, to go to Lincoln. I want to enlist in one of the services myself.'

For a moment he stared at her, then he sighed. 'Well, I shall be very sorry to lose you, Miss Holmes. You are an excellent and trustworthy worker, but I can fully understand that things are somewhat difficult for you now.' He smiled wryly. 'Probably both here and at home, so yes, you may have the day off. Good luck, and don't forget I am willing to write a glowing testimonial for you should you need it.'

As she turned to leave, he said, 'May I ask why you're going all the way to Lincoln?'

'I don't want anyone in Skegness seeing me volunteering. A lot of people know me here.'

'Would Grantham do instead? If it would help you, I shall be going there tomorrow afternoon to see my elderly mother. I go about once a month on half-day closing. She lost a much-loved brother in the Great War and she is getting very jittery about another war coming.' He sighed.

'I'm sorry to hear that,' Carolyn murmured. Even though her uncle Harold had served in that conflict, he had returned, albeit somewhat changed. But he had come back. So many had not.

'Mother told me last time I saw her about a notice in the *Grantham Journal* about a recruitment drive at the barracks in Grantham. I'd be happy to give you a lift there if you like.'

For the first time in over a week, Carolyn smiled genuinely. 'Thank you. That's very kind of you. And in that case, I'd be able to work the morning as usual.'

'It's no more than you deserve. You know where I live, don't you?'

Carolyn nodded.

'Come straight to my house when you leave work.'

The following morning, Carolyn parcelled up her Sunday-best dress and coat and managed to sneak it out of the house without her mother noticing. As she left, she called back over her shoulder, 'I might be late tonight, Mam. I'm going to Mrs Fox's and then I'll call in on Grandad.' She wasn't sure what time she would get back to Skegness – that rather depended on Mr Williamson – but she didn't want her mother sending out a search party.

At work she hung her clothes in the cloakroom for the creases to drop out and, as closing time approached, she grabbed a quick sandwich and changed into her Sunday clothes. Arriving at Mr Williamson's house, she left her bicycle propped against the side wall outside and walked round to the front. She was about to knock when the door opened and Mr Williamson smiled down at her. 'Very prompt as always, Miss Holmes. Then we'll be off.'

As they drove, Mr Williamson said, 'May I suggest you try the barracks first? If they can't help you there, I'm sure they will be able to direct you to wherever you need to be. There may be a proper recruitment centre somewhere in Grantham by now. If there isn't, people say you can go to the Labour Exchange, but I think, in this case, your first port of call should be the barracks.'

'I had thought of asking at the police station, but your idea is better, seeing as your mother saw that notice.'

'I'll drop you at the barracks, then, and pick you up there too. Shall we say five o'clock? I'm sure you can amuse yourself in the town until then. It's not very far to walk from there, if you've time to kill. Will that be all right?'

'Perfect, Mr Williamson. Thank you.'

It was over an hour after Mr Williamson had left her outside the imposing building that Carolyn at last found herself sitting in front of a uniformed army officer. She wasn't sure of his rank, but she thought he looked very important. He was distinguished-looking, with silver hair and a small moustache. His blue eyes searched her face keenly.

'Miss Holmes, is it? We haven't actually got a recruitment drive here at the moment, but when the soldier on guard duty told me that you were asking about volunteering and that you'd come all the way from Skegness to do so, I thought it only fair that I should at least have a chat with you.'

'Thank you, sir,' Carolyn replied.

'My name is Major Jefferson, once retired but now back to serve my country in any way I can. So, how can I help you?'

'I would like to volunteer for one of the services, preferably for the ATS.'

A small smile made his eyes twinkle. 'Ah, that is the women's branch of the army. A good choice, if I may say so. Are you aware of what they do?'

Carolyn nodded. 'I've read in the newspapers that

they need clerks and telephonists, amongst others, and I thought I might have the skills they need.'

The major picked up a pen and drew a notepad towards him. 'Right, let's start with the basics. Name, address, date of birth and your current occupation, for starters.'

'Carolyn Holmes, Willow Cottage, Gibraltar Road, Skegness. My date of birth is the sixth of June, 1920, and I work for F. W. Woolworth as a clerk in their office.'

'So you're quite good with figures, then? Anything else.'

'I've been taking lessons in touch-typing and Pitman's shorthand.'

'What are your speeds?'

'Not that fast yet, I'm afraid. About sixty words a minute in shorthand and thirty words a minute in typing, but in both I try to aim for accuracy rather than speed.'

He nodded, his head bent over the page as he wrote.

Carolyn licked her lips. 'And I've been learning Morse.'

The major's head shot up and there was no doubting the spark of interest in his eyes. 'Have you really? How did that come about?'

'My brother's been teaching me. He's an amateur wireless enthusiast and has all the equipment set up in our front room. We live close to the coast – literally just over the sandhills – and he can pick up shipping in the North Sea.'

'He's not in the forces, then?'

Carolyn laughed. 'He's only fifteen. He's still at the local grammar school. His science master got him interested and they've built a wireless receiver-and-transmitter set together. Mr Fox also taught him Morse.'

'So, this Mr Fox – he's not in the forces either?'

'I think he was in the Great War and – and I think perhaps he was injured because he walks with a limp.'

'Ah,' the major murmured. 'Poor fellow.' He was thoughtful for some time before adding, 'Now, I will put your name and details forward and you'll hear something in due course. I'm sure the ATS will be delighted to have you. But in the meantime, I have a colleague who I'm sure would be very interested in paying your brother a visit, and probably Mr Fox too. He will be most interested to see what they're doing. I may well ask him if I can come with him.'

'They're – not going to be in trouble, are they?'

The major chuckled. 'Far from it, my dear. My colleague will want to see if they can be recruited in a civilian capacity. It sounds as if they're both ideally placed to help, though if it came to that, no doubt they would both have to sign the Official Secrets Act. Probably your parents too.'

He stood up and held out his hand. 'Good luck, my dear. Perhaps we shall meet again.'

Carolyn was then shown into a room and given a brief medical examination. The man – Carolyn wasn't sure if he was a doctor or not because he didn't introduce himself – listened to her chest, looked into her eyes and passed her as A1.

'You'll get your call-up papers in a couple of weeks or so,' he said gruffly.

Thirteen

'Where have you been until this time of night?' was her mother's greeting when Carolyn arrived home. 'I know you said you were going to be late, but I hadn't realized just how late you meant.'

'It took longer to get back and then I had to cycle home . . .'

'What on earth are you talking about, Carolyn?'

'I've been to Grantham to enlist in the ATS – the Auxiliary Territorial Service.'

Lilian's mouth dropped open then, recovering herself, she grabbed Carolyn's arm and dragged her into the kitchen where Eddie was sitting by the fire reading the newspaper he now brought home from his father's each evening.

'Eddie!' Eddie's peace was shattered in a moment at the sound of his wife's irate voice. 'D'you know what your stupid daughter has done now? It's not enough that she's refused the best offer of marriage she's ever likely to get, but she's gone and joined the ATS. She's been all the way to Grantham without telling us. Aye, and I know why, an' all. Because we'd have stopped her, that's why. You're still under-age, Carolyn. You're not twenty-one until June.'

With a sigh of resignation, Eddie folded the

newspaper. 'Actually, Lilian, you're wrong there, because I wouldn't even have *tried* to stop her.' He smiled up at his daughter. 'Well done, love. Did you get in?'

'I – I think so. I'll get a letter—'

'Not if I can help it. I'll burn it,' Lilian snapped.

'You'll do no such thing, Lilian.' Eddie's tone was firm, something that Carolyn didn't hear very often from her gentle, unassuming father. 'On two counts. You'll not interfere with what Carolyn wants to do and besides, if you destroy an official letter, you could get yourself arrested. And while we're on the subject, I shall be joining the Home Guard in Skegness. I won't be called up, but I want to do my bit.'

Lilian glared at her husband but said nothing.

'There's – there's something else, Dad.'

'Lilian, get the lass her tea and she can tell us when she's eaten. I bet you haven't had much to eat all day, have you, love?'

Carolyn shook her head and her father added, 'No, I thought not.'

Half an hour later, Carolyn went into the front room. She tapped Tom on his shoulder. He looked up and lifted one of the headphones away from his ear. 'What?'

'Can you come into the kitchen? I've got something to tell you all.'

'Give me ten minutes.'

She nodded and left the room. 'Tom'll come in a moment,' she told her parents. 'He should hear this as well.'

As they waited, Lilian said, 'This is all about Peter, isn't it?' She was a little calmer now, but there was still an edge to her tone. 'I've had Phyllis here ranting and raving again. I hope you know how very much you've disappointed both Phyllis and me—'

'Ah,' Eddie butted in with relief. 'Here's Tom. Come and sit down, lad. Carolyn has something that she wants us all to hear.'

Over the next half an hour, Carolyn recounted all that had happened that day, ending, 'Major Jefferson said a colleague of his would likely come to see Tom and probably Mr Fox too. He might come with him. He thinks you might both be able to help the war effort.'

'I won't have Tom going away. You had no right to say anything about your brother, Carolyn. You might get us all into trouble.'

'Actually, I asked the major that and his exact words were "far from it". He thinks we're ideally placed here on the coast to listen in to messages in the North Sea. I think they'll want Tom – and possibly Mr Fox too – to do it officially.'

'But he's not old enough . . .' Lilian began.

'Age will have nothing to do with something like this, Lilian,' Eddie put in. 'It'll be his capabilities they'll want to test.'

'But – but he's got school to go to.'

'They'll understand that. They won't interfere with his schooling. Most likely they'll give him a timetable he can manage for listening in. Let's just wait and see, shall we?'

*

The major and a colleague, who was dressed in the uniform of an army captain in the Royal Signals, arrived just over a week later on the Saturday morning. Lilian opened the door to them and found herself flustered by the arrival of the two smartly dressed men.

'Can I get you a cup of tea? Something to eat?' she asked, fussing around them and inviting them to sit down by the range.

'A cup of tea would be most welcome, Mrs Holmes. Thank you,' Major Jefferson said and introduced his colleague. 'This is Captain Delaney. He is from a department that is very interested in what your son is doing, if what I understood from your daughter is correct.'

'She'd no right to say anything about our Tom. He's only fifteen. I won't have him being taken away from home. He's still at school and doing very well.'

'Please don't concern yourself, Mrs Holmes. It's what he is already doing at home that interests us. Now, is he here?'

Lilian sighed. 'Finish your tea and I'll take you to him.'

Five minutes later, Lilian opened the door into the front room and ushered the two men in. They were met by the blipping from Tom's wireless and saw the young boy hunched over his notepad, writing swiftly. They stood quietly until he had finished and had removed his headphones. He jumped visibly as his mother spoke; he had been unaware of anyone entering the room, so engrossed had he been. He turned and looked up at the two strangers.

110

Captain Delaney moved closer, casting an expert's eye over Tom's wireless equipment.

'My word, young man. You are well set up, aren't you? Did you build this yourself?'

'With Mr Fox's help.'

'Ah yes, we know about Mr Fox. We're going to see him after we've talked to you.' The captain pulled up a chair and sat down beside Tom. 'Now, tell me what sort of messages you've been picking up . . .'

The major turned to Lilian. 'I'll think we'll leave them to it, Mrs Holmes. This will get far too technical for me and, if I'm not being too cheeky, I would love another of those delicious scones you gave us and a second cup of tea.'

Lilian preened and led the way back into the kitchen.

Eddie arrived home for his dinner while the visitors were still there. He shook hands with Major Jefferson, who told him, 'You have every reason to be very proud of both your children. Your daughter's skills will be most useful in the service she has applied to join and Tom can even play his part from home, young though he still is. I do hope this has your approval?'

Eddie didn't even glance towards his wife before saying, 'Of course. Anything we can do to help. There is just one thing; I wouldn't want anything he does for you to interfere with his normal schoolwork. We're very hopeful that he will stay on to take his Higher School Certificate.'

'We'll do our very best to make sure that what we

want him to do will not interfere with his schooling.' The major smiled. 'We need bright young men like him. We're on our way to meet Mr Fox now, but I can tell you that we hope to enlist both Mr Fox and Tom to work for us from their own homes. We will draw up a timetable for them both. It will probably be a couple of hours each evening for Tom – say six to eight o'clock – with some time on Saturdays and Sundays. We will talk to Mr Fox about what he is able to do. You should also know that, unfortunately, we may have to remove the transmitter from Tom's equipment, but,' he added hastily, 'it'll only be for the duration of the war.'

'What about the messages they get? I mean what do they *do* with them?'

The major smiled. 'You've probably noticed that there is, at the moment, an army – er – *presence*, shall we say, at the Point. We will arrange for a despatch rider to pick up Tom's notes each evening after he finishes his session and then pick up Mr Fox's too and take them to wherever they need to be. You can leave all that to us.'

'What will he need? Plenty of paper and pencils, I expect,' Eddie asked. Lilian was taking no part in the conversation but she was listening intently.

'If you could provide him with pencils, we'll see that he gets everything else he needs and he'll receive instructions as to what we want him to do and how to do it. There is just one thing, though. Anyone who lives in this house will be required to sign the Official Secrets Act and that means that you must not breathe a word about this to anyone, not even to relatives.

You're nice and remote out here, so it shouldn't be much of a problem for you.'

Now Lilian spoke for the first time since Eddie had arrived home. 'His grandfather knows about his wireless set. He bought a lot of the equipment for him. I mean, it was just a boy's hobby – then.' The tone of her voice told the three men in the room that she wished it was still just that.

'I understand,' Major Jefferson said. He was thoughtful for a moment before adding, 'It might be as well for him to sign the act too. And now, we'll thank you for your hospitality, Mrs Holmes, and be on our way.'

'There's just one more point,' Eddie said. 'I know it's a long way off yet, but what will happen when Tom gets to eighteen? I wouldn't want him to be seen by the locals as a shirker.'

The major smiled. 'As you say, it's a way off yet, Mr Holmes, and we all hope the war will be over by then. But if it isn't, we'll make sure Tom is protected.'

Fourteen

'Ah, do come in,' George Fox greeted the two men as he opened the front door of his house, which was set up on a ridge overlooking the North Sea at the northern end of the town. They had left their vehicle on the road and walked up the sloping driveway to the house. 'I've been expecting you. Tom said you might be visiting us both.' Limping a little, George led the way through the hall and up the stairs to a bedroom that looked out over the sand dunes and the sea. 'This'll be what you've come to see, I expect.'

The major and the captain leaned over the wireless equipment. 'You certainly know how to construct a transmitter and receiver, sir,' Captain Delaney said. 'Though I'm afraid we may have to remove the transmitters, both yours and Tom's – though, on second thoughts, perhaps we could leave you with yours. It might come in useful at some point. I'll speak to my superiors about that.'

George inclined his head but said nothing.

The major gave George their names and then went on, 'So, you've helped young Tom to build his own set and you've also taught him Morse?'

'That's right. He's an able pupil – a quick learner. So is his sister.'

'Ah, yes. I've met her,' Major Jefferson said.

George nodded. 'Yes, Tom told me how this has all come about. She's applied to join the ATS, I understand.'

The major didn't reply; it didn't do to tell people much, but, of course, he was obliged to explain how they planned to utilize Tom's abilities and George's too.

'We're suggesting that young Tom should listen in from six to eight each evening. He's assured us he can manage that without disrupting his homework needs. Then, if you could do from eight to ten, the despatch rider can pick up Tom's notes at about nine-thirty and then come on here to collect yours. As regards the weekend, Tom says he can do two to four each afternoon. Would you be able to work around that, sir?'

George nodded. 'That would suit me nicely. I could probably do twelve to two and four to six on both days, if you like, and I can certainly do the evening hours in the week you suggested.'

'That would be excellent. Thank you. We would also need you and your wife to sign the Official Secrets Act and what you are doing must not be talked about to anyone, is that understood?'

George nodded. 'Yes, I understand, although it might be as well to involve my headmaster – both for my sake and for Tom's. I'm sure he would be willing to sign the Act too if it were necessary.'

George and Tom started 'doing their bit' for the war effort even before Carolyn got her papers. She carried on working at Woolworth, but the atmosphere was uncomfortable. She had to put up with the other girls sniggering behind their hands and casting arch looks towards her. So it was a great relief when a letter arrived in March together with a railway warrant telling her to report for her basic training in two weeks' time. Carolyn heaved a sigh of relief. Now she could hand in her written notice.

'I'm sorry to see you go, Miss Holmes, but I understand your reason,' Mr Williamson said, shaking her hand. 'Good luck.'

'So, you're off then,' Lilian said.

'Yes, Mam. Do I look all right?'

'You do, but I'm surprised you're going in your Sunday-best clothes. What'll happen to them when you get issued with your uniform? They might get lost.'

'I'll try to keep them safe and bring them home when I get some leave, but I want to look smart, Mam. I want to make a good impression.'

Lilian sniffed. 'Well, that's understandable, I suppose. Off you go, then. I can hear your grandad's truck arriving to take you to the station.'

Carolyn kissed her mother's cheek and hurried outside. She'd said goodbye to her father and to Tom before they'd left for work and school, so there was only her mother to wave her off.

'You look nice, lass.' Frank smiled. 'You'll look even smarter in uniform.'

They didn't talk much on the short journey to the station, but she could see in his eyes that her grandfather was feeling her going. When they parted, he

116

hugged her tightly and whispered, 'Now, you take good care of yourself and write to me every week. No excuses now.'

'I will,' Carolyn said, her voice a little husky. 'I promise. And you take care of yourself too.'

As she boarded the train, she glanced back to give him a final wave and was touched to see how old he was looking now. The last six years since her grandmother had died had certainly taken their toll on him. While he had plenty of family nearby to look out for him, he still lived on his own and it was an empty house he went back to every evening.

Carolyn had been sent to Leicestershire for her basic training, the place where the Leicester Regiment had their home. Stepping down from the train in Loughborough, she was relieved to see a group of young women on the platform who, she guessed, were on their way to the same place. They were, in the main, smartly dressed and chatting easily to each other, even though at the moment they were strangers. Transport had been arranged from the station – they all climbed into the back of a troop carrier – and, arriving at the barracks, they were shepherded towards the canteen.

'Hello. I'm Beryl.'

Carolyn glanced up from her lunch as, without invitation, a short, rather plump but beautifully proportioned girl with blond hair, blue eyes and a wide, red-lipsticked mouth plonked her tray down on the table. She was dressed in a floral summer dress and a small, dainty hat perched cheekily to one side of her head. She wore white gloves and high-heeled shoes. Her outfit didn't look quite right for March, which could still be cold, Carolyn thought as Beryl sat down and held out her hand. 'You're Carolyn, aren't you? I heard someone call you that. Where are you from?'

'Erm,' Carolyn hesitated for a moment, unsure just how much information they were supposed to reveal. Having been exposed already to the Official Secrets Act because of Tom's work, she was aware how careful everyone had to be. She took a deep breath and went on, 'Skegness on the Lincolnshire coast.'

'Are you really? I've been there. My family went there one summer for two weeks' holiday in a caravan.' She pulled a face. ''Spect we won't be going for a bit now, though, will we? Unless, of course' – she giggled – 'you were to invite me to stay with you.' She laughed even louder at the startled look on Carolyn's face. 'Don't mind me. I'm only teasing. I'm a cheeky cow. Everyone says so, but I'm quite harmless. I'm from Sheffield, but I expect you can tell that from my accent.'

'Your city was badly bombed last December, wasn't it?'

For a moment, the girl's face clouded. 'It was, but we were lucky. Nothing fell in our street.' She paused and then, regaining her cheerful attitude, said, 'What d'you think to all this, then? Going to like it, are you?'

Carolyn smiled. She couldn't help it. The girl was so friendly and bubbly, it would be hard not to respond. Besides, Carolyn had no intention of snubbing her approach; she had been feeling a little homesick already and needed a pal. She'd never travelled very far from her home town before. 'I think it'll be all right. Everyone seems very friendly.'

'I suppose the real test will be where we get posted to eventually. I expect I'll end up as a clerk somewhere.'

'What did you do before?' Carolyn asked.

'I was a Comptometer operator.'

'What's one of those? I've never heard of it.'

'It's like a big adding machine, but it does subtraction and multiplication too. It was invented and made in America, but firms here have started using them. I worked for one of the big firms in Sheffield and they used them for stock control.'

'So you're pretty nifty with your fingers, then?'

The girl smiled in acknowledgement and asked, 'What do you do, or rather what *did* you do?'

'I worked in our local Woolies, first as a shop assistant then in the office, but I learned to touch type in my own time and I do shorthand.' Carolyn said nothing at present about her knowledge of Morse code, but she had already decided to apply for whatever course there was for that after her initial training when, no doubt, there would be a selection process.

'You're sure to be sent somewhere as a clerk too, then,' Beryl said.

Carolyn smiled, but she still said nothing about her ambitions within the service. There would be time for confidences later, when she got to know Beryl a little better.

Fifteen

'Let's stick together,' Beryl said as a young woman in uniform, whom they later found out was called a section leader, led them out of the canteen and towards the army hut where they would sleep for the next few weeks. They were shown how to stack their bedclothes.

'There's a kit inspection every morning and you must learn how to do it properly,' they were told.

Carolyn and Beryl chose adjoining single iron beds.

'This is going to be strange, sleeping in a room with so many other girls,' Carolyn murmured, but Beryl said nothing; she seemed to be concentrating on learning how to fold her sheets and blankets correctly, in the pattern the officer was explaining.

'Grey blanket on top, then a sheet . . .' Beryl was muttering.

There was a lot of laughter in the line of girls when they collected their kit.

'Just look at these,' Beryl trilled as she held up a pair of voluminous khaki knickers. 'Passion killers, if ever I saw them.'

The giggles rippled down the line, suppressed only by a glare from the officer overseeing the procedure.

Carolyn loaded everything over her arm; underwear items, a jacket, pyjamas, skirts, shirts with separate collars, ties, three pairs of thick, khaki stockings, a warm greatcoat and heavy lace-up shoes. The list went on until they could hardly carry everything.

'Don't forget your kitbag, helmet and gas mask, girls,' someone at the back of the line trilled and everyone took up the chant.

'Don't forget your gas mask . . .'

'What on earth are these?' Beryl said loudly, picking up a pair of heavy shoes. 'I'm never going to catch a feller wearing these.'

'You're not here to "catch a feller",' the young woman in uniform behind the trestle table overseeing the distribution of kit snapped. 'You're here to help win the war.'

But Beryl was unfazed. 'And these?' Now she held up a pair of plimsolls. 'For PT, I suppose.'

The girl in the line behind Beryl giggled. 'Or for marching.'

Beryl turned to her with wide eyes. 'Marching? I thought that was what these awful shoes were for.'

'Usually, yes, but my sister joined the ATS last year and they had to catch a train in the early hours one morning and they had to march through the town in plimsolls so's not to disturb the townsfolk. Anyway, word must have got around somehow that they were leaving, because there were a lot of the residents on the streets to wave them off anyway.'

'Fancy,' Beryl murmured and moved on.

At the end of the row of tables, a different ATS girl, who looked immaculate in her uniform, said, 'You'll need these too. This is what we call a "housewife". It's a small sewing kit and there's also a button stick.'

'What's that used for?' Carolyn asked as she picked it up. It was a flat piece of metal with a slit up the middle.

'For polishing your buttons, to stop you getting the brass cleaner onto the clothes.'

'How ingenious,' Carolyn murmured.

Their weeks of basic training were filled with medical examinations and fitness tests and an awful lot of marching and drill, taken by a gruff male sergeant who barked orders in a loud voice and gave no quarter to the fact that they were female. But, gradually, the girls learned their left from their right and all turned in the same direction at the same time. There were also aptitude tests to see which branch of the service might suit each girl the best.

'What do you think those hearing tests were for?' Carolyn said.

'To make sure we can hear the enemy coming,' Beryl quipped.

'No, I'm being serious. They asked me to identify all sorts of different sounds.'

'Yeah, me too.'

'Did everyone have to do those?'

Beryl yawned. 'No idea. Sorry, Carolyn, I'm whacked.'

With all the physical activity and the IQ tests too, they all fell exhausted into their beds at night.

'I can't even be bothered to sort my biscuits out to be comfortable,' Beryl said sleepily, referring to the three three-foot squares that made up a so-called mattress.

'Just so long as you're up bright and early for the daily hut inspection,' Carolyn murmured from the next iron bed. Each morning the three 'biscuits', pillow, sheets and blankets had to be laid out on the bed in a certain order, while each girl stood by the bed with buttons and shoes highly polished. There were regular kit inspections, too, where everything had to be laid out in a specific way for an officer to check for anything missing or in need of repair.

The only reply from Beryl was a groan followed by, 'Roll on Saturday, when we can take the bus into Leicester and spend our hard-earned pay.'

'That won't take long,' Carolyn muttered. 'I earned more than twice as much at Woolies.'

But now there was no response from the next bed, only a gentle snore.

After the first weeks of drilling on the parade ground, a lot of the girls were limping.

'I'm not sure which is hurting the most,' Beryl moaned. 'My arm from the inoculations with that blunt needle or my feet. I've got a blister on my heel the size of a penny.'

'I'll get you a bowl of warm water,' Carolyn offered.

When she returned, a girl sitting next to Beryl with her feet in a bowl of purple water said, 'Here, have a drop of this,' as she held out a small bottle.

'What is it?' Beryl asked a little suspiciously.

'Not sure,' the girl said cheerfully. 'But my dad

uses it in the garden and he swears by it if he gets any sort of blister or sore. He insisted I bring some with me. "You'll get blisters when you start square-bashing," he said and he was too damn right.'

'Thanks,' Beryl said.

'You don't need much – just a few drops – and you can use my old towel to dry your feet when you've had a good soak. About ten minutes is enough. But it can turn towels a funny colour and you don't want to be on a charge for damaging ATS property.'

'Why haven't you got blisters, Carolyn?'

'I think my feet are pretty tough from tramping around the fields at home in wellies.'

'I'm so fed up with all this marching. When do we get to do something different?' Beryl moaned as she dried her feet after soaking them.

'Funny you should say that,' Carolyn said. 'I've heard on the grapevine that tomorrow we're going to have some sort of special training.'

'What?'

Carolyn shrugged. 'Don't know, but we can only hope that it gives our feet a rest.'

The next day, as the girls lined up on the parade ground, they were issued with gas masks.

'I'm not sure I like the look of this,' Beryl murmured.

'Be careful what you wish for, don't they say?'

'Yeah. Maybe we should have stuck to drilling.'

'Too late. Come on, we'd better keep up.'

They ran across the open space to a hut at the far side where their section leader was standing.

'This morning,' the young woman said in a clear voice, 'we're practising being caught in a gas attack. You will enter the hut and once inside remove your gas mask for a few moments – not too long, mind – so that you experience what a real gas attack would be like. And I'd like you to go in in pairs. Watch out for each other just as you would if it was a real attack. Apart from anything else, this should serve to remind you to always have your gas mask with you, no matter where you are. Now,' she pointed at Beryl and Carolyn, 'since you two were the last to arrive, you can go in first.'

'Right, let's show 'em, Carolyn. Hang on to the back of my jacket. We'll get in, count to twenty and then take off our masks. All right?'

They pulled on their masks and, with Beryl leading the way, they went into the darkened hut. Carolyn caught hold of Beryl's jacket as she began to count to twenty. She could hear her friend muttering, but through the mask the words were indistinct. She removed her mask and at once the gas stung her eyes.

'It's tear gas, Beryl. Let's get out of here.'

'Give it a few seconds more,' Beryl spluttered, moving towards the door at the far end of the hut, opposite to where they'd entered. 'Don't want 'em thinking we're a couple of cowards.'

By the time they staggered out of the hut, they were coughing and their eyes were streaming. One or two of the other girls standing in line turned pale.

'It's not that bad,' Beryl wheezed when she had regained her breath. 'Better to know what we're in for.'

Her words gained a smile and a nod from their section leader. 'Go and get something to drink,' she said.

'Thanks,' Beryl said, and as they walked away, she muttered, 'Well, if that show of leadership doesn't get me a stripe, I don't know what will.'

At the end of the weeks of basic training and their passing-out parade, when everything from shoes to buttons had to be shining, they were both posted to the Chilwell ordnance factory in Nottinghamshire.

'You as a filing clerk,' Carolyn said, unable to hide the disappointment in her tone. 'And me as a short-hand typist.'

'At least we'll still be together.' There was a tinge of doubt in Beryl's voice, as if she thought that perhaps Carolyn didn't want to be with her.

'Yes, we will be, and I'm really glad about that,' Carolyn's smile was genuine, 'I just so wanted to become a wireless operator. Still, never mind.'

'Maybe the tests we took weren't up to scratch.'

Carolyn shrugged. 'I don't suppose for a minute they'd tell us, even if we asked.'

'You bet they wouldn't. "You're in the army now and you'll do as you're told",' Beryl said, mimicking a superior officer's voice and they both dissolved into laughter.

Sixteen

'We're not allowed any leave, it seems, until the end of June,' Carolyn told Beryl when they had settled into their new posting. Carolyn found herself in a small typing pool with three other ATS girls producing small labels for the spare motor parts being sent out to various war zones. It was repetitive and boring – not at all what Carolyn had hoped to do.

'It's amazing what noise four typewriters can make when we're all going at full speed. My head's positively aching,' Carolyn moaned to Beryl at the end of their first day.

'I know. I have to come into your room quite a lot to those filing cabinets against the back wall. It's a right racket. What was it you were saying about leave?'

'Evidently, we're not allowed leave until we've done three months' service. That takes you and me until the end of June and then we don't get very long.'

'I'll have to stay here, though,' Beryl sighed.

'Will you? Why? Oh sorry, I shouldn't have asked. It's none of my business.'

Beryl smiled weakly. 'It's just a bit difficult.'

Carolyn waited but no further explanation was

forthcoming, so she thought quickly. She was sure it would be all right to take Beryl home with her. 'Come home with me, but we're not very grand, I'm afraid. We live in the back of beyond and we might have to share my bed, though it is a double.'

Beryl stared at her, open mouthed. 'D'you really mean it? I mean, won't your mother mind a complete stranger turning up on her doorstep unannounced?'

'No, I'm sure she won't. Besides, it's a few weeks before we can go, so I've time to write and ask her.'

'What about the rest of your family?'

'There's just my dad and a brother, Tom. He's fifteen.'

'D'you get on all right with him?'

'Fine. We're great mates.' She bit her tongue, not yet ready to confide in Beryl what her brother was actually doing with his hobby, which had become so much more important now. Besides, she had signed the Official Secrets Act. Instead, she said, 'He's still at school. He's taking his School Certificate any time now and he'll be staying on into the sixth form. My mother insists!'

'And your dad?'

'He works for his own father, who has a joinery business on one of the main roads leading out of town. Mam's dad – he's a widower – has a farm. We live in one of its cottages on the road leading out to the Point.'

'I remember that. We went there when we were on holiday that time. Lovely place, but a bit wild for me. I'm a city girl, really.' Beryl paused and then asked, 'Have you got a boyfriend?'

'No.'

Beryl waited but Carolyn said no more. 'That was a bit sharp,' Beryl ventured. 'Been let down, have you?'

Carolyn sighed. 'No, but I had a bit of bother over a lad I'm friendly with.'

'Well, I won't pry . . .' Beryl said, but the look in her eyes told Carolyn that the girl was itching to know more. 'Look, I know I come across as a chatterbox and a bit of a scatterbrain, but I can keep my mouth shut when necessary. We'll all have to keep lots of secrets soon enough in this game, won't we?'

'I'm very good friends with a lad called Peter . . .' Carolyn paused and sighed. 'Both our mothers have been – well, pushing us together for years.' She smiled wryly. 'They've almost planned the wedding, but Peter and I had a long heart-to-heart talk and we both agreed that although we are extremely fond of each other and the very best of friends, neither of us wants to marry the other.'

Beryl snorted ironically. 'I don't believe girls and boys can ever be friends.'

'Why ever not?'

She shrugged. 'Because sooner or later one of them will start to get romantic feelings for the other and if it's not reciprocated, then there's real trouble and what was once a nice friendship goes out the window.'

'I can see how that might happen, but in our case we really are just friends. Ever since we were kids,' Carolyn went on. 'He worked for my grandfather. He and his widowed mother live in a tied cottage on the farm. But at the beginning of this year, he

129

volunteered for the services and his mother blames me for, as she said, refusing his proposal. The daft thing is, Peter never proposed, but she caused trouble for me at work. She came into the store one day, shouting her mouth off and – well, it made things very uncomfortable for me. So, I volunteered too. Don't get me wrong, I would have done so eventually anyway. I wanted to do something for the war effort. I just did it a bit sooner than I might have done. By the way, please keep all this under your hat. My family don't know about Peter's mother making a scene at Woolworth and I don't want them to. My mother's not one to take things lying down. There'd be an unholy row with Peter's mother and my poor dad and grandad would be caught in the middle of it.'

'I won't breathe a word.' Beryl promised and then frowned. 'Will his mother still be able to live in the cottage if he's gone?'

'Oh yes. Grandad wouldn't turn her out and, besides, she cleans for him and works in the dairy.'

The merry smile was back on Beryl's face. 'So if you're sure it'll be all right, I'd love to come with you.'

Although Carolyn hadn't minded in the least telling Beryl about her own family, she was still puzzled as to why the girl said little or nothing about her own.

'We'll visit my grandad first,' Carolyn said as they stepped off the train. 'He likes pretty girls.' She laughed. 'In the nicest possible way, I mean. Now let's see if we can hitch a lift to the farm. It's a long way.'

'After all the route marching we've done over the last few months, I'm sure it'll be a doddle. Thank goodness the ATS shoes are *sensible*. I hated them at first – and giving up my lovely high heels – but now I know just why they have to be so sturdy.'

Frank flung open the back door of the farmhouse when he saw them crossing the yard. 'Come in, come in.' He opened his arms wide as if to embrace them both. He kissed his granddaughter on both cheeks and shook Beryl's hand warmly.

As if to confirm Carolyn's words, he chuckled and said, '*Two* beautiful girls visiting me. How lucky am I? Sit down, both of you. I'll make some tea and yar mam left me some freshly baked muffins this morning.'

'I'll do it, Grandad. You sit and talk to Beryl.'

'Eh, I've missed you, lass,' he murmured, touching Carolyn's cheek with gnarled fingers.

She grinned at him. 'No one to do the washing-up, eh?' But they exchanged a loving look that said that was definitely not the reason.

While Carolyn busied herself in the scullery, she heard Frank and Beryl chatting amiably. As she went back into the kitchen, carrying a tray, she heard Beryl say, 'We've been lucky that we've been posted together . . .' The girl seemed about to say more, but with a swift glance at Carolyn, she fell silent.

'How long are you likely to be wherever it is you are at the moment?' Frank asked. 'I've heard that the forces have a habit of shifting folks from one place to another quite regularly.'

Beryl shrugged. 'They haven't said.' She glanced at Carolyn, unsure how much to say in front of Frank, but he helped her out by saying, 'I'm not going to ask any questions. I know how secretive everything has to be.'

'It's just boring clerical work, Grandad,' Carolyn said as she set the tray down. 'But I am using my shorthand and typewriting skills now.'

Beryl pulled a face. 'And I am learning the skill of keeping numerous files in apple-pie order.'

As he bade them goodbye at the back door, this time he kissed both girls on the cheek saying with a chuckle, 'Be good and if you can't be good, be careful.'

'He's a diamond, your grandad.'

'He's taken a shine to you, I can tell,' Carolyn said, laughing.

As they were about to head towards Carolyn's home, two figures appeared in the yard.

'Oh, there's Uncle Harold and Adam too. We must have a word with them.'

'Can't shek 'ands, miss,' Harold said to Beryl when she held out her hand. 'They'm mucky.' He nodded to Carolyn. 'You all right, lass?'

'Yes, thank you, Uncle. Are you and Aunty Eve well?'

'Aye, fair to middlin', ta.'

Carolyn turned to greet her young cousin. 'I can see this young scallywag is in fine fettle. I reckon you've grown even since I last saw you.'

'He keeps shooting up,' Harold said. 'His mam can't keep pace with his clothes. And eating! I dorn't know where he puts it all.'

Adam greeted them both with a wide grin, his brown eyes glinting a welcome. His shock of red hair peeked out from beneath his flat cap and freckles peppered his nose and cheeks. He was indeed tall for his age. It was obvious that farm work was already beginning to make him broad-shouldered and strong.

'You want to get your Tom out into the fresh air,' the young boy said. 'He's getting round-shouldered and pasty-faced bein' indoors all the time, crouched over—'

'Adam!' his father snapped, a warning note in his tone, but Adam only grinned afresh and winked at Carolyn.

'Come on,' Harold said brusquely. 'Pigs won't feed theirsens and there's the cows to milk yet.'

He nodded a farewell and turned away.

'Don't mind Uncle Harold,' Carolyn said as they walked away. 'He can be a bit grumpy. I expect he's missing Peter. His workload will have fallen heavily on Uncle Harold and Adam now.'

'Why don't they get a couple of land girls?' Beryl said with a laugh. 'Your grandad would like that.'

'I bet he would, but Uncle Harold wouldn't. His views on women working are just the same as my mam's. A woman's place is in the home.'

'Oh heck. One of those, is she? I reckon I'd better turn round and catch the train back to Nottingham.'

'Don't be daft. What you do is no business of hers, though I should warn you she might have a go at me.' Carolyn paused while she jumped over a puddle in the rutted lane. 'There is something I should tell you about before we get there.'

133

'Go on. I'm all ears.'

'Adam nearly let it out just now before Uncle Harold shut him up.'

'This sounds intriguing. Do tell.'

'You remember that when we arrived at Chilwell, we had to sign the Official Secrets Act because of all the confidential paperwork we'd be dealing with?'

Beryl nodded.

'Well, my whole family have had to sign it too.'

Beryl's eyes widened. 'Whatever for?'

'My brother, Tom, is a wireless enthusiast.'

'Go on.'

'With the help of his science teacher at school, he built a transmitting and receiving set. And now he listens in to shipping in the North Sea, but you can't breathe a word about it. You do realize that, don't you?'

'Do the authorities not know, then?'

'Oh yes,' Carolyn said airily. 'He's working for them now.'

Beryl's face was a picture.

Seventeen

To Carolyn's surprise, Lilian made her unexpected guest very welcome, readily involving her in the family.

'I've baked a special cake as it was Carolyn's twenty-first earlier this month. I thought we'd have a bit of a celebration now. Better late than never, eh? It's not up to my usual standard though' – she pulled a face – 'with all this wretched rationing.'

Lilian fussed over Beryl, serving her a generous slice of meat and potato pie and piling more vegetables onto her plate than the girl had ever seen at one mealtime. As they all sat down to eat, both Eddie and Tom joined them.

'It's nice to see a fresh face,' Lilian said. 'I'm not usually much of a mixer. I suppose being brought up in the wilds out here, you get used to your own company. But I have to admit I look forward to seeing the nice young soldier who calls every evening to take Tom's notes. Where he takes them, I don't know, but they obviously go somewhere and presumably they're quite important because—' Lilian broke off abruptly and she clapped her hand over her mouth. 'Oh my!'

'It's all right, Mam, Beryl knows what Tom's doing.

I told her before we got here. We've learned very quickly not to say anything about anything to anybody, so don't worry. I just hope you haven't said anything to Mrs Carter. She's a blabbermouth, if ever there was one.'

Lilian glanced away. Her lips were tight as she said, 'I don't see much of her now. I thought we were friends once, but she hardly speaks to me these days. I avoid going up to the farm when I think she'll be there. Before, I used to go up there early deliberately for a chat and a cuppa. But now . . .'

'I'm sorry, Mam,' Carolyn said quietly. And she was. She hadn't wanted to be the cause of her mother losing her friend, but Lilian only shrugged. 'If her friendship was that fickle, it wasn't worth having. Now, Beryl, love, have a bit more cake to finish off with. I baked it this morning, so it's nice and fresh. We're lucky we live on a farm,' she went on. 'We have to stick to the regulations, of course, but we have a plentiful supply of vegetables and whatever fruit is in season.'

'We won't be able to go picking blackberries at the Point anymore, though,' Carolyn said mournfully. 'I used to love doing that.'

'There'll still be plenty of hedgerows on the farm loaded with blackberries when the time's right,' Eddie reminded her. 'There's always lots on the lanes I cycle to work on.'

'Carolyn tells me you're a wheelwright, Mr Holmes,' Beryl said, smiling prettily at Eddie. 'Forgive my ignorance, but, being a city girl, I haven't a clue as to what that is exactly.'

'In the past, it was mainly making wheels for farm carts and suchlike. Mind you, the local wheelwright was usually the funeral director for the area too. We still are, and now our work includes general carpentry and joinery. There are a couple of builders in Skegness, who use us to do the woodwork in the houses they build.'

'It sounds like a thriving business. Is it yours?'

'My father's. He's still quite active, but I expect I shall take it over one day.'

'How lovely to keep it in the family.' Beryl glanced at Tom across the table. 'And I expect you will hand it to your son one day.'

Before anyone else could answer, Lilian cut in, 'Tom's clever. We're hoping he'll go to university.'

Beryl could feel the sudden tension in the air, so she said no more. She could be very tactful when it suited her. As she sat back in her chair at the end of the meal, she said, 'That was absolutely wonderful, Mrs Holmes, thank you. And now, Tom, I want you to show me this wireless set of yours. And don't worry, I won't breathe a word about it outside this house. I can be a bit of a chatterbox, but I do know how to keep secrets.'

Tom beamed and led the way into the front room. He, Carolyn and Beryl spent the rest of the evening listening in to his wireless. He even let them have a go at reading some Morse. Carolyn hadn't forgotten what he had already taught her and even Beryl could pick out a few easy letters by the time Carolyn yawned and said, 'Well, I'm for bed.'

The girls snuggled down together in the double

bed in Carolyn's room. They talked for a while, but they were both so tired that they soon fell asleep.

Carolyn and Beryl enjoyed the short holiday and when the time came for them to leave, Carolyn said, 'Mam's brought a message from Grandad. If we walk to the farm, he'll take us to the station in his farm truck.'

As the family stood on the doorstep to wave goodbye, Beryl said, 'You've got a lovely family, Carolyn.'

Seeing them for the first time through someone else's eyes, Carolyn wrinkled her forehead. 'They're all right. Mam seems to have lightened up a bit. She virtually killed the fatted calf for you.'

Beryl chuckled. 'They certainly all made me very welcome. Thanks for asking me, Carolyn.'

'No problem. If we stay together, you're welcome to come again, but I really think that next time we get a decent leave, you should go home to see your folks.'

Beryl, negotiating a muddy puddle, didn't answer.

One Saturday afternoon, early in September, there was a loud knock at the door of the Holmeses' cottage.

'Captain Delaney. Oh, and Major Jefferson too. How nice to see you again,' Lilian gushed as she opened the back door to the two officers. 'Please come in.'

'We were in the area,' the captain explained, 'so we thought we'd call in to see how Tom is progressing.'

Lilian smiled as she shrugged. 'As far as I know,

all right. His workings are still collected daily and he sometimes gets letters – though I don't know what's in them,' she added hurriedly.

The two men smiled but said nothing.

'He's been working a lot of extra hours through the summer holidays but now he's back at school – he's in the sixth form now – he's had to drop back to his two hours each evening, but he still does a few more at the weekend.'

'We understand, Mrs Holmes,' the major said smoothly. 'And, rest assured, we want Tom to continue his education as much as you do.'

'That's a relief. Now, let me get you both some tea and I've a sponge cake just out of the oven. A wartime recipe, I'm afraid, but it's not too bad. Please, go through.' She waved her hand in the direction of the front room.

When the two men entered the room, it was to see Tom hunched over his set, headphones clamped to his ears, writing furiously. They had to wait a few moments before he stopped writing and glanced up, becoming aware of their presence. He pulled the headphones from his ears. 'I think he's stopped,' he said, without greeting his visitors. 'There's this frequency I follow regularly and I almost feel as if I've got to know a particular operator. I always know when it's him. I can recognize his touch.' Tom grinned. 'I've nicknamed him Klaus.'

Captain Delaney smiled. 'That's what a lot of our operators say. They call it his "fingerprint" or his "fist". It's the way he transmits Morse or the same pattern of words he uses either at the beginning of a message or at the end that they can identify him by. Good work, Tom. Not all operators have that skill. We feel it's something that can't be taught, but well done and keep on it.'

'We were in the area,' Major Jefferson put in casually, 'so we thought we'd come and see if you were getting along all right. Is there anything you need?'

Tom wrinkled his forehead and flicked back the flop of his hair. 'I don't think so. A few pencils would come in handy. Dad has to keep buying them for me.'

'Sorry, old chap. All our operators have to provide their own.'

'How is your sister getting along?' Major Jefferson asked. 'She must have finished her basic training now.'

'All right, I guess. She's working as a shorthand typist, but she won't say where she is. She and her friend Beryl are still together. She – Beryl – was a Comptometer operator before she joined up. I expect they're in some office somewhere.'

A fleeting look of annoyance crossed the major's face and Tom knew a moment's fear. Perhaps he had said too much. But Major Jefferson's anger was not directed at the young man or what he had said. Having interviewed Carolyn himself, the major had considered that she would be an ideal candidate for specialized training as a wireless operator. And it sounded from what Tom had said as if her friend was worth a trial too. Surely they had not slipped through the net of IQ and aptitude tests?

Though he said no more, Major Jefferson pursed his lips and promised himself he would find out exactly where Carolyn Holmes and her friend were. With his contacts, he thought, it shouldn't take him long.

'Holmes – Morley. CO's office now,' the supervisor in charge of the typists bellowed from the front of the room.

'But, I haven't . . .' Carolyn, sitting at her typewriter, began, while Beryl slammed the drawer of the filing cabinet at the far end of the room and headed for the door.

'Now, Holmes! When the CO says "Jump" we just say "How high?". Go.'

As they hurried past her, they both heard her mutter. 'I don't know what the pair of you have been up to but it must be something serious.'

They entered the CO's office, saluted smartly, stood to attention and waited while the officer finished reading the letter he held in his hand and glanced up at them.

'It seems that your tests on leaving basic training have been reassessed. You are being posted to Trowbridge with immediate effect.'

Beryl opened her mouth and then closed it again. They were constantly being told they should not argue with an order or even ask questions. But a small smile quirked at the corner of the officer's mouth. Now his smile broadened as he said, 'Just between these four walls – and I really mean that – you are being sent for special training to become wireless operators.'

The two girls glanced at each other. Now Carolyn dared to ask, 'Learning Morse, sir?'

'Oh, I expect so,' he said airily. 'Now, off you go, the corporal in the outer office will give you your travel warrants as you leave. Finish off whatever you were doing and then be ready at seven tomorrow morning to be taken to the station. Good luck.' He did not add what he was thinking: you might need it.

As the two girls left his office, the officer picked up the telephone and asked for a number. When it was answered all he said was, 'Your two pigeons are flying.'

Outside his office, the two girls clutched each other.

'At last,' Carolyn said, and Beryl added, 'Come on, let's get out of here.'

Eighteen

'Our travel warrants say we've to go to London first,'
Carolyn said as, early the following morning, they
waited for transport to take them to the station in
Nottingham.

'That's a bit odd, but you know what train services
are like just now. They're being diverted all over the
place because movement of troops and equipment
comes first.'

'Do we have to change anywhere else?'

Beryl shrugged. 'I haven't a clue. Several times,
probably. I'm completely lost here. Now, if it was
Sheffield . . .'

'I expect it will take us most of the day to get
there. Do you know where Trowbridge is?'

'Wiltshire, I think.'

Carolyn had been right. They didn't arrive until
the evening, trudging uphill towards the barracks
carrying their heavy kitbags.

'You'd've thought there would have been some
sort of transport to meet us,' Beryl muttered.

'Maybe they're not expecting us. It did seem to
happen in rather a rush.'

But on arrival at the guard house, they were directed around the barrack square to the women's huts.

'Which one d'you suppose we're in?'

'Dunno. Let's knock on one of the doors and ask. Someone will know.'

'Hopefully,' Beryl murmured. Her eyes were already dark-ringed with tiredness.

Carolyn knocked softly on the door of the nearest hut. She didn't want to wake anyone. Although it wasn't late, she knew how tired the girls might be.

It was opened by a tall, thin girl.

'Oh hello, you must be the new arrivals. We've been expecting you. I'm Noreen Hunter, by the way. You're not in this hut.' She stepped across the threshold and closed the door behind her. 'You're next door. I'll take you there.'

'Thanks,' Beryl muttered and picked up her kitbag again.

'Have you had anything to eat?'

'Yes. The WVS were on the last station handing out tea and sandwiches, so we're fine, thanks.'

Noreen knocked on the door of the next hut and Carolyn and Beryl were welcomed inside.

'I'll leave you in Polly's capable hands,' Noreen said. 'See you tomorrow. Get a good night's sleep if you can. It's all "go" here.'

The girl Noreen had introduced as Polly ushered them inside, where the other girls they were to share with were getting ready for bed.

'I'll show you the bathrooms and toilets,' Polly said, 'and then I expect you'll want to get to bed. You both looked shattered and I'll warn you now the work's interesting – and they tell us it's going to be very useful – but it's intense. Your head will be buzzing by the end of the day. Get some sleep whenever you can.'

They returned to the hut to find that two iron beds at the far end had been left for them. As they passed down the centre of the room, the other girls waved or nodded hello, but they were all about to go to bed. Carolyn and Beryl undressed quickly, each pushing their belongings into a box at the side of the bed and hanging up their uniforms.

Despite the gruelling journey and the strange surroundings, they were both asleep in minutes.

The following morning, Polly led them to the cookhouse for breakfast. 'The food's not up to much here.' Polly grimaced. 'They seem to boil or fry everything, but we do have a canteen where you can buy cakes and, of course' – now she laughed – 'if you can get into the town, there's beans on toast to be had.'

The remainder of their first day was spent with the inevitable route march, drill and PT.

'But when do we get to do what we came here for?' Beryl muttered. 'I want to get on with learning Morse and now I've been told you and me have to join two other girls to do spud-bashing. As if that's going to help the war effort when we're supposed to be training to be specialized operators of some sort. I mean, what exactly are we being trained *for*?'

Carolyn shrugged. 'I don't suppose they're going to tell us until we reach the required standard. But Polly said this is the Special Operators Training Battalion.'

'And that is?'

'We've got to know how to maintain a wireless set and learn direction finding – whatever that is. And we've got to be able to read Morse at eighteen words per minute at the very least, so she said.'

Beryl gaped at her. 'Crikey! That sounds fast. What can you do?'

'Not sure, but Tom thinks I can do about twelve.'

'Right, then. You're going to have to help me catch up with you, because I'm determined we're going to stay together. I'm not getting left behind while you swan off to some fancy job without me.'

'If we can wangle it, we'll do extra practice.'

'You're on.' Beryl grinned.

The girls sat in rows at long tables, each with a set of headphones to receive messages and a telegraph key for transmitting. They were also given pencils and a pad printed with a grid.

'Now,' the instructor explained. 'The messages come in five-letter blocks, so if you miss a letter, you must leave a space. Don't forget the messages have to be decoded and the decoder must know when there's a letter missing. Let's make a start.'

'Ah,' Beryl murmured. 'Now I understand the reason for the grid.'

The learning process was intense and both Carolyn and Beryl – and all their fellow ATS girls – ended each day with bleary eyes and a buzzing in their heads.

'The work you'll be doing is vitally important,' their instructor told them repeatedly. 'Mistakes could cost lives – many lives. We have to be sure you can do this in your sleep.'

'I already am doing so,' Beryl muttered, but not loud enough to be heard.

'D'you think we're going to be taught how to send messages as well as receive them?' Carolyn said.

'Polly – the fount of all knowledge – said we'll do a bit but not much. We've got to concentrate on listening and writing it all down. By the way, do you understand what these Q codes are that we've got to learn by heart?'

'Polly said . . .' Carolyn began and they smiled at each other. 'Well, she does know a lot and she seems to be right in everything she says.'

'Thank goodness for the Pollys of this world,' Beryl murmured. 'Go on.'

'She says they are international signals to send instructions or special messages to the receiver. They're all three letters and all start with a Q. Like QRS asks them to "send slowly".'

'And we have to learn them by heart?'

' 'Fraid so.'

'So, not only have we got to learn the Morse for all the letters of the alphabet and numbers nought to nine, but we also have to learn these special codes too?'

Carolyn nodded.

'But there are dozens of them,' Beryl groaned.

'About a hundred, Polly says,' Carolyn said cheerfully. 'And then there's all the other stuff. Map reading, direction finding, electromagnetism . . .'

'Stop, stop. Enough.'

One or two of the girls couldn't stand the intensity of the work and were sent back to their previous postings, but Carolyn and Beryl ploughed on, determined not to be beaten. In the friendliest of ways, they vied with each other and spurred each other on. Although they had yet to be told what they would actually be doing, they both clung to the knowledge that eventually it would be, as their instructor kept impressing upon them, vital and important work. And that the need for speed and accuracy was paramount.

The two girls, keen to learn everything they could and to get the highest marks in the daily tests for speed and accuracy, were encouraged by an enthusiastic instructor, Lance Corporal Gladys Finney. Very recently the names of the various ranks of the ATS had been changed to the same as those in the British Army.

'Thank goodness for common sense,' Beryl had muttered when they'd heard. 'I never did understand the difference between a Chief Volunteer and a Sub-Leader, but now I know exactly what a lance corporal or a corporal is.'

Lance Corporal Finney encouraged their enthusiasm and often allowed them to work on their Morse together when perhaps they should have been running, drilling or spud-bashing.

'I don't know how she's managing it, but I'm so thankful she is,' Beryl said. 'If there's one thing I hate doing, it's peeling mounds of potatoes. Though I don't mind the drilling. It's taking inches off my waistline.'

What the two girls didn't know was that their instructor had had a quiet word with her sergeant.

'Those two girls – Holmes and Morley – have got real talent, ma'am. I think one of them has had previous knowledge of Morse somehow and the other one is catching her up fast.'

The sergeant had nodded. 'Well, encourage them in any way you can, but don't allow it to upset the other girls in the squad. I want a happy team, not one where there are festering resentments because they feel some are getting preferential treatment.'

'I'll have a quiet word with them both and see what we can work out between us. They have such promise, though, it'd be a shame for them not to reach their full potential.'

And so, without causing any ill-feeling amongst the other girls, Carolyn and Beryl managed to wangle extra time to practise their Morse skills. And it wasn't just Morse. They had to understand direction finding and map reading. Luckily, they both mastered those too. But they were careful always to join in the marching and drill and always attended the church parades on Sundays. They joined their squad's hockey team so that they didn't appear to be stand-offish and even made sure they did their fair share of potato peeling, but they were excused from fire-watching duties which they both hated. If anything suffered, it was their leisure time because they sneaked away to do extra Morse practice.

But one Saturday afternoon, Beryl said, 'Carolyn, I've had enough of being a goody two shoes. Let's go to the pictures with the other girls. Polly says they have fish and chips on the way home.'

Carolyn rubbed her eyes. 'Sounds like a great idea.'

She paused and then said, 'You know, I'd love to see a bit more of Wiltshire. It looks like a lovely county with undulating green hills – so different from the flatness of Lincolnshire where I live.'

'I'd love to see the famous white horse carved into the chalk,' Beryl sighed, 'but I expect they'll have covered that over because of the war. It'd be too much of a landmark for enemy aircraft.'

'I think there's more than one, isn't there?'

'Really? I hadn't heard that.'

'And then there's Stonehenge. I wonder what they've done with that?'

'No idea,' Beryl said losing interest. 'Come on, let's get ready to go out.'

It was a merry band of six girls, including Polly and Noreen, who set off into the town on a cold November afternoon to enjoy a proper break from their studies and the never-ending sound of dots and dashes in their ears. Outside the picture house they linked up with four young men from the barracks, who later insisted on paying for the girls' fish and chips and walking them back to the barracks.

'Was that chap I saw you with nice?' Beryl whispered as they got ready for bed.

'Yes, but not *that* sort of nice,' Carolyn giggled. 'Fergus, with a broad Scots accent, but he was very polite and courteous. Took my arm as we crossed the street. That sort of thing. What about you?'

'I think his name was Clifford, but he was like an octopus. Hands everywhere. And he wanted to kiss me "goodnight".'

'And did you let him?'

'Of course. Why not?'

Carolyn didn't quite know how to respond, but there was no need to, as at that moment the lights went out.

Nineteen

Just before Christmas 1941 – the third Christmas of the war – Beryl had mixed news for Carolyn. 'I've heard we're not going to be allowed home for Christmas, but there's a rumour going around that we're probably going to be posted some time fairly early in the New Year, though there's no news yet as to where we're going. I do hope we'll still be together.'

'Me too.'

'The girls are saying that they think we'll be given a seventy-two-hour pass to visit our families the weekend before we go to – wherever we're going.'

'That'll be to make up for us having to miss Christmas at home, I expect.' Carolyn paused and then asked, 'Shall you go home to see your folks this time?'

Beryl shook her head and avoided meeting Carolyn's gaze. 'No, it's a long way for such a short time.'

That was true, Carolyn thought, but so was the East Coast of Lincolnshire, which was much more difficult to get to as it involved several changes. It sounded to Carolyn as if Beryl was making excuses not to go home. She wondered why.

'Never mind. Come with me again. You'll be very welcome.'

'Are you sure?'

'Beryl,' Carolyn laughed, 'I've never seen my mother make such a fuss of a visitor. Believe me. It won't even matter if it's at short notice. So, will you come?'

Now Beryl turned to face her. 'Just try and stop me.'

'But before that,' Carolyn reminded her, 'we'll have all the tests to do.'

Beryl groaned.

'The first is going to be on direction finding. Come on, they're taking us out in jeeps with a wireless set to plot the position of a signal . . .'

Only an hour or so later, Carolyn and Beryl were walking back towards the barracks. 'Well, that was easy enough.'

But it seemed that the 'getting back' wasn't quite so easy for all the girls; some got completely lost and were late returning.

'It's all right for us,' Beryl laughed, commiserating with those in trouble with the sergeant. 'Carolyn lives in the country. She's like a homing pigeon, but if I'd been on my own, I don't think I'd be back yet.'

'The real tests will be tomorrow. Our Morse-listening skills. We've to take Morse for half an hour and then be tested on the Q codes too.'

'Early night for me, then,' Beryl said and Carolyn agreed.

The following day passed in rather a blur and all the girls were convinced they'd failed the tests, but the next morning they were to find that out of their group twelve had passed, including Carolyn, Beryl and Noreen. The rest were to be returned to their previous postings or training centres.

Those who had completed the course successfully had to read and digest the Official Secrets Act and then, fully aware of just how serious this now was, they had to sign it yet again.

'I suppose each place we go to wants us to sign it specifically for them, but I feel,' Beryl said soberly, 'as if I am signing away the next few years of my life.'

'I think we probably are,' Carolyn said, equally as solemn.

'We're really part of something now, though, aren't we, even if we don't know quite what yet.'

They were given the badge of the Royal Corps of Signals to wear over their left breast pocket.

'More brass to clean,' Beryl chuckled, but there was pride in her tone now.

'I really don't mind that,' Carolyn said. 'The navy and white flashes we're to wear on our sleeves are rather smart though. They make me feel rather important now, though why they should, I really don't know.'

'Polly says we've got a proper trade now. We're Special Wireless Operators and members of the Royal Corps of Signals. And, best of all, we get a pay rise. The higher our Morse speed the more money we get.'

'Really?' Carolyn grinned. 'Then I'm glad we gave up a lot of our spare time to improve.'

'But what are we actually going to *do*?' Beryl asked for the umpteenth time.

'No doubt they'll tell us in their own good time.'

'Perhaps we're going to be spies.'

'I doubt it. I would expect they have to be able to send messages as well as receive.'

'Well, we did a bit of that.'

'Yes, but don't you realize we weren't *tested* in transmitting?'

Beryl gaped at her. 'No, you're right. We weren't. So . . .'

'Don't ask, Beryl, it'll only get you into trouble. We'll find out soon enough.'

Two days before they were due to go on the promised leave at the end of February, Beryl said, 'We've got our posting and we're to go straight there after our leave. You'll never guess where?'

'Go on.'

'Back to Leicestershire,' Beryl said excitedly. 'It's not far from where we did our basic training and . . .' She grabbed hold of Carolyn around her waist and pulled her into a jig. 'Best of all, we're going there together.'

'That's marvellous.'

They danced around for a few minutes before stopping and leaning breathlessly against each other.

'Not that I don't want you to come home with me, but you have got time to see your family. Goodness knows when we might get a decent leave again.'

Beryl's face fell. 'I – I don't think I will. Travelling's so difficult just now with all the troop movements and I wouldn't like us to be late reporting to our new place of work – the War Office Y Group at Beaumanor Hall. It wouldn't look good to get off on the wrong foot.'

Carolyn had the distinct feeling that there was more behind Beryl's reluctance to go home for a short visit, but she did have a point; they certainly didn't want to be reprimanded for late arrival before they'd even started working there.

'Right then, you're coming home with me, as long as you don't mind sharing my bed again.'

Beryl laughed loudly. 'Since we've been sharing one on and off for weeks to keep warm in these draughty huts I don't think another couple of nights will matter. Thanks, I'd love to come.' She patted her stomach. 'Even if it's only for your mother's delicious pies and puddings.'

Two days later, with an unusual splash of extravagance, they shared a taxi to get them to Carolyn's home. They had more luggage with them this time as they were reporting at Beaumanor Hall straight after their leave.

'I don't think we'd better tell anyone exactly where we're going,' Carolyn said as they climbed out of the taxi in front of her home.

'We can just say somewhere in Leicestershire, can't we?'

Carolyn nodded. 'I expect that'll be all right.'

'We've got a bit of news too,' Lilian told them as they sat around the tea table. 'Your grandad has had a telephone installed. He says he needed it for the farm but he's told your dad that he wants you to ring him regularly to let us all know how you are.'

'My goodness, that must have cost him a bit! I mean, we're not even close to the town.'

Lilian shrugged. 'I haven't asked him. But will you do that, Carolyn? Telephone him regularly?'

'Of course, Mam. We'll go and see him while we're here. And we'll go and see Grandpa and Granny Holmes too. We'll make the last day a visiting day.'

The two days went very quickly, but on the last afternoon, after visiting Frank, Carolyn and Beryl cycled further on across the fields via the rutted lanes towards the main road.

'Does your dad cycle this way every day?'

'Yes, just morning and night on three days a week when Granny feeds him at dinner time. The rest of the time he cycles home at dinner time as well. Granny Holmes is a jolly little woman, whereas my grandpa is quieter.'

'Like your dad, then. He doesn't say a lot, does he?'

Carolyn wrinkled her forehead. 'No, I suppose he doesn't. I'd never really thought about it before, but now you mention it, he's not very talkative.' She chuckled. 'Maybe he can't get a word in edgeways with Mam, Tom and me.'

Beryl laughed with her. 'There is that.'

Beryl was made as welcome by Carolyn's Holmes grandparents as she had been by Frank. They lived in a house next door to the workshop over which hung the sign: *Norman Holmes and Son, Wheelwright and Joiner*. Norman was tall and thin and slightly stooped. He was clean shaven and his grey hair was thinning. Dorothy was always smiling and welcoming. From the moment her visitors stepped through her back door, she never stopped talking.

'I can see why your dad's a quiet one,' Beryl whispered. 'He never got a word in while he was growing up either.'

Carolyn hid her smile. She'd never realized it before; it took an outsider to see her family's character traits.

'It's lovely to see you – both of you. We heard about Frank getting the telephone installed at the farm, so we've decided to do the same here. It'll be a big help for the business and there'll be no excuse for you not to keep in touch, Carolyn. And with your dad being here six days a week, we can soon get messages to your parents. I'll let you know the number as soon as we have one . . .' On and on Dorothy prattled, but, Beryl thought, it was such lovely friendly chatter that she felt as if she were enveloped in a warm, cosy blanket. Carolyn's family had all made her feel so very welcome.

It was going to be even more difficult for her to put off inviting her friend to visit her own home in Sheffield.

Twenty

The train journey from Lincolnshire back to Leicester took longer than it would have done by motor car, but then it was the only way the girls could travel. As, at last, they stepped off the train in Loughborough, they were surprised to see several other girls already on the platform.

'Look,' Beryl grabbed Carolyn's arm, 'there's Noreen from Trowbridge.'

'Oh yes – and I recognize one or two others too, but I don't know their names.'

'There aren't many of us, though, are there?'

'Come along, you two,' Noreen's voice rose above the general chatter, 'we've been waiting for you. The troop carrier's outside.'

The vehicle trundled along narrow lanes until it came to a stop in the centre of a small village.

'Here we are,' the ATS driver called out merrily. 'This is our headquarters.'

As they climbed out of the back of the carrier, Beryl exclaimed, 'A pub! You've got to be joking.'

'It's not a pub at the moment,' their driver explained. 'It's been altered to fit our needs, but you're all likely to be billeted in the village. Come on, I'll take you in to meet our commander, Miss Everatt.'

She lowered her voice. 'She's a nice old stick if you toe the line, but don't get on the wrong side of her.'

The new arrivals trooped into the building, expecting to see a little grey-haired old lady; instead, they were greeted by a woman in her late thirties or early forties, looking extremely smart in her well-fitting uniform and wearing a broad smile of welcome.

'You must all be tired and hungry. Go and have a meal in the mess and I will see you after you have eaten.'

An hour later, as she stood before them, the commander explained what would be happening over the next few days. 'Corporal Johnson will take you to your billets down the road. Try to get a good night's sleep. The work you are here to do is very intensive, but also extremely important.' She paused a moment and glanced around at the puzzled faces. 'I can see from your expressions that you still haven't been told what the work is.'

A murmur of 'No, ma'am' rippled around the room.

'Have you all signed the Official Secrets Act?' There was now a unanimous 'yes' before she went on. 'What you will be doing is highly sensitive and most secret. You must not tell anyone – not even your families – what you are doing, or even where you are, nor must you talk to the locals about what goes on at Beaumanor.'

Carolyn breathed a sigh of relief. Thank goodness she and Beryl had said nothing about their posting at home.

'You are now part of the War Office Y Group and

you will be listening in to enemy messages in Europe and even as far away as North Africa. This, as you can imagine, requires monitoring twenty-four hours, seven days a week, so this is divided into four watches working in six-hour shifts on a three-week basis, but the times change each week. It sounds a little complicated, but you'll soon get the hang of it. We do advise you to get as much sleep as you can during your off-duty hours . . .' She smiled as she added, 'I do understand you will need some leisure time, but please be bright-eyed and bushy-tailed when you report for duty. I do have to fit in drill and PT from time to time, but I try to keep that to a minimum.' She paused a moment and cleared her throat as if what she had to say now was a little embarrassing. 'Our ATS girls are a relatively new addition here. Beaumanor was manned solely by male civilian operators, known as Experimental Wireless Assistants, until we began to arrive here last month.' She paused again. 'Some of the EWAs are, shall we say, a little less than welcoming. This is because – and I have to admit they have a point – our training has not been as good as it might have been. Some of the girls have had to go for additional training in Loughborough.' She glanced around the room. 'So, if this happens to you, don't be upset. You wouldn't even be here if you hadn't passed the tests, but it might be that some of you need a little extra help to reach the standard required here. Once you start work, you must not discuss it with anyone other than the sergeant of your watch or the supervisor of your hut. Not even with me. But if you have any other sorts of problems, then you come to me or my officers.'

She then read out all the names and to which watch they were all assigned.

'You'll be working at Beaumanor Hall about a mile and a half away and will be picked up by troop carrier at twelve forty-five tomorrow for your first week of shifts, which start at one p.m. You will all be issued with a special pass, which you must carry with you at all times or you won't be allowed in. Corporal Johnson will take you to your billets, which are all within easy walking distance from here.'

Carolyn, Beryl and Noreen had been assigned to 'C' watch and were also to be billeted together in a tall house with bay windows at the front. Carolyn and Beryl shared the first-floor front bedroom and Noreen had a smaller room at the back.

'Still with iron bedsteads and boxes for our belongings, I see,' Beryl said, as they glanced around the room. 'But it's a step up from a hut.'

Breakfast, they had been told, was in the mess back at the pub and they would have the morning to themselves as long as they were ready and waiting for the troop carrier.

'Let's have lunch,' Carolyn suggested, 'at about twelve, and then we'll be ready for the transport.'

'Good idea,' Beryl and Noreen, who had now attached herself to them, agreed. The two friends didn't mind. Noreen was a nice girl and fitted in with them. She didn't seem to have made a particular friend at Trowbridge – or, if she had, that friend had not been posted with them here.

*

The following morning, they were driven to the hall in about ten minutes. There were three other girls on the same shift who were also from their billet. It seemed as if those who worked together stayed together, which made sense to Carolyn and Beryl.

'Oh my,' Beryl breathed as they clambered out of the back of the carrier. 'It's a stately home.'

One of the girls introduced herself as Judith and told them she was the sergeant of their watch. She laughed now at Beryl's envious look at the big house. 'That's not where you'll be working, though. The house was taken over by Military Intelligence and there are people who work there – admin, an ops room, directional finding – oh, all sorts of things we aren't privy to, but we need to go round the side of the house to the huts in the field there. Come on, follow me.'

'Not huts again,' Beryl groaned.

But when they walked around the corner of the house and came out into the field it was to see several brick buildings dotted around the edge, some still under construction.

'They're being built to look like farm buildings – barns, stables or cottages. The walls are extra thick for blast protection, though I have to admit the roofs aren't, so if one got a direct hit . . .' Judith said no more but the newcomers understood.

'That one over there' – she flung out her left arm – 'built to look like a cricket pavilion, complete with painted clock, is the teleprinter room where all our messages go initially. We're in the hut over there that's built to look like workmen's cottages. D'you know, they even leave a couple of milk bottles outside to look like the place is lived in? Full in the morning and empty at night.'

'How ingenious,' Carolyn murmured.

As they walked across the grass, they glanced around them, seeing tall, thin aerials dotted around the area.

'There's just one thing I ought to warn you about,' Judith told them. 'I doubt we'll get much more now – we're well into spring – but when it snows, you mustn't walk across the open spaces to get to your hut. Tracks might be seen from the sky.'

Automatically, they all glanced up as if expecting to see a plane appear out of the clouds.

'What about like now?' Carolyn asked. 'I mean, if a spotter plane went over, it would look a bit strange to see a lot of figures moving towards the huts, wouldn't it?'

'That's a good point. Just hide amongst the trees if you hear one.'

Judith opened the door and ushered them into the set room. It seemed rather gloomy at first because the only windows were rather small and high up. There were two rows of twenty receivers down the long, rather narrow room. Thirty-six were in use, with four being left as spares. At the end nearest the door where they entered were two desks. A man sat at one and Judith indicated that the other was hers. The man, whom the girls presumed to be the supervisor, glowered up at them. 'Ah, three more useless women, I take it.'

But Judith only laughed as she introduced him.

'This bundle of laughs is Graham Lawrence. If you ever get a word of praise out of him, it'll be like a gold medal at the Olympics.'

He gave an expressive sigh, gestured to a small room where they saw that they could hang up their outdoor wear and then, with yet another sigh of resignation, he pointed to the far end of the room and then at Carolyn. 'You go down there. You're to take over from Bill. I suppose you do know how to take over from an operator on a busy shift?' Without waiting for her answer, he then allocated positions to both Beryl and Noreen.

'I've got an ATS girl,' Noreen whispered.

'Lucky you,' Beryl muttered as, with a determined expression, she headed down the room towards the corner opposite to where Carolyn was being sent.

Carolyn hovered near the man towards whom she had been directed. She was relieved to see that the set was very similar to those she had worked on at Trowbridge and even to the one Tom had at home. She breathed a sigh of relief. At least she knew how to work it. The operator was writing furiously, obviously in the middle of taking down a message. With his left hand and without looking up at her, he indicated two blank writing pads, both of which Carolyn recognized. One was the log sheet which she filled in as best she could and then she pulled the message pad towards her. With her right hand poised over the now familiar grid printed in red, she was ready to start writing. With her left hand she gently removed one of the headphones from the operator and pressed it to her own ear. She was lucky. It was a clear signal.

Immediately, she began to write, her hand moving swiftly across the page writing down the letters in blocks of five just as they had been taught. After a while she became aware that the man had stopped writing and had torn off the top sheet of his pad beneath which was a carbon copy. He put the top page into a tray on the top of the wireless set. It was picked up almost immediately by a young ATS girl who, Carolyn found out later, was called a 'runner'. Indeed, the girl scurried away, collecting other sheets as she went, before hurrying to the back of the room where she rolled them up and put them into a metal container which she pushed into a tube. This, Carolyn also learned later, was a pneumatic tube connected to the teleprinter room.

Carolyn continued writing without stopping for ten minutes, but then the wavelength fell silent. Although they hadn't been taught much about tuning in at Trowbridge, Carolyn had learned it from her brother, so she reached up to the dial and gently turned it this way and that, trying to locate the station she had been listening to, or to pick up another.

She felt a gentle touch on her arm and turned to look into Bill's kind, brown eyes. He was somewhere in his forties, she reckoned, with dark brown curly hair and a smile that made his eyes crinkle.

'Don't stray far from the frequency we're on,' he said softly. 'I'm supposed to stay on it as much as possible.' His smile broadened. 'By the way, well done. You're the best ATS arrival I've seen yet.'

'Thanks. Will you tell the supervisor that? He greeted us as "three more useless women".'

Bill laughed softly. 'Take no notice of Graham Lawrence. He's had to take a lot of flak from Station X – that's where our messages go – for the work not being up to standard. It's not your fault – or ours – that they haven't quite got the training up to standard yet. We've had to send a few girls who came here to Loughborough for further training, but I can see that you won't need it. What about your friends?'

'They're both about the same standard as me. The three of us passed out top of our group.'

'Right. I'll be off, then, as I can see you'll be all right. I'll see you around.'

Carolyn put the headphones on and began to listen in again.

Twenty-One

It was a busy shift and when the time came to hand over to the next operator, Carolyn's head was buzzing, but she was happy. She didn't think she'd made many mistakes – if any. She'd only had to leave two blank spaces during the whole of her shift. She and Beryl had sat across the room from each other the whole time but had not been able to speak. As they walked back across the field towards where the troop carrier would pick them up, Beryl said, 'Whew, that was what you'd call a "baptism of fire", wasn't it?'

'It was certainly busy. How d'you think you did?'

'All right, I think. Luckily, the reception was good. I hate it when there are atmospherics and you can't hear the Morse properly. I know we're supposed to be able to cut out the hissing and whistling and concentrate on the Morse, but we're bound to miss bits, and it's not really our fault.'

'Yes, mine was clear too,' Carolyn said. 'I'd love to know what the messages were, wouldn't you?'

'Yes, but that's for the clever folk at this mysterious Station X to work out. Good luck to them, is all I can say.' Beryl yawned. 'Come on, let's get back and see what there is for dinner.'

When they entered the mess, Noreen and Judith were already sitting at the table.

'Hello, you two. How did you get on?'

'It was hectic.' Beryl smiled, sitting down on the opposite side of the table to the other two girls. Carolyn sat beside her.

'I got put with a right grumpy sod,' Beryl went on, 'but he did have the grace to unbend a little when he saw that I knew what I was doing. Luckily, the signal was clear. He told me it was coming from North Africa.'

'Bill seems nice,' Carolyn put in.

'Bill Graves. Yes, he's lovely,' Judith said. 'Most of the men are OK but some are a bit frosty with us. They don't like the idea of women coming here.'

'I presume you mean the supervisor, for one.'

'Exactly.' Judith leaned forward and lowered her voice. 'Though to be fair, he's got a bit of a problem on his hands. Some of the first arrivals were pretty useless. You can't blame the men for resenting us if we can't do the job properly.'

'That's true.' Beryl glanced up at Judith to ask bluntly, 'Are you any good?'

Judith smiled. 'I'm the sergeant of the watch, so I don't actually do much intercept work now. But I noticed you, Noreen, were getting along fine.'

'I'm not as good as these two, though.' Noreen nodded towards Carolyn and Beryl. 'Came out top of the class at Trowbridge, they did.'

'Wow!' Judith's eyes widened. 'That's fabulous. How many words a minute do you do, then?'

Carolyn and Beryl glanced at each other, a little

embarrassed now, but Noreen answered for them without any trace of resentment. She sounded as proud of their achievements as if they were her own. 'Like I say, they're good. About twenty words a minute, isn't it, girls?'

'That *is* good. If you can reach twenty-five words per minute, you'll get a pay rise.'

'Mm,' Carolyn murmured, 'but I expect we still won't please Mr Lawrence.'

The girls would have been surprised, however, if they could have overheard the conversation taking place between Bill Graves and his supervisor at that very moment.

'So what about the new girls who arrived today?' Graham Lawrence asked. 'Pretty useless, I expect.'

'Far from it,' Bill said. 'John's told me that the one called Hunter will be all right, given a bit of time to settle in, but the other two – Holmes and Morley, is it?'

'Don't tell me.' Graham rolled his eyes. 'They're rubbish.'

'On the contrary. Holmes, who took over from me, was excellent. About twenty words per minute and – as far as I could tell – accurate. John said the same of Morley, even though he admitted to being a bit brusque with her at first.'

'I must admit,' Lawrence said grudgingly, 'all three of them kept their heads down all the way through the shift. And it was a busy one today.'

Bill hid his smile as he said casually, 'You know, Graham' – the two men had become friendly and now called each other by their Christian names – 'I think we haven't given these young women a fair chance.' Tactfully, he included himself, even though he had never been a part of it. 'We're totally forgetting how tough we found it at the start. Some of us – and I include myself in that – were abysmal to begin with. But we worked hard and we gave ourselves time to learn. Given a bit more time, I'm sure all these girls – especially Holmes and Morley – promise to be as good as any man we've got on site.'

'You surprise me.' Graham was silent for a moment, feeling a twinge of guilt for his own greeting of the newcomers, before unbending a little to add, 'But I'm pleased to hear it.'

That evening, Carolyn walked down the road to the small village shop, where there was a phone box, to ring Frank as she had promised. After their usual greetings, she said, 'I haven't got long, Grandad, and I can't tell you where we are or what we're doing, but Beryl and I are still together. We get a forty-eight-hour pass about every six weeks, so we might try to get over to see you then.'

'Let me know if you want me or your uncle to pick you up anywhere and be sure to bring Beryl, unless she wants to visit her own family.'

'I will.' As she replaced the receiver, Carolyn was thoughtful. What she hadn't told Frank was that she and Beryl had already discussed how they would get to the East Coast. Travelling there was difficult and protracted at the best of times and it was exacerbated by the war.

'We'll hitch,' Beryl had said. 'We'll be together and everyone stops to help girls in uniform.'

Carolyn had agreed with her friend, but she wasn't sure her family would.

Cocooned in their own little circle, the girls heard little from the outside world. By the time they read the newspapers or listened to the BBC, the news was always several days old. They'd heard about the fall of Singapore before they'd arrived here, but now it felt to them as if the war wasn't going on anymore. At least, not where they were. They didn't hear about Bomber Command launching a round-the-clock campaign against enemy arms factories, or the British Commandos' attack on a Nazi U-boat base. On a lighter note, they didn't learn until much later about the British Board of Trade dictating that skirt hems should be shorter and menswear should no longer have double-breasted jackets or trouser turn-ups. All in the cause of saving fabric. And yet, the ATS girls were at the heart of it. It was strange that although they were so closely connected to the progress of the war, they knew very little about what was actually happening. The messages they took down so faithfully were a complete mystery to them.

'It's all gibberish,' Beryl said as they walked across the field at the end of their first month. 'I just wish sometimes we knew what they were all about.'

'It's probably best we don't know. At least we can never be accused of giving away information.'

'That's true, but I never tell anyone what we're doing. Do you?'

'Heavens, no,' Carolyn said. 'They don't even know at home exactly where we are, and certainly not what we're doing. I didn't even tell them about our training at Trowbridge. We'd probably end up in the Tower of London if we tell anybody anything.'

'You're right, of course,' Beryl smiled, 'but that doesn't stop us going out and having a bit of fun. We've got quite a few hours off now until our next pattern of shifts start, though I don't think it's long enough to go home. It's about another two weeks before we can apply for a forty-eight-hour pass. So, let's go and find Noreen. I reckon she's the one who knows where the action is.'

'You're on.'

'No time like the present. She's just ahead of us. Let's catch her up and we can ask her.'

It turned out that the nearest 'action' was to be had in Loughborough. The next time the three girls had a few hours off in the evening, they went into the town to a dance at the Town Hall. It seemed as if all the servicemen and women in the area were there with only a few locals able to get in.

'There aren't many fellers in civvies, are there?' Beryl remarked.

'They're probably away in the forces,' Carolyn said, glancing around at the few girls in pretty dresses. 'While their girlfriends are flirting with the guys in uniform.'

Beryl chuckled. 'But have you noticed, it's us girls who *are* in uniform who are getting all the attention. Look out, there're a couple of lads coming towards us. I bags the tall one . . .'

Twenty-Two

'Carolyn, I've organized a double date for us,' Beryl began and, before Carolyn could protest, she rushed on, 'Please say you'll come. I so want to get to know Jeff better – a lot better – and I thought it would be so much easier if we went out as a foursome.'

Carolyn was not angry; she was amused. 'So, who am I getting lumbered with?'

'His friend. You know, the tall, dark-haired one. I think his name's Michael.'

Carolyn nodded, trying to sound nonchalant. 'You mean those two RAF lads who were at the dance last week?' She smiled to herself. Carolyn hadn't really wanted to go dancing; she had never learned the proper steps, but nowadays the floors were so crowded with servicemen and women looking for some fun that it didn't really matter. She was secretly delighted to be paired with Michael. Trying to look as if she wasn't staring at him, she'd taken in every detail of his appearance that night. She'd thought him the most handsome man in the room, with film-star good looks, sleek black hair and dark eyes. He was courteous and charming too, but it had been his brooding eyes that had captivated her.

Beryl's beau, Jeff, was nice-looking, a little taller

than Michael, with light brown hair and hazel eyes. Both young men were resplendent in their RAF uniforms, but Jeff didn't make Carolyn's heart leap at the sight of him as Michael did. The two young men arrived in a car borrowed from one of Jeff's mates to pick up the girls. They roared down the quiet village street, coming to a skidding halt in front of the billet.

Michael proved to be all Carolyn had hoped he would be. He took her arm as they crossed the street towards the nearest pub and made sure she was comfortable before he sat down himself. Beryl, however, seemed really smitten with Jeff even though he didn't seem as thoughtful as Michael. Carolyn watched as Beryl hung on Jeff's every word and gazed up at him adoringly, even though this was only the second time that they'd spent any time together. *Oh dear*, Carolyn thought, *if she's like this on a first proper date, what on earth is she going to be like if the friendship progresses?* Perhaps, she thought, Beryl had had little experience with men. Although they were already good friends, Carolyn still didn't know an awful lot about Beryl's home life or her background. She'd never spoken about having a boyfriend before, not even when Carolyn had confided in her about Peter. Beryl was strangely reticent about her family and her friends back home.

As they arrived back at the girls' billet, Michael said, 'May I see you again, Carolyn?'

'That would be lovely.'

'Perhaps' – he hesitated – 'without the others next time?'

175

In the darkness of the blackout, he wouldn't be able to see her smile, but she squeezed his hand in silent agreement.

'Oh, Carolyn,' Beryl clasped her hands together, her eyes shining, 'I think I'm in love. Jeff is just wonderful. I've never met anyone like him before. He's asked me out again. D'you mind? I mean, he wants us to be on our own.'

'Of course I don't,' Carolyn said, making it sound as if she were being very generous, but in fact she was secretly pleased. She waited for Beryl to ask her if she was going out again with Michael, but the question never came; the girl was too wrapped up in her own romance.

The two girls began to see the young RAF men whenever they had time off that coincided. They didn't spend so much time together in their off-duty hours now, but because they worked together on the same shift and shared a bedroom, their firm friendship endured.

Even though they were now stationed closer to Carolyn's home than they had been, leave that allowed time to go home only came around about every six weeks or so. They hadn't used their first forty-eight-hour pass during April, preferring to explore the countryside and the delights of the two nearby cities, but the next time a longer leave of three days occurred, Carolyn said, 'We've got the weekend off, so I'm going home this time. You're welcome to come with me.'

'Not this time, but thanks. I – um – might go to

see my folks.' Beryl smiled archly. 'What about Michael? Are you taking him with you?'

Carolyn hesitated. She and Michael were growing closer, it was true, but she wasn't quite ready to introduce him to her family. She wasn't sure what sort of reception from her mother awaited any young man who wasn't Peter Carter. 'Not this time,' she answered. 'I might tell them about him first and see how the land lies. What about you? Are you taking Jeff to meet your folks?'

'Lord, no,' Beryl answered before she stopped to think. Her swift, unguarded reply needed clarification. She sighed. 'Like you, it's a bit soon.'

Carolyn didn't question her any more. Her answer seemed credible because it was the same reason as hers. And yet, although she couldn't put her finger on it, Carolyn felt there was something more than her friend was telling her.

Their work was hard and intense, but the times out with Jeff and Michael were oases of rest, relaxation and fun. Occasionally, they still went out as a foursome, but usually they went out in their separate pairs. As she had told Beryl, Carolyn was not quite ready to take Michael home with her, so when the three days' leave came, she went to Skegness alone. On arrival at the railway station, she rang her grandfather from a telephone box in the town, knowing that Frank or Harold would be only too pleased to collect her in the farm's truck.

Sliding into the seat beside Frank, she leaned across and planted a kiss on his weathered cheek.

'It's good to see you, lass. How're things?'

'Fine. The work's hard, but we find time to have a bit of fun too.'

Frank chuckled. 'And might that "fun" include a boyfriend or two?'

Carolyn laughed too. 'Grandad, really! I'm not that sort of girl.' She paused and then added, a little shyly, 'But there is one young man I see quite a lot of when we're off duty at the same time.'

'Tell me about him.'

'His name is Michael and he's tall, dark and handsome . . .'

'Would he be anything else?' Frank teased.

'But he's also polite and charming.'

'That's good. Has he got a good sense of humour?'

'Yes, he has. We laugh a lot together. Why do you ask that?'

'Because, in my book, a good sense of humour is what carries a couple through the bad times as well as the good. A marriage doesn't end with a fancy wedding. It's only just the beginning and, to my mind, an ability to see the funny side of whatever life throws at you is more important than good looks.' There was silence between them until Frank said, 'So, you haven't brought him home to meet us yet, then?'

'No, Grandad. I wanted to tell all of you about him first. I – I need to see how Mam will react.'

'Ah!' Frank said understandingly. 'Now, sadly, though she's me daughter and I love her dearly, your mam hasn't got that all-important sense of humour I was talking about. She sees life as one long battle, which is rather sad.' He sighed. 'I don't understand why both of my children are rather – what's the word – dour.' He sighed heavily. 'Harold used to have a sense of humour before he went to war. He came back very changed, Carolyn, from the young man who went away. I hope that doesn't happen to you young ones this time around.'

'They must have gone through horrific experiences in the trenches, Grandad,' Carolyn said quietly. 'This war's bad – of course it is – but it's different somehow.'

They were both silent for a few minutes before Frank said, 'Your grandma and I could always see the funny side of anything that happened. Even if things went wrong on the farm, we'd always try to have a laugh.' He chuckled. 'I remember in 1912 we had the most awful wet summer and the harvest was all but ruined. But yar grandma said, "Frank, love, I reckon we'd better start building an ark".'

Even though he was smiling at the memory, he wiped a tear from his eye and Carolyn realized how much he still missed his wife.

As he drew the vehicle to a halt outside Carolyn's home, Frank leaned across and squeezed her hand. 'Tell them about Michael, lass, but I should tell yar dad first. He'll understand and back you up if it's needed. Besides, it's high time all this nonsense about you and Peter stopped. Me an' yar dad can see that.'

Carolyn sighed. 'Oh, I wish it would.' Again she leaned across and kissed his cheek. 'Thank you, Grandad.'

'Good luck,' he called to her as she alighted from

the truck's cab. Giving him a cheery wave as he turned the truck and drove off, Carolyn picked up her kitbag and went towards the back door to face the lion – or rather lioness – in her den.

Twenty-Three

'When do you go back?' Lilian asked after she'd greeted her daughter. Carolyn hid her smile. She knew her mother didn't mean it, but rather than asking 'How long can you stay?' the way she phrased the question sounded as if she wanted her gone.

'I'll have to leave early on Monday morning. Grandad picked me up from the station and he said he'll take me back there.'

'How did he know when to meet you?'

Carolyn grinned. 'This new telephone is very useful.'

'Oh yes. I was forgetting. I haven't quite got used to the idea yet.' Lilian paused. 'No Beryl with you this time?'

'No, she thought she might go home to see her family in Sheffield.'

'It's a shame you can't stay another couple of days until your birthday, but I've made you a cake. You can take it back with you and share it with Beryl.'

The Holmes family spent a pleasant evening around the range exchanging news, though Tom had to complete his two-hour stint tuned in to the wireless. After all the usual pleasantries and Carolyn catching up with how all the members of the family

181

were, the conversation inevitably turned to the war and its progress – or otherwise.

'It sounds as if the Russians are holding their own,' Eddie said. During the last week in May, the newspapers had been full of war news, both good and bad for the Allies.

'Just,' Carolyn said solemnly, repeating only what she had read. She sometimes gleaned a little more at work, not from the messages she took down – they were still a mystery – but from her colleagues, though she still had to be careful not to repeat any of that information. 'We're not doing so well against Rommel in Libya though, are we?'

'True, but it was in yesterday's paper that the RAF have inflicted grievous damage on Cologne,' Eddie said.

'It saddens me, though, that we have to demoralize the ordinary people to win the war.'

'Well, that's what they tried with us. Have you forgotten the London Blitz? And then there was Coventry, and Sheffield, and – oh, a host of other cities,' Lilian said defensively. 'Don't try to tell me they've played fair.'

Carolyn sighed. 'Sadly, there's nothing fair in war. I don't suppose there ever has been.'

At about nine-thirty, a knock came at the back door and Lilian jumped up. 'That'll be Steve.'

As his wife hurried to open the door to their visitor, Eddie said, 'He's the young soldier who collects Tom's notes most nights. He's stationed at the Point, though what's really going on there none of us can find out.

Nice young feller. Got a wife in Hull, apparently.' He smiled. 'Yar mam's taken to him. She likes spoiling him. She bakes three times a week now, just so she can load him up with cakes and scones to take back to camp.'

'Does that bother you?'

'Heavens, no. I'm only too pleased to do whatever we can to help the lads in the services.' He glanced at her. 'I only hope someone where you are is being as nice to you.'

Before she could answer, Lilian came back ushering in a stocky young man with fair hair and smiling eyes. He was only a couple of inches taller than Carolyn, but his build was broad and strong. 'This is Steve Wilson and this is our daughter, Carolyn. As you can see, she's in the ATS. She's got leave for the weekend.'

'Pleased to meet you, miss.' His handshake was strong and warm. He had a Yorkshire accent that was a little similar to Beryl's but somehow not quite the same. But then she realized that Steve was from Hull, whereas Beryl was from Sheffield. No doubt the accents were just slightly different.

'Sit down, sit down,' Lilian said. 'I'll get you something to eat.'

Carolyn listened in amazement. She could hardly believe the change in her mother. Lilian was positively animated.

'That's very kind of you, Mrs Holmes, but I can't stay tonight. I'm a bit late and I've got to call at Mr Fox's yet and then ride to . . .' He grinned. 'Well, I can't tell you that, but it's quite a distance.'

'Surely you've time for a cuppa?' Lilian's disappointment was palpable.

'Oh, go on, then.' He sat down beside Carolyn and grinned at her. 'Where are you based, then?'

She laughed. 'Now, you should know better than to ask.'

'Aw sorry. Comes natural to ask, doesn't it?'

As they chatted, Tom left the room and came back with a sealed envelope which Steve put straight into an inside pocket. 'I hope this is worth my long ride. It's starting to rain out there.'

Now it was Tom's turn to laugh and say, 'I couldn't possibly say.'

Steve pulled a comical face and then said, 'Well, one thing I can tell you that wouldn't be giving away any secrets is that whenever I arrive at wherever I'm going, they grab the two envelopes – yours and Mr Fox's – and rush off with them as if they can't wait to tear them open and find out what you've sent. So, yes, I think what we're all doing must be valuable.'

At that moment, Lilian returned carrying a cup of tea and a bulging paper bag.

'I've put some scones for you in here. You might feel peckish before you get back.'

'You're very kind. Thank you. I wish my Sally could bake like you. She's a grand lass, but she's no cook.'

'Have you heard from her recently?' Eddie asked.

Steve shook his head. 'No. Post is a bit hit and miss. Sometimes you don't hear for ages and then four letters arrive all together. It's a worry though. Hull's had quite a lot of bombing and although I've made sure Sal and her mam have got a good shelter to go to, I do worry about both of them, 'specially if I don't hear.'

'Do all your family live in Hull?' Carolyn asked.

His face sobered suddenly and he shook his head. 'I haven't got any other family. Only Sal. I was brought up in the orphanage in Hull. My dad was a sailor and was lost at sea just before I was born and my mam died of tuberculosis when I was about one, so I've been told. I don't remember her.'

'Oh that's so sad,' Lilian said. 'Didn't you have any aunts or uncles?'

Steve pulled a face. 'To be honest, I've no idea. Obviously, no one who was willing to take me in. Times were hard then,' he said with a shrug. 'If there *was* anyone, then I can't blame them for not wanting to take on another mouth to feed. But my family now is Sal and her mam. She lives in the same street, just a couple of houses away, which is nice for Sal while I'm away. They're very close and they both have a lot of friends, so Sal's got plenty of company and help if she needs it.'

Steve finished his tea and stood up, 'Well, I'd best be off. See you tomorrow.'

As Lilian saw him to the door, Carolyn murmured, 'He seems a nice feller.'

Eddie nodded. 'Yar mam's very taken with him. Fusses over him like a mother hen.'

'Well, that's nice. He's a long way from home.'

Eddie nodded but said no more as Lilian returned and sat down by the fire. 'He's such a nice lad. Shame he's married. You could do worse than find yarsen someone like him, Carolyn, if you're set on refusing Peter's proposal.'

'Lilian, love, Peter hasn't proposed to her. She's told us that.'

'Ah well, that's as maybe, but I'm not sure I believe her. It's not what Phyllis says.'

Eddie frowned. 'As far as I know, our daughter has never lied to us in her life. And I don't think for one moment that she is doing so now.'

Lilian shot him a fearsome look, but she said no more. There were times in their married life when his voice took on a firm tone that caused even Lilian to remain silent. This was one such moment.

'Mam,' Carolyn said quietly, 'I promise you I'm telling you the truth. If only you and Mrs Carter would accept it.'

Lilian sniffed. 'Well, I suppose I might – in time – but I don't think Phyllis ever will. She'd banked on his being married to you and staying safely on the farm here. But now he's gone to war, she's frightened to death that he's going to be killed.'

There was silence in the room before Carolyn licked her dry lips and said, 'Actually, I have met someone.'

Lilian said nothing, but Eddie said, 'Have you, love? Tell us about him.'

'His name's Michael Dunkley. He's in the RAF and stationed at – well, I don't know exactly where, but it's not far from where we are. And – and he's very nice,' she finished lamely. She found it hard to put into words – especially to her mother and father – just how she felt about Michael.

Lilian stood up suddenly. 'I'm going to bed and it's high time you were going up, Tom. You're looking tired.' She paused by Carolyn's chair and looked down at her, anger sparkling in her eyes.

'Mind you don't come home with yar belly full, girl, because if you do, you're out on your ear.'

The door slammed behind her. Tom whispered goodnight to his father and sister and followed her. Eddie and Carolyn sat in silence for a long time. At last, with a heavy sigh, Eddie said, 'I don't know how much you know, love, but that's not what her parents did when she – when we . . . your grandad didn't even raise his fist to me, let alone get out his shotgun. They just organized a quiet wedding and built an extension on his farmhouse at the southern end.'

Carolyn nodded. She knew the part of the farmhouse her father was referring to. Although it had not been used in recent years, the rooms were always given a good spring clean every year.

'When you were about three,' Eddie went on, 'this cottage became free and your grandad made it and a bit of land around it over to Lilian. There were no recriminations, no disappointed looks, no threats of being turned out. They just helped us. My parents too. But if you check our wedding date and your birthday, you'll see that there is only a good four months between the two. But I would advise you not to let it happen, love. It's not the best way to start a marriage.'

'Oh Dad, I'm sorry.'

'Don't be, love. It wasn't your fault. It was ours, all ours.'

They were silent again for a while before Eddie said softly, 'So, tell me about Michael. I do want to hear.'

They sat talking for another hour until Carolyn yawned and said, 'We really should go to bed, Dad. You're up early every morning and I ought to go and see Aunty Eve tomorrow.'

As she kissed his forehead and turned towards the door, she didn't see his anxious gaze following her.

'Did you go home?' Carolyn asked Beryl when she returned to Beaumanor.

Beryl shook her head. 'No. It – er – didn't work out. I spent some time with Jeff and, to be honest, the rest of the time sleeping.' She paused and then asked, 'Did you tell your family about Michael?'

'Yes.'

'And how did they take it?'

'Dad was fine about it – wanted to know all about him – but Mam, well, she was a bit nasty. I think it's because she's still upset about Peter and me not getting married.' She paused and then asked, 'Won't your parents at least be interested to know about Jeff?'

'No, they won't,' Beryl said shortly and turned away abruptly. 'Sorry, I've got to go.'

By the time Carolyn reached the set hut to report for duty, Beryl was already hard at work with her headphones on, scribbling furiously. It wasn't until their break that Carolyn was able to say, 'I'm seeing Michael briefly tonight. What about you?'

'Well, I'm not seeing Michael. He hasn't asked me.'

Carolyn laughed, pleased that her friend's good humour seemed to have been restored. 'No, silly, I meant are you seeing Jeff?'

'Not tonight. He's on duty. Maybe next time we get an evening that coincides. Anyway, have a good time. And don't do anything I wouldn't.'

The next time the girls had a thirty-six-hour leave Beryl said a little self-consciously, 'I won't be back tonight. I've applied for a sleeping-out pass. Jeff has got leave to coincide with mine and we're heading into the country. He's booked two rooms at a little hotel in Derbyshire . . .' Carolyn noticed that she laid heavy emphasis on the word 'two'. 'He's been able to borrow that car again from his mate, so we're travelling in style.' Beryl was busy packing her kitbag for her night away so they had time for a quick chat. Carolyn sat on her bed and watched her friend folding her underwear neatly.

'Are you sure you're allowed to go that far? We were told we had to stay around here.'

Beryl shrugged. 'No one'll know. It's not far and I'll be sure to be back in time for our next shift.'

Carolyn sighed inwardly. She didn't want to be a spoilsport, but she hoped her friend wasn't heading for trouble. 'Don't forget your gas mask and do you want to borrow my little torch? It might come in handy.'

'Please, if you don't mind. I ought to get one for myself, but I never seem to get round to it. Thanks, Carolyn. Right, I think that's everything.' As they both heard the sound of a car pulling up below their window, Beryl said, 'Now, I'd better be off. Don't want to keep him waiting.'

Carolyn hugged her and went downstairs to wave her off.

'Don't come outside,' Beryl said, when they reached the hallway. 'It's raining.

'All right. Have a good time.' Carolyn switched off the light in the hallway, pulled the heavy blackout curtain back and opened the front door for Beryl to slip out. She watched as her friend ran to the waiting car. She closed the door and leaned against it for a moment, letting out a huge sigh.

'I just hope she's back in time for work and that no one else finds out where she's been,' she said quietly to herself.

Twenty-Four

'So, did you have a good time?' Carolyn asked Beryl when she rushed into the hut just before they were both due to start their first shift after the thirty-six-hour break. Beryl had obviously only just made it back in time; she still had her kitbag with her, which she tried to stow out of sight in the cloak-room.

'What? Oh – er – yes.' But Beryl was avoiding her friend's gaze. Instead, she deflected the attention back towards Carolyn. 'What did you do? Did you go out with Michael?'

'Yes, we went to a concert in the De Montfort Hall in Leicester.'

'And did you want to go to that? You don't seem a lover of classical music to me.'

Carolyn shrugged. 'I don't mind what we do. I'm happy just to be with him. We're going dancing next time we both get a decent leave.'

'I thought you weren't too keen on dancing.'

'Michael's teaching me.'

Beryl pulled a face. 'You've got it bad, girl.'

Carolyn blushed. 'I have, haven't I? It's proved one thing for me, though.'

Beryl raised her eyebrows. 'What's that?'

'If this is what really being in love is like, then I was certainly never in love with Peter.'

Carolyn thought about the butterflies in her stomach every time she was due to meet Michael: how, when she saw him walking towards her, her legs felt weak, as if they were going to give way at any moment. When he kissed her and held her close, she felt as if a thousand stars were bursting in the heavens. Every moment apart from him felt like wasted time. She counted the days, the hours, even the minutes, until the next time they would be together.

'So, is everything all right between you and Jeff? When are you seeing him again?'

'Same time as you see Michael, I expect.'

'They don't seem to do a lot of flying, do they? I mean, they seem to get a lot of time off. More than we do.'

Beryl stared at her. 'Don't you know what they both do?'

Carolyn shook her head. 'No, I've never dared to ask them.'

'Where they are is mainly a training base, mostly for Polish units, Jeff said. I think they're both in-structors. Right, we'd better get to work. We'll catch up later. Tell you what, we'll all go dancing together. I'll ask Jeff if he wants to go.'

Carolyn opened her mouth to speak, but Beryl had turned away to sit down in front of her wireless set. When she put her headphones on, Carolyn knew any more conversation was impossible. She sighed. Michael wasn't too keen on them sharing their

precious time with other people. He liked to have
Carolyn all to himself. The thought made her feel
warm and fuzzy inside.

Carolyn didn't have a chance to tell Michael that
Beryl and Jeff would be joining them, and when the
four of them met up on the following Saturday
evening, Michael's face was thunderous. 'What on
earth are they doing here?' he hissed.

'I'm sorry. I didn't think you'd mind.'

'Well, I do,' he said shortly. 'I want you to myself.'

For once, the warm and fuzzy feeling didn't
happen. Beryl was her friend and she'd thought that
Michael was good friends with Jeff; it was how they'd
all met. Surely he didn't mind being with them for
an evening now and again? But it sounded as if he
minded very much.

'Come on, let's dance,' he said as he stood up and
held out his hand to her.

'I – I'm sorry. I can't do this one. It's a tango.'

For a moment, Michael glowered, before saying,
'Then I'd better find someone who can.'

'Oh Michael, please . . .' Carolyn began, but he'd
already turned away from her.

She felt her face burning with embarrassment. Why
was he being so horrid? He knew she couldn't dance
at all before he met her. He'd taught her the waltz,
the foxtrot and the quickstep. It was hardly her fault
she didn't know any other dances yet. She pushed
her way through the chattering girls, who were still
ranged along the side of the dance floor waiting for
someone to invite them to dance. No doubt one of
them would end up in Michael's arms, she thought

bitterly. She found the cloakroom, but it too was crowded with girls applying make-up or combing their hair. She dived into one of the cubicles and locked the door. She dug her nails into the palms of her hands; someone had once told her that that could stop you crying. It seemed to work, for the tears that had welled in her eyes didn't fall.

When the noise outside the cubicle's door lessened, Carolyn ventured out. There was only Beryl there, washing her hands and smoothing her hair.

'Hey, there you are. I've been looking for you. I saw Michael dancing with another girl. Everything all right?'

Carolyn forced a smile, though it was rather a watery one. 'Yes, fine. I can't do the tango.'

Beryl pulled a face. 'That's no reason for him to dance with someone else. A bit mean, I call that.'

'No, no,' Carolyn said hastily. She didn't want Beryl speaking to him about it. 'It's fine. Really. He's a good dancer. There's no need for him to sit out the ones I can't do.' She gave a forced laugh. 'I'm not the jealous type.' Though in her heart she knew that wasn't true. The thought of another girl in his arms was a physical pain.

After Carolyn had washed her hands, Beryl said, 'Come on. Let's go back. I think they're playing a waltz. You'll be all right with that.'

When they returned to the dance floor, they found Michael and Jeff sitting at a table together. As they approached, both men got up. Michael was smiling now and holding out his arms. 'Now this one you *can* do, because I taught it to you.'

Gratefully, Carolyn slipped into his arms and he nestled his cheek against her hair and held her close. They were together for the remainder of the evening, Michael sitting out those dances she couldn't do yet.

'We'll have to have a lot more lessons,' he murmured as they danced the last waltz together at the end of the evening.

'That'd be lovely,' she said, the earlier hurt forgiven, if not quite forgotten.

As they got ready for bed, Beryl said hesitantly, 'I hope you don't mind me saying this, Carolyn, but Jeff said he'd prefer us to go out as couples, like we were doing, not in a foursome. He found this evening a bit – a bit – awkward.'

'Oh Beryl, I'm so relieved you've said that. It's exactly how Michael feels too.'

The two girls laughed, then Beryl said, 'You know why that is, don't you?'

'Well, not really. Why?'

'Because they want to have their wicked way with us, that's why.'

Carolyn looked shocked. 'Oh, I'm sure you're wrong. Michael's not like that.'

Beryl smiled smugly. 'I'm telling you, that's the reason. You wait and see.'

The two girls had settled into their life at Beaumanor. More ATS girls arrived on a regular basis and a few of the civilian men began to leave. Although the work was intense, there was still time for fun, even sometimes on site.

'Let's sneak into the house,' Carolyn said one day, greatly daring. 'I'd love to see inside.'

'Are we allowed? I don't want to be on a charge and I certainly don't want to be stopped by an MP and his Alsatian dog.' Beryl shuddered. 'They scare me, especially if I meet one in the dark.'

'Look, there's Bill just coming down the steps. He'll take us in.'

'Oh I don't know . . .'

But Carolyn was already waving animatedly. 'Hey, Bill . . .'

He saw her, waved back and came towards them. 'What are you two doing here?'

'We want to take a peek in the house. Can you take us in?'

'Don't do anything that will get you into trouble,' Beryl said swiftly.

Bill smiled, his eyes twinkling. 'Of course, I'll give you a conducted tour. and no, it won't cause any problems. There are rooms we won't be able to go into, though, but you'll get a good idea of what the house is like.'

They followed him up the steps and into an entrance hall with a beautiful white fireplace and then into a much bigger, but rather gloomy hall in the centre of the house. The two girls gasped at its magnificence. On the right-hand side, a flight of dark wooden stairs led up towards a boarded-up window, then divided into two, continuing up to left and right to where a cantilever balcony ran round the whole square of the hall at first-floor level.

'What's behind the boards?' Beryl asked.

'A wonderful painted window. Sadly, you won't see it until all this madness is over, but it's well worth protecting. It looks, at first glance, just like a stained-glass window, but it's been very cleverly painted to look just like the real thing.'

'I'll come back one day and see it,' Beryl murmured.

'Just look at the size of that chair,' Carolyn exclaimed pointing to a huge chair set against the wall to one side of the stairs. 'Who lived here? Giants?'

Beryl was already going towards it and climbing up onto the seat. 'Come on, Carolyn. There's room for both of us. In fact, I think there's room for most of the watch.'

They sat in the chair, looking just like two naughty, giggling children. Bill laughed too. 'I wish I'd got my camera.'

They climbed down, still laughing, and returned to where Bill was standing. He pointed up to the ceiling with carved panels and to the carved bulls' heads set around the cornice. 'You'll see that motif repeated all around the house.'

'Does it have any significance?'

Bill wrinkled his forehead. 'Just an emblem of the family's strength, I suppose. No one argues with or confronts a bull, do they? Now, I can take you into one or two rooms, but not all of them, obviously.'

He took them into a well-proportioned room to the side of the main entrance. 'This was where the last owner of the hall had his office. Sitting here he could see whoever was coming or going.'

'He could keep an eye on everything, you mean.

How clever. I'm surprised the commander doesn't have his office in here.'

Bill chuckled. 'He does have a room overlooking the entrance, but it's a bedroom on the first floor. Now, I can show you the library with another lovely white fireplace and then only the cellar, which is a very good air-raid shelter and a store for ammo. The Beaumanor unit of the Home Guard have use of it too for storage.'

They trooped after Bill, fascinated by the rooms he was able to show them. Lastly, he led them out into the courtyard, where the buildings were now used as stores, the Motor Transport office, maintenance and other workshops.

'Thanks, Bill,' they said as they left. 'It's been interesting to see how things work behind the scenes.'

'I'm just off into Leicester on my motorbike, if either of you fancy a trip. Can't take both of you, I'm afraid.'

Both girls laughed. 'Another time, perhaps, Bill, but thanks.'

As they parted, Beryl said, 'What a nice man he is. I wonder if he's married.'

Twenty-Five

'Darling, you're free on Sunday, aren't you? It's your forty-eight-hour leave, isn't it?' Michael asked.

'Yes. I was thinking of going home.'

'Oh no, you're not,' he said, but it was with a laugh. 'I've organized something rather special for Sunday. I've borrowed a mate's motorbike. You're all right riding pillion, aren't you?'

'I never have, but I'll give it a go.'

'That's my girl. The only thing you have to remember is to put your trust in me and lean the same way I do when we're cornering. If you try to sit up straight, you'll have us both off. I thought we'd go into the countryside. Shame to waste all this lovely weather. And I've booked us lunch at a lovely hotel in the middle of nowhere. We'll not bump into people who know us.'

Carolyn wondered why this mattered. It was common knowledge that they were going out together. She'd never tried to hide it, so why . . . ?

'I'll pick you up about ten?' He squeezed her hand. 'And don't wear your uniform. Come in a pretty dress.'

'Oh but . . .' Carolyn began, but he was already striding away. Carolyn bit her lip. She only had the one dress with her; the one she wore to go dancing if they decided to go in civvies. She sighed. It wasn't really suitable for a Sunday lunch out or riding on the back of a motorbike. She went in search of Beryl.

'I need a new summer frock for Sunday. Are you free to come with me?'

'We're both off on Wednesday afternoon, aren't we? Have you got enough coupons?'

'Yes. I've hardly used any. We spend most of our time in uniform.'

'Right. You're on.'

The girls spent a happy afternoon shopping in Loughborough. Beryl, caught up in the excitement of buying new clothes, spent all her coupons and most of her money. Carolyn was more careful. She bought a pretty floral summer dress and a pair of sandals with low heels.

'I'll draw a line down the back of your legs on Sunday,' Beryl promised, 'so that it looks like you're wearing stockings.'

Carolyn laughed. 'I've got some gravy browning left. I'll paint my legs and you can do the line down the back.'

She was ready and waiting by the time Michael rode up on the noisy motorbike.

'I thought I told you to wear civvies.'

'I am, but my uniform coat is the only one I've got and I thought it would be draughty on the back of your bike.'

He frowned. 'You won't need a coat. It's July, for Heaven's sake.'

'The weather's been so changeable lately. I thought it might rain.'

'Darling, it's the middle of summer and we're not going far. Go and hang it up in the hall. You can leave your headscarf on. Your hair might get blown a bit.'

She shrugged but did as he had asked. When she returned, he said, 'Remember what I told you about leaning with me.'

She sat behind him and put her arms around his waist, laying her head close to his back. She liked the feel of his body, even through the thick clothing he was wearing. They rode into the countryside for several miles until he turned in at a gate leading up a driveway to a country hotel.

She climbed down and he parked the bike to one side of the front door.

'Did I do all right?' she asked, linking her arm through his.

'Not bad.' There was a note of surprise in his tone. 'I think you've ridden pillion before.'

'No, I haven't. I just tried to do what you'd told me.'

He laughed and tweaked her nose playfully. 'Mind you always do.'

As they stepped through the double doors into a spacious hall, Michael muttered, 'There'll be a powder room somewhere for you to do your hair. Yes, look, over there. I'll check in with reception and find out where the restaurant is.'

In the ladies' powder room there was a plush carpet and fancy gold-framed mirrors above the

201

washbasins. Carolyn applied fresh lipstick and combed her hair. Returning to the reception area, she found Michael waiting for her, and in the restaurant, a waiter in a black suit and bow tie ushered them to a table for two in the bay window looking out over a smooth lawn and well-kept garden.

'This is a lovely place,' she said, glancing round. 'I've never been anywhere so grand.'

'Nothing but the best for you, my darling.'

The waiter approached them again, carrying a menu and a single red rose wrapped in cellophane. 'The gentleman ordered this for you, madam.'

'Oh, how beautiful. Thank you, Michael.'

'Would you like to order now, sir?' the man said, handing the only menu to Michael.

'Thank you. I'll order for both of us,' he said and then sat for several moments while the waiter still hovered.

'Madam will have the roast chicken breast and I will have the steak, medium rare, and I'll have a half-bottle of the Merlot and a glass of house white for madam.' Michael closed the menu folder with a snap and handed it to the waiter, who gave a little bow and moved away.

Carolyn was a little disconcerted that Michael hadn't asked her what she would like to eat or drink but she had never been entertained in such a fancy restaurant. Perhaps, when a gentleman took a lady out to lunch, this was the way things were done.

'Thank you for the rose, Michael.'

He inclined his head in acknowledgement.

'This is really the first time we've had a chance to sit and talk,' she said. 'Before, when we've gone out, it's been to the cinema, or dancing, or to the concert, and you can't hold a proper conversation then.'

'Or we've had other people with us,' he said pointedly. He reached across the table and took her hand. 'It's nice to be on our own.'

Carolyn laughed. 'Evidently Jeff feels the same. They don't want to make up foursomes anymore either.'

'So, what do you want to talk about?'

'I know so little about you – what you did before you joined the RAF, what you plan to do after the war . . .'

'I didn't join of my own free will. I was called up.' There was a bitterness to his tone.

'Where are you from?'

'Lincoln.'

'Oh that's funny.'

'Why?'

'Because I live in Lincolnshire. On the coast near Skegness. So what did you do in Lincoln?'

'I worked for my father. He owns a building firm. And one day it'll be mine, as I'm his only son. Only child, in fact. He's built it up from nothing and we live in a very nice house now, not far from the cathedral. He's done very well for himself and married into a good family. My mother's distantly related to the current chancellor. What about you? What sort of background do you come from?' There was suddenly a scathing tone in his voice as he added, 'I presume you didn't actually go out to work?'

Carolyn bristled. 'Of course I did. I worked for Woolworth in the town.'

'Woolworth! Oh I know it – the department store. Don't tell me you worked as a shop assistant.'

'That's how I started, but then I moved into the office.'

'I suppose that's a bit better.'

'What on earth do you mean, better?'

'We-ell . . .' He shrugged.

'Woolworth is a very good company to work for,' she said defensively. 'They care about their staff and treat them very well.' She bit her lip. She was on the point of confiding in him the reason she had left the firm, but something held her back. It hadn't been because of anything that had been caused by the management or staff. It had been Peter's mother who had caused the embarrassment. In fairness, Mr Williamson had wanted her to stay on.

'It'll be a nine-day wonder, Miss Holmes,' he'd said. 'They'll soon have something – or someone – else to gossip about.' But by then Carolyn had already volunteered for the ATS.

Michael's only reply now was to shrug again.

The meal was lovely and Carolyn had to admit that Michael had made a good choice for her, though she would have liked to have had the chance to see the whole menu for herself. After they'd both finished a lovely pudding too, they sat lingering over their last glass of wine.

Carolyn leaned forward. 'There doesn't seem to be much in the way of shortages here.'

Michael smiled knowingly. 'No, and I doubt there

will be; the hotel will have a way of obtaining whatever it wants.' He paused and then added, 'If you're ready, we'll go up.'

Carolyn blinked. 'Up? Up where?'

'Upstairs. I've booked a room for the afternoon.'

'A – a room? Whatever for?'

'Just so we can have a nice kiss and a cuddle with some privacy and comfortable surroundings. I'm getting rather sick of having to say goodnight to you outdoors.'

Carolyn eyed him suspiciously. 'Is that all?'

He didn't answer her directly but countered, 'Don't you want that too?'

It would be nice, she thought, to be in his arms without worrying if someone was going to discover them at any moment, but she felt herself blushing. What on earth would the hotel staff think? Her heart began to beat a little faster as they left the dining room and mounted the stairs to the second floor. It was a lovely room, overlooking the grounds at the front of the hotel.

'There's a bathroom just along the landing,' Michael said as he took off his jacket and placed it on the back of a chair.

Carolyn scuttled out, thankful to have an excuse to leave him for a few moments. When she returned to the room, he was standing in front of the window. She glanced nervously towards the bed, but it was just as it had been. He turned from the window and held out his arms to her and she went into them willingly.

He kissed her gently and she felt her heart melt

and her knees turn to jelly. His kisses became more ardent and his hands roamed over her body, lighting a flame within her. Gently, he began to undo the buttons down the front of her dress. She gasped as he touched her bare breast. She felt a sliver of delight course through her and she opened her mouth beneath his. Then, suddenly, he was lifting her up and carrying her to the bed. He set her down on the floor briefly while he flung back the covers and then picked her up again and laid her gently on the bed. They lay together, kissing and holding one another close, their bodies melding together. Then his hand pulled up the skirt of her dress and he ran his hands up her thighs . . .

Suddenly, realization struck her and she tried to push him away. 'No, Michael. No. . .'

'Oh darling,' he murmured against her mouth. 'Please. I'll be careful. I won't hurt you. Just trust me. I want you so much . . .'

Carolyn struggled against his strong arms. 'No, no. I'm not like that. I won't.'

He gripped her arms tightly and flung his leg over her, twisting himself to lie on top of her.

'No, Michael, no. Please don't.'

But he was taking no notice of her desperate pleas. He was tearing at the bodice of her dress, ripping the fabric.

'I'll scream.'

'No one will hear you – or take any notice. We're on the top floor.'

She opened her mouth and at once he covered it with his hand, muffling any sound she might make.

Carolyn stopped struggling. She stared up into his dark eyes. Thinking she was giving way to him, he removed his hand from her mouth. With a strange calmness now, she said, 'I never had you down as a rapist, Michael.'

Suddenly, he was still. Then slowly he sat up, straddled across her, his full weight on her legs. He raised his right hand and slapped her hard across the left side of her face. He rolled over to the other side of the bed, got up and adjusted his own clothing. He put on his jacket, glanced around to make sure he hadn't left anything, and left the room, slamming the door behind him.

She lay there for a long time, trying to come to terms with what had just happened. Somewhere far below the window she heard the sound of a motorbike starting up and leaving, the sound growing fainter and fainter.

After a while she sat up and swung her legs over the side of the bed, but when she tried to stand, she found her legs were still trembling. She took a few steadying breaths and tried again. This time she gained her feet. She stumbled to the door, opened it and glanced up and down the corridor. Thankfully, there was no one about. She used the bathroom, bathing the side of her face with cold water. It was bright red and she knew that soon she would have an awful bruise. However was she going to explain that away? She returned to the bedroom and sat for some time until she felt calmer. She stood up and decided to make the bed before she left, but, to her horror, she saw that there were some brown marks on the sheets where her legs had been. Some of the gravy browning had rubbed off when he had sat on her. She sighed and left the bed unmade. The maids would change the sheets anyway after the room had been occupied, she knew, but she was mortified to imagine what they would think had happened there. And it almost did, she thought bitterly. As she stood in front of the long mirror in the wardrobe, she saw that the side of her face was swelling now and looking redder than ever. Then she noticed the tear in the front of her dress. She tucked the torn flap into the top of her brassiere. It didn't look too bad. She picked up her handbag and the key to the room and walked out, leaving the red rose, which was beginning to wither already, on the dressing table.

Downstairs, she hovered in the reception area until there were no other residents about. Then she approached the desk.

Keeping her head bent she murmured, 'I'm checking out.'

'Oh, yes, Mrs Smith. I just need to check whether everything has been paid.'

Mrs Smith? Good heavens! Carolyn was shocked. He'd thought of everything. He'd planned this whole thing.

She was shaking visibly now. Surely he hadn't left her to pay the bill? But to her relief the girl said, 'Everything was paid in advance, Mrs Smith. That is our usual policy when we – um – don't know the people involved.'

Carolyn nodded and began to turn away, but the receptionist said – rather gently, Carolyn thought –

'Madam, is everything all right? Can I – help you with anything?'

Now it was just two young women, one concerned about the other. 'Please can you tell me which road I take to get to Quorn?'

'Of course, madam.' Tactfully, she had ceased calling Carolyn 'Mrs Smith'. She gave directions and then added, 'Is there anything else?' She leaned across the counter and, although there was no one else within earshot, she whispered, 'I can give you a couple of safety pins.'

Carolyn glanced down. The front of her dress had slipped out of its moorings and was hanging down. Hastily, she pushed it up and held it. 'Oh, please. That would be so good of you.' Tears filled her eyes at the unexpected kindness of a stranger.

The girl left for a moment and went into the office behind the reception desk, returning to hold out two large safety pins. 'There you are, madam.'

With trembling fingers, Carolyn tried to pin the torn cloth back into place.

'Here, let me help,' the girl said gently. 'There's no one about.' After fastening the pins, the girl said, 'There. That looks a lot better. Are you sure you're going to be all right? Would you like me to get you a taxi?'

Carolyn shook her head and then wished she hadn't. It hurt. 'I'll be fine. I'm used to walking.'

'It's a fair way, though, and it's looking like rain.'

'I'll be fine. Honestly.' Carolyn couldn't wait to put distance between her and the hotel and she didn't want to admit that she had very little money with her, probably not enough to pay for a taxi. 'Thank you so much for your help.'

'Not at all. See you again some time.'

Carolyn smiled weakly. Not if she could help it, she thought bitterly.

She left by the front door, walked down the short driveway and turned in the direction the girl had indicated.

She'd covered about half a mile when she felt the first large spot of rain on her face.

Twenty-Six

It was raining stair rods, as Granny Holmes would have said. At the thought of her family, Carolyn felt a sob catch in her throat. She struggled on, bending her head against the lashing rain. Ahead she saw a flash of lightning, which was closely followed by a rumble of thunder. Within minutes she was literally soaked to the skin, her thin cotton dress plastered to her body. The gravy browning was running down her legs in streaks and her pretty new sandals were ruined. She squelched along until she came to a huge tree at the side of the road. She knew it was dangerous to shelter under a tree in a thunderstorm, but she was beyond caring now. She just wanted some shelter, even if only for a few moments.

She leaned against the tree, shivering and sobbing uncontrollably now. Then, in the distance, even above the noise of the storm, she heard the sound of a motorbike coming closer. Now she began to shake with fear as well as with the cold and wet. She tried to get round to the back of the tree trunk to hide, but it was close up against a barbed-wire fence and there was no space.

The noise came closer and the machine drew to a

halt. She heard the rider stop the engine, dismount and come towards her.

'Carolyn? Whatever are you doing all the way out here in this?'

Carolyn let out a huge breath. It wasn't Michael. She recognized the voice. It was Bill Graves. With a cry of relief she flung herself against him, sobbing into his wet leathers. Awkwardly he put his arms around her. 'Come on, lass. Let's get you back. Here, have my coat.'

She lifted her head. 'No, Bill, no. I'm wet through already.' She was feeling stronger already now that help was at hand.

'I insist. You're shaking with cold. You'll catch your death, if you haven't already,' he said firmly as he removed his top coat and held it out for her to slip her arms into the sleeves. As she hugged it around her, she had to admit she did feel warmer already.

'Now, let's get you onto my pillion and we'll get you back to your billet. It won't take long.'

For the second time that day, Carolyn sat behind a man on his motorbike and wrapped her arms around his waist. By the time they arrived back, even poor Bill was wet, though he'd had a jerkin below his top coat which had kept the worst of the rain from soaking him through.

'I'm going to find Beryl and get her to come and help you.'

It seemed an age but in fact it was only a few minutes before Beryl burst into the bedroom they shared.

'Bill said . . .' she began and then stopped as she

took in the sight of her bedraggled friend. 'Oh my goodness, whatever's happened?' Without waiting for an answer, she went on, 'Tell me later. Let's get you out of those things and into a hot bath.' She poked her head out of the door. 'Noreen . . .' she called.

'Oh please, Beryl, don't . . .' Carolyn began, but her weak protest went unheeded. Beryl either wasn't listening or was deliberately taking no notice.

'Noreen, go and organize a hot bath, if you can. Carolyn's in a dreadful state. She's soaked through. Looks as though she's had some sort of accident. The side of her face is all bruised.'

Noreen came to the door, took one look at Carolyn, then scuttled off, calling back over her shoulder. 'I'll get her some hot milk and whisky, if I can find any.'

'Come on, you. Let's get you out of those wet things. Put your dressing gown on and go along to the bathroom.'

'It'll get messed up.'

'It'll wash.'

Carolyn was still shivering when the two girls took her to the bathroom and helped her to climb into a hot bath. She lay back and closed her eyes.

'Here, I've brought you some of my bath salts,' Noreen said.

But before she could tip some into the water, Beryl said, 'Let's wash her hair first, then she can have a good soak. Have you got any shampoo?'

'Yes, I'll get it.' Noreen hurried away again.

Carolyn felt so weak and exhausted that she

submitted to their ministrations with gratitude. They helped her out of the bath and dried her as if she was a small child.

'I've filled my hot water bottle and put it in her bed,' Noreen said as they slipped Carolyn's nightdress over her head and held out a dressing gown for her. 'Yours needs washing. Borrow Beryl's and now I'll go and fetch her that mug of hot milk. I've managed to scrounge some whisky too.'

'You're a good sort, Noreen,' Beryl said. 'Thanks.'

In bed, Carolyn began to feel more human again and the other two girls sat beside her as she drank the hot milk and whisky that warmed her even more. She could sense that both girls were dying to ask questions, but they didn't. When Carolyn handed the empty mug to Noreen, with a husky 'Thank you', Beryl said, 'Right, now lie down and try and get some sleep. You look all in. Luckily, you're not on shift until Tuesday, so you've time to feel better. Will you be all right? I'll have to go soon. I'm on at seven. I wouldn't normally be, but someone's called in sick and as I wasn't doing anything, I said I'd stand in.'

'I'll look in on her,' Noreen promised. 'If there's anything you need, Carolyn, just say, won't you?'

Carolyn nodded, lay back against the pillows and whispered, 'Thank you, both of you,' before her eyes closed.

When she woke several hours later it was dark. She was hot now, yet still shivering, and she knew she'd caught a chill. Noreen came in several times through the night and the following morning, when

Carolyn showed no signs of improving, Beryl insisted that the commander should be informed. 'You won't be fit for work tomorrow, Carolyn. She ought to see you for herself. She might think you need a doctor. I certainly do.'

Carolyn felt too ill to argue and later, when Miss Everatt visited, and then a doctor, she could hardly raise herself for the doctor to listen to her chest, or answer their questions.

'I'll sign her off for a week,' he said. 'It's no good her trying to come back too soon.' He regarded the commander over the top of his spectacles. 'She has to be fit to do – whatever it is she's doing here.'

'Quite so. I'll reorganize things so that her shifts are covered.'

'We'll do extra,' both Beryl and Noreen offered when they heard.

'That's good of you both. I'll bear that in mind. In the meantime, keep your eye on her and make sure she takes the medicine the doctor has left for her.'

'We will,' they chorused.

'By the way,' the commander asked as she turned to leave. 'Do you know what happened to her face?'

Beryl met her gaze squarely, 'No, she hasn't said.'

Miss Everatt nodded briefly and turned away. As she disappeared down the stairs, Beryl muttered so that only Noreen heard, 'But I've got a bloody good idea. And if I catch up with him, he'll wish he'd never been born.'

But it seemed that Michael had disappeared. The next time Beryl saw Jeff, he told her, 'Just left on Monday morning. All I heard was that he'd got trouble at home – a family bereavement or something – and had been given compassionate leave.'

'Will he be coming back?'

'I've no idea. We weren't that close. Only mates who worked together and then, of course, we met you two girls.' He grinned. 'But then neither of us wanted to carry on with foursomes.'

'I gathered that,' Beryl said tartly.

'What's up, Beryl? You seem all uptight.'

Beryl opened her mouth, was actually on the point of spilling it all out to him, but some instinct made her hold back. She knew what fellers were like. They'd stick together and make out that whatever had happened was all Carolyn's fault. She smiled weakly, 'Oh nothing really. I just wondered where he was, that's all. Carolyn hasn't heard anything from him for a few days. She's not very well and I – er – wanted to let him know.' She shrugged and forced herself to sound nonchalant, when inside she was seething. Carolyn was still suffering the after-effects of whatever had occurred on Sunday, though she still hadn't confided in Beryl what exactly had happened. She was out of bed now, but felt very weak and shaky and the doctor had approved another week off work.

A week to the day since the unfortunate outing, Carolyn got dressed and went down to the mess for Sunday dinner. How different it was to last week, she was thinking.

'Do you feel up to a little walk in the garden?' Beryl asked her when they returned to their billet. 'It's a lovely day and quite warm. It'll do you good.'

Carolyn gave a tremulous smile. 'Yes, nurse. Whatever you say, nurse.'

Beryl hugged her arm. 'That's the spirit. I'll fetch your coat for you. You stay here . . .'

'No – no, Beryl. Don't leave me on my own.'

Beryl, who'd already gone a few paces, stopped and turned to look back at her friend. She came back to her and took Carolyn's cold hands into hers. 'You'll be all right,' she said gently, guessing the reason for Carolyn's fear. 'He's not around. He's gone.'

'Gone? Are you sure?'

Beryl related what Jeff had told her.

'But he might come back. He . . .'

'I don't think so. Not really.' Pointedly, she let her eyes stray to the fading bruise on Carolyn's face. 'Do you?'

She felt the tension leave Carolyn's hands and saw the girl visibly relax as she let out a huge sigh.

'Sit here on the chair by the front door while I get our coats in case it turns a bit chilly, but there are plenty of folk passing in and out. You'll be fine and I won't be long. I promise.'

Only minutes later, when they were walking around the garden at the back of the house, Beryl linked her arm through Carolyn's. 'Now, are you going to tell me what happened? Don't, if you don't want to, but I'm your friend and I hate to see you hurting like this. Besides, I'm a nosy cow and I want to know, but I am also very good at keeping secrets. We all are. That's why we work here.'

Carolyn was silent for several minutes before saying haltingly, 'I'll tell you, but I don't want anyone else to know. Not even Noreen. I know she's our friend and she's been good to me this past week, but . . .'

Beryl patted her hand. 'A confidence is a confidence, in my book. It'll go no further; I give you my word.' She giggled. 'I'll sign the Official Secrets Act again, if you want.'

'You see, everyone – well, a lot of people – would say it was my own fault,' Carolyn began hesitantly. 'That I – I asked for it, or at least was daft enough to get into a position of being – of being . . .'

'Tell me from the beginning and I'll tell you if you were daft or not.'

Carolyn gave a watery smile. She drew in a deep breath. 'Michael asked me to go out with him for the day last Sunday. On his motorbike. He insisted I wore a pretty dress – not my uniform. Definitely not my uniform. He didn't even let me take my coat, even though we were on a motorbike. I didn't think much of it at the time. It was a warm day and he was in a smart suit, though I noticed he wore his leather jacket over it. He'd booked lunch at a very posh hotel out in the countryside. It was lovely but . . .'

'Go on.'

'Well, he was very – bossy. I'd never really noticed it before, but now, thinking back, he always chose where we went out, what we did, even where we sat in the cinema or the theatre. And on Sunday he chose from the menu for both of us. I never even had the chance to look at it, let alone decide for myself.'

'Reasonable so far, I suppose, though I'd have snatched the menu and had a look myself. But that's just me. Sorry, I shouldn't interrupt.'

'He gave a me a single red rose and we had a very nice lunch, but then I found out he'd – he'd booked a room upstairs for the afternoon.'

Beryl said nothing. Now she just waited for Carolyn to finish the tale in her own time without interruption.

'It was all right at first. He said it was just so we could have a kiss and a cuddle in private – in comfort. You know?'

Beryl nodded, but still she kept silent while Carolyn went on, explaining everything that had happened before ending, 'Oh Beryl, I was so shocked. I stayed there in the bedroom for a while and when I went downstairs the girl behind the reception desk was so kind. You wouldn't expect such kindness from a complete stranger, but she was lovely. She gave me two safety pins and helped me fasten the front of my dress.'

'I wondered about them. I think I began to guess a bit of what might have happened when I saw your torn dress and the bruise on your face. Go on.'

'She offered to get a taxi for me, but I hadn't enough money with me.'

'Yer daft 'aporth. Someone would have paid it for you when you got back here.'

'I – I didn't want anyone else to see me other than you and, of course, Bill.'

'He's been asking after you all week.'

Carolyn gave a wan smile. 'That's kind of him. And I hardly know him either. We've only exchanged a few words when I've taken over from him at work and, of course, that time he showed us around the big house.'

'I can't get over that rat just leaving you high and dry . . .' Beryl laughed wryly. 'Well, you were not exactly dry, were you? I think you got a chill but I think you were also suffering from shock. Still, you're on the mend now.' She hugged Carolyn's arm to her side. 'Don't ever let a man do owt to you that you don't want him to. I mean, if you're willing, that's different.'

They walked on in silence until Carolyn burst out, 'I'm glad if he has gone. I don't want to see him again. Not ever.'

Twenty-Seven

'So, are you going to report him?'

Beryl had deliberately left raising the delicate subject for several days. Carolyn was now much stronger and had returned to work, though the supervisor and her friends were keeping an eye on her to make sure she was fit enough to cope with the intense pressure their work demanded.

They were sitting together in the mess after their shift. They had both finished eating and were enjoying a cup of coffee. Carolyn stirred hers thoughtfully.

At last she said slowly, 'No. I've thought about it a lot, but you know what would be said: that I'd asked for it. Going up to the bedroom he'd booked for the afternoon wasn't exactly sensible, was it? I don't know how I could have been so stupid.'

'You trusted him, that's how.'

'I did. I took what he said at face value. That it'd be nice just to be on our own for an hour or two. Warm and dry. I never thought . . .' Her voice trailed away and she shook her head as if even she couldn't believe she'd been so foolish. 'I mean, it's not as if I don't know all about the birds and the bees.' She smiled ruefully. 'Helping with the work on a farm, you can't help but know.'

'True, but you're not streetwise, are you? Living out there in the wilds, I don't expect you've met many fellers, let alone been out with them. If this Peter you talk about was the only one you knew outside the family – and he sounds so nice – you can't be blamed for thinking all men are the same as him. But, believe me, love, they aren't.'

For a moment there was a hardness to Beryl's tone and her eyes glittered with something akin to a bitterness that Carolyn couldn't understand.

'So, you're not going to do anything about it, then,' Beryl added in a more normal tone.

Carolyn shook her head. 'But I tell you what I am going to do; I'm going to learn from it. I was lucky. He didn't manage to – well, you know – and that's the way it's going to stay until I find someone I really want to marry. Someone who loves and *respects* me as well.'

Carolyn did not miss the look of scepticism in her friend's glance. 'He'll have to be someone very special to fit that bill,' Beryl murmured.

'Indeed he will,' Carolyn said firmly.

'We can apply for a forty-eight next week,' Carolyn said. 'Are you going home?'

Beryl glanced away and wriggled her shoulders. 'I – I don't think so. It's a long way to go.'

'No further than my journey. Actually, it's probably not as far. Or at least it's a more straightforward one.'

Beryl did not answer.

'Oh I get it.' Carolyn grinned. 'You want to stay here with Jeff.'

'No. He's on duty most of the weekend.' Beryl hesitated and then asked tentatively, 'Could I come home with you, Carolyn?'

'Of course you can. I think Peter might be home on leave.'

Beryl's eyes sparkled. 'Ooo, I can't wait to meet the young man who has caused so much trouble.'

Carolyn laughed. 'It wasn't his fault. Or mine. It was our mothers getting their heads together and trying to organize our lives.'

They travelled to Lincolnshire together, successfully hitch-hiking all the way. But not a word about their journey was said at home.

'It's the uniform that does it,' Beryl laughed. 'Have you noticed how the lorry drivers almost stand on their brakes to stop?'

Beryl was welcomed warmly once more and when they went to see Frank the following morning, he kissed them both. 'Nice to see you again. How're things?'

'Fine, Grandad. What about here?'

'Same as ever. Well, almost. We're busy with the harvest at the moment but we're a bit late with it this year. We've had such a lot of bad weather recently.' He eyed them archly and then chuckled. 'We've got a couple of land army girls. They're doing all right, but it seems it takes two to replace young Peter. They're causing a bit of a stir in the neighbourhood. Seems they like to work hard and play hard too. Town'll never be the same again, your Uncle Harold ses. And as for young Adam, well, he's besotted with both of them.'

Carolyn's mouth dropped open. 'But he's only . . .' Then she laughed. Time had marched on while she had been away and her cousin Adam was now eighteen. Of course he was interested in girls.

'Where are they billeted?'

Frank gave another deep, rumbling chuckle. 'With yar uncle and aunt.'

'Oh my! We're going to see Aunty Eve when we leave here.'

'I'm pleased to hear it. Yar aunt was a little put out she's yet to meet Beryl.'

'I'll mind we see everyone this time.'

'Including Peter?' Frank said mildly.

'Including Peter,' Carolyn laughed. 'Beryl can't wait to meet him.'

Frank's eyes twinkled. 'Well, if you tek a shine to him, lass, and get any ideas, you'll have to get past his mother first.'

Carolyn glanced at Beryl. She expected her friend to say that she'd already got a boyfriend, but Beryl was strangely silent.

As they left, Frank said, 'Peter arrived home last night and he was here bright and early to do a stint on the farm while he's here. Glutton for punishment, that one. He's helping us with the harvest. Ses he's missed it. You'll find him in the top field and your aunt should be at home. She's a grand lass, is our Eve. You'll like her, Beryl. I never thought she'd take to the country life, but she has. Mind you, she always dresses to kill and nips into town at every opportunity. Not like our Lilian. She avoids going anywhere, if she can. Doesn't like the hustle and bustle in the town, 'specially in the summer when all the visitors are here.' He chuckled. 'Hates having to walk in the gutter then like all the locals do.'

'Do the locals really walk in the gutter, Carolyn? Whatever for?' Beryl asked in astonishment as they left the farmyard and took the path that led to the furthermost fields belonging to Frank. It also took them very close to where Carolyn's uncle and aunt lived, killing two birds with one stone as Carolyn said.

'Because the visitors, bless 'em, are on holiday, so they're ambling along, window shopping or sight-seeing while the residents are in a much greater hurry, so it's easier to walk in the gutter than to keep dodging round the strollers on the pavement.'

'Oh. I'd never have thought of that.'

'There's Peter.'

'He looks busy.'

They stood watching him, shading their eyes against the glare of the early evening sun as Peter collected the stooks of wheat, throwing them up in a single smooth movement onto the top of the cart which was drawn by two shire horses. The cart moved slowly while one of the land girls stood on top of the growing stack, spreading them evenly. Peter was bare chested, his muscles rippling under his tanned skin which glistened with a healthy sweat from his labour.

'He's a nice-looking feller,' Beryl murmured. 'I'm surprised you didn't fall in love with him, Carolyn.'

'Now, don't you start . . .'

'Only kidding, but do introduce me.'

As they neared him, Carolyn called out, 'Hi, Peter.'

He looked round and grinned. 'Hello, Caro. And this must be Beryl I've been hearing so much about from your grandad?'

'Indeed it is. Peter, meet Beryl; Beryl, meet Peter.'

'It's good to see you, Beryl.'

'Likewise,' Beryl said. She nodded towards the cart. 'That looks like hard work.'

'It's what I've always been used to, so it's nice to keep me hand in when I come home.'

'D'you miss it?' she asked him.

He pulled a face. 'I do, but I honestly felt I had to do my bit.'

'Wouldn't you have done that by working on the farm?'

Peter sighed. 'Yes, I know. I've heard that argument a lot – especially from my mother – but I did what I felt was right, and . . .' he added with a saucy smile and glanced pointedly at Carolyn, 'it had nothing to do with being jilted.'

They laughed together and then Carolyn said, 'We'd better let you get on. We're on our way to see Aunty Eve. We might see you again. We're here until Monday morning.'

'So am I. What about a trip into town tomorrow evening? Can't make it tonight. We've got to get this load to the stack yard. Looks like being a late finish, though Mr Harold and Adam'll be there to help when they've finished the milking. But tomorrow, I'll take you both to the pictures. Tell you what, we'll go a bit earlier and have afternoon tea before we go to the cinema. My treat. And see if you can prise young Tom away from his wireless for the evening, though

I doubt you will. He's certainly doing his bit, young as he is, but I do worry about him not getting out much. I don't mean for exercise – he gets plenty of that cycling to and from school – but he doesn't get a lot of fun time.'

'I'll ask him, Peter, but I doubt he'll come. He's so dedicated to what he's doing.'

As they waved goodbye to the girl on the top of the stack and walked away, Beryl murmured, 'Is it common knowledge what Tom's doing?'

Carolyn sighed. 'It's difficult keeping secrets around here, believe me, but what I do know is that it will go no further than just our small community. It won't even get as far as the town. Here we are. This is where Uncle Harold, Aunty Eve and Adam live.' Carolyn tapped on the back door and opened it, calling out, 'Are you home, Aunty Eve?'

'Come away in,' a merry voice answered. 'And this must be the famous Beryl.'

Beryl glanced at Carolyn and raised her eyebrows, but her friend only laughed. 'That'll be Adam telling his mam all about you.'

Eve Atkinson was about forty, Beryl surmised. Her green eyes were sharp and perceptive and Beryl could see that no one would be able to hide anything from her for long. She wore the usual wrap-around overall that farmers' wives seemed to favour, but beneath it was a pretty floral dress. She wore black-and-white shoes with a two-inch heel and silk stockings. *Oh my*, Beryl thought, *Carolyn's aunt actually has real silk stockings.*

'Come in, both of you. No need to stand on

ceremony here. Now, miss' – she wagged her finger at Carolyn – 'why has it taken you this long to introduce me to Beryl?'

'I'm sorry, Aunty Eve, time just seems to slip away when we're here.'

Eve gave a mischievous smile and her eyes twinkled. 'Ah well, I forgive you this time, but don't let it happen again, mind.' She turned her attention to Beryl to appraise her from head to foot. 'Aye, our Adam's right. You are a pretty girl. You make a good pair. I bet all the fellers are after you two.'

Both girls laughed a little nervously. Neither of them wanted to share their romantic adventures, especially not Carolyn. 'We've got a couple of land army girls billeted with us. They could easily have stayed at the farm. Your grandad's got plenty of room, much more than we've got here, but the sour-faced woman who brought them said primly that she couldn't allow them to stay in a house with a single man. I ask you, how ridiculous is that? He's over seventy. What on earth did she think they were going to do? Have a threesome?'

Beryl stifled a giggle and glanced at Carolyn; a look that said, *By Heck, your aunt doesn't mince her words, does she?*

'Anyway,' Eve went on, 'we're lumbered with 'em.' Then she smiled. 'Actually, I don't mind. They're nice girls and Adam thinks the sun shines out of them. Perhaps you'd like to go out with them one evening. They go into town at the weekend.'

'We're already going to the cinema tomorrow night with Peter,' Carolyn said.

Eve raised her eyebrows. 'Peter, eh? So, tell me, what's really going on between you and Peter? We've had such a shenanigans here about the pair of you. Phyllis and Lilian are hardly speaking to each other. You'd think·they had more to worry about with a war on, but, I have to admit, we all wondered why he disappeared into the army so quickly and then you were hot on his heels volunteering for the ATS.'

Carolyn sighed. 'The trouble is, Aunty Eve, no one will believe what we're telling them.'

Eve put her head on one side. 'Try me.'

Carolyn sighed but repeated what she had already told other members of her family on several occasions. When she had finished, Eve shrugged her shoulders and said, 'Well, I believe you. And so should your mother and Phyllis Carter, but I rather suspect it's because they don't want to. You stick to your guns, lass, especially if Peter is of the same mind.'

'He is, Aunty Eve. I promise you he is.'

Twenty-Eight

Frank allowed Peter to borrow the farm truck to take the girls into the town the following evening. The three of them squashed onto the bench seat as Peter negotiated the bumpy road. The weather was dismal, but he knew the road so well and there was very little other traffic.

They went into a cafe just opposite the Tower Cinema, where Peter and Carolyn had been the day the bombs fell on the centre of the town. They were served tea and fancy cakes. They were all in civvies. Even Beryl had managed to squeeze into one of Carolyn's summer dresses – the marching and PT had certainly trimmed her shapely figure. And, luckily, they took the same size in shoes, so she had borrowed a pair of summer sandals too.

'This is a rare treat,' Beryl said, biting into a cake with undisguised relish. 'We don't get this sort of food where we are, do we, Carolyn?'

'Nor us.' Peter grinned. 'Make the most of it.'

The three of them chatted easily, swapping stories about their lives; at least as much as they thought it safe to tell anyone else, even someone who was also serving their country.

'Do you remember the last time we were here, Caro?'

'How could I forget? Let's hope it doesn't happen again today.'

Peter cocked his head on one side as if listening for aircraft overhead. 'No, all clear so far.'

'What happened?' Beryl asked.

Between them they related the story of their previous trip to the cinema. 'We never did get to see that film, did we?' Carolyn ended.

In the cinema, Peter sat between the two girls, solicitously talking to first one and then the other. As they came out into the darkness of the street, he held out his arms to them both. 'Take my arm. I don't want you falling over. Now, can anyone remember where we left the truck, or would you like to go for a drink first?'

'Ooh, a drink, I think,' Beryl said at once. 'Don't you, Carolyn?'

'Rather. Lead on, Macduff.'

The pub they chose was crowded with a few local men and several RAF lads who were billeted in the town for training. There was also a group of four or five young men in army uniform. Carolyn guessed they were from the Point with a few hours' leave to come into town.

'Hello, here comes another of the yokels too yellow to join up,' one of the blue-uniformed young men said. He lurched towards Peter, the pint of beer he held slopping over the side of the glass.

'Leave it, Alf. We don't want to cause trouble,' one of his mates said, putting a restraining hand on Alf's arm. 'We have to live in this town, remember.'

But Alf was already half drunk and too far gone

to listen to reason. 'Why should we be up there in the sky every day, risking our lives to save you shirkers.' His lips curled. 'And who are these two? They're not in uniform either.' He smirked. 'But mebbe they bring comfort to the troops in other ways, eh? But you want to be careful of the company you keep, girls. What was it they said in the last war? Any girl seen with a man not in uniform ought to be ashamed of herself. Well, the same goes for this war in my book. Get yourselves someone you can be proud of.'

'Alf, let it go . . .'

Ignoring his friend's pleas, with a quick movement, Alf threw the rest of his beer over Peter. There was a moment's stunned silence in the bar and then everyone seemed to move at once. The other local men, not in uniform, slammed down their pints and moved towards the RAF men; even the army chaps moved forward too and, with fists starting to fly, a fight broke out, though who was on which side it was hard to say. One of the army men detached himself and grabbed the two girls by the arms.

'Come on, Carolyn, and your friend. Let's get you out of here.'

'Steve – it's you,' Carolyn said, allowing him to hustle the two of them outside onto the pavement. 'But what about Peter?'

'It's all right. My mates are on his side. I told 'em he's in the army. Pity he didn't wear his uniform tonight.'

'But we ought to—'

'You both stay here. I'll go back and see what's happening . . .' But there was no need, for at that moment, two of the army lads came out with Peter between them. He was walking a bit unsteadily and holding his nose, which appeared to be bleeding.

'He'll have a right shiner in the morning,' Steve said cheerfully. 'But no real harm done, apart from bruised pride. How are you getting home?'

'We came in my grandad's truck. Peter drove us here.'

'I don't reckon he'd better drive you back. He's a bit groggy. Look, I'll drive you all back.'

'We won't all get in the cab, will we?'

Steve grinned. 'Then one of you will have to sit on Peter's knee.'

They walked to where they'd left the truck.

'It's very good of you, Steve, but I'm sure I'll be fine now,' Peter said, but he talked thickly through his bruised nose.

'I think it's best if I take you. Don't want you running off the road in the blackout. Is this it? Now, you get in first, Carolyn, then Peter – and Beryl, you climb in onto his knee. I'll drive very carefully and just hope a copper doesn't catch us. It's bad enough only being able to use side-lights. I've never known anywhere so pitch-black as it is here.'

Peter was still holding a bloody handkerchief to his nose, but he put his arm round Beryl to steady her as she perched on his knee.

Steve drove to Carolyn's home first to drop the two girls off and then to the cottage where Peter lived.

'How are you going to get home?' Peter asked thickly.

'Don't you worry about me.' Steve grinned. 'All this route marching and training we do, that bit of a walk's nowt. Now, go in and get a cold compress on that nose. Night, Peter.'

'Night, Steve, and thanks.'

Peter watched as Steve walked away and was swallowed up by the darkness. With a sigh he turned and let himself into the cottage. Thankfully, his mother was already in bed, but the following morning he had to face her.

'Whatever were you thinking, taking both girls out? Is that why you got into a fight?'

'Don't ask, Mam.'

'Remember who you're talking to, m'lad. I'm still your mother, even if you are the big man in uniform now.'

'Aye, and if I'd gone out in it last night, this wouldn't have happened. It was some RAF lads who started it. They called me a shirker but the army lads came to my rescue. Thanks to Steve, they knew I'm one of them.'

Phyllis sniffed. 'Well, I don't know what your commanding officer's going to say when you turn up looking like that.'

Peter grinned ruefully. 'I was wondering exactly the same thing.'

The girls and Peter left Skegness on the same early train on the day they all had to be back, but parted at Peterborough, neither telling the other where they were bound.

'I'll see you again soon, I hope,' Peter said, kissing them both chastely on the cheek. As he slung his kitbag onto his shoulder and strode away from them down the platform, Beryl gazed after him.

'He's every bit as nice as you said he was,' she murmured. 'If only . . .'

'What?'

'Oh nothing. Come on, let's go and get a cuppa. Our connection's not due for half an hour.'

It wasn't until they were sitting on the train that Carolyn realized no one at home – not even her father or grandfather – had asked her about her 'young man in uniform'. She wasn't to know that Beryl had managed to speak to Frank, warning him that the friendship hadn't worked out and that it would be better not to ask questions about the young man.

'But she's all right?' Frank had asked worriedly.

'She's fine. I promise you,' Beryl had said, smiling, and Frank had squeezed her arm in gratitude.

'You're a good friend, Beryl lass. She's lucky to have you.'

'As I am to have her.'

The two girls were plunged straight back into the hectic routine at Beaumanor. The traffic – the messages coming through – seemed heavier than ever. While both girls were highly proficient at their work now – both had the fastest and most accurate speed of all the ATS girls – they were still shattered at the end of every shift.

'Thank goodness for a few hours off,' Carolyn

yawned. 'I'm for a sleep, Beryl, but are you seeing Jeff?'

'Yes. He's borrowed a mate's car and we're going out into the countryside for an hour or two.'

'Just don't be late back, that's all.'

'I feel awful going out with him now and leaving you all on your own. It was different when . . .' She paused tactfully.

'When Michael was around, you mean?' Carolyn put her arms around Beryl and gave her a quick hug. 'Don't be daft. I'm just glad to see you happy with a nice chap who's good to you. There'll be someone out there for me one day, but for now, I'm just happy to go out and about on our hours off, get home on our longer leaves, and to feel we're really doing something to help the war.' She laughed. 'Exactly what it is, none of us know, but it must be useful to someone somewhere.'

'The mysterious Station X,' Beryl murmured.

Through September and into October 1942, the news from the war front was not encouraging. Appalling news reached the Allies that German SS troops had slaughtered thousands of Jews in the Warsaw ghetto and a tremendous battle was being fought for the occupation of Stalingrad. The Russians were clinging valiantly to their city, but it was rapidly becoming a gigantic mound of burning rubble. Towards the end of October, however, General Montgomery, who had been appointed Commander of the Eighth Army in August, began to make headway against the enemy at El Alamein in North Africa. At the beginning of

November, Monty, as he was affectionately known, led his army to break through Rommel's front line and the enemy were reported as being in full retreat. It was a major victory for the Allies and brought renewed hope.

'Got him.' Beryl's tone was triumphant and those who were not glued to their headphones smiled. They knew what she meant. She had been following a particular operator whom she had come to recognize by the way he transmitted. She'd lost him for a while but now it was obvious that she'd found him again.

Later, as they walked round the perimeter of the field, Beryl explained it to Carolyn. 'There's this operator on one of the frequencies I follow regularly. He's so slapdash I'm surprised they don't remove him. Mind you, I hope they don't, because he's a joy to intercept. D'you remember us being told at Trowbridge to watch out for repetitive words? Well, this one sends a seven-letter word at the end of every message. I'm sure it's his girlfriend's name or something.'

'Station X must be delighted. They must need that sort of thing to help them crack the codes.'

Even though there was no one near them, Beryl lowered her voice. 'Do you know where – or what – this mysterious Station X is?'

'Not a clue,' Carolyn said cheerfully. 'All I know is that all the pieces of paper the runner collects from our trays are then sent down the tube to the teleprinter room, from where they're sent on immediately. And then, each night, a despatch rider takes the actual pieces of paper to Station X.'

'Every night?'

'Yup.'

'Golly. The messages must be important to do all that.' Beryl chuckled. 'Isn't that what they call "belt and braces"?'

Carolyn laughed. 'It is. Being doubly careful. By the way, have you heard we're going to be issued with men's battle dress now we're into autumn and even men's underwear, because it's so cold in the huts.'

'Thank goodness. I wonder why they aren't better heated?'

'No idea, but warmer clothes will help. I'm going to treat myself to some fingerless gloves. I'll get you a pair, if you like.'

'I would like. Thanks, Carolyn.'

'I'll get Noreen a pair too. Her fingers were blue with cold yesterday.'

'Come on, let's run, else we'll miss the transport.'

As the weather turned colder, the girls would go to the canteen as often as they could for a hot cup of tea. On one such day in November, Carolyn and Beryl sat together at the end of a particularly hard shift. Beryl stirred her tea thoughtfully, even though there was no sugar in it. With no warning, she suddenly blurted out, 'I've got to ask for compassionate leave sometime soon. I – I need to go home.'

Carolyn had noticed that Beryl had not been her usual bubbly self for a couple of weeks. 'Oh dear. That sounds as if something's wrong.'

'I – um – think there is, so I'd better go and sort it out. Look, I don't want to say any more just now,

Carolyn, but I'll – I'll tell you when I get back. And before you offer, I don't want you to come with me. This is something I've got to do on my own.'

'Well, good luck, then.'

Beryl pulled a face. 'I think I'm going to need it,' she muttered.

Twenty-Nine

'Hello, Beryl? You're back quicker than I thought you'd be,' Carolyn greeted her friend when she arrived back at their billet after only one night away. Carolyn had thought that Beryl would be away for at least the whole seventy-two hours she'd been granted on compassionate grounds. 'Everything all right?'

'I only wish it was,' the girl muttered and dropped her head.

Now she looked more closely, Carolyn could see that her friend was really upset. Her eyes were red and swollen from crying. She took Beryl's bag from her and linked her arm through hers. 'Come on. Let's go and get you a nice hot drink in the kitchen and you can tell me what's happened.'

Fresh tears sprang to Beryl's eyes. This was so unusual that it must be something really serious.

'Is there something wrong at home?' Carolyn asked as she pushed Beryl gently into a seat and busied herself making them both a drink.

'No – yes. Oh Lord!' Her tears flowed freely now and Carolyn stopped what she was doing to put her arm around her friend's shoulders.

'Let's go and find a quiet place and you can tell me what's happened. There are too many people coming and going in here. Even our bedroom can be like Piccadilly Circus, with Noreen running in and out whenever she feels like it. Let's go for a walk.'

Beryl sobbed now and clung to Carolyn's arm. Carolyn was shocked; this was so unlike the cheerful, outgoing girl. Now, she was really worried.

As they walked down the road towards the river, arm in arm, Beryl's sobs ceased, but she kept her head down as if she didn't want anyone to see her. They sat down on the bank. Carolyn held her friend's hand and patted it. 'You can tell me anything. Is it to do with Jeff? A trouble shared and all that . . .'

Beryl hiccupped. 'Sort of, but the trouble's all mine. My – my father made that very clear.'

Carolyn stared at her. 'Oh no!' she whispered. 'You're not – you're not . . .'

Beryl nodded and said bitterly, 'Yes, I am. I'm in the pudding club and there's no mistake because I've seen a doctor.'

'Oh Beryl. But – but Jeff's a good sort. He'll marry you.'

Beryl shook her head. 'No – he won't. Jeff is not "a good sort". He's not the man I thought he was. He's married,' she ended flatly.

'Married! Oh my Lord, I didn't expect that.'

'Neither did I,' Beryl said bitterly. Then she sighed heavily, 'Though I did expect the reception I got at home. My dad has turned me out. I'm not to "darken their door again". Not ever. Oh Carolyn . . .' She leaned her head against Carolyn's shoulder and wept afresh. 'Whatever am I going to do? They'll turn me out of the ATS when they find out and now I've nowhere to go.'

'You've never said much about your family, but surely they won't do that, will they? I expect they're just shocked. They'll come around.'

But, suddenly, Carolyn was unsure herself as her mind flitted back to the time when her own mother had said that if she went home 'with a belly full', she'd be turned out.

Beryl raised her tear-streaked face. 'I've never said much about my family and I've never gone home before when we've had leave, because – because I didn't want to.'

'Go on,' Carolyn said softly.

'I'm sorry, Carolyn. I should have trusted you. I've not been entirely honest about my family. I left home under a bit of a cloud. My father is a very strict disciplinarian. Oh he's a good dad in a lot of ways. He provides for us. We've never gone hungry, but he rules our whole family with a rod of iron, including my poor mam.' Beryl's eyes clouded as she thought about her mother. 'I worried and worried about leaving her when I joined up, but in the end, Carolyn, I just had to get away.' She laughed wryly. 'Talk about this chap Hitler being a dictator; he could take lessons from my dad.'

'Have you got any brothers and sisters?'

'Yes, one of each. I've just turned twenty-one. Robin's eighteen months younger than me and Rosie is fourteen.'

'They'll look out for your mam, won't they?' But before Beryl could answer, Carolyn added, 'Oh, but perhaps your brother will be called up, will he?'

'I'm not sure. He's working in a factory that has turned over to war production, so he might not be. Mind you, he might want to join up, like I did, and for the same reason.'

'What . . . ? I mean, how . . . ?' Carolyn began and then fell silent. Prickly though her relationship with her own mother was sometimes, she couldn't imagine leaving home because of it, and her dear, placid father had never even raised his voice to either her or Tom.

'What does he do, you mean?' Beryl guessed what she was trying to ask.

'Well – yes.'

Beryl's pretty mouth twisted with bitterness. 'How long have you got? For a start, he gets in some filthy moods, usually after he's had a drink or six or when Sheffield United have lost a match.'

'Does he – did he – hit your mother or you?'

'Not Mum, no, but he used to smack us kids across the back of the legs when we were small.'

'Yes, my mam did that, but never my dad. He only had to look at me with such an expression of disappointment and I used to dissolve into tears.'

'My father is so controlling, Carolyn. Everything has to be just as he wants it. For heaven's sake, I'm twenty-one now, but I still had to be in no later than ten o'clock every night. He wanted to know who I was going out with and where I was going. And as for boyfriends, well, you could forget that. So, you can see why I'd rather stay here than go home, can't you? I only joined one of the services to get away from home. He couldn't stop that, though he had a damned good try. He went to the recruiting office where I'd signed on and played merry heck with them, but as I was over eighteen, he couldn't do anything about it. I was never allowed out in the evenings – not even to go out with girlfriends. Once I got home from work, that was it.'

'What about your brother and sister?'

'The same. Once they were home from school, they weren't allowed out again. Not even to play with the other kids in the street.' She paused and then added, huskily, 'So you see, when finally I got away from home, I went a bit wild. I'd never been allowed to have a boyfriend. Not even a friend who was a boy, like you and Peter. And I was so naive. I mean, I knew the facts of life. It was all drilled into me – especially by my dad – that I mustn't let a boy anywhere near me. I thought for a long time that you got pregnant by kissing.' She smiled wryly. 'But it was told to me in such a way that it sounded horrible and dirty and disgusting. There was nothing about loving and being loved. And when Jeff came along . . .' Tears sprang to her eyes yet again. 'He was so kind and thoughtful and gentle, I just fell in love with him. He promised he wouldn't hurt me. That he'd be careful . . .' Her voice faded away to a whisper. 'And I trusted him.'

'Did you – did you know he was married?'

Beryl looked up sharply. 'Heavens, no! I wouldn't even have gone out with him at all if I'd known that.'

There was a long silence. Beryl dried her tears and blew her nose hard. Then she straightened her shoulders. 'You won't tell anyone else, will you, Carolyn? Not even Noreen.' Over the time since Carolyn's misadventure, Noreen had become a closer friend to both of them than before, but not as close as Carolyn and Beryl were to each other.

'Of course not, but what are you going to do?'

'I'll stay on here until they kick me out, which they will do, once they get to know.' She sighed. 'Then I expect I'll have to find a mother-and-baby home somewhere. After that, well, I don't know.'

'Have you really got no other relative who'd help you? No grandparents or aunts?'

Beryl bit her lip as she shook her head. 'I think my mother has a sister somewhere but they fell out when she married my dad. In fact, her whole family cut her off.'

Carolyn gaped at her. She hadn't realized just how lucky she was to have a close-knit family. Oh they were a bit of a pain sometimes, especially when her mother tried to organize her life, but she'd never believed that they would turn her out if she got into trouble, despite what her mother had warned. But now a little seed of doubt began to grow. Would they have reacted the same as Beryl's parents had done if she had found herself in trouble?

'Look, we should have a forty-eight coming up soon. I'll be going home,' she said. 'Want to come?'

Beryl shook her head. 'Not this time, thanks. I couldn't face them. I wouldn't be able to keep it from them. They're such lovely people. In fact, you can tell them, if you want to. I don't expect they'll want to see me again, but they'll have to know sometime.'

'Will you be all right on your own, though?' Carolyn asked worriedly.

'Yes. I'll offer to do extra duty. There's always someone off ill this time of the year. It'll keep me busy. I won't have time to think.'

'What – what about Jeff? You have told him, haven't you?'

Beryl nodded. 'Oh yes. I couldn't wait to tell him. I was so excited. I thought we'd be married straight away and we'd live in a little cottage with roses round the door and be such a happy little family.' Bravely now, she held the tears back. 'Oh Carolyn, why was I so stupid?'

'It's not your fault. We were both too trusting.'

'Grandad.'

'Yes, lass? What is it, cos I can see summat's bothering you? So, out with it.'

They were sitting in front of the range on the Sunday afternoon before Carolyn was due to return to Beaumanor Hall the following morning.

'It's Beryl. She's in trouble.'

Frank packed his pipe slowly and when it was lit, he said, 'Tell me about it, love.'

As Carolyn explained what Beryl had told her about her family and about Jeff, who'd misled her so cruelly, Frank stared into the fire. He didn't interrupt once and when she had finished, there was a long silence between them. 'So,' he said slowly at last, 'she's nowhere to go?'

'No. She says she'll have to go into a mother-and-baby home.'

Frank winced. 'They'll make her have the bairn adopted, whether she wants to or not. Does she – does she want to keep it?'

'Actually, she's not said. She probably doesn't even know herself yet. I wouldn't at this stage.'

'No, but she'll feel differently once the little mite arrives. I can guarantee that.'

Carolyn smiled. Her grandfather had always been fond of children. One of her earliest memories was of him bouncing her on his knee playing 'Horsey, Horsey'.

After another thoughtful silence, Frank said, 'Are you sure she's no other relatives she can go to?'

'She said not.'

After another long pause he said, 'Then, Carolyn, you can tell her that she can come and live here with me, the bairn too.'

Carolyn's eyes widened in surprise. 'Are you sure, Grandad?'

'I wouldn't have offered, lass, if I wasn't.'

'But – but what will Mam and Uncle Harold say?'

'It's nowt to do wi' them. I'm still in charge of my faculties. I like Beryl. Despite what's happened, she's a nice lass. I reckon her parents have let her down first and foremost, keeping her penned up so she didn't have a chance to get to know the way of the world. And then this feller, well, he's a wrong 'un. Getting another lass in the family way when he's already married. I ask you. I don't blame her but she's the one left in disgrace.' He glanced at her.

'Now, you go back tomorrow morning and tell her, but leave telling yar mam to me. All right?'

Carolyn stared at him and then, smiling, she nodded and whispered huskily, 'Thank you, Grandad.'

'She won't be coming for a bit, will she?'

'No, she's going to stay on in the ATS until it – her condition – becomes obvious and then she'll have to leave.'

'That gives me a bit of time to get things ready.'

'What – I mean – how . . . ?'

Frank chuckled. 'This is a big house, lass. More than half the rooms aren't used now.' He prodded the air with his pipe towards the south. 'You maybe haven't been to that end of the house recently, but it's where your mam and dad lived when they were first married.' His eyes softened. 'You were born here, love. I wouldn't have minded you all staying here for good. It was what your grandma wanted too in the end. She was upset at first, like any mother would be, but I talked her round and once they were married, she couldn't do enough to help them. But your mam wanted her own place, so I gave them the cottage and a bit of land for their lifetime.'

Carolyn wrinkled her forehead. 'Yes, Dad told me a bit about it not long ago. I don't remember living here, though.'

'No, you probably won't. You were only about three when you all moved out. Anyway, what I'm coming to is that the rooms at the far end of the house are already self-contained. There's a small kitchen, living room and two bedrooms and a bathroom above. We have to share the same staircase but, other than that, it's all separate. There's even an outside privy just near the back door of the kitchen. So you see, Beryl will be fine there. But you'd best tell her just one thing: I don't want any rent off her, but I would hope she'll be able to do a little work about the place – once she's over the birth, of course. She'll get plenty of food from the farm and I'd give her a small wage. She'll need a bit of money of her own to buy things she'll need.'

'But what will everyone say?'

'I wouldn't give a brass farthing for what anyone else says. Not even your mam or your uncle. I'm far too old to worry about my reputation and as for hers . . .' He shrugged.

Carolyn sighed heavily as she finished his sentence for him, 'It's in tatters already.'

As she left, she hugged her grandfather hard. 'I don't know how to thank you. And nor will Beryl.'

'Don't forget – not a word to your mam. This is our secret. For the moment anyway.'

Thirty

'Where's Beryl?' Carolyn asked Noreen when she got back to the billet.

'In her room. She's got some sort of stomach bug. Keeps being sick, she says, and she looked as white as a sheet this morning. Mr Lawrence has given her the day off. She's neither use nor ornament in that state.'

Carolyn hurried to the room they shared. She found Beryl lying on her bed, her face swollen from shedding copious tears. She paused a moment in the doorway, her heart turning over at the sight of her friend in such hopeless distress. She closed the door and moved to sit on the bed at Beryl's feet.

'Now, you. Sit up, I've got something to tell you.'

Beryl groaned. 'Leave me alone. I just want to die.'

'No, you don't. At least you won't when you hear what I've got to say.'

'It can't be that good.'

'Oh it is. It's better than you could ever imagine.'

Even in the depths of her misery, Beryl was intrigued. Slowly she pulled herself up and leaned against the bedhead. 'Has Jeff come back and said he's going to divorce his wife? Because if that's what you're going to say, then I don't believe you.'

'No, sorry, it isn't that.'

'Don't be sorry. I don't want to spend the rest of my life with such a lying bastard.'

'Now, just listen and hear me out, will you?' Swiftly, Carolyn told her all that Frank had said and, while she talked, Beryl's mouth dropped open.

'You're not serious. *He* can't be serious.'

'Grandad never says anything he doesn't mean. I promise you.'

'But – but – why? He hardly knows me. Why would he want to help *me*?'

'He took a liking to you and I think . . .' Here she hesitated.

'Go on,' Beryl prompted.

'I've never told anyone this . . .'

'I won't say a word. You know I won't.'

Carolyn took a deep breath. 'I volunteered for the ATS because of something that happened at work. It was when all the trouble blew up about me and Peter. His mother came to where I worked . . .'

'Woolworth?'

Carolyn nodded. 'She caused a dreadful scene. I was so embarrassed, I just had to leave. Amongst all her accusations against me about Peter, she said something about my parents. She implied that my birth was too soon after their marriage, if you know what I mean. And then, a while back, my father admitted that there was rather a short time between their wedding date and my birthday and then, yesterday, when we were talking, Grandad confirmed what Dad had said and that we lived with him and Grandma until I was about three years old. I can't remember it, but I expect it explains his understanding of – of the situation you're now in. He and Grandma stood by their daughter and now he wants to help you because your parents won't. Sorry if that sounds a bit blunt.'

'Don't apologize. It's true. What a wonderful man he is and you're the most wonderful friend anyone could have.'

She flung her arms around Carolyn and they hugged each other. 'You helped me when I most needed it, Beryl. That's what friends are for.'

'I must write to him and thank him for such a generous offer. I'll tell him I'll work so hard for him, his house will shine like a new pin and I'll help out on the farm anywhere he wants me to.' She shook her head again, 'I just can't believe it. He hardly knows me.'

Carolyn chuckled. 'You're soon going to know each other a whole lot better.'

The two girls laughed together. It was the first time in weeks that Carolyn had seen Beryl laugh.

'Father, have you quite taken leave of your senses?' his daughter demanded.

'Far from it,' Frank said calmly, puffing at his pipe as he sat across the hearth from Eddie after Sunday lunch at their cottage.

Lilian sat down heavily, quite forgetting that there were the dirty pots to wash up and put away. 'I don't believe it.'

'What don't you believe?'

'That you can be so – be so – gullible. Eddie – talk to him. Tell him he's making a big mistake.'

Eddie glanced at Lilian and then sighed. What he was about to say would undoubtedly land him in hot water with his wife, but he had to be honest. He thought for a moment and then turned his answer into another question. 'Why do you think he's making a mistake?'

'She's a little gold digger, that's why. And no better than she should be. Getting herself pregnant and then looking for some senile old fool to take pity on her.' She turned her attention back to Frank. 'She's got family of her own, hasn't she?'

'They've turned her out.'

Lilian sniffed. 'Well, I can't say I blame them for that.'

Frank glanced at her and then looked away again before saying quietly, 'Really, lass?'

Eddie shifted uneasily in his chair and although colour suffused her face, Lilian wasn't done yet. 'Does Harold know?'

'Not yet, but he will by later today. I intend to call in to see him and Eve on my way home.'

Lilian jumped up. 'Well, if I can't say anything to make you change your mind, I'd best get on with my work. Where's Tom disappeared to?'

'Front room,' Eddie said. 'He always does two hours at the wireless on a Sunday afternoon instead of the evening, if you remember.'

'Oh yes. And Steve will be calling in later for his notes as usual. At least that will be something to look forward to. I hope he'll have time to have a bit of tea with us. I've made a trifle.' She sniffed. 'Such as it is, with all the shortages.'

When the two men were alone, with only the sound of clattering crockery coming from the scullery, Eddie asked softly, 'Are you really sure about this?'

'As sure as I was about not turning me own daughter out when she was in the same predicament. That was a bit different, though, I grant you, as you were willing – and able – to marry her.'

Eddie looked uncomfortable again but said nothing. With feigned casualness, Frank said, 'The way Lilian reacted makes me think she wouldn't take kindly to Carolyn being caught in the same way.'

Eddie shrugged and sighed. 'In that case, I'd have to stand up to her, wouldn't I?'

Frank chuckled, feeling suddenly sorry for his son-in-law. 'Let's hope it never comes to that, eh?'

'Amen to that,' Eddie said with feeling.

'So,' Frank said when he'd finished explaining to Harold and Eve, 'that's what's going to happen. Lilian's not happy about it but, like I told her, I'm still in charge of me faculties at the moment. And although it's not going to make any difference to my decisions, I'd like to know what you think.'

Eve jumped out of her chair, crossed the hearth and planted a swift kiss on the top of Frank's head. 'I think what I've always thought. That you're a lovely man and I'm so grateful to be part of your family and that you're my Adam's grandfather.'

Frank reached for her hand and kissed her fingers. 'And I am lucky to have you as my daughter-in-law. We understand one another, you and me, don't we, lass? We both call a spade a spade.'

Eve laughed aloud. 'Aye, or a bloody shovel.' Despite her fancy clothes and make-up, she was blunt and outspoken, but you knew where you stood with her, Frank thought. She was easier to deal with in some ways than his own daughter.

'What about you, Harold?' he asked his taciturn son.

'I can't see owt wrong with it, mesen. It'll be nice for you to have someone living in the house. Company, like. As long as you don't mind a screaming kid. Will she do a bit of work about the place, d'you think?'

'Once she's fit again after she's had the bairn, yes. I've made that very clear to Carolyn. The lass will have to earn her keep.'

'And she'll live in the rooms where Lilian and Eddie first lived, will she?' Eve asked.

'That's what I thought.'

'Then I'll come across and help get them cleaned. It's a big job for Phyllis on her own.' She chuckled. 'And Phyllis Carter will certainly have plenty to say about this when she finds out.'

'I expect you know all about this madcap scheme of your dad's, then?' Phyllis was standing in Lilian's kitchen, her hands on her hips. 'Has he gone soft in the head in his old age?'

'He's just helping Carolyn's friend out for a while. I don't expect it'll last very long.' Even though she agreed with Phyllis, Lilian felt obliged to defend her own father. Finding fault within the family was one thing, allowing an outsider to do it, was quite another. 'A girl like her won't want to be trapped out here in the middle of nowhere. Once she's had the kid and probably had it adopted, then she'll be off back to the bright lights.'

Phyllis sniffed. 'You reckon? I'm not so sure. She'll have her eye on the main chance, you mark my words.'

Lilian paused in polishing the brass fender around the hearth. 'Whatever d'you mean, Phyllis?'

'An old man and a pretty young girl living in the same house. That's why the authorities wouldn't let the land army girls live with him, even though there's plenty of room in the farmhouse. A sight more than at Harold's place.'

'If you're going to cast aspersions on my father's integrity, Phyllis Carter, you can leave right this minute.'

But Phyllis stood her ground. 'I'm not, Lilian, but it's how it *looks* to folks. There'll be gossip.'

'Aye, I'm sure there will be and you'll be the one spreading it, I've no doubt. Can't wait to impart a bit of juicy tittle-tattle, now can you? Unless, of course, it's about your own family, then it's a different matter.'

'If you're going to be like that, Lilian, I will go.'

'Oh for Heaven's sake sit down and don't be so huffy.'

While Lilian put the kettle back on the hob and laid out cups and saucers, Phyllis said slyly, 'Eve's been across this morning to clean out the rooms for this Beryl. You know, the ones you had years ago.'

Lilian stopped and stared at her. 'Has she indeed?' She stood for a few moments in thought, then she shrugged and said, 'Oh well, it saves me a job, I suppose.'

'I've been helping her. Mr Frank wants us to give 'em a lick of paint.'

'Paint? He's going to a lot of trouble for a girl he hardly knows.'

'She's Carolyn's friend, isn't she?'

'Well, yes, but . . .'

'Mebbe it's not just this Beryl who's in trouble.'

Lilian glared at her. 'What are you insinuating, Phyllis?'

'Oh nothing,' Phyllis said airily. 'Just that I agree with you – it's a lot of trouble to go to for a complete stranger.'

When Phyllis left half an hour later, Lilian was still frowning over their conversation. She'd go and see Eve, she decided, as she seemed to be involving herself in all this. The sisters-in-law had never really hit it off. Where Lilian was concerned, there had always been the shadow of Harold being the one who would inherit the farm. They were both strong-willed women, who weren't afraid to speak their minds. In the past, they had often disagreed, but now, Lilian thought, they should unite as a family. Two hours later, she was sitting in Eve's kitchen and coming straight to the point.

'Not often you come to see me, Lilian,' Eve said bluntly. 'To what do I owe this pleasure, as if I didn't know?'

Ignoring the sarcasm, Lilian said, 'It's about this business with Father and this girl.'

Eve raised her eyebrows. 'You're making it sound

as if there's a lot more to it than there is. He's taken pity on a girl who's in trouble. That's all.' Pointedly, she added softly, 'Not the first time, is it?'

Lilian coloured. 'That was different. That was family. He's only met this girl a couple of times.'

'But she's Carolyn's friend. Actually,' Eve hid her smile as she added with deliberate casualness, 'I rather liked her too.' She knew it was naughty of her, but she enjoyed winding Lilian up. She decided, in that moment, that she would befriend Beryl. It wouldn't do her any harm in Frank's eyes either. There was nothing devious or scheming in Eve's thoughts. She had no ulterior motive. With no parents of her own still alive, she looked upon Frank as her father and loved him dearly. She would do anything to please him.

Thirty-One

It was amazing that no one – not even Noreen – guessed Beryl's condition. She had managed to hide the early morning sickness she suffered during the first three months and even when she began to put on a little extra weight, no one remarked about it.

'I think it's because I'm a little plump anyway,' Beryl confided to Carolyn just before Christmas. 'I didn't expect to be able to hide it this long, but now I can't fasten my jacket properly, it's going to be noticed.'

Neither of the girls got leave over Christmas, and they both worked solidly over the holiday period. But just after New Year, the commander called Beryl into the headquarters.

'Sit down, my dear.' The woman was kindly. 'Morley, I'll come straight out with it. Are you pregnant?'

Beryl bit her lip and nodded. She was no longer reduced to tears by the very mention of the fact. Now, with Frank's kind offer, she had somewhere to go and she even had the option to keep her baby, if she wanted to. She still hadn't decided that. She rather thought she wouldn't know what she wanted to do until she held the baby in her arms.

The woman sighed. 'Then you do know you will have to leave us, don't you?'

'Yes, ma'am.'

'Do you have somewhere to go? Are your parents standing by you?'

Beryl cleared her throat. 'My parents have thrown me out, but I do have somewhere to go.'

'Ah,' Miss Everatt smiled, 'then the young man is doing the honourable thing, is he?'

Beryl shook her head 'No, ma'am. He – he can't. He's already married.' She looked up swiftly and met the steady gaze of the woman sitting opposite her. 'I didn't know that when I – when I . . .' Her voice faded away.

'I see. Well, you're not the first naive girl to be caught out by sweet words and empty promises and, sadly, you won't be the last before this war is over.' She paused and then said, surprisingly gently, 'I'm sorry, Beryl, but I will have to ask you to leave by the end of the week.'

'I understand, ma'am.' She smiled tremulously. 'I – I've done well to hang on this long.'

'Does no one know?'

'Only Carolyn Holmes.' Now her eyes filled with tears. 'She's the best friend anyone could have. It's her family who have offered me a home.'

'Then you're very fortunate. And are they willing to let you keep the baby?'

Beryl nodded.

'Then you are doubly fortunate.'

'I'll come with you,' Carolyn said as she watched Beryl pack up her belongings. 'Help you get settled in. We're lucky it's fallen on one of our forty-eights, but Ma'am has granted me an extra day's compassionate leave to help you.'

'She's been remarkably kind,' Beryl murmured. She was feeling a little apprehensive now. She had never lived in the countryside before and she realized that the Point would be very bleak in the winter. There would be no one of her own age around and, while she knew Frank would make her welcome, she wasn't sure about the rest of his family. But when they arrived at the farm the following afternoon, not only was Frank standing on the doorstep to greet her, but Eve was beside him.

Beryl couldn't stop her eyes filling with tears. Their kindness touched her far more deeply than had her father's outrage. Eve put her arm around the girl. 'Come on, love. Everything will be all right. I promise. Mr Frank and I will look after you. Let me show you your rooms while Carolyn has a chat with her grandad.'

Eve opened the door that led out of Frank's kitchen into the small hallway. To the left were the stairs leading to the upper floor and to the right, opposite the foot of the stairs, was the front door leading into a large greenhouse built against the west-facing wall of the house. 'Lovely place to put a baby in its pram when the weather's bad,' Eve remarked as she closed the front door again and opened the one leading into the extension to the farmhouse that had been built over twenty years earlier. 'And this is where you'll be. You're quite self-contained, though you have to use the same staircase to get to the bedrooms. There are two that'll be yours and there's a little bathroom.

I'll take you up there in a minute but first, this is your sitting room.'

Beryl stepped inside and gazed around her. 'I don't believe this,' she whispered. 'It's wonderful.'

'And through here is a little kitchen, fully fitted out with a small range so you can do your own cooking, if you want, though I expect you'll be cooking for Mr Frank and yourself in his kitchen. I think that's what he wants you to do. Everywhere's furnished, of course, but we haven't presumed to buy anything for the baby, cots and prams and suchlike. We thought you'd like to do that yourself, but I'll come with you into town, if you'd like me to.'

'Oh I would, Mrs Atkinson,' Beryl said.

'Do call me Eve. I can't be doing with all that "Mrs" stuff. Most folks call me Eve.'

'Would – would *Aunty* Eve be all right?'

'Fine by me, if that's what you'd prefer. Now, you get unpacked and settle in. The back door in your little kitchen leads outside to the rear of the house and the privy is just along the path to the right. No indoor toilet, I'm afraid, but Mr Frank has installed a little bathroom upstairs, so you're all nicely self-sufficient. But don't feel you have to stay in here all the time.' Eve's smile widened. 'Mr Frank's looking forward to having you here. He'll enjoy the company and, to be honest, Harold and me are pleased someone will be here with him. I'm often worried that if he was taken ill, none of us would know.'

'I want to help out around the house and the farm too, if I can be of use.'

'There's always plenty of work to do, even though we've got two land army girls at the moment. They're all right, but even the two of them don't get through the work that Peter Carter did. Just one word of warning, don't tread on Mrs Carter's toes. She cleans for Mr Frank and works in the dairy too. If you take my advice, ask her what you can do to help *her*.' Eve gave a broad wink. 'Get on her right side from the off.'

It seemed, however, as if Phyllis hadn't got 'a right side' for Beryl to get on. From the moment they met, Phyllis's hackles rose and, however pleasant and willing Beryl tried to be, she couldn't seem to please the woman.

'Don't think we don't all know what you're doing,' Phyllis said the first time the two women were alone together. 'Trying to get your claws into an old man and his money.'

Beryl gasped and sat down suddenly on the nearest chair. 'It's nothing like that, Mrs Carter.'

'I'm surprised young Carolyn has been duped,' Phyllis carried on as if she hadn't heard her. 'But then she's a silly girl who doesn't know what's best for her. She'll get 'ersen into trouble an' all, I shouldn't wonder, and then my Peter won't want owt to do with her. *He* wouldn't touch soiled goods. Cos that's what you are now. No decent man will ever look at you.'

Beryl hung her head. Everyone else had been so kind. Even Lilian. Even though her welcome had been a little cooler, it hadn't been nasty like this.

'Are you keeping it?'

'I – I don't know yet.'

'You want to get rid of it. It'll be a millstone round your neck. Have it adopted.'

Beryl was not one to tell tales anyway – she never had been, even at school – so she kept silent about Phyllis's needling. On it went, day after day, until Beryl had almost decided to pack her few belongings and leave. It would mean finding a mother-and-baby home, but surely anything was preferable to this woman's spiteful tongue. At least all the girls there would be in the same boat, as the saying went. But one day, when they were working together in the dairy and Phyllis had raised her voice above the noise of the butter churn, a figure appeared in the doorway and stood listening quietly.

'Mrs Holmes is wise to your little games, miss,' Phyllis was saying. 'Don't think you can pull the wool over my eyes or hers. I'm putting her right. I tell her every little thing I see going on here. Bought you a brand-new cot for your little bastard, hasn't he, when a drawer out the dressing table would do. I 'spect it'll be a posh new pram next. My God, you've got him wrapped round your little finger and no mistake.'

Suddenly, Frank's voice boomed from the doorway, making both women jump. 'That's enough, Phyllis. Leave what you're doing and go. Just get out of my sight and don't bother coming back, if that's how you're going to treat Beryl. She's here at my invitation and what I choose to do to help her is no one else's business. Especially not yours.'

Phyllis turned to face him, her face contorted in fear and anger. 'No fool like an old fool, is there,

Mr Frank? She'll take you for every penny she can. And what'll be left for your own family then, eh?'

'I won't . . .' Beryl was in tears now. 'I wouldn't.'

But neither of them were listening to her; the quarrel was now between Phyllis and Frank. He was icily calm. 'And was that why you were so keen for your son to marry Carolyn? Did you think he'd be set for life by marrying my granddaughter? Phyllis Carter, you're a mean-spirited woman and vicious with it. The wonder is that you've given birth to a young man as nice as Peter. He's a good lad and, if it wasn't for him, I'd be giving you notice this minute to leave your cottage. But he's fighting for his country and I won't turn his mother out of her home while he's away. But I don't want to see you here again. You're done working for me.'

Phyllis's face turned first deathly white and then bright red. She flung her arm out towards him. 'You see? You see what she's done? You're turning your back on someone who's given you loyal service for over twenty-five years. Me and my husband, before he was daft enough to volunteer and get himself killed. And then my son. My family's devoted themselves to you and this is how you repay me when a little slut worms her way into your life.' She stepped towards him and shook her fist in his face. 'Just you wait till my Peter gets home on his next leave. You haven't heard the last of this.'

Her anger carried her out of the dairy but not towards her own home. Instead, she headed towards Lilian's cottage while, in the dairy, Beryl was still crying. Frank put a kindly hand on her shoulder.

'Don't waste your tears on that woman. She's showing her true colours now.'

'I don't want to cause trouble amongst your family and friends, Mr Atkinson.'

'You aren't doing, lass. Not amongst those who matter to me. And do call me "Mr Frank".'

'But – but I didn't want her to get the sack. I mean, a lot of what she says is true and it's what a lot of other people will be saying.' Her voice dropped to a whisper. 'Even my own family.'

She cleared her throat and squared her shoulders. 'I promise you I'm not a gold digger. I'm very grateful for all your kindness and generosity, helping me over a bad patch, but once I'm on my feet, I'll be on my way. I'll have the baby adopted and then I'll be free to do whatever I like – or whatever they'll let me. Maybe they'd even have me back in the ATS.' She gave a wry little smile. 'I am very good at what I was trained to do, even though I say it myself.'

Frank looked sorrowful. 'Don't make any hasty decisions about the bairn yet, love. It's a big thing to give away your own flesh and blood. Adoption's a big step. You're not allowed to know who has taken the kiddie and you'd probably never see them again. Do you really want that?'

Beryl shrugged. 'Do I have any choice? An unmarried mother with a child is always going to be shunned.'

'Not by everyone,' Frank said quietly. Then, more robustly, he added, 'Just promise me one thing.'

Beryl looked up at him with reddened eyes and tear-stained cheeks. 'Anything, Mr Frank.'

'That you'll wait until the baby is born and give yourself a bit of time afterwards before you make such a huge decision.'

'I . . .' Beryl hesitated. She didn't want to go against Frank's advice, not after everything he was doing for her, 'But I might get fond of it and then – and then I wouldn't want to give it up.'

Frank said nothing. He just smiled down at her and touched her cheek and Beryl understood. That was exactly what Frank was hoping would happen.

Thirty-Two

'Lilian! *Lilian!*'

'Whatever's the matter, Phyllis? Has a bomb dropped somewhere?'

'You could say that.' Phyllis sat down at the kitchen table and made herself at home, 'Your father's only gone and sacked me, that's all.'

Lilian gaped at her. 'Why?'

Phyllis wriggled her shoulders. 'Cos I had a go at that little slut that's trying to worm her way into his life – and take all his money, I shouldn't wonder.'

Lilian sat down slowly, her gaze still on the woman who was sometimes a friend, sometimes an enemy. Phyllis was a strange woman. The way she was talking was as if she was jealous . . . And then Lilian realized. That's exactly what Phyllis was. Jealous. Now she recalled all the times when Phyllis had been there to help Frank after his wife had died. How she had cleaned his house for no payment in the early days, cooked him nice meals, done any shopping in town he'd needed. Lilian had suspected as much before but now it was obvious. It had been Phyllis who had been trying to ingratiate herself with Frank. Although she was a good few years younger than he was, it would have been quite understandable if he had wanted to take a second wife in his loneliness. And Phyllis had put herself into the position of being prime candidate. But now there was a younger, much prettier girl actually living in the same house.

Lilian smiled inwardly as she delivered what she knew would be a fatal blow to Phyllis's hopes. 'Don't worry. No one could ever take my mother's place in my father's eyes or in his affections. I think this thing with Beryl is exactly what it seems; he's just trying to help a young lass who's got herself into trouble.'

Phyllis wasn't about to give up so easily. 'He's lavishing a lot of money on her. A brand-new cot and it'll be a new pram next, I shouldn't wonder.'

Lilian shrugged. Inside she was still aggrieved, but she'd decided not to share her own thoughts and feelings with Phyllis anymore. She no longer trusted the woman; if, in fact, she ever had.

'You've changed your tune, Lilian. You weren't too pleased when I was helping Eve to paint the rooms for her coming.'

'So, why were you helping, if you're so against her coming here?'

Now it was Phyllis's turn to be evasive. 'It was what your dad wanted and I – I was only trying to please him.'

I bet you were, Lilian thought grimly, but she said nothing.

'I thought he was just trying to freshen the rooms up a bit,' Phyllis went on. 'Like you would for anyone, but I didn't realize he was going to start spending his hard-earned money – your inheritance, Lilian – on her like he is doing. After all these years, after all

that me and my family's done to help him, this is
how he treats me over a little slut like her. Just wait
till my Peter comes home on leave. He'll have summat
to say about all this.'

'Have you heard anything from him lately?'

'Yes, he hopes to get a seventy-two-hour pass in
a few weeks' time. He'll be coming home for a couple
of nights then. Just wait till I tell him what's been
happening. He'll not stand by and let his mother be
treated like this, I can tell you.'

At Beaumanor, in her off-duty hours, Carolyn was
lonely. She missed Beryl more than she would have
thought possible. It wasn't as if she hadn't formed
other friendships. Noreen was a good friend; they
got on very well together and she now shared the
bedroom with Carolyn. They grew closer in the days
after Beryl left – but she wasn't Beryl. She hadn't got
Beryl's spark that had always made Carolyn laugh
and keep her spirits up through the hardest of times.
There had been – still was – a very special bond
between the two girls who had met at the very start
of their time in the ATS. They had been lucky to be
able to stay together through all that time. There
were other girls, too, with whom Carolyn was
friendly, but no one could take Beryl's place. So now,
rather than mope, Carolyn looked for other interests
that were available during their off-duty hours. She
had always enjoyed cycling, even to and from work
in Skegness on the coldest of winter days. It had
never appealed to Beryl, so now Carolyn bought a
second-hand bicycle and joined the Beaumanor

Cycling Club. They went out into the surrounding countryside and to Bradgate Park. When someone found out about her typing skills, she was persuaded to help out with the publishing of the *Beaumanor Staff Magazine*, though she shied away from actually writing articles or producing drawings for it. So her days were busy, but she still couldn't help missing her best friend.

She and Noreen went often to one of the cinemas in Loughborough or to concerts in Leicester or Nottingham but neither of them wanted to go dancing very often.

'I've got a boyfriend back home,' Noreen explained. 'Well, sort of. I don't want to risk getting close to anyone else. Alan and I are very fond of each other and if the war hadn't got in the way, we'd probably have been married by now. But . . .' she sighed, 'when he went into the RAF, we both decided not to take it any further. Not yet. He's on bombers and they – they . . .' She hesitated and swallowed hard. 'Don't have a very good survival rate.'

'Oh Noreen, I'm so sorry. But, actually, it suits me too.'

Carolyn had told her a little about what had happened that day, but not every detail. She just said that they'd had a falling out after lunch and he had ridden off on his motorcycle leaving her to find her own way back to Beaumanor. Noreen accepted Carolyn's explanation though the girl was shrewd enough to guess that there was more to it than just that. But, wisely and kindly, she asked no more questions.

Strangely, Carolyn missed Michael too. They'd had some good times together before – her mind shied away from remembering. Keeping busy was her salvation and there was always work to do. She took on extra shifts if needed. Just to fill her time. But a couple of weeks after Beryl's departure, Noreen said, 'Are you off on Saturday evening, Carolyn?'

'Yes, why?'

'A small group of us are going dancing in Loughborough. Would you like to join us?'

'Well . . .' Carolyn paused. It was high time, she told herself sternly, that she buried her demons. Going to the same place where she had gone so often with Michael would be painful, but it should be faced. 'Yes, I would,' she said before giving herself any more time to think about it. 'Thanks for asking me. Who else is going?'

'A couple of the other girls we work with and three of the lads, but no strings. We just want to have a good time. Personally, I don't believe in wartime romances. They can end so badly.'

The girl was fishing for information, but Carolyn didn't rise to the bait. Instead, she said, 'You're absolutely right, Noreen.'

'What *really* happened between you and Michael?' Noreen was no longer trying to be subtle. 'He doesn't come around anymore.'

'Oh, it wasn't working out. We had a big row when he took me out to lunch and he just went off on his motorbike.'

'Yes, you told me that, but you came back that day in such a dreadful state.'

Carolyn forced a smile. 'If you remember, I got caught in a thunderstorm.'

Noreen eyed her sympathetically. She obviously guessed there was more to the story than Carolyn was telling, and she was worried about her friend. 'Has he gone away? Servicemen – or women – can't just up and leave. Not unless they're pregnant, of course.' That was a bit of a dig at Beryl, Carolyn knew, but again she chose to ignore it. 'Did he get a posting and, if so, how did he wangle that and so quickly?'

'Honestly, Noreen, I've no idea. I haven't seen him since. When I surfaced again after being ill for a while, he wasn't around. I think they were both – Michael and Jeff – stationed at Hucknall, so it's far enough away from here for us not to bump into each other. '

'He wasn't around *at all* after that day you came back in such a state. He never even came to see if you were all right.'

Carolyn shrugged. Now, at least, she could be completely truthful. 'I've really no idea where he went or what happened. Jeff told Beryl that he'd got compassionate leave to go home. A death in the family, I think.'

'You sound as if you don't care.'

Now Carolyn met her gaze. 'I don't,' she said shortly.

Noreen shrugged. 'Oh well, you'll be all right on Saturday. Bill's going. The one you usually take over from at work and who brought you home that day. He's a bit older than us, but he's really nice. You'll be quite safe with him.'

And she was. Bill stuck to her side all evening. He danced with her for most of the evening and bought her drinks, shepherding her to the buffet when it was served. But he was comfortable to be with. Carolyn didn't feel any pressure; he was just being friendly and nice. They talked and talked, telling each other about their homes and families when they sat out for one or two of the more energetic dances. 'I can't do this one,' Carolyn said when a tango was played. 'But please ask someone else if you want to.'

'I don't,' he laughed. 'I can't do it either and this sort of dance doesn't suit my size-twelve feet. I'm best with a waltz or a quickstep at a push. So,' he asked as they watched the dancers from a small table at the side of the room, 'what did you do before the war came along and put a stop to all our ordinary lives?'

Carolyn told him how she came to be at Beaumanor Hall. There was no need for secrecy between herself and Bill; he still worked on the same shift and she took over from him when it was her turn. There wasn't usually much time for chat, only occasionally, when the traffic was quiet, did they have the chance to talk.

'So, what did you do?' Carolyn asked him when she had come to the end of telling him her life story to date.

He grinned lopsidedly. 'You're never going to believe this, but I come from a farming family too.'

'Never!' Carolyn laughed aloud. 'Now, don't tell me it's in Lincolnshire. Let me guess . . . Norfolk, because just now and again, I catch a Norfolk accent.'

'Guilty, m'lord. We're pig farmers with turkeys for Christmas. We do grow crops, but they're mainly for feeding the animals. We have a few cows as well, but the focus is pigs.'

'I like pigs. They're lovely creatures. Grandad has a few, but not many, and a few cows and sheep.' She was quiet for a moment and then she murmured, 'It'll be lambing time next month. That always starts in February on my grandfather's farm. I shall miss being there.' Suddenly she felt very homesick. She'd always loved that time of the year.

They talked for the rest of the evening, dancing occasionally when there was a dance they both knew. How different he was to Michael, Carolyn thought. She couldn't help making a comparison. Michael had been so controlling. Everything had to be done just his way. And his varying moods were like a switch being flicked. One moment he'd been all charm and courtesy and then the next, when something didn't go just his way, he'd been moody with ill-concealed irritation. In contrast, Bill was easy-going. At the end of the evening, they dispersed back to their billets with no more than a chaste kiss on the cheek. Only one couple disappeared into the darkness to be alone together for a few minutes.

'Don't get caught, you two,' someone called after them cheekily. 'Sarg might be on the prowl.'

'It's been a lovely evening, Bill. Thank you.'

'We'll do it again some time,' he said casually. 'Good night, Carolyn.'

'So?' Noreen demanded as they got ready for bed.

'I had a great evening.' Carolyn smiled. 'Thanks for asking me along, Noreen.'

'But what about you and Bill?'

'What about me and Bill?'

'Well, I mean, is there a blossoming romance there?'

'No, there isn't. He's very nice and I'd like him as a friend, but no more. What about you?' Adroitly, Carolyn avoided telling Noreen what Bill had already confided in her earlier that evening. He was a lovely man, but now she knew they would only ever be good friends.

'I told you, I've got a boyfriend. I'm not looking to get serious with anyone here.' Noreen yawned. 'But it was a good evening. Night, Carolyn.'

'Night, Noreen, and thanks again.'

Thirty-Three

When Carolyn took over from Bill at the start of her next shift, he whispered, 'I've got two free tickets for a concert on Sunday at the De Montfort Hall. Would you like to go with me? It's Anne Ziegler and Webster Booth.'

Carolyn's face lit up. 'Oh yes, I've heard them on the wireless, but I've never seen them live. They're married, aren't they? To each other, I mean.'

'Not sure, but I think so.'

'I'd love to go. Thank you, Bill.'

'We put a list up on the noticeboard for anyone interested to add their names and there's already enough for us to get transport there and back.'

It was a wonderful evening. The magnificent music in the beautiful hall transported them far away from the tensions of their work and from thoughts of the war.

'And you still keep telling me there's nothing going on between you and Bill,' Noreen teased when Carolyn crept into their bedroom late that night.

'Oh sorry, did I wake you?'

'No. Not at all, I've been reading. To be honest, I'm a bit like a mother hen. I can't settle until my chick is safely back home.'

Carolyn could have been irritated by Noreen's fussing, but she wasn't. Instead, she laughed and said jokily in return, 'That's nice of you, Noreen, but please don't turn into my mother, will you?'

Noreen, with good grace, laughed too. 'No, I promise. It's just that I knew you were going into Leicester and with the bombing and everything . . .' Her voice faded away but, without meaning to do so, Noreen had brought the war back into Carolyn's mind.

While Carolyn had been sitting in the De Montfort Hall listening to the wonderful singing, Steve had been knocking on the door of her parents' cottage.

'Come in, Steve. Have you time for a bite to eat? I've kept a plate back from teatime for you,' Lilian said as she opened the door. 'Tom says he's going to be a bit longer tonight. Evidently, he thinks he's picked up something that could be quite important.'

'Righto, Mrs Holmes.' He hesitated. 'I wouldn't say "no" to a bite, thank you, but you really mustn't do it every night, you know. I'm starting to feel very guilty about eating your food with all this rationing.'

Lilian flapped her hand in a dismissive gesture. 'Don't you worry about that. We live on a farm. Sit down, I'll get it out of the oven.'

'Have you heard from Carolyn recently? I expect she doesn't get home very often.' Steve said as he sat down at the table. 'Travelling on public transport can be a nightmare these days. Thank goodness I've got my motorbike for when I want a quick trip home to Hull.'

'As far as I know, she's fine. She rings her grandad quite often and he relays any messages. But goodness knows when she'll get leave again – at least, long enough to get home. There, you get round that.'

'Thank you. It looks wonderful.'

Tom came into the room as Steve was finishing his meal. He laid the usual brown envelope on the table. 'Sorry if I've kept you waiting, Steve.'

The young soldier grinned. 'I've been quite happy. Your mam's been feeding me again. Right, then,' he added, getting up. 'I'll be off.' He tucked the precious envelope into a brown leather pouch that would go into the pannier on the back of his motorcycle. In half an hour's time, another similar one from Mr Fox would join it and then he would ride through the night to hand it to the officials. What happened to this paperwork then, he didn't know. It was all very hush-hush. He couldn't even tell Tom and Mr Fox where he took the results of the hours they spent crouched over their wireless sets.

'He's such a nice young fellow,' Lilian said as she cleared the pots away. 'It's a pity he's married. He'd have been a nice boyfriend for Carolyn.'

Eddie, seated by the fire, rattled his newspaper. 'Now, Lilian, no more matchmaking, please.'

Tom, completely uninterested in boyfriends for Carolyn, or girlfriends for himself at the moment, if it came to that, yawned. 'I'm off to bed, Mam.'

'Night, love. Sleep well.'

Tom nodded. That was one thing he was thankful

about. As soon as his head hit the pillow, he was asleep and slept soundly until the following morning. He was usually up with the lark to follow the regular pattern of his days now. Cycle to school and then home again in the late afternoon. A couple of hours homework and then two or more hours listening in to any enemy signals he could pick up. It was getting easier now. He could sometimes recognize the same German operator on the same wavelength. He couldn't, of course, decipher the code used but sometimes the same series of letters came through. He guessed that this was the operator's call sign and then, very often, there were the same two words at the end of the message. Tom thought that these might spell out '*Heil Hitler*'. He was always pleased when this happened. He thought it would be very helpful to those who had to decipher the codes. They were known as 'cribs', Mr Fox had told him.

Tom slept soundly, completely unaware of the sad news that would alter his contented routine the next day.

'Hello,' Lilian said, when she opened the back door at just after nine o'clock the following evening. 'It's Gordon, isn't it? You've been before when Steve's had a night or two off, haven't you? Where is he tonight, then?'

'He's had to go home suddenly. He heard this morning that Hull was bombed in a raid on Friday night. And he can't find out if his wife and her mother are all right. So, he's been given leave to go home.'

Lilian's mouth dropped open and her hand

fluttered to cover her mouth in shock. 'Oh no! How dreadful.' She stood staring at the young soldier.

'Er – sorry to trouble you, Mrs Holmes, but I'm doing the run tonight. I've come to fetch your son's notes.'

'Oh – of course. I'm sorry. It was such a shock. Do come in. Let me mash some tea. Tom's not quite ready yet. Oh dear. What dreadful news. Eddie . . .' She led the way into the kitchen. 'Eddie, poor Steve's had to go home. There's been an air raid in Hull and he's had no news of his family.'

Startled, Eddie looked up. 'I'm sorry to hear that.' His glance went beyond his wife to the soldier whom he'd seen only once or twice before. He couldn't for the life of him remember his name.

'Hello there, young feller,' Eddie greeted him, getting up. 'Good to see you, though I'm sorry for the circumstances. Keep us posted, if you hear anything about Steve, won't you?'

Gordon nodded. 'I will, Mr Holmes, though I think, whatever's happened, Steve will have to come back eventually.'

Eddie sighed. 'Aye, it's sad times indeed when a young feller can't stay and look after his family. Anyway, sit yarsen down and have a cuppa. I don't think Tom will keep you waiting long.'

Conversation was stilted. Lilian and Eddie didn't know how to talk to Gordon. They had developed such an easy, friendly relationship with Steve – he had become almost like one of the family – but now they had to deal with a comparative stranger. And the circumstances in which they were meeting were sad and difficult. It was a relief when Tom appeared from the front room and handed over the brown envelope.

'No Steve tonight?' he asked innocently and turned pale when Lilian explained.

'Right, I'd best be on my way,' Gordon said. 'Thanks for the tea, Mrs.'

'You do know to call at Mr Fox's, don't you?' Tom said.

'Oh yes.' The young soldier grinned. 'I've done this run before. And then I'll be on my way to Waddington.'

As Gordon left, Tom murmured, 'I don't think he should have told us that, do you, Dad?'

'Probably not, son, no, so . . .' He lowered his voice. 'Not a word to your mam.'

They could still hear Lilian bidding Gordon good-night at the door.

'What's at Waddington, Dad?'

'An RAF station. I think it's a bomber station. I expect that's where he's going.'

Tom shrugged. 'Oh well, that's nowt to do with me, is it?'

'No, you just do what they've asked you to do and don't ask questions.'

'Do you think that's where Carolyn is?'

Eddie sighed. 'I've really no idea and, again, best not to ask.'

Lilian came back into the room. 'That's awful news, isn't it? I do hope his wife is all right.'

'What family has he got?' Tom asked. 'I've never really had a chance to talk to him like you have.'

'He's married but they haven't any children as yet. His mother-in-law lives in the same street a few doors away from them,' Lilian said. 'That's all I know. He told us he hasn't got any other family.'

'Let's hope for the best,' Eddie said.

Tom nodded. 'I've just got a bit of homework to finish.' He grinned. 'But as it's for Mr Fox, I don't expect I'll be in trouble. But I'll see if I can get it done and then I'm off to bed.'

'I'll bring you up some hot milk,' Lilian said. 'You must keep hearing dots and dashes ringing in your ears.'

Tom laughed. 'Yes, I do a bit. Thanks, Mam.'

As they heard his footsteps going up the stairs, Eddie murmured, 'He's a good lad. We've got a good couple of kids.'

Lilian wriggled her shoulders. 'As long as madam doesn't get hersen into trouble like . . .' She gestured her head in the direction of her father's farmhouse.

Eddie retreated behind his newspaper.

During the early weeks of 1943, there was a feeling of optimism that perhaps the course of the war was turning in favour of the Allies. After Monty's victory at El Alamein the previous November, people began to dare to hope. Though she had never said anything to anyone – not even to her closest colleagues – Carolyn had often wondered if at that time she'd been picking anything up from German operators attached to Rommel's army. She knew she was receiving German messages from North Africa and she kept to the same frequency for much of the time, having become familiar with a particular operator's 'fist', as they called it – his way of transmitting. But after El Alamein, her particular contact disappeared and she had to become familiar with other operators. She often wondered, even in later years, what had become of the man whom she'd felt she'd come to 'know'. She hoped he hadn't been killed. Though an enemy, he was still someone's son or brother or even husband.

Through January there were significant victories for the Allies as their troops captured Tripoli and, at the very end of the month, the RAF launched two daylight bombing raids on Berlin, disrupting broadcasts being made by Goering and Goebbels celebrating ten years of the Nazi regime. Then, the Germans surrendered to the Red Army at Stalingrad and, a few days later, the Americans won a gruelling six-month battle for Guadalcanal as the Japanese withdrew from the Solomon Islands.

But still the messages came thick and fast through Beaumanor on their way to Station X.

Thirty-Four

Peter jumped on the train for Skegness as it was about to depart.

'Just in time.' The man on the platform with the whistle to his lips grinned. 'Don't want to leave one of our brave lads waiting for the next train.'

'Thanks, mate.' Peter waved his hand in salute. As the train gathered speed, Peter moved through the carriage.

'Excuse me, is this seat vacant . . . ?' he began as the girl in ATS uniform turned to look up at him. 'Good Lord! Carolyn! What are you doing here?'

'Same as you, I suspect. Got a forty-eight this weekend, so I'm going home to see how they're all getting on.'

When Peter had stowed his kitbag in the shelf above them and settled himself into the seat beside her, he said, 'So, tell me what's been happening. Mam's letters have been a bit odd just lately. I've got a feeling things aren't quite right. That's partly why I've got leave to come home. Not exactly compassionate leave, but I did tell Staff Sergeant that I was a bit anxious about my mother. He's a good sort. There's not much happening for us at the moment,

285

so there was no problem about me having two days off.'

'Has she told you about Beryl?'

'No, she's never mentioned her.'

'Ah. Then I'd better fill you in . . .'

For the rest of the journey, Carolyn told him as much as she knew about what had been happening at home, ending with, 'I got a letter from Mam only yesterday saying that Grandad has dismissed your mother after overhearing her being unpleasant to Beryl. I don't know any details other than that.' But Carolyn could guess. She'd been on the receiving end of Phyllis Carter's vitriolic tongue herself.

'Good Lord! He hasn't given her notice to quit the cottage as well, has he?'

'I don't think so. I'm sure he wouldn't do that.'

'Oh dear. It looks as if I'm walking into a hornet's nest.' He sighed. 'I'll try and sort it out, Caro.'

Phyllis must have been watching out for him, for when Peter walked up the path, the front door was flung open. She hurried towards him and threw her arms around him.

'Whatever's the matter, Mam?'

He and Carolyn had decided that he should pretend to know nothing about what had happened; that way he would hear his mother's version.

'Frank Atkinson – that's what's the matter . . .' And out it all spilled, scarcely before he'd got in through the door.

'Now, calm down, Mam. Make us both a cuppa and we'll sit down and talk about it.'

'Calm down, you say? How can I keep calm when he might turn me out of me home?'

'He won't do that . . .'

'Huh! I wouldn't be too sure. No fool like an old fool, Peter. And he's making a proper idiot of himself over this girl and no mistake.'

'Why are you so against her, Mam? She's just a lass who needs a bit of help. And she's Carolyn's friend. Why shouldn't he help her, if he's a mind to?'

'Now don't *you* go feeling sorry for her, else she'll have her claws into you.'

'You really have taken a dislike to her, haven't you? I just don't understand why.'

'She's a little slut, that's why. I shouldn't wonder if she hasn't led Carolyn astray.' She cast a glance at her son, but he kept his face impassive. 'After all this family's done for Frank Atkinson. Your dad worked for him and then you. And both of you used to work long hours for no extra pay and I've done my bit and then he treats us like this.'

'I'll go and see him tomorrow.'

'I don't reckon it'll do any good . . .' Phyllis said mournfully. Now she was feeling sorry for herself. None of this was her fault. It was all that wretched girl's doing.

'Now then, Peter. Good to see you. How's things?' Frank's greeting was the same as ever, with no sign of any rancour towards him. Peter shook Frank's proffered hand.

'A bit boring, if I'm honest. Life in the army is OK, but we don't seem to be doing anything.'

Frank didn't laugh. Instead, he was very serious as he said, 'I'm sorry to say that if and when you do have to "do" something, it will be far from boring. Be careful what you wish for, Peter.' There was a pause before he went on. 'I expect you've come to see me about your mother, have you?'

'Well – I – er – I'm concerned about what's been happening.'

'To put it bluntly, she's taken an exception to Beryl and I think it's best if they keep their distance from one another. I've said I'll help the girl and I'm not going to go back on my word.'

'I think she's worried about you as much as anything.'

Frank stared at him for a moment and then laughed. 'I can guess what she's thinking. She more or less said as much. But I know exactly what I'm doing. I'm not being duped by a scheming hussy, I promise you. She's just a young lass who's made a mistake. She's not the first and she won't be the last. Her own family refuse to stand by her, so I'm just lending a helping hand. A good Samaritan's hand, if you like. In my book, Peter, it's no good going to church every Sunday if you don't intend to try to follow what the preacher tells you. Now, I'm not one to bear grudges, so you tell yar mam that she can come back and work in the dairy, if she likes. Beryl can cope with the housework, so there'd be no reason for them to meet very often. But I don't want any more of her nonsense like we had the other day and you can tell her that. Now, come along in and see Beryl. She's turning out to be quite a good little cook, which, I have to admit, has surprised me.'

Beryl was busy kneading bread at the kitchen table when Frank led Peter into the kitchen. She looked up with fearful eyes, but relaxed when she saw the broad smile on the young soldier's face.

'You carry on, Beryl,' Peter said. 'I'll mash us all some tea, shall I?'

'That'd be nice. Carolyn came earlier. She said you were home on leave for a couple of days.' She bent her head again and concentrated on the dough.

Frank sat down in the chair near the range and Peter, after setting out teacups on the opposite side of the table to where Beryl was working, sat opposite him. 'So, how are things on the farm, Mr Frank? How are the two land army girls getting on?'

Frank chuckled. 'Aye. They're pretty lasses. Easy on the eye, you might say, but they don't know much about farm work. It takes them both to do what you used to do, lad. Still, they do their best and we'd be hard pressed without them, 'specially at lambing time, which, as you well know, Peter, will start in a couple of weeks or so.'

'I'll see if I can get a longer leave and come and help. If not now, then I'll certainly do my best to be here at harvest again. I do miss life on the farm,' he added pensively. 'I sometimes wonder if I did the right thing in joining up.'

'You've got to do what your conscience tells you, lad. I was sorry to see you go – you know that – but I admire you for doing what you thought was right.'

Beryl stepped between them to put the dough, covered with a cloth, in the hearth to prove.

'Shall I make the tea?'

'No, no,' Peter jumped up, 'I said I'd do it. You sit down, Beryl, for a minute. It's not the first time I've made tea in this kitchen, is it, Mr Frank?'

The three of them sat together, but the conversation centred around the farm. Finishing his drink, Frank got up. 'I'll just go and check on what the girls are doing.'

Peter began to rise too, but Frank said, 'No, no, you stay and chat to Beryl. I'm sure she'd like a bit of young company.'

'I just wondered if I can do anything for you while I'm home?'

'I wouldn't dream of it, lad, not this time. You've not got long as it is. But if you can get some leave at harvest time, that would be great. See you later, Peter. Take care now.'

'I will, Mr Frank. Thank you.'

As the door closed behind him they sat in awkward silence until they both spoke at once with the very same words. 'I'm sorry . . .'

Embarrassed, they both looked at each other and then glanced away. 'You go first,' Beryl murmured.

'I'm sorry to hear my mother has been unpleasant towards you.'

'And I'm sorry she's upset about me being here. I'd leave if I had somewhere else to go other than a mother-and-baby home, but to do that would seem so ungrateful to Mr Frank.'

'Of course it would. You mustn't even think of it.'

Beryl gave a tremulous smile and risked a glance at him. He was so nice and he was good-looking, too. She wondered why Carolyn hadn't wanted to marry him. He was just the sort of man she, Beryl, would love to marry. She sighed inwardly. If only she hadn't been so stupid as to fall for Jeff's sweet nothings. And they had proved to be exactly that: worth nothing.

'Do you think you'll like living in the countryside?' Peter said, interrupting her reflective thoughts. 'It must be very different to what you're used to.'

'It's the complete blackness at night that frightens me a bit. I mean, in the city there's always a sort of glow – right through the night. Not now, of course, with the blackout and everything, but normally it never seems to get completely dark there. Not like here. And in the daytime too, the sky is so huge.'

Peter laughed. 'I'd never thought about it before, but I see what you mean. It's the opposite for me. When we go into towns or cities now, I feel hemmed in. I long to push my elbows out' – he demonstrated – 'to make more space.'

'But the sunsets here are something else. I stand outside my back door just watching the sun go down. The colours are amazing. I've never seen anything like it before.'

They laughed together, an easy, companionable laugh.

'Would you – like to come to the cinema tonight? I'm sure Mr Frank would lend me the truck. It's too far for you to walk. And I'm sure he could spare the petrol.'

Beryl's eyes widened. 'Oh no. I can't. I mustn't. I mean . . . What would your mother say, for a start?'

Peter's smile widened. 'I'm a big boy, Beryl. Mam is going to have to come to terms with that. I make my own decisions now.' He was thoughtful for a moment. 'What about a little walk, then, later this afternoon? Just round the fields, if you're shy about meeting anyone.'

'Don't you mind being seen with me? I mean, people will gossip. They – they might even think the baby's yours. There's no hiding it now, is there?'

Peter shrugged. 'I don't mind what they think. Folk will always make up their own stories anyway. So, what d'you say?'

'All right,' she said shyly.

'I'll come across at about three. Will you have finished everything you have to do by then?'

Beryl nodded. 'I'll get everything prepared for Mr Frank's tea, but I must be back by five to cook it. He likes it on the table by six.'

'We'll make sure not to be late.' Peter got up. 'I'd best let you get on now. See you this afternoon, then.'

She watched him walk away with long strides, his arms swinging easily, almost as if he were marching. She smiled faintly. Perhaps he was. He must have done so much square-bashing recently that it had become second nature to walk like that.

Beryl turned away from the kitchen window to return to her bread making with a sigh. If only, she thought, my baby was Peter's, how wonderful life would be.

*

'Did you see her?' Phyllis demanded almost before Peter had stepped across the threshold.

'I did.'

'And?'

'And what, Mam?'

Phyllis wriggled her shoulders. 'What did you think of her?'

'Exactly the same as I thought before. She's a nice girl who's made a mistake. That's all there is to it.'

'But – but what about her living there? With Mr Frank? Don't you think she's a little gold digger?'

'No, Mam, I don't. I think it's what Mr Frank says it is. It's a lass – a friend of Carolyn's – who needed a helping hand.'

Phyllis sniffed. 'Aye, and she's helping herself, I shouldn't wonder. I hope he's locked away his silver and his wife's jewellery.'

Peter wagged his forefinger at her. 'That's slander, Mam. You want to mind what you're saying.'

'I've nowt else to lose. I've lost me job . . .'

'Not really, at least not all of it. Mr Frank says you can carry on with the dairy work, if you want, and Beryl will cope with the housework. That way you can keep out of each other's way – which, he thinks, would be for the best.'

'Oh so I'm pushed out of the house, am I? Only good enough to work outside in the cold dairy?'

Peter sighed heavily. 'Oh Mam, can you really not be a little more understanding towards Beryl?'

'No, I can't. Folks should wait until they're married before – before . . .'

'Mam,' Peter said gently, 'there's a war on. None

293

of us – not even civilians with all this bombing – know if they're going to see tomorrow. They don't want to wait. They can't. Life's got to be lived in the here and now.'

Phyllis stared at him and turned pale.

Thirty-Five

'So, where do you want to go?'

'Just round the fields, like you said. Not – not anywhere public. You can tell me what crops are going to be grown this year.' Beryl laughed. 'I always thought cabbages and potatoes just came from a shop. I never really thought about them being *grown* in fields, picked and sent to market.'

'Tattie picking, as we call it, is quite hard work. That's in October. It's back-breaking, until you get used to it. But I shall miss it this year, though I have said I'll try and get leave at harvest time in August – if I haven't been posted overseas by then.'

Beryl felt her heart plummet. 'Overseas?' she whispered hoarsely. 'Where? To France?' Although Peter had not been involved in the Dunkirk evacuation, it was still raw in everyone's minds.

'Sadly, not yet. I think it will be at least a year or so before we can set foot in France again, but we've heard that more of our lads are being sent to North Africa.'

'Oh my,' Beryl breathed. 'That sounds a long way away.'

As they walked along the edge of a field, Beryl stumbled.

'Here, take my arm. Can't have you falling. Maybe we should have stuck to a proper lane.'

'No, no, this is lovely.' She slipped her arm through his. 'I like you telling me all about the crops and the hedgerows and all the wild flowers that'll soon be growing. Go on.'

They walked slowly, with Peter describing the work on the farm and all that grew there and even the wildlife that the area attracted. 'You'd love it at the Point. It's one of my favourite places – Carolyn's too – but it's off limits at the moment.'

'Mr Frank – that's what he's told me to call him; he says Mr Atkinson is too formal.'

'Yes, it's what most folk call him. Go on.'

'Mr Frank thinks it's the army practising and training there and there's some sort of coastal defence battery there too. We do hear the guns sometimes.'

'Yes, I think he's right.' They walked on again, coming full circle. They were almost back at the farm.

'Beryl,' Peter blurted out just as they reached the gate into the yard. 'Will you write to me?'

She looked up at him. 'If – if you're sure that's what you want, I'd love to.'

'I'm sure. It's lovely to get letters and – and I want to know how you get on. Tell me everything, won't you?'

Beryl nodded and the warmth of his concern melted a little corner of the ice block that her heart had become.

On the Sunday afternoon, Peter went again to the farm to say goodbye to Beryl and to tell Mr Frank that his mother would be coming back to work in the dairy the following morning. What he didn't say was that it had taken him almost an hour to persuade her to return.

'I'm teking Carolyn for the early train, lad. A' you going on the same one?'

'Yes, Mr Frank.'

'Right. I'll pick you up, then.'

Early the following morning, as Frank's vehicle drew up outside their home, Peter hugged his mother. 'Now, Mam, no more falling out with Beryl.'

Phyllis sniffed.

'If you do, Mam, he'll sack you for good this time.'

'And turn me out of the cottage an' all, I suppose.'

'I don't think he'd do that, but I wouldn't risk it, if I were you. Just go and do your work in the dairy and keep out of her way.'

He wanted to say more, about how he liked Beryl, but he knew he couldn't. Their blossoming friendship must remain a secret for the moment, especially from his mother.

Phyllis was busy in the dairy when a shadow appeared in the doorway. She looked up to see Beryl standing there. Phyllis paused in her churning.

'I've brought you a cup of tea and some biscuits,' Beryl said quickly. 'And before you say anything, let me just say this. Please. I know you don't like me and I do understand why, though you're wrong to think I mean to harm Mr Frank in any way. That's the last thing I'd do. If you need to come into the house for anything, I'll go to my rooms and keep out of your way. Please believe me, Mrs Carter, I don't want to cause anyone any trouble.'

Phyllis glared at her for a moment. Her mind was working quickly. No, she didn't like the girl, but she wasn't doing herself any favours by antagonizing Mr Frank. Secretly, she had harboured hopes that perhaps they would become close after his wife died, that he might even ask her to marry him. But, if she was honest, it hadn't looked likely to happen, even before this girl had come on the scene.

Phyllis nodded briefly. 'All right. We'll call a truce and we'll keep out of each other's way. But don't think I won't be keeping an eye on you, m'girl, because I will, an' if I see anything untoward, I'll be telling his daughter, so you'd best watch your step.'

'That suits me, Mrs Carter. I'll put your tea and biscuits down here.' With that, Beryl left the dairy and headed back to the kitchen. It wasn't quite what she really wanted, but it was the best she could hope for just now.

She allowed herself a little smile as she went back into the kitchen to peel potatoes. It was a start, but she rather feared that if Phyllis got to hear of Beryl's growing friendship with Peter, then feathers would certainly fly again.

It was a month before Steve appeared again at the back door of the Holmes's cottage.

'Oh you're back,' Lilian said unnecessarily. 'Come in, come in. Sit down. Are you all right? What happened? Are your wife and her mother safe?'

298

Steve's head dropped as if to hide his face.

Lilian led him into the kitchen where Eddie was reading his paper by the fire. He glanced up as Steve entered. 'Hello, son . . .' he began, but seeing the expression on the young soldier's face, he fell silent. Steve sat down heavily in a kitchen chair, resting his elbows on the table.

'No, Mrs Holmes . . .' His voice was husky with emotion. 'I'm sorry to say they're not all right.'

Lilian sat down opposite him, staring at him, not knowing what to say. For once in her life, she kept silent. Eddie, too, just listened.

'Our house took a direct hit,' Steve said haltingly. 'The whole street was badly bombed. My mother-in-law – even though she was in the Morrison shelter I'd put up for her – was trapped and badly injured. She died two days later in hospital without regaining consciousness.'

'And – and your wife?' Lilian asked softly.

Steve couldn't speak for a few moments and when he did, his tone was a mixture of sadness and yet anger too. 'She – she – Sal – was found in bed. And there was someone else with her . . .' He gulped and paused again. 'A man. He was dead too. It seems she'd been having an affair. A neighbour told me.'

Lilian reached across the table and took his hands. 'Oh Steve. I'm so, so sorry.'

'That's why I've been away so long. I still had to arrange the funerals, you see. For Sal and my mother-in-law. And I had to find out who the man was – it was no one I knew. But, thankfully, my neighbour knew him. It had been going on for some time, so

299

she said. The police took over after that – as regards him, that is.'

'That's dreadful. You poor, poor boy.'

Steve pulled his hands away from her and covered his face. He sat there, motionless and silent now, while Lilian made him a cup of tea with an extra teaspoonful of her precious sugar ration.

'There, drink that,' she said, putting the cup in front of him. 'Do you want anything to eat?'

Steve shook his head.

Eddie levered himself up from his armchair and took a seat at the table. He didn't know what to say but he felt he had to make some gesture of support.

Steve took a gulp of tea and then set the cup back in its saucer. His hand was trembling as he did so.

'Is there anyone else supporting you?' Eddie asked at last.

Steve shook his head. 'As you know, I was brought up in an orphanage and haven't any family of my own. Sal and her mother were all the family I had.'

Tears filled Lilian's eyes. She rarely wept, but this was such a sad story and she had become so fond of Steve.

'I've lost everything,' he said. 'The house is just a mound of rubble and we couldn't even find any belongings.' He gave a wry smile. 'Not that we had much, you know.'

'Just excuse me a minute,' Eddie murmured. 'I think I'd better tell Tom.'

Eddie disappeared into the front room and was gone for some time.

'A lot of the houses in our street were damaged,'

Steve went on. 'Several folk were badly injured too. I knew all of them.' He paused and then burst out angrily. 'It should have been me, not them. Being a soldier and in a war, it's to be expected, but killing innocent women and children in their own homes. It's – it's obscene. I'm ashamed to admit I never thought about it much before. You know, you hear on the news about London and other big cities being bombed and the loss of life there, but until it happens to you, you don't really take it in. You don't *feel* it.'

'Yes, I know just what you mean,' Lilian whispered. 'We're so lucky here. There's been a bit of bombing in the town and one or two lives lost, but nothing's come close to us. Eddie built an Anderson shelter in the garden, but we rarely use it.'

Eddie came back into the room, with Tom close behind him carrying the brown envelope, but instead of his usual cheery grin, his face was solemn. He stood near Steve's chair and put his hand on his shoulder. 'Dad's just told me. I'm so sorry.'

Steve nodded, unable to speak for a moment. 'Thanks,' he said hoarsely at last.

'I'm surprised you've come back.'

Steve shrugged. 'The army's been very good actually. I got extra compassionate leave to – to bury them before I came back. There was no one else to do it, you see. Besides,' he added, more strongly now as he got up, squared his shoulders and took the envelope from Tom, 'I've still got a job to do and it's good to be back amongst my mates at camp and – and you all too. You've been very good to me. I – I'd like to think we're friends.'

'Oh we are, we are,' Lilian said quickly.

As he made to leave, she hugged him and Eddie held out his hand. 'Now, if there's owt we can do for you, lad, you only have to say.' Eddie never said much, but when he did speak up, it always meant something.

'Thank you, Mr Holmes. I appreciate that. Maybe . . .' Steve hesitated.

'What is it, lad? Speak up.'

'It's just . . . when I get leave, I shan't want to go back to Hull, not straight away, anyway, if I ever do. It – it'll be too painful. I was just wondering if Mr Atkinson might have a bit of work for me on the farm.'

'What did you do before you joined the army?'

'I was a ship's carpenter.'

'Good Lord, were you really?'

'Yes. Why? You sound surprised.'

'No, no, it's not that,' Eddie said hastily, 'it's just that that's what I do. Well, not a *ship's* carpenter, but I work with my father in the family business. We're wheelwrights and joiners. I'm sure we'd be glad of an extra pair of hands when you're free. If you wanted to, that is?'

'I'd be glad to have something useful to do, Mr Holmes, and I love working with wood.'

'That's settled, then. I'll have a word with my dad tomorrow, but I'm sure he'll be pleased to hear it. He was grumbling only yesterday that we ought to take on a young apprentice.'

When Steve had left them, roaring off into the night on his motorcycle, Lilian was thoughtful.

'Now what are you cooking up in that head of yours?' Eddie teased her. 'Cos I can see it's something. I know that look.'

'I'm very sorry for his loss,' she said, 'of course I am, but if he's nothing to go back to Hull for when all this is over, maybe he'd like to come here and work for you and your dad.'

'I think you're getting a bit ahead of yourself, Lilian love. This war's got a long way to go yet.'

Lilian said nothing but Eddie couldn't stop her mind running riot.

Thirty-Six

When lambing time was in full swing, Beryl watched in amazement as everyone was involved. Frank was often out all night alongside Harold and Adam. Even the land girls worked late into the night. And Eve, still wearing make-up and with her hair neatly curled, came to the farm, donned wellies and tramped out to the barn with hot drinks and food for those keeping watch over the animals.

'What can I do?' Beryl asked, feeling helpless.

'Keep the drinks coming, love, and make a nice hot stew, if you will, and some baked potatoes.' Frank smiled. 'That'll keep us going.'

Beryl stayed up all night too, feeling she couldn't go to bed while everyone else was working and now there was something really useful she could do. At about three in the morning, Eve came back into the kitchen carrying a newborn lamb.

'We'll have to rear this one by hand. The mother's had three lambs and sheep are only designed to suckle two.' She put the lamb into Beryl's arms and set about finding the feeding paraphernalia, which Frank kept on a shelf in the pantry.

'I'll show you what to do.'

'Oh Aunty Eve. I can't do that.'

'Course you can, love. There's nothing to it.'

'Can't you take it home with you?'

'I would, but I've already got two to take. Their mother's an old ewe and she doesn't look too good. I think we're going to lose her. Now, let me explain . . .'

For the next half-hour Eve showed Beryl how to prepare a bottle and then how to feed the lamb. 'She needs to be kept warm and she'll want feeding every few hours. Mr Frank would be so grateful to you, Beryl, if you can save this lamb for him, 'specially if he's likely to lose a ewe.'

It took a while and a lot of patience to get the tiny animal to suck the teat on the bottle, but at last she was feeding hungrily.

'There you are, you see. We'll make a farmer of you yet.'

Beryl smiled weakly, but she had to admit there was something very satisfying about helping to save a young life. Frank didn't have a huge flock of sheep as sheep farming went – he did a little bit of everything – but all his sheep seemed to decide to give birth at different times of the day and night.

Over the following days, Beryl was fully occupied helping with the lambing and caring for her particular charge until it was old enough to be weaned.

'You've done a grand job, lass,' Frank said as they watched the healthy lamb frolicking in the field with the others. 'It helps make up for the owd ewe we lost. This little lass can take her place.' He paused a moment and then asked casually, 'Did you have a name for her?'

Beryl hesitated for a moment before saying. 'Yes, I called her Rosie after my – my little sister.'

There was a long silence between them before Frank asked softly, 'Do you ever hear from any of your family?'

With tears in her eyes, Beryl shook her head. 'No,' she said hoarsely, 'but then I don't really expect to.'

Frank patted her shoulder and his voice was a little unsteady as he said, 'Ne'er mind, love. We're your family now.'

'Now then, love. How're things? Managing all right, are you?'

Eve opened the back door and walked straight into the farmhouse kitchen.

Beryl straightened up from putting a pie in the range oven and turned to greet her visitor. She winced a little and rubbed her lower back.

Eve eyed her speculatively. 'You're getting big now, lass. How much longer have you to go?'

'Only about a couple of weeks or so, I think. I've just made a pie out of a chicken Mr Frank killed.' She pulled a face. 'I'm getting more used to farming ways, but I can't bring myself to do that yet.'

'Best not, then,' Eve laughed. She put a basket on the table and began to unload it. 'I've brought you some apples from our orchard picked last autumn and bottled by my own fair hands. You can make pies, or crumbles, or even just stewed apples and custard.'

'I can make custard now. Phyllis told me how.'

Eve's eyebrows rose. 'You two getting along better now, are you?'

Beryl smiled. 'A bit. We keep out of each other's way most of the time, but I catch her watching me sometimes and if looks could kill . . . Let's just say I'd be feeling a bit poorly.'

'Mm,' Eve said thoughtfully. 'So, your cooking and baking's coming along nicely, is it, despite all the rationing?'

'I keep trying to learn new things.'

'There's a little trick I've discovered on how to save on our precious rations,' Eve said as she watched Beryl prepare to roll out pastry. 'If you're interested.'

'Of course, Aunty Eve. I'm always willing to learn.'

'Yes, I have noticed,' Eve murmured. She was becoming very fond of this city girl who was trying so very hard to fit in with what must be, to her, strange surroundings. 'When you cook mince,' Eve went on, 'let it cool and then skim off the fat from the top and use it to make pastry for a pie. A savoury pie is best. It's nice with a leek and potato pie. I've tried it and there were no complaints.'

Beryl smiled to herself. She doubted anyone in Eve's household would dare to complain about her cooking, not even her husband.

'Thanks, I'll try that.'

'Erm . . .' For a brief moment Eve seemed strangely reticent. 'Do you mind if I say something?'

Beryl smiled at her with the kind of full, wide smile she hadn't felt much like displaying lately. 'From you, Aunty Eve, I don't mind anything.'

'Well, I'm a dab hand with my sewing machine,' Eve said, carefully leading up to what she wanted to say.

'That's good with all this "make do and mend" advice. I'm not bad with a darning needle, but I've never had a chance to learn how to use a sewing machine. Sorry – I'm interrupting. Go on.'

'I can't help noticing that you don't have many clothes. That dress you've got on has seen better days.' Eve couldn't help her usual bluntness coming out.

Beryl pulled a face, but she was still smiling. 'No, I haven't got many and most I can barely get into now. I bought one or two things in . . .' She stopped. She really shouldn't say where. 'In the nearest town to where we were, but other than that, no. I only had my uniform.'

Eve's face lit up. 'Then I can help you. I love dressmaking and sewing. And knitting, if it comes to that. It's my hobby.'

Now Beryl laughed out loud. 'You mean to tell me you have time for a *hobby* with everything else you have to do?'

'I *make* time, Beryl. Whatever else you do in life, love, always make sure you take some time out for yourself – for hobbies or interests or whatever. And my hobby just happens to be doing something useful as well, especially in these times.'

'But I'd need to get some material.'

Eve's smile now widened into a positive beam. 'Because I've done dressmaking for years, I have a contact on the markets – Deirdre. She knows exactly the sort of thing I like and always saves me fabrics for when she comes to our town.' Eve winked at Beryl and tapped the side of her nose. 'And she does me a special discount in exchange for a few eggs. Tell you what, come across to our place when you've time and I'll take your measurements.' Then she chuckled. 'Though your waist won't be exactly right at the moment, will it? I'll make you a couple of blouses and a wrap-around skirt for now and, once you've had the baby, I'll make you some dresses and skirts and knit you a jumper or two. I'm sure Deirdre will be able to find something you'll like. And she sells wool too.'

Tears prickled at the back of Beryl's eyelids. 'Thank you, Aunty Eve. That would be wonderful.'

Eve sat and talked a while longer with Beryl but as she left she saw Frank coming out of the tractor shed, wiping his hands on an oily rag.

'Morning, Dad,' she called cheerily and walked towards him. She had always called her father-in-law 'Dad'. Her own parents were both dead and he had been as good to her as any father.

'Hello, love. What brings you here?'

'I've brought some bottled apples for Beryl to use.'

'She's getting quite a dab hand in the kitchen and she seems to enjoy it.'

Eve moved closer. She didn't want to be overheard and she wasn't sure if Phyllis was here this morning or not. 'Dad, will you promise me something?'

'I will if I can, love.'

'Beryl's getting quite close now and I want you to fetch me when she starts in labour.'

'Even if it's in the middle of the night?'

'Yes, even then.'

'Shouldn't I ring the midwife first?'

'Yes, of course, but then come and fetch me.'

'But that'd mean leaving her on her own.'

'We're only a few minutes away in your truck.'

'That's true. I'll mek sure I've always got plenty of petrol in it.'

The two smiled at each other. 'Poor lass,' Frank murmured. 'No mother around to be with her.'

'That's exactly why I want you to fetch me. I like the girl. She's not a bad lass, even though some around here seem to think she is. She made a mistake, that's all.' Eve paused and then asked, 'Is she going to keep it?'

Frank frowned. 'At the moment she says she's going to have it adopted, but I'm rather hoping that once she holds the little mite in her arms . . .'

'That's exactly what I'm hoping, Dad.'

Over the next week or two, Beryl visited Eve regularly. Soon, in the wardrobe in her bedroom, there hung three new cotton blouses, a skirt and a tailored jacket.

'I'll make more when you're back to your normal size.'

'Oh Eve, you're so clever. I wish I could do something useful like this.'

'Can you knit?'

'Sort of. I'm not very good.'

'Then you can borrow some knitting needles from me and some wool and practise. Start with a jacket for the baby. I've plenty of patterns. I'll look out some easy ones. And if you get stuck, you know where I am.'

How kind everyone is, Beryl thought, as she walked

home across the fields from a visit to Eve's. She stopped suddenly, surprised at her own thoughts. Yes, she did think of Frank's farm as 'home' now. But, she asked herself, as she moved on again slowly, was that wise? Was it safe to get too attached to living here?

Thirty-Seven

But the arrival of Beryl's baby didn't happen as Frank and Eve had hoped. It was a bright, fine day in early April and Beryl had been feeling a nagging pain in her lower back since she'd got up. After breakfast, Frank had set out early to give instructions to the two land army girls in one of the far fields. He would be gone for the rest of the day. And neither Harold nor Adam were in the yard. There was only Phyllis, who was just finishing up in the dairy before coming into the house for a cup of tea, then setting off home. Beryl would be alone for two or three hours until Frank returned.

They sat in awkward silence, while Phyllis drank her tea. As she rose to go, Beryl said tentatively, 'Mrs Carter, could you call at Mr Harold's on the way home, please? It's on your way, isn't it?'

'Why?' Phyllis asked sharply.

'Just tell Aunty Eve . . .' Beryl began, but whatever she had been going to say ended up with a cry as pain stabbed her groin. She clutched the edge of the table and bent over.

'You've started, haven't you?'

'I – think so,' Beryl gasped. The pain had receded now and she stood up.

'There's no need to trouble Mrs Atkinson,' Phyllis said. 'She's enough on her hands with her own family and them two girls lodging with her. I can help you.'

'Oh please, I . . .'

'Get yourself up to your bedroom. And put a waterproof sheet on the bed. We don't want Mr Frank's mattress getting spoiled. And find some towels. I'll get the kettle and a couple of pans of water on the go.'

Beryl heaved herself up the stairs to her bedroom. This was the last thing she wanted: Phyllis standing over her while she gave birth. If only she could get word to Eve or even if Mr Frank would come home. But there was no way either was going to happen.

She did as Phyllis had instructed. Then she undressed and put on her nightdress and dressing gown. Despite the warmth of the day she was shivering – more, she thought, from fear than cold. She didn't want to lie on the bed yet, so she walked around the room, pausing at the window, longing to hear the sound of the farm truck returning. But the yard was silent. How she wished Eve was on the telephone, but only Frank was. Then another thought struck her. She fished in her handbag and found the scrap of paper she'd been given at the doctor's surgery. It was the number of a local midwife. Pushing her feet into her slippers, she went back downstairs and into the kitchen where the telephone sat on a dresser.

'What are you doing? You ought to be lying down.'

'I'm just going to ring the midwife . . .'

'You'll do no such thing. Midwives costs money. Mr Frank has spent enough on you already. Giving

313

birth is a natural thing. There's no need for anyone else to be here.'

'Oh please, Mrs Carter . . .'

'I've had a baby myself. I know what happens. Just do as I say.'

'But what if – what if something goes wrong?'

As another pain gripped her, Beryl didn't see the gleam in the other woman's eyes, but all Phyllis said was, 'You'll be fine. You're a strong, healthy lass. Just go and lie on your bed and try to relax. You can't fight the pain – it makes it worse. Just go with it.'

Beryl hauled herself back upstairs and lay on the bed. She breathed in and out deeply and tried to relax as Phyllis had told her, but doubt niggled at her. Was Phyllis actually giving her good advice?

The pains came at regular intervals, but there were several minutes between each one, when Beryl was able to lie quietly. But when the pain started, she couldn't stop the groans. Why didn't Phyllis come to check on her? As the afternoon light began to fade, Phyllis had still not come to see how she was. Had she gone home? Had she left her all alone in the house? She tried to get up off the bed, but another stab of pain made her flop back against the pillows and cry out. As the contraction eased, she called out, 'Mrs Carter? Mrs Carter, are you there?' But there was no reply from downstairs. And then she felt a wetness between her legs. Fear flooded through her. Oh no, she must be bleeding and she didn't think that was right. There would be blood, of course, but when the baby came, not before.

Beryl began to cry and, as another pain swept through her, she cried out aloud, 'Help, please help me.'

Alone in the kitchen, Phyllis heard her cries but merely smiled to herself. The slut was paying for her moments of pleasure now, wasn't she? Maybe she'd behave herself in future. She hadn't heard the truck come into the yard and didn't realize that Frank was back until the back door opened. She had no time to scuttle upstairs and make out that she had been with Beryl all the time. Instead, she grabbed the kettle as if she were busy making preparations.

'Oh Mr Frank . . .' she began, but at that moment a loud scream from upstairs rent the air.

'What's going on?'

'It's her. She's gone into labour . . .'

Almost before Phyllis had finished speaking, Frank was hurrying upstairs and flinging open the bedroom door.

'Help me, please help me. I'm bleeding . . .' Beryl cried, hysterical now.

Frank moved to the bedside and threw back the blanket Beryl had pulled over herself. Relief flooded his face. 'It's all right, lass. Yar waters have broken, that's all. Yar not bleeding. Now, how often are the pains coming?'

Now that the solid presence of Frank was with her, Beryl calmed down a little. 'It feels like all the time, but I – I suppose it's still in waves, though they're very close together now.'

'I'll telephone the midwife. You just try to relax, lass. I'll be back in a minute . . .'

Beryl lay back and closed her eyes. She'd be all right now Frank was here. He wouldn't leave her on her own. She heard distant voices and knew that Phyllis was still there. What a cruel, vindictive woman she was, Beryl thought as the pain subsided for a few moments and gave her temporary respite. How could any woman leave another in such distress? Phyllis had borne a child herself. She knew what the pain was like. How, she thought, had such a nasty woman given birth to such a nice young man as Peter? Another contraction began as Frank came back into the room.

'Midwife won't cycle right out here now it's getting dark, so I'm going to fetch her in my truck. I'll be as quick as I can.'

'Mr Frank . . .' Beryl gasped and reached for his hand. 'Please – get Aunty Eve to come over.'

He looked into her eyes and read the fear there, guessed that things were not all that they should be between her and Phyllis. 'I'll call in on me way.' He patted her hand. 'Don't fret, lass. I'll get her.'

He hurried out of the house without another word to Phyllis. Once he'd gone, she just sat down at the kitchen table and picked up the newspaper again.

Frank drove the truck hard along the rutted lane towards Harold's house. He left the engine running as he hurried up the path and banged on the door. Adam opened it. 'Come in, Grandad. What's to do?'

'Is yar mam here?'

'Yes, of course . . .'

Frank raised his voice. 'Eve – Eve?'

Eve appeared from the scullery drying her hands on a towel. 'Hello, Dad, what's the matter?'

'It's Beryl. She's in labour and she's close. Phyllis is there, but I don't reckon she's been helping her. Can you go across straight away? I'm going to fetch the midwife. I've telephoned her, but she won't come out here now because it'll likely be dark before she can cycle home.'

'Of course,' Eve said at once, untying her apron. 'I'll go at once. I'll cycle across. It'll be quicker. You get off, Dad . . .'

Only ten minutes later, as Frank pushed the old truck to its speed limit towards town, Eve was letting herself in through the back door of the farmhouse. She moved deliberately quietly; she wanted to see just what was happening before anyone realized she was there. At once, she heard Beryl's anguished howls echoing down from the bedroom. The door into the kitchen was ajar and she pushed it further open without making a sound. Phyllis was sitting at the table, reading the newspaper, acting as if she was oblivious to Beryl's cries. Anger surged through Eve, but she forced herself to tiptoe back to the outer door, open it again and close it with a bang. This time she marched into the kitchen to see Phyllis lifting the kettle from the hob.

'Just making the poor lass a cuppa, though I don't expect she'll want it,' Phyllis said brightly.

'How is she?'

'Meking a lot of fuss, as you can hear, but it is her first time. Well, as far as we know,' she added, snidely.

'I'll go up to her.'

'Don't you want a cuppa first?'

But Eve had gone, hurrying upstairs towards the shrieks of fear and pain. 'I'm here, Beryl love. Everything'll be all right. Mr Frank's gone for the midwife.'

Beryl reached out with a trembling hand. 'Oh Aunty Eve. Thank goodness. I've been on my own all the time and I'm terrified. I'm sure I'm bleeding . . . Aagh!'

'Let's have a look at you.' Eve pulled back the blanket and laid her hand gently on the girl's abdomen. She could feel the swell of the contractions coming close together now.

'Everything's fine, I'm sure. You're not bleeding. It's your waters, that's all, and that's perfectly normal. Baby won't be long coming now.'

'Mr Frank said that was what it was, but I can't raise myself up enough to look.'

As the pain subsided for a brief moment, Beryl lay back against the pillows, her hair wet from the sweat beading her forehead and running down her temples into it.

'I'm just going to get some warm water and a flannel to bathe your face.'

'Don't leave me, Aunty Eve. Please don't go.'

'I'm going nowhere, love, I promise you. Not until it's all over.'

Returning only seconds later, she said, 'Phyllis is making tea, but I've brought you a glass of water. I think it's better for you.'

Beryl drank gratefully. 'I'm so thirsty. Thank you.'

318

Eve's anger and disgust rose again, especially when Beryl asked, 'Is she still here? I thought she must have gone home. I've been shouting and shouting and she didn't come.'

Eve said nothing – for the moment. Now was not the time to start an almighty row and that's what it would be.

'Oh, ooooh . . .'

'Just try to relax, let yourself go limp and ride with the pain. It'll not be long now and Mr Frank should be back with the midwife very soon.'

But it was another half an hour before Eve heard the welcome sound of voices in the kitchen and footsteps coming upstairs.

'Now then, lass . . .' A large, round-faced woman with a beaming smile, dressed in navy blue and carrying a bag, bustled into the bedroom. 'Oh hello, Eve. Mr Frank said you'd be here though I'm surprised to see m'lady hanging around downstairs. Anyway, let's get to work. Eve, love, get me some hot water in that bowl on the washstand and some more towels wouldn't go amiss. Now – Beryl, is it? My name's Mrs Wing, but you can call me Kath.'

Swiftly and expertly, she examined Beryl. 'Eeh, you're well on, lass. I should have been called a couple of hours back. But not to worry. All is well and going normally.'

Now that both Eve and the midwife were with her, Beryl felt much better. She could even withstand the pain, for the fear had gone.

'Now, love, I want you to do exactly as I tell you. I'm going to tell you to push when a contraction comes and then to stop pushing and to pant. Can you do that, d'you think?'

'I'll try.'

'Good lass. Right, now here we go . . .'

It wasn't very long, though it seemed an age to Beryl, until Kath said, 'The head's born, lass. One more big push when I tell you and he'll be here.'

Beryl heard a mewling cry and both Kath and Eve laughed. 'My word,' Kath said, 'he's making his presence felt already. Ah, now here we go. Push, lass. Push now.'

Beryl felt the baby slide out of her with a great whoosh and then the cries grew stronger.

'You have a beautiful baby boy, lass. Eve'll get him cleaned up and wrapped up warm while I see to you and the afterbirth and then you can hold him.'

'I don't want to.' Beryl squeezed her eyes shut. 'I don't want to see him.'

'Well, I'm afraid you'll have to, love,' Kath said briskly. 'You'll need to feed him. Poor little mite won't survive, if you don't.' She glanced at Eve, before adding, 'You've got some lovely friends to help you, I can see that. And you can't shock me, lass. I've seen it all. Babbies born out of wedlock, babbies born in wedlock but they're not the husband's. And there's been a lot more of both while this wretched war's been on, I can tell you. Poor little mites who are number seven or eight in the family and aren't wanted. Mothers fair worn out with childbearing. Now, can you cough for me?'

Beryl opened her eyes and looked up at Kath standing beside her. 'Cough? Whatever for?'

'It helps the afterbirth come away. Just give it a try.' Beryl coughed weakly. A pause and then Kath said, 'That's a good girl, here it comes.' After a few moments, while she examined the afterbirth, Kath said, 'That's lovely. All in order. You're all set to have more babies.'

'There won't be any more,' Beryl said grimly.

'Oh, you'll feel differently when you meet a nice young man and fall in love.'

'I thought I already had,' Beryl said piteously and then the tears came.

Thirty-Eight

'Dad,' Eve began as they sat together later over a small glass of sherry to 'wet the baby's head', as Frank said. There were only the two of them in the kitchen now. Phyllis had gone home soon after she'd heard of the baby boy's arrival. Eve was thankful she hadn't seen her again; she wasn't sure she would have been able to hold her tongue. One day, Phyllis Carter, she promised herself, you and me are going to have it out. But for now, she sat with Frank.

'We've got a problem with Beryl.'

'Have we, love? I thought Nurse said everything was fine.'

'It is – physically. Everything went well and the baby's fit and healthy. Eight pounds, Kath said.'

'Then . . . ?'

'She won't have anything to do with the little chap. She turns her head away and won't even try to feed him.'

'That's serious,' Frank said worriedly.

'All she'll say is that she wants to have him adopted. Before you took her home, Kath said that if Beryl's really serious, she can put her in touch with someone who arranges such things.'

'Aye, but not for a few weeks at the earliest. She's got to feed and care for him now.'

Eve sighed heavily. 'I've tried everything I can think of, Dad. Perhaps you can have a go.'

'I most certainly will.'

He got up as if to go and speak to Beryl that minute, but Eve said, 'She's sleeping now. Leave it until she wakes up. Baby's asleep too so there's no problem for the minute. Let me get you something to eat. You've had no tea, have you?'

Frank gave a wry laugh. 'D'you know, lass, I never even thought about it, but I am a bit peckish, now you mention it. But I'll be fine, you'll be wanting to get back home.'

Eve waved her hand in a dismissive gesture. 'They'll be fine, Dad, they're big enough to look after themselves for one evening. And the girls are there. They'll look after Harold and Adam. Now, let me find something for us . . .'

After an hour, leaving Eve to do the washing-up, Frank tiptoed into Beryl's bedroom and sat down beside the bed, determined to be there when she woke up. He didn't have long to wait before Beryl stirred and opened her eyes.

'Now, lass,' he said kindly, 'how are you feeling?'

'Not bad. A bit sore. And . . .' Embarrassed, she stopped, but Frank guessed her meaning.

'Aye, them'll feel as if they're bursting, but once you feed the little man, they'll be better.'

'I don't want to,' Beryl blurted out. 'I'm not going to.'

'Well, that's a shame.' Frank still kept his voice

low, his tone mild. 'Young 'uns need their mother's milk, 'specially the first feed.'

'Can't he be fed with a bottle, like we fed that lamb?'

Frank wrinkled his forehead as if thinking. 'We could, but it's not the same and, if you remember, the reason we had to feed that lamb with a bottle was because the mother couldn't feed three young 'uns. And then we lost a ewe too, didn't we, so hers had to be bottle fed? Now, you're fit and healthy, so the nurse said. There's no reason why you can't feed him.'

'I'm going to have him adopted.'

'Well, if you still feel that way in, say, six weeks' time, then I'll help you do it.'

'Six weeks! You're saying I've got to look after him for six weeks?'

'About that,' Frank said as calmly as he could. 'As I understand it, if you'd gone into a mother-and-baby home, you'd have had to look after him for about that time until they found some adoptive parents.'

At that moment the baby began to whimper. Frank made no move to go to him and as the minutes passed by, the child's whimpers became pitiful cries. At last, Beryl said, 'What's the matter with him?'

'I expect he's hungry,' Frank said, forcing himself to sound casual and still remaining seated.

Beryl gave a huge sigh. 'Oh all right, then, you win.'

Frank almost leapt up. 'I'll get Eve. I don't want to embarrass you, lass.'

He hurried out and only a couple of minutes later,

324

Eve came into the room, went straight to the cot and lifted the baby out. Wrapping him warmly in a blanket, she laid him in Beryl's arms, his head crooked against her breast.

'Try him on the left side first. There . . . Ah look at the little mite, he's that hungry he's nuzzling you already. Oh bless him, he seems to know exactly what to do. Some babies can take an awful lot of encouragement before they feed properly. Adam was a nightmare when he was born.'

As the baby sucked and pulled at her breast, Beryl looked down into the bright blue eyes staring up at her. He had wispy blond hair and fair skin. He resembled her and for that she was grateful. Her fear had been that he would look like Jeff and be a constant reminder. The child waved his arm as he suckled. With a tentative gesture, she put her finger into his palm and his tiny fingers closed around hers. And still, he gazed up trustingly into her face.

'Oh Beryl,' Eve said in a husky voice. 'He's perfect. What are you going to call him?'

'Call him? Shouldn't I leave that to his adoptive parents?'

'Well, no, love. He has to be registered. It's the law. You'll have to give him a Christian name and he'll be given your surname to start with. You can't put the father's name on the birth certificate unless, of course, he agreed to it.'

'He wouldn't and, besides, I wouldn't want it.'

When the child finished feeding, Eve showed Beryl how to wind him and to change him. 'You put him back in his cot,' Eve said, pretending to be busy tidying away the baby paraphernalia. Beryl laid him gently in the cot and then stood looking down at him for a few moments. Then, wordlessly, she got back into bed and lay staring at the ceiling.

'Now,' Eve said, 'I'm just going to pop home and fetch an overnight bag. I'm going to stay here for a couple of nights until you're stronger.'

'I'll be all right, Aunty Eve. I'm sure I'll sleep through the night.'

Eve laughed. 'You easily might, but his lordship won't. He'll be awake and hungry in three or four hours.'

Beryl sat up and stared at her aghast. 'Three or four hours? All through the night?'

''Fraid so.'

'And how long will that go on?'

'It depends. Some babies start to sleep through the night in about two or three months or so. Some take longer.'

'Two or three *months*? Oh well, that settles it, then. He'll be gone in six weeks and you can tell Mr Frank that right now.'

Beryl settled back against her pillows and closed her eyes. The conversation was at an end.

Phyllis arrived the following morning at her usual time. She lingered at the gate when she saw the postman cycling along the lane towards the farm, wobbling unsteadily on the rutted ground.

'Morning, Mrs Carter,' he called cheerily as he neared her. 'Nice day.'

'It is, Mr Taylor.' She stretched out her hand. 'I'll take those in for you. Save you the trouble.'

'That's good of you. Thanks.' He handed her a bundle of letters. 'Shall I give you yours now, an' all?'

'You can. Save you a trip up my lane, won't it?'

He sorted through the mail and handed her two white envelopes. 'I see there's one from your Peter. Writes to his mam regular as clockwork, doesn't he? He's a good lad.' Then he winked at her. 'I see there's one in his handwriting, if I'm not mistaken, for the young lass who's staying here. Beryl, is it?'

Phyllis stared at him and was about to say, 'I certainly hope not,' but then she thought better of it and just smiled weakly at him.

'I expect they've got friendly, have they? Well, best be on me way. Morning to you, Mrs Carter.'

As he pedalled away, Phyllis stepped back behind the hedge that bordered the yard and rifled through the letters. There were several bills addressed to Frank and then she found the white envelope with Peter's handwriting addressed to Beryl.

The little slut, Phyllis thought. *How dare she? And how could he be so stupid?* His visits to the farm when he'd been on leave hadn't been so innocent after all. Helping Mr Frank, indeed! She separated the letter from Frank's mail, put it with her own and slid it into her coat pocket. It would never reach Beryl; Phyllis would burn it, but first she would read it to see just what exactly was going on. She pulled in a deep breath. Before that, though, she had to plaster a smile on her face and act the concerned neighbour.

She let herself in by the back door. Eve was in the scullery washing up breakfast pots.

'I could have done that, Eve. There's no need for you to have come across this early.'

Eve turned her head and Phyllis saw her eyes were glittering with anger. 'I've been here all night and I've no intention of leaving her to your tender mercies until she's a lot stronger.'

Phyllis pretended to frown and tried desperately to look concerned. 'Nowt wrong, is there? She was all right when I left.'

'Aye she was, but no thanks to you. You'd left her yelling out in agony and hadn't even bothered to go and sit with her.'

'Well, they all make a lot of fuss and noise, these young lasses.'

'Do they now? And how would you know?'

Phyllis's valiant efforts to show empathy died. Her face twisted. 'It's no more than the little slut deserves. She had her pleasure, now she's got to pay for it.'

'Look, Phyllis, go to the dairy and do your work and then go home. I won't have you in the house again.'

Phyllis folded her arms across her chest. 'Oh aye, and who's going to make me, eh? It's not your place to order me about.'

'Mebbe not, but I know I'd have Mr Frank's backing. So, I suggest you go to your work and then leave. I've no wish to be vindictive, Phyllis, and I wouldn't want you to lose your job or your home, but you're not welcome in here while you treat that lass as you have been doing.'

'What's so special about the little trollop, I'd like to know.' As she moved, Phyllis felt the rustle of Peter's letter in her pocket; she could hardly wait to get home and read it.

She turned to leave but as she did so, Eve called after her, 'Oh and I'll be staying until Mr Frank gets back this afternoon and I'll be here in the morning before he leaves.' Eve said no more but her meaning was clear. As she'd said, she had no intention of leaving Beryl alone with Phyllis.

Phyllis slammed the back door and marched across the yard to the dairy. But she was smiling grimly. She fingered the letter in her pocket. She'd put a stop to that nonsense. She didn't know quite how, yet, but she'd do it. She didn't want her Peter mixed up with the likes of Beryl.

Thirty-Nine

That same evening, Tom was late home from school and Lilian was becoming anxious. He hadn't arrived by the time Eddie came in from work.

'Where can he be?' Lilian said, meeting her husband at the door. 'He never stays this late.'

'He'll have stayed behind with his mates, or maybe he's gone to Mr Fox's. I shouldn't worry, love.'

'But he's due to do his two-hour stint on the wireless soon. He wouldn't miss that.'

'Ah, I see. Well, you do have a point there. But if I cycle into town, I don't know where to look for him. He could be anywhere.'

'You could ask Dad if he'd let you borrow the truck to go and look for him.'

'Yes, I'll do that, but let me grab a bite to eat and a cuppa and then I'll go.'

'Oh, all right,' Lilian said, though she couldn't hide the reluctance in her tone. She wanted Eddie to go and look for Tom that minute. 'You get washed at the sink. I'll dish up your tea. It's all ready.'

Eddie was just wiping the last of the gravy up with a slice of bread when a knock came at the back door. They glanced at each other. That couldn't be Tom; he'd have walked straight in.

'Oh my, something must have happened,' Lilian gasped as she hurried to answer it.

A tall, broad policeman stood there. Before he could speak, Lilian blurted out, 'Is it Tom? Has there been an accident?'

'You are Mrs Holmes, I take it?' he said in a gruff voice. 'You're Thomas Holmes's mother?'

'Yes, yes. What's happened? Is he – is he hurt?'

'Your son is quite well, Mrs Holmes. He's at the station being questioned and we need either you or his father to be with him as a responsible adult. He is only seventeen, I believe?'

Lilian and Eddie glanced at one another. They'd been worried that Tom was approaching the age when he could be called up. Even though they had been assured at the start of his wireless operations that this was unlikely because of the work he was doing here, they were still uncertain. Tom was due to sit his Higher School Certificate this summer and then he would be leaving school. In normal times, he would be applying for university, but the family had agreed that the work he was doing was far more important. Very soon he would be sitting crouched over the receiver for longer hours than he had done up to now.

'I'm sure there'll be schemes for young men like you to go to university after the war,' Eddie had said. Lilian had said nothing; what her son was doing was keeping him safely at home and that was all she wanted at the moment.

But now, as they faced the young constable on their doorstep, they both wondered if the time had come when the authorities would demand that he be called up as soon as he was old enough, and that was only four months away.

Eddie had come to stand behind Lilian and he now asked, 'Questioned? What about?'

'That I can't say at this point, Mr Holmes, but if you would come with me to the station . . . ?'

'I'll go, Lilian,' Eddie said. 'You stay here. I'll just get my coat, officer.'

The man nodded and turned away to go back to the police car standing in the lane.

'Oh Eddie,' Lilian clung to his arm for a moment, 'whatever can have happened? Surely he's not in trouble. Not our Tom. He's a good boy.'

Eddie patted her hand. 'Try not to worry, Lilian love.' And with that, he was gone.

The hours that followed were torture for Lilian; it was terrible just waiting and not knowing what was happening.

In the police car, Eddie tried again to find out what the trouble was, but the constable either genuinely didn't know or he wasn't telling. 'The inspector will explain it all to you, sir,' was all he would say.

Arriving at the station, Eddie was shown into an interviewing room where Tom, wide-eyed and white-faced with fear, was waiting.

'Oh Dad!'

'It's all right, son,' Eddie said calmly. 'Whatever it is, we'll sort it out. I'm here now.'

'It's about Mr Fox,' Tom blurted out. 'There are all sorts of rumours flying around school. He didn't come in this morning. One of the lads from the year above us lives in the same street and he saw a police car taking Mr Fox away early this morning. It looked like he was being arrested. They're saying at school that he's a spy and now they want to question me. Dad, I swear I'm not a spy. At least, not one for the enemy.'

'Of course you're not, lad.' Eddie felt relief wash over him. 'You've only been doing what the authorities have asked you to do. I know that. We'll soon have all this straightened out.'

They sat down and waited for twenty minutes before a rotund inspector entered the room. He sat down opposite them with a file of papers in front of him.

'Good evening, Mr Holmes,' the man said formally.

'Oh hello, Derek.' Eddie knew the inspector well. 'What's this all about, then?'

The two men had been at school together and occasionally still met for a pint and a game of darts in one of the pubs in town. Derek was normally jovial and friendly, but today, Inspector Derek Spencer's face was solemn.

'Thank you for coming in. We need to ask Thomas some questions about his activities listening in to messages and his association with Mr Fox, but we needed either you or his mother with him as he is classed as under-age.' The inspector turned his attention to Tom. 'Now young man, tell me exactly how you got involved in becoming a VI?'

Tom blinked. 'A what?'

'A voluntary interceptor. That's what they call you, isn't it? You listen in to radio frequencies to pick up enemy messages.'

'Yes.'

'And how did you get into doing this?'

Tom hesitated. He didn't want to 'tell tales' on Mr Fox.

'Tell the truth, Tom,' Eddie said calmly. 'You've done nothing wrong. Not that I can see, anyway. And don't worry, Derek will be bound by the Act in his position. You can be honest with him – with Inspector Spencer.'

Tom took a deep breath. 'I've been interested in being a radio ham for about six years, ever since I started the grammar school at eleven. Mr Fox, the science master, took a lesson about it one day. He brought some of his own equipment into the school to show us all. I got hooked on it and with his help' – he glanced briefly at Eddie – 'and with Dad's approval, I started to build my own wireless transmitter and receiver in our front room and Dad put up an aerial near the tree in our back garden. You can't really see it from the road. The top bit that sticks out looks just like a bit of branch. I've still got the receiver, but the authorities removed my transmitter for the duration.' Tom's face fell, looking as if he didn't quite believe what he was about to say next. 'They say I'll get it back – eventually.' Tom explained how he had been visited by two army officers after Carolyn had volunteered for the ATS.

'So you were aware that what you were doing should be kept secret?'

'Not at first, no, but I do now. I mean, before the war started and even for a while afterwards – it was just transmitting to contacts around the country or even in other countries and having a chat. You know, other wireless enthusiasts like me. But after the two army chaps had visited, I had to sign the Official Secrets Act when I started listening in officially.'

'We all did,' Eddie put in.

'Where exactly is Carolyn now?' Derek asked mildly.

Eddie smiled wryly. 'We don't know, inspector. Because she learned shorthand and typing and Tom also taught her Morse, I'm guessing she's engaged on some sort of secret work too. She joined the ATS, but we have no idea where she is or what she does. She just arrives home on leave now and again and that's all we know.'

'I see.' Thoughtfully, Derek leafed through the papers in front of him. 'Getting back to how you got started . . . wireless equipment of this nature is very expensive.' His penetrating gaze rested on Eddie.

'We built it up slowly, buying him bits and pieces for birthdays and Christmas. His grandad chipped in and Mr Fox gave him a few parts too.'

Derek leaned his arms on the desk and stared straight into Tom's eyes. 'So, how did you come to be listening in to German transmissions?'

Tom explained about the two army officers who had visited and how they had arranged for a soldier stationed at the Point to come each evening to collect Tom's notes.

'They showed me which frequencies I should listen to and we arranged that I should be on duty from six to eight o'clock every evening and for two hours each day at weekends and that Mr Fox would do other hours around the times I do.'

'The soldier who collects Tom's notes most of the time is a very nice young man,' Eddie put in, 'but a few weeks back he had to go home to Hull on compassionate leave following a bad air raid. His wife and his mother-in-law were killed.' He hesitated to say any more. Surely what had happened to Steve could have no bearing on what he and Tom were here for. 'He was away for a while, but he's back now,' Eddie went on. 'We're all fond of Steve. He's become like one of the family. The one that took his place temporarily was Gordon. He still fills in now and again when Steve is off duty. He's likeable enough, but we haven't got to know him as well yet.'

'Do you speak or understand German, Thomas?' Derek asked, with a sudden added sharpness to his tone.

Tom shook his head. 'No, we only learn French at school.'

'But you've learned Morse code outside school. Have you also learned German?'

'No. I understand the odd word but all the Morse messages are in code anyway.'

'So, how do you know that the messages you are so carefully recording are of any use at all?'

Tom shrugged. 'I don't. I just copy down what I hear as accurately as I can onto the forms they send me, seal them in an envelope and hand them to whoever collects them every night.'

Derek allowed himself a small smile. 'So, you've

no idea whether the words are German, Double Dutch or Gobbledegook.'

Tom, feeling the tension in the room relax a little, smiled too. 'No, sir. I don't. The only thing I do know is that I sometimes get a note back from whoever they're sent to telling me to tune into a particular frequency and to stay on it until they tell me different, so I did wonder if that had given them something useful.'

'I think,' Derek said slowly, 'that perhaps it did.' He glanced from Tom to Eddie and back again. His serious face was back. 'What I am about to tell you now is in the strictest confidence. You must not discuss it with anyone outside this room, not even with your wife, Eddie. But since you tell me that you have both signed the Official Secrets Act, I am permitted to tell you.'

The use of Eddie's Christian name now eased the stress that both he and Tom were feeling. There was a definite relaxation and the inspector was now treating them as confidants, not suspects.

'It was in fact, Tom, one of your transcripts that first alerted the authorities to a spy attempting to enter this country by landing on a deserted part of this coastline. I know you don't transmit messages now, but Mr Fox does. He, too, picked up similar messages, which somehow he obviously understood because he replied, giving coordinates as to where the German might land so as not to be detected. Evidently, he met him and took him to his house. An anonymous phone call, made from a call box that same night – or rather in the early hours of the morning – was received at our police station suggesting that we should investigate Mr Fox's home. It was a woman's voice. We don't know who it was, but we intend to find out. Armed police surrounded the house and the German was found hiding in the loft.'

'Is it true, then, that Mr Fox has been arrested as a spy? That's the rumour going around school.'

Derek grinned widely now, but all he would say was, rather pompously, 'He is assisting us with our inquiries. And now, Tom, thank you for your help. You are free to leave, though we may want to speak to you again.'

Tom and Eddie rose slowly. 'Am I allowed to continue with listening in, then?'

'Oh yes. Most certainly. In fact, I think you may receive a visit from the authorities asking if you could do longer sessions now that Mr Fox might – erm – be off the airwaves for a while.'

'Oh Tom! Thank goodness!'

Lilian flung her arms around him and hugged him hard. A little embarrassed by his mother's display, Tom wriggled free. 'It's all right, Mam. I haven't done anything wrong. I just told them everything I knew. It's Mr Fox I'm worried about though. I think he's still there. At the police station, I mean.'

'Oh never mind him,' Lilian snorted. 'Whatever he's been up to is his business as long as he hasn't involved you. That's all I care about.'

Eddie and Tom exchanged a glance. They didn't agree with Lilian, nor could they tell her anything; they had been sworn to secrecy by the inspector.

'So, what happened? What was it all about?'

'Basically, Mam, they just wanted to check up on what I'm doing.'

Lilian frowned. Tom was avoiding looking her in the eyes. She knew when her son was lying – or, rather, not telling her the whole truth. She turned towards Eddie, but he too was suddenly busy reading his newspaper.

'Are neither of you going to tell me, then?' she snapped.

'It was Derek Taylor who interviewed Tom and, like the lad says, love, it was just to ask him about his wireless operations. They have to know what's happening on their own patch, now don't they?'

'I suppose so.' Lilian was still not convinced. 'All right, then,' she conceded reluctantly at last. 'As long as you can assure me that you're not in any kind of trouble, Tom, I won't ask any more.'

Tom gave her a quick grin and disappeared into the front room. He was already late tuning in and now he intended to do two hours extra to cover Mr Fox's time too.

Forty

'I expect you've heard that the little slut has had her bastard?'

The afternoon following Tom's visit to the police station, Phyllis arrived to see Lilian after she had finished her work in Frank's dairy. Knowing nothing of the events of the previous night in the Holmes's household, she launched straight into what concerned her the most: Beryl.

'Dad told me when he called this morning,' Lilian said.

The two women were sitting together in Lilian's kitchen.

'And your Eve is making such a fuss over her an' all,' Phyllis went on, eyeing Lilian to gauge just how her words were being received. She was not disappointed.

Lilian sniffed. 'Oh aye, my dear sister-in-law will be getting her feet well and truly under the table.'

'I thought she'd already managed that,' Phyllis said slyly. 'What with Harold being the one who'll inherit the farm.'

'Aye, well, that's another sore point, as well you know, Phyllis.'

'So what are you going to do about Beryl?'

'There's nothing I can do, is there? Unless you have any bright ideas.'

Phyllis was thoughtful for a moment before saying quietly, 'Lilian, can I tell you something in the strictest confidence?'

'Of course.'

'Peter's been writing to the little bitch.'

'Peter? Your Peter?'

'Yes, my Peter. Can you believe it? I must say I'm surprised at him. I don't think the army's doing him any good.'

'But why? Why's he writing to *her*? I mean, they hardly know each other.' She paused and then added, 'Do they?'

Phyllis sighed. 'On his last leave, he spent quite a lot of time at the farm. I *thought* he was helping your dad out. At least, that was what he said.'

'And you think he spent time with Beryl?'

'He must have done, Lilian, or he wouldn't be writing to her, would he? I did know he took both Carolyn and Beryl to the pictures one night some time ago. Got into a fight, he did. Came home with a bloody nose. I bet that was *her* fault.'

'Did he? Carolyn never said anything.'

'Well, she wouldn't, would she? She'd stick up for her friend. Besides, they've all got very secretive since this wretched war started. They're getting out of our control, Lilian, and I don't like it.'

'How did you find out about him writing to her?'

'I ran into the postman at the farm gate one morning and he gave me the letters to take to the house. There was one with Peter's handwriting on it addressed to her.'

'Did you give it to her?'

'No, I did not,' Phyllis said hotly, quite oblivious to the fact that she had done anything wrong.

'You read it?' Lilian said. She didn't see anything amiss in that; it was exactly what she would have done in the same circumstances.

'I did and then I burned it.'

'What did it say? I mean, was it all lovey-dovey?'

'No, to be fair, it wasn't. It was just a friendly letter. But it should be *Carolyn* he's writing to, not that little whore.'

Lilian shrugged. 'Maybe he is. Nothing comes here for her now, but then it wouldn't, would it?'

'Can you find out?'

'What? If they are writing to each other?'

When Phyllis nodded, Lilian said, 'I'll ask her next time she comes home on leave.'

'Huh! I expect she'll be rushing up to the farm to see Beryl when she does. It's all Carolyn's fault the girl is even here, isn't it?'

'Don't you worry, Phyllis,' Lilian said. 'I shall be having words with her about it anyway.'

Oblivious to the events that were happening at home, Carolyn filled the time when she was not either working or sleeping with activity. With the arrival of the warmer April weather, she joined Bill on his motorcycle jaunts into the countryside, her arms around his waist, her head pressed to his back. He was so easy to be with and, soon, all thoughts of

Michael faded. They played tennis, with Bill helping her to improve her backhand; they went for long walks together talking about anything and everything; they attended concerts in Leicester and occasionally went dancing; but Carolyn's thoughts were never far away from her friend Beryl. She longed to hear news of the baby's arrival. Surely, she thought, it must happen soon.

At the same time that Lilian and Phyllis were having their conversation about the developing friendship between Peter and Beryl, George Fox was still sitting in a cell at the police station wondering just how he had got himself into this mess. He had been there for almost thirty-six hours now, since the police had called at his house during the early hours of the previous day. It hadn't gone quite according to plan. He was worried about Tom; he hadn't wanted the young boy to be involved, but he understood from what he'd overheard that the police had taken Tom from school to the police station the previous afternoon. Other than that, he didn't know what had happened to the boy. He himself had not been officially arrested; not yet. But George could imagine the rumours flying around school now. The headmaster, Mr Milner, was fully aware of his and Tom's activities, although he was ignorant of the recent events. He had, behind the scenes, been instrumental in helping to obtain equipment for Tom to build his wireless set. 'It's good for a boy to have an interest,' he'd said to George. 'You never know, it could lead to a career for him.'

What Mr Milner had not envisaged, George thought ruefully, was that it might lead to a prison cell. It wasn't the most comfortable place to spend thirty-six hours, though he had to admit he had been very well treated. The food was adequate. He'd been brought an extra blanket when he said he was cold, though no one had told him anything about what was happening, even though he had been treated with courtesy. He sighed. To be fair, he knew exactly why he was being held.

George glanced at his watch. It was almost six o'clock now. He doubted he would get home to tune in at his usual time that evening. He'd already missed one session the previous day. He just wished he knew what was happening to Tom. He felt responsible. Damn it! He *was* responsible.

He heard footsteps and a key turning in the lock. The door swung open and a police constable said courteously, 'Would you come with me, Mr Fox? The inspector would like a word.'

Relieved to be out of the cell, George followed him down the corridors, up some stairs and into an interview room.

'Inspector Spencer will be with you in a moment.' The constable left the room but did not, George noticed, lock the door. He waited another twenty minutes before Derek Spencer bustled into the room.

'Good evening, Mr Fox. I'm sorry to have kept you waiting so long, but I needed to speak to young Tom first.'

'Is he all right? He's not involved in this, you know.'

'He's fine. He went home with his father last night.'

George sighed with relief. 'Thank goodness. All the boy does is copy out the Morse signals and send them off with the courier. I don't think he can understand their meaning, not even the ones in plain text. He hasn't learned any German and I don't think he knows where they go to either.'

'But you do?'

'Oh yes. The army officer who set all this up told me a little more than he told Tom. Captain Delaney. I'm sure if you get in touch with him, all this can be straightened out.'

'Maybe so, Mr Fox, but first I would like you to tell me what has been going on and why you ended up with a German spy hiding in your loft.'

George smiled. 'With pleasure, inspector, but first I must ask you something. Have you signed the Official Secrets Act? Because if you haven't, then I am afraid I can't tell you anything.'

As the sun began to sink low in the western sky, Frank stood leaning on his farm gate, puffing at his pipe and enjoying, for the umpteenth time in his long life, the magnificent Lincolnshire sunset. Although he wasn't a widely travelled man, he didn't think there could be a better sunset in the world. One to equal it, perhaps, but not to better it. But tonight he was worrying about Beryl and her bairn. He had persuaded her to write to Carolyn and he had posted the letter himself earlier that day. He hoped his granddaughter would be able to get leave to come home and help him sort out the problem. If only, between them, they could persuade her to keep the baby.

With a sigh, he turned away, reluctant to leave the magnificent scene before him, but there were more pressing matters at the moment. The sunset could wait; it would still be there tomorrow and all the days after that.

He entered by the back door to find Eve washing up the tea things. 'You get off home now, love. Harold must be wondering if he's still got a wife.'

'If you're sure you'll be all right, then I will. She's feeding him now regularly, so that much is all right, but she's still saying she wants to have him adopted.'

'I got her to write to tell Carolyn and I posted the letter today.' He smiled conspiratorially at Eve. 'I'm just hoping it will bring Carolyn running.'

Eve pulled a face. 'I sure she will, if she can get permission. They can be a bit sticky about leave.'

'I know, but from what Carolyn said last time she was home, they've got quite an understanding officer in charge of them.'

'We can but hope,' Eve murmured as she hung the tea towel up to dry. 'I'll be off then, but don't hesitate to fetch me if there's a problem.'

Inspector Derek Spencer smiled across the table at George. 'All police officers are bound by the Official Secrets Act, Mr Fox, so fire away. I'm all ears.' He sat back in his chair and folded his arms, settling down to listen to George's story.

'In the summer of 1914,' George began, 'I had just become fully qualified as a science teacher, but when war broke out I volunteered for the Signals Corps. I'd always been interested in communications and foresaw huge potential in that field. After the war, I obtained teaching posts as a science teacher. I came here from the Magdalen School when this grammar school first opened. In my spare time I built wireless transmitters and receivers. I might add here that I was always on the lookout for any pupils who had a similar interest to myself. I also joined the Radio Society of Great Britain. At the outbreak of *this* war, many of our members had to relinquish their transmitters, including Tom, much to his disappointment, though he was allowed to keep his receiver for reasons which you now know. Because of my background, the authorities allowed me to keep my transmitter.' He smiled. 'And also, because I am fluent in German – and French too, as a matter of fact – I have extra duties that Tom knows nothing about. Nor do the couriers who collect our paperwork each night.

'Most of the signals we receive are in Morse and are also encrypted, so even I can't understand them, but occasionally we'll get a message in plain text – usually in German, of course. Tom won't understand those messages either, but I do. About a month ago, I started getting messages which seemed to indicate that the enemy were trying to arrange for a spy to come ashore somewhere along the East Coast and were trying to locate a suitable spot. I immediately got in touch with Captain Delaney and we devised a plan. It seems that Tom had also received some encrypted messages about the same thing, though of course he wasn't aware of it. These were deciphered at . . .' He paused and then changed the direction of his conversation, 'Well, we'd better not say quite where, but they confirmed the messages that we had both picked up.

'Our plan was that I should reply to these messages offering to pinpoint a place very near here where the spy would be able to land in secrecy. I can't tell you how we did this. I just followed Captain Delaney's instructions. He, I believe, had help and advice from someone higher up the . . . What shall we call it? The secrecy chain. We didn't, of course, want our spy blundering ashore at the Point where the army have training facilities – as, no doubt, you know, inspector.'

Derek nodded but remained silent.

'After a couple of weeks and a great many messages going back and forth, my contact evidently believed that I was genuine. We finally arranged that he should land just north of the Point and that I should meet him.'

'Why were the police not informed then? We could have been ready and waiting for him.'

George smiled and said gently, 'Inspector, no disrespect, but it would only have taken one tiny, careless slip – something like a movement in the bushes by one of your men – to have alerted him. He would then not have come ashore and we would have lost him.'

Derek had the grace to smile. 'Point taken. I suppose ten or twenty policemen in their size twelves blundering about on the sandhills in the dark would not have been the best idea. Go on, Mr Fox.'

'I met him and took him to my house, fed him

and then hid him in the loft. I did not want to leave the house for two reasons. One, I wanted to be sure he remained where he was and two, I didn't want him to suspect that I was reporting his arrival so, to that end, I stayed in the loft with him. But by prior arrangement, my wife left the house and called you anonymously from a phone box. And there you have it, but I want to reiterate that Tom had no involvement at all. All he does is what he's been asked to do. Monitor the airwaves on the frequencies he's been given for a couple of hours a day and hand over his notes to the courier who calls at his house each night.'

'And the couriers knew nothing about this either?'

'Not as far as I am aware. I don't see how they could have done.'

Derek was thoughtful for a moment before saying slowly. 'Well, I believe your explanation, but I am sure you will understand that I have to verify what you have said with this Captain Delaney.'

'Of course, I wouldn't expect anything less. May I borrow your writing pad and pen?'

Puzzled, the inspector pushed the items across the table. Swiftly, George wrote down a telephone number from memory.

'This is Captain Delaney's number. I was given this to contact him in case of an emergency and I think this warrants that term, don't you?'

'Thank you, Mr Fox. I will contact the captain as soon as possible. In the meantime, I am afraid you will have to stay in custody.'

'Understood. May I ask you one question? What will happen to the young fellow who came ashore?'

'He'll be taken down to London for questioning.'

George sighed. He hoped they wouldn't be too brutal with him. He'd seemed a good sort of chap, who was only doing what he believed was his duty for his own country. George was escorted back to the cell, but he was sure that now it would only be for a few hours more.

Forty-One

'There's a letter for you,' Noreen said, holding out an envelope to Carolyn. 'I think it's from Beryl. I recognize her handwriting.'

Carolyn tore open the envelope in her haste. 'I wonder . . .' she murmured.

Noreen was just as curious as she hovered in front of Carolyn. 'Well?' she said impatiently as Carolyn scanned the page. 'Has she had the baby? What did she get? Are they all right? And what has she called him or her?'

Carolyn looked up and smiled. 'A baby boy and they're both fine.' Then her face clouded, 'But she hasn't named him because she says she's not keeping him. She's going to put him up for adoption.'

Noreen snorted. 'That's terrible. She made a mistake – we all know that – but she's no need to compound it by giving him away. Your family are standing by her, aren't they? Even if her own aren't.'

'Yes, yes, they are.'

'Then I think you'd better see if you can get some leave and go home and talk some sense into her. Talk to Ma'am. She's very understanding. Giving him away, indeed! The very idea.' Noreen was positively bristling with indignation.

'Yes,' Carolyn said slowly. 'I think you're absolutely right. I'd better get home as soon as I can.'

On the journey home, Carolyn had time to think. Life was so hectic. There was hardly a minute to talk during working hours; everyone concentrated so hard on their job and, by the end of a shift, their heads were still buzzing from the crackling in their headphones and the intense effort of trying to separate the Morse from the interference. But now she couldn't wait to see Beryl again and meet the new baby, though she was worried about her friend's plan to have the little boy adopted. Carolyn was determined to make her change her mind.

'See what trouble you've caused?'

Carolyn hadn't been in the house many minutes before Lilian began to have 'words' with her. Two weeks after receiving Beryl's letter, Carolyn had managed to get home.

'Eh?' Carolyn blinked. She was mystified. 'I haven't any idea what you're talking about, Mam. How can I have caused trouble? I'm not even here most of the time.'

'Getting round your grandad to give that little madam a home.'

'I didn't ask him, Mam. He offered.'

'Same difference. You knew he was a soft touch and would take pity on the girl if you told him her sob story. What about her own family?'

'They threw her out, as did the ATS when they found out. She had nowhere to go.'

Lilian sniffed. 'Well, I don't blame any of them. It's what I would have done if it had been you.'

Carolyn shot her mother a sideways glance but said nothing. It was enough, though, to make Lilian's cheeks turn red. She changed the subject. 'Are you writing to Peter? I bet he's glad of letters.'

'He is and, yes, we do write now and again. Just between two friends, Mam, so don't start getting any ideas. He's finding army life all very boring at the moment. He wishes he could get into the action somewhere.'

'Oh my goodness, I do hope not. Phyllis will have a ducky fit if he gets sent abroad and into the fighting.'

Carolyn reached for her coat. 'I'm just off to see Grandad and Beryl and the new baby. Has she chosen a name for him yet?'

'I really have no idea.'

'Have you seen him?'

'Why on earth would I want to do that?'

'Do you mean you haven't been to the farm since he was born?'

'I go to see your grandad now and again.'

'Now and again? But you used to go almost every day to take him his dinner.'

There was a sharp edge to her tone as Lilian said, 'I'm rather surplus to requirements now. The girl did all his meals until she went into labour and ever since then, your Aunty Eve has been there a lot of the time.'

Carolyn said no more. She got the feeling there was more to this than her mother was saying. Never

353

mind, she told herself as she buttoned her coat, she would soon find out.

She cycled to the farm, then entered by the back door.

'Hello, Aunty Eve. How lovely to see you . . .' She gave Eve a swift hug. 'I must see Beryl and the baby and then we'll have a chat.'

Eve laughed. 'Up you go. I'll put the kettle on.'

Carolyn opened the bedroom door to see Beryl sitting up in bed, breastfeeding the baby. As she glanced up, her eyes filled with tears to see Carolyn standing there. 'I knew you'd come as soon as you could.'

'You couldn't keep me away,' Carolyn said. She tiptoed across the room and sat down on the bed, leaning forward to look at the child. 'Oh Beryl, he's gorgeous. And so *big*. However much does he weigh?'

'He was eight pounds when he was born, the midwife said.'

'That's a good weight for a first baby.'

'How do you know so much about it all?'

Carolyn laughed. 'You don't grow up on a farm without learning such things.'

She gazed down at the two of them before saying. 'I'll leave you to finish feeding him and then I'll come back. Aunty Eve is just making a cuppa. I'll bring you one up.'

Back downstairs, Eve said, 'You're looking a bit peaky. Are they working you too hard?' She laughed as she added, 'At whatever it is you're doing.'

'We do work very hard, Aunty, but I can't tell you anything about it or even where I am. Sorry.'

'I quite understand, love.' Eve sighed.

'It's very good of you to look in on Beryl and the baby, Aunty.'

'I'm here to look after Beryl and the bairn when your grandad has to be out.'

Suddenly, Carolyn was worried. 'Is something wrong with one of them?'

'Heavens, no. They're both thriving and eating us out of house and home.' Her face clouded for a moment. 'Though she is saying she wants to have him adopted and neither your grandad nor I can change her mind. But, we're working on that. No, the real trouble is Phyllis Carter. I haven't said much to your grandad, though I think he's guessed what's going on.'

'So, what *is* going on?'

'Let's just say, Phyllis is less than kind towards Beryl and her baby. Poor lass went into labour during the afternoon. Your grandad was out and there was only Phyllis here. From what Beryl says – and she hasn't said very much – Phyllis did stay here in the house, but she left her alone in the bedroom. Even when the contractions got worse and Beryl cried out for her, she didn't go to her. She wouldn't even let Beryl call the midwife. It wasn't until Dad came home and found out what was happening that anything was done to help her. From what I can make out, if he hadn't come back home when he did, poor Beryl might have given birth completely on her own. Of course, Phyllis made out she'd been looking after her, but I don't think she had. All Beryl will say is that she didn't think Phyllis could hear her, but I heard her quite clearly the minute I came through the back door and I found Phyllis sitting reading the newspaper in the kitchen and taking no notice of Beryl's cries. Maybe you can get a bit more out of the lass than I can. She clams up when I ask her. Doesn't want to tell tales, I expect. Anyway, I've been coming every day since she gave birth to be with her while Dad's out in the daytime.'

'Oh Aunty Eve, how good of you.' Carolyn hesitated and then added, 'Mam says she's not been across.'

Eve's mouth tightened and she glanced way. 'No, she hasn't.'

'Look, if you want to get off home now, I can stay with Beryl until Grandad gets in. I want to see him anyway. And I'll come again tomorrow, if you like.'

'That'd be a big help, love, if you could. Dad's around most of the time on a Sunday, but he still has to see to the animals. Thanks, I'll take you up on both today and tomorrow. I've let things slip a bit at home. Not that Harold or Adam have grumbled. They're being very good about it. Harold never says much,' she smiled fondly, 'as you well know, but he's a kind man at heart. Just not very talkative.' She laughed. 'But he always says I do enough for the two of us. Talking, that is. And, of course, the girls' – she was referring to the land army girls lodging with them – 'are there. They've been good too. They've kept things ticking over, you might say, but they can't do everything I do. I'll just say cheerio to Beryl and then I'll get off.'

The two women went upstairs.

'I'm going now, love, but Carolyn's going to stay with you now until Mr Frank gets home and she'll come again tomorrow, so I'll see you on Monday.'

'How good you all are to me,' Beryl said huskily. 'I don't deserve it.'

'We'll have no more of that talk,' Carolyn said. 'Now, let me have a hold of my godson while you drink your tea.'

Beryl's eyes widened. 'Eh?'

'Well, I do hope you're going to ask me to be his godmother. I'd be most hurt if you don't.'

Beryl was still staring at Carolyn when Eve wiggled her fingers in farewell and slipped out of the room.

'I hadn't thought about anything like that,' Beryl said. 'Won't his adoptive parents want to do that sort of thing?'

'Oh Beryl, you're not still thinking of doing that, are you? Not after you've seen him – held him – fed him.' Carolyn reached out to take the infant into her arms as Beryl handed him over. She looked into his big blue eyes staring up at her. He waved his chubby arms and wriggled in her grasp. 'My word, he's strong for a little 'un. You're going to be a real bruiser, aren't you . . . ? Oh, I don't know his name.' She glanced at Beryl. 'What are you calling him?'

Beryl shrugged.

'I think you'll have to call him something, Beryl. He's nearly three weeks old now and he'll need to be registered very soon. In fact, I can do that for you on Monday, if you like. I haven't got to go back until Tuesday morning. Would you like me to?'

'I really don't care one way or the other.'

'Let's think of some names, then. What about calling him after your father?'

Beryl snorted. 'I'm not calling him after him or any of my family, thank you very much. I'd sooner call him after your grandad, if he wouldn't mind.'

'Of course he wouldn't. He'd be honoured.'

'Honoured? To have his name used by a little bastard?'

'Oh Beryl. Don't talk like that.'

'That's what Mrs Carter calls him.'

'Does she now?' Carolyn said gently, putting the baby against her shoulder and patting his back. 'Tell me about Phyllis Carter. You know how good I am at keeping secrets. Nothing you tell me will go beyond these four walls.'

Haltingly at first and then in a flood of words, as if it were a relief to talk about it, Beryl told her all that had happened since she had come to live at the farm.

'But Peter's nice,' she ended. 'He – I – he and I have been writing to each other since he went back. He usually writes to me every Sunday, although I haven't had a letter for a couple of weeks now.'

'That's great,' Carolyn said and Beryl could see that her delight was genuine. 'But I wouldn't let his mother know, if I were you.'

'No, I won't.'

'So,' Carolyn went on, as the baby's eyes began to close and he fell asleep against her, 'what about a name? Is it Frank, then?'

'Has your grandad got a second name?'

Carolyn wrinkled her forehead. 'I think his proper

358

name is Francis James, but he's always been called "Frank". You could always call the baby "James".'

Beryl was thoughtful for a few moments before murmuring, 'Jamie's a nice name for a little boy, isn't it?'

'Yes, it is. You could always christen him "James", but call him "Jamie".'

'If Mr Frank doesn't mind, then that's what I'll do, but – but I don't think the vicar will agree to christen him properly, will he?'

Carolyn chuckled softly, so as not to wake the sleeping child nestling against her neck. 'It's a rector we have here, but you leave him to Grandad. He'll soon sort him out.'

'I suppose I should do the right thing by him,' Beryl murmured. 'I'll certainly get him registered.'

'I'll do that for you on Monday, if you give me all the details they'll need. Do you want a second name?'

Beryl shook her head. 'No, James will be enough. Like I say, his – his adoptive parents will probably want to change it anyway.'

Carolyn rocked the baby gently. 'Beryl, are you really sure that's what you want to do?'

Tears filled Beryl's eyes and ran down her cheeks. 'No, Carolyn,' she burst out. 'I'm not sure at all, because – because I can't stop myself loving him.'

Forty-Two

'Hello, lass. I heard you're home for a couple of days. Come to see Beryl, have you?'

'And the baby . . .' Carolyn kissed Frank's leathery cheek. 'And you, of course.'

'Nice little thing, isn't he?'

'Grandad,' Carolyn said, lowering her voice almost to a whisper, even though Beryl was upstairs, 'you want her to keep the baby, don't you?'

'Of course I do.' His reply was swift and firm. There was no doubting Frank's sincerity. 'A baby should be with its birth mother, even if the father's done a bunk.' He sighed. 'But she's adamant she's going to have him adopted.'

'I don't think she's as sure as she was before he was born. She's wavering.'

Frank's eyes lit up. 'Really? Are you sure, lass?'

'What was it Grandma used to say about babies – "They bring the love with them"?'

Frank's tone was pensive as he remembered his wife. 'Aye, she did and she was right most of the time, wasn't she?'

Carolyn chuckled. 'I think she could be again, but what you have to decide is how you want to help her if she does decide to keep it?'

'You mean, tell her she can stay here as long as she wants?'

'Can she?'

'Of course. I enjoy her company. She's a nice lass.' He eyed his granddaughter for a moment before saying softly, 'I reckon young Peter's taken a shine to her, an' all.'

Carolyn's eyes widened. 'Better not let his mother hear that.'

Frank snorted. 'I won't.' He paused and then added gently, 'You don't mind, though?'

'Heavens, no. I'd be delighted. I've persuaded her to give the baby a name and let me register him on Monday in town. She wants to call him James after you, but he'd probably be known as Jamie. Would you mind?'

Frank beamed. 'Mind? I'd be thrilled.'

'You'd better tell her that and also that she can stay here. I think that might just sway her decision about having him adopted.'

'I'll have a chat with her later after I've had me tea, because I can smell something very tasty coming from that oven.' He nodded towards the range.

'I'll be off, then. I've set the table for you and taken Beryl something to eat. I think she plans to be up and about very soon now. I've promised to come across tomorrow to give Eve a break.'

'If you could just be around while I feed the animals and go to church, then I'll make sure I'm here the rest of the day,' Frank said casually, but Carolyn had the feeling he'd guessed exactly what had been going on with Phyllis, even if he didn't know the details, and he'd also realized what Eve had been trying to do.

When Frank had finished his tea, he went to Beryl's bedroom. Although she had been getting up and dressed for several days now, she still hadn't ventured downstairs except to visit the outside privy. It seemed as if her bedroom was her sanctuary.

'There's no need to stay in here, love. You can bring Babby down into the kitchen.'

Beryl smiled tentatively. 'I wasn't sure. I'll bring him back here if he starts to cry.'

'No need,' Frank said placidly. 'I'm used to it. I had two of me own and Carolyn lived here for a while when she was little. And besides, I wouldn't mind having a hold of him, if he wakes up. Come on, let me carry his Moses basket for you and we can have a nice chat by the fire.'

He set the cradle on the table and they sat either side of the fireplace.

'I'll not smoke while the little 'un's here,' Frank said. 'Not good for his little lungs.'

Beryl gazed into the fire, watching the flames leaping. 'Carolyn said I should think of a name for him. She's going to register him for me on Monday. She – she said she didn't think you'd mind if I called him after you. Your second name is James, isn't it?'

'It is and I'd be over the moon.'

'I'd register him as James, but call him Jamie.'

'I like that. Jamie it is, then.'

They sat for several minutes, an easy silence

between them. Only the crackling fire and the baby's snuffles disturbed the silence.

'I know you've talked about adoption, Beryl love, but if you should change your mind, I want you to know you can stay here for as long as you want.'

She glanced up at him and tears filled her eyes. 'Are you sure? Really sure?'

'I am.'

'It'd just be until I can find work and get my own place . . .'

'That's not going to be easy with a bairn, now is it?' As always, Frank spoke his mind, but his words were said with gentle understanding.

Beryl shook her head. 'No, it isn't,' she whispered. 'Especially when they find out I'm still a "Miss".'

'There's going to be a lot more like you before this war's over. Folks are going to have to get their heads round it. The worst is going to be for those servicemen, who come back from the war and find their wives with a bairn which obviously isn't theirs.'

'I didn't know he was married,' she blurted out. 'He never said until I told him about the baby.'

Frank sighed. 'There's all sorts of deception, love, and that's one of the cruellest. But it's hardly your fault.'

'Not that part, no, but I should have been a good girl. Like Carolyn.'

Frank said nothing, though he was pleased to hear it all the same.

'So,' he said at last, 'are you going to keep him? He's a grand little chap. You should be proud of him and you can carry on being my housekeeper. Officially.'

'What about Mrs Carter?'

'What about her?'

'Well – she used to do housework for you, didn't she?'

'She did, but I don't want her in my house anymore, even if you don't stay. She can keep her cottage and carry on with the work in the dairy, but other than that, no. And you needn't do any dairy work, so you can keep out of her way. And don't think anyone's been telling tales out of school, because they haven't.' He tapped the side of his nose. 'But I wasn't born yesterday and I've seen and heard enough to guess exactly what's been going on between the two of you, even if I don't quite know all the details, so don't you worry about it anymore.'

'If you're really sure, Mr Frank, then I'd love to keep him and stay here.'

'That's settled, then. It'll be a healthy life for him, growing up on a farm. And when he gets to school age . . .'

Beryl began to laugh and cry at the same time. 'Oh Mr Frank, I don't know how to thank you.'

'No thanks needed, lass. We'll get on very nicely together. You'll see.'

When Carolyn arrived back home from the farm, Steve was sitting at the table, drinking tea and eating scones. She knew all about his sad loss and even about his wife being found with someone else. Steve was suffering a double blow of the worst kind. This was the first time she'd seen him since it had happened. She didn't quite know what to say; she didn't want to keep reviving the bitter memories and yet she felt it would be unfeeling not to mention it at all.

'Hello, Steve,' she said carefully. 'How are you?'

Steve shrugged. 'Oh – you know.'

As Lilian slipped out of the kitchen, Carolyn sat down opposite him. 'I was so sorry to hear the awful news.'

'Thanks, Carolyn. That's kind of you. It helps being back here. Your parents have both been so kind and your dad has found me some work with him when I have time off. It means I'm not at a loose end. There's nothing to go back to Hull for now. Nothing at all. And it's actually worse when I'm there.'

'Yes, I can understand that,' she said gently. 'Are you helping out at the joinery, then?'

Steve nodded. 'Yes, it's what I did before I joined up.'

'Fancy that. That's a bit of luck, isn't it? I bet Dad and Grandpa are pleased for an extra pair of hands. Dad was telling me when I was home last time that they're busier than ever. He thinks everyone is really getting into this "make do and mend" directive.'

'Yes, instead of buying new. I see what you mean. I hadn't looked at it like that, but I guess he's right.'

There was silence between them as their gaze met across the table. 'Would you – would you like to go to the pictures one evening? I've got a couple of nights off from Tuesday. Gordon will pick up Tom's notes then.'

Carolyn smiled. 'I'd really like that, but I have to go back early on Tuesday morning. This has been a 'specially granted leave for me to come to see Beryl. I've been very lucky to get it. But perhaps next time I'm home?'

For the first time in weeks, Steve smiled too.

Carolyn's next seventy-two-hour pass came only a few weeks later, at the end of May, but the way her shift pattern fell gave her a little longer at home. Peter came home for a brief leave at the same time.

'How lovely,' Phyllis enthused when he arrived. 'I've got so much planned for us to do. I thought we'd take a trip out into the countryside. I'm sure Mr Frank would let us have the truck for an afternoon. And then there's a good film on at the cinema. You wouldn't mind taking your old mam, would you? It's ages since I went to the cinema. And—'

'Mam, I thought I'd lend Mr Frank a hand.'

Phyllis flapped her hand. 'Oh there's no need. He's got the land army girls now. He won't need you.'

'He can always use an extra pair of hands, Mam, but yes, I'll take you to the pictures. We'll go tomorrow night, because I have to go back early the next morning. Short visit this time, I'm afraid.'

But you'll have time to go and see that little trollop, I bet, Phyllis thought sourly, but she had the good sense, for once, to keep silent.

Only ten minutes after entering his home, Peter was leaving it again on his way to the farm. Phyllis watched him go with bitter resentment.

'Whatever are you doing here?' Beryl greeted him as she opened the door to his knock.

'I told you I was coming this weekend. Didn't you get my letter?'

'No, I didn't. I haven't had one in weeks.'

'Really? I've written to you every Sunday, though I haven't had one from you for quite a while either. They must be getting lost.'

'To be honest, I haven't been able to write to you recently. I've been busy with the baby. Anyway, come in. It's lovely to see you.'

'And it's lovely to see you. I can't wait to see the baby.'

'I'm calling him "James" after Mr Frank. That's his second name, though I plan to call him "Jamie".'

'That's nice. I like it. Please can I meet him?'

When Peter was holding the baby, Beryl said, 'I was going to have him adopted but Carolyn persuaded me not to and Mr Frank says I can stay here as long as I want. I'm to be his housekeeper.'

Peter glanced up, though it was an effort to tear his gaze away from the infant in his arms. He seemed entranced by the baby. 'That's very good of him.'

'Isn't it? He's been so kind to me. And Aunty Eve too. She came over every day after the birth until I felt strong enough to be up and about.'

'Didn't my mother help you? She's here every day, isn't she?'

Beryl turned her head away. 'She was here for a while,' she said vaguely. She didn't want to speak ill of his mother, especially not to him.

'Have you got a pram for him, yet?'

'No, but Mr Frank says we'll get one this week.'

'Let me get that for you.'

'Oh no, Peter. It's very kind of you, but I couldn't let you do that. What would people think?'

'I don't give a damn about what people think or say. I'd really like to, Beryl. Please let me.'

'You shouldn't spend your army pay on me. You need to help your mother.'

'Mam's all right. She's still doing the dairy work here, isn't she? Or are you taking over that?'

'No, no,' Beryl said hurriedly. 'Only the housework. I won't be helping in the dairy at all.'

'So, there you are, then. All sorted out very nicely, isn't it, Jamie?'

The baby gurgled as Peter rocked him gently. As Beryl watched them, tears sprang to her eyes. If only, she thought, if only Peter was Jamie's dad.

Forty-Three

'Peter's asked me to go to the pictures with him in town tomorrow night,' Beryl told Frank, 'but I don't think I should leave Jamie.'

'Of course you should. You need a bit of fun, lass. As long as you feel well enough to go. He'd be all right with me, if you feed him just before you go, but I tell you what, we'll ask Eve to come over. I'm sure she won't mind.'

Eve was delighted. 'I'll always help out in any way I can,' she said, when Beryl asked her tentatively. 'You only have to ask.'

Just like Frank – and it seemed Peter, too, now – Eve was quite besotted with the baby and delighted to hear that Beryl had decided not to have him adopted. Carolyn arrived at the farm more frequently during her leave than she would usually have done and even Eddie called in on his way home. It seemed they all wanted to see the baby, apart from Phyllis and Lilian.

'Mam,' Peter said the following morning, 'I'm taking you out to tea this afternoon instead of the pictures tonight. All right?'

'No, it isn't. I really wanted to see that film. Why, might I ask?'

'Because I'm taking Beryl. It's time that poor girl had a bit of fun.'

Phyllis's face twisted. 'Poor girl, indeed! She's a little slut who's had plenty of *fun* and look where it's got her! I'm surprised at you, Peter, I really am, wanting anything to do with a girl like her. And disappointed in you too. I don't think the army's doing you any good at all. Breaking a promise to your mother in favour of that – that *whore.*'

Peter glared at her, but did not react to her harsh words. Instead, he said shortly, 'Well, do you want to go out for tea or not? Mr Frank's lending me the truck for the rest of the day.'

Phyllis glared back at him, but she knew when she was beaten. Peter was no longer the biddable little boy he had once been. If only he and Carolyn had been sensible and were now engaged like she and Lilian had wanted, none of this would have happened. He wouldn't have gone into the army and Carolyn wouldn't have gone into the ATS and brought home that little slut either. Why did youngsters never listen to their parents, who always knew best?

That afternoon Peter took Phyllis to the restaurant in one of the nicest hotels in town overlooking the sea.

'You wouldn't know there was a war on, would you?' he tried to joke as he held the chair out for her. 'Until you see all the rolls of barbed wire along our lovely beach. Now, what are we having? Their cream teas are a speciality here, I understand. Or at least, they were before the war.'

The atmosphere between them throughout what turned out to be an unexpectedly delicious tea was strained. Phyllis hardly spoke. Peter tried to make conversation but with only monosyllabic answers from his mother, he gave up eventually. He was determined not to pander to her. All his young life he had obeyed her every whim, but now he was a grown man prepared to go to war for his country. He had a right to choose his own friends – even girlfriends.

'Right,' Peter stood up as they both finished eating, 'I'll just pay the bill. Is there anywhere in town you want to go while we're here? Any shopping you want to do?'

For a brief moment Phyllis hesitated. Then she pursed her mouth and said, 'No, thank you.'

Peter sighed inwardly. 'Fair enough. But now's your chance, if you wanted any heavy bags transporting.'

'I manage perfectly well,' she said tartly. 'I'm hardly a weakling, lifting all those heavy churns in the dairy. Besides, I have to manage my shopping when you're not here, don't I? And walk miles to do it.' It was another barely disguised barb at him for leaving her in the lurch when he'd volunteered.

Peter didn't rise to her bait. He knew she could get a lift into the town any time she needed it and, besides, most of her food came directly from the farm. For other things, she could always get a delivery. She had no need to walk miles with heavy shopping bags, but Peter realized now that his mother loved to play the martyr.

'Right, I'll drop you off home.'

As he drove, Peter said tentatively, 'Mam, I really wish you'd try to be a bit more understanding towards Beryl. She's just a lass who made a mistake. She was deceived. The chap was already married but he didn't tell her.'

'You seem to know a lot about it.'

'We've been writing to each other.'

Don't I know it, Phyllis wanted to say, but she pressed her lips together to stop the words being spoken.

'You're my mother and I'll always love you and see that you're cared for, but I'm not your little boy anymore. I've got to make my own decisions. Can't you see that?'

'All I can see is that you're going to ruin your life. I've done my best for you, Peter, and it hasn't been easy. But since you no longer want to take my advice, then you'd better get on with it. Anyway, we're home now . . .' she added as Peter pulled the truck to a stop outside their cottage. 'I'd better make a start on our dinner.'

'I won't be in for dinner, Mam. Besides' – Peter patted his stomach – 'that tea's about filled me up.'

'Taking *her* to a fancy restaurant, are you?'

'No, just the pictures,' Peter said quietly. Then he added wickedly, 'This time.'

Eve stood in the doorway with Jamie in her arms to wave them off.

'I don't like leaving him,' Beryl said worriedly.

'He'll be fine with Eve. Besides, we won't be gone that long. He's just had a feed, hasn't he? He'll probably sleep until we get back. Now stop fretting and enjoy yourself. I hear it's a good film.'

Beryl smiled. 'I will. It's kind of you to take pity on me.'

Peter laughed aloud. 'What I feel for you, Beryl Morley, is not pity, I assure you.'

Beryl felt herself blushing, but a small smile curved her mouth.

When Peter had parked the truck, they walked to the cinema hand in hand.

'There's a bit of a queue,' Peter said. 'I hope we're going to get in.'

'Look, there's Carolyn in the queue with that soldier who helped us last time.'

As they passed them on their way to the back of the line, they stopped for a brief word.

'Fancy seeing you here.' Peter smiled, kissed Carolyn's cheek and shook Steve's hand. 'We'd better get to the back. See you later. Maybe we can give you a lift home.'

'We've got our bikes,' Carolyn said.

'No problem, they can go in the back of the truck and we can all squash in the front.' Peter grinned sheepishly. 'We've done it before.' The four of them laughed easily together, remembering the evening Peter had got into a fight. This time, he was wearing his uniform.

They didn't try to sit near each other in the cinema, respecting that each couple probably wanted to be on their own – or at least not sitting next to people they knew. But at the end of the programme, Peter and Beryl waited outside to meet the other two.

'The truck's parked just round the corner. Where are your bikes?'

'Down the side of the cinema. I'll get them,' Steve said.

He was gone only a few minutes and then the four of them walked to the truck. Piling the bikes into the back, they squeezed into the front bench seat, giggling at the tight fit.

'Just so long as you leave me room to drive,' Peter joked. This time it was Carolyn who sat on Steve's knee, while Beryl snuggled up close to Peter.

'I hope the police don't stop us,' Carolyn said. 'We could be in trouble for this. I'm sure it's not safe.'

Steve said nothing. He had been interviewed recently about his duties as courier, picking up the notes from both Tom and Mr Fox. All had been well, but he didn't want to come to the notice of the local bobbies too many times.

'Just drop us near Carolyn's home,' he suggested. 'I can cycle to the Point from there quite easily.'

Realizing that the young soldier probably wanted to share a goodnight kiss with Carolyn, as indeed he did with Beryl, Peter did as he was asked. On the way between Carolyn's home and the farm, he pulled the truck to a halt, switched off the engine and took Beryl into his arms.

'Are you really sure about this, Peter?'

'I've never been more sure about anything in my life. Now, are you going to let me kiss you or not?'

Outside Carolyn's home, Steve was a little more circumspect. It was only recently that he'd lost his wife in the most hurtful of ways and he didn't want

374

to be making declarations to Carolyn that were perhaps borne out of grief and loneliness and not a little bitterness.

Instead of making any attempt to kiss her, he squeezed her hand and said, 'Do you mind if we take this very slowly, Carolyn? I like you – I like you a lot, but . . .'

'I know and I quite understand. It's what I'd prefer anyway. Everything is so uncertain just now, isn't it?'

Steve breathed a sigh of relief. 'I may be posted any time, but I'd like to keep in touch. May I write to you?'

'I'd like that.'

'Shall I send letters here for you?'

'No. I'll see you tomorrow night when you visit Tom. I'll write the address down for you. And now, I'd better go in. Thank you for a lovely evening. Good night, Steve.'

She leaned across the space between them and gave him a peck on the cheek.

Forty-Four

In the middle of May 1943, the German and Italian troops in North Africa had surrendered to the Allies and Carolyn found that she had lost all contact with those operators she felt she had come to know. The retreating German army had changed position frequently. When Carolyn returned from her brief leave, it was to find herself with a whole new set of challenges. It seemed she was now intercepting messages from Northern Italy.

'I suppose I'd got comfortable with North Africa,' she moaned to Noreen as the summer progressed. 'This is stressful.'

'Never mind. There's an impromptu cricket match taking place tomorrow afternoon. Some bright spark had the idea that because the teleprinter room is disguised as a cricket pavilion, we ought at least to have a match in the field now and again. Bill's playing,' she added archly.

'Then I'll definitely be there,' Carolyn said, hiding her mischievous smile as she saw the smug expression on Noreen's face. 'But can they find enough space between the aerials?'

'Oh I expect so. Someone will have measured out a pitch of sorts.'

The cricket match was deemed a huge success by everyone. Several of the girls – including Carolyn and Noreen – set up a trestle table with a tea urn and cool drinks. They ferried sandwiches and cakes from the canteen on the opposite corner of the field. The ATS girls had all been careful to dress in civvies – pretty summer dresses – and somehow, most of the cricketers had managed to beg or borrow 'whites'. The snacks provided were welcomed eagerly by both teams. It was a friendly game with no time limit set; a casual village cricket match.

'Well, if spotters fly over today, all they'll have to report back is that the British still have time to play cricket,' Bill chuckled as he sat on the grass in front of the 'cricket pavilion', balancing a cup of tea in one hand and a plate with two scones in the other.

Carolyn sat beside him. 'From what the papers say, the war is going a little better for us now, isn't it?'

'I think so, but we still have to get a foothold back in Europe. We can't begin to say we're winning until we do that.'

'When do you think that might happen?'

'Not until next year. Next summer, I'd guess.'

Carolyn was shocked. 'Another year?'

'There'll be a helluva lot to organize. The Americans will have to be a part of it. A huge part, I'd say. And just think of all the troops you'd have to get across the Channel ready to fight stiff opposition when they get there. And the backup they'd need. Constant supplies of equipment, fuel, food. It'll be a gigantic undertaking. And then, sadly, they'll have to make plans for bringing the wounded back because, I'm sorry to say, there are bound to be a lot of casualties.'

'I presume they'd go across at the narrowest part. Dover to Calais.'

'Common sense would tell you that, yes. But in war, the most obvious choice is not always the best. You need to be devious and completely unpredictable. And in that case, you don't take the most obvious route. Well, that's just my humble opinion anyway.'

Carolyn was thoughtful before saying quietly, 'I think you're right. But another whole year to wait.'

'Yes, and then it's likely to be another year or so after that. Hitler is not going to give in easily. And neither, I'm afraid, is Japan. Still, it helps if we can have days like today when we can forget about the war for an hour or so.'

'You're right. I shouldn't have brought the subject up.'

'Don't apologize. It's good to talk things through sometimes.'

There was a brief silence between them before Carolyn asked, 'Who thought of the cricket match?'

Bill chuckled. 'You'll never believe it, but it was Graham Lawrence.'

'Really? But I have to admit he does seem to have lightened up a bit.'

'Well, he's got nothing to grumble about anymore. The ATS girls we're getting now are so much better qualified.' He grinned. 'They're *almost* as good as you.'

A companionable silence fell between them until Bill asked, 'How are things at home?'

Carolyn gave a deep sigh. 'Fine, but it'll be harvest soon and I'll miss it. It was one of the times of the year on a farm that I loved the most. That and lambing time.'

'I know. Me too.' Bill seemed about to say more but a shout came across the field.

'Come on, Bill. Luke's out. You're next in.'

Bill adjusted his shin pads and hauled himself to his feet. 'Better go.'

Carolyn smiled up at him. 'Good luck.'

Beryl had already learned so much about the farming year. When she had arrived in January, Frank had been busy with general farm maintenance; making sure any machinery was repaired and in good working order for the rest of the year. Then had come the time when cows began to calve and the lambing season began too. That was when she had really begun to feel part of Frank's world. She learned when the various crops had been sown and would be ready for harvesting; when haymaking would happen and when the trees in the orchard would bear fruit. And always, every day, there were the animals to care for.

When the day came for the harvest to start, Beryl tucked Jamie into the pram and followed Frank down the lane to the field to be cut first. Pulling the pram into the gateway, Beryl's glance swept the field. Already Harold was scything the edges of the wheat field. The two land girls were following behind him gathering up the cut grain and tying it into bundles.

'Is he going to cut the whole field by hand?' Beryl asked.

'No, lass,' Frank said. 'He's just making a path for the reaper to make a start. Adam should be here any minute with it. I reckon I can hear the tractor coming from their yard.'

'I ought to be helping you,' Beryl murmured. 'I could do what the girls are doing.'

'No, I don't want you hurting yourself. It's too soon and you have to think about having more babies in the future.'

Beryl cast him a wry glance but said nothing. The chugging of the tractor came closer and they moved out of the way for Adam to turn into the field.

'You just keep us supplied with drinks and snacks through the day, love. That's the best way you can help, and Eve will be along later at dinner time with pasties and ale.'

Beryl nodded. 'Yes, she's already told me what I've to bring, but I just wish I could be of more practical help.'

Frank chuckled. 'And how d'you think we'd keep going if you and Eve didn't feed us, eh? Nowt can keep going without being fuelled, not even that there tractor. Now, I'd better be off and do me bit.'

Beryl glanced at him to see the broad smile on his face. Frank was at his happiest at the busiest times in the farming year. He was content with his lot; she could see it in his face. How she envied him.

'Mebbe you'll be able to help us next year,' Frank said as he turned away towards where Adam was manoeuvring the tractor and reaper-binder into position.

Beryl stood watching for an hour until Jamie began

to whimper that he was hungry. She was fascinated to watch the machine cutting the wheat, tying it into sheaves and then spitting each one out for the land girls to gather and set up in stooks, the ears pointing to the sun to dry. As Jamie's cries became more insistent, she turned reluctantly towards the farmhouse.

Next year, Frank had said. Where would she be by this time next year? Beryl wondered. She was beginning to get surprisingly settled here. If she wasn't careful, she wouldn't want to leave. Not ever.

Peter arrived home on a three-day leave just in time to help with the final stages of the harvest.

Frank was delighted to see him home to lend a hand. 'Peter's the best I've ever seen at building a stack. Even better than I was in me younger days.'

'You've been lucky with the weather, Mr Frank,' Peter said when he visited the farm the same evening he arrived home.

'We have,' Frank agreed. 'But there's rain forecast for the end of the month.'

'We'd best get a move on, then. I'll be here bright and early in the morning.' Peter rubbed his hands together. 'I can't wait to get a pitchfork back in me hands.'

And I can't wait to see you stripped to the waist wielding one on top of a stack, Beryl mused, but she kept such thoughts to herself. Instead, she said aloud, 'Carolyn wanted to be here too, but she can't get leave this time.'

Peter grimaced. 'That's a shame, but I'm not

surprised.' He exchanged a knowing look with Beryl but said no more.

It was a very busy few days for all of them. Even Beryl was kept fully occupied helping Eve to keep the workers fed and watered, never mind attending to the farm animals too.

'I don't know how you do it,' Beryl said, wiping the sweat from her forehead after helping Eve to deal with a particularly awkward cow at milking time, when the menfolk were still busy in the fields late into the evening.

'What? Milk Buttercup? I can teach you, if you like.'

'Yes, please. I'd like to feel I can help out on the farm as well as keep house for Mr Frank, though,' she added with a wry smile, 'I don't want to tread on Mrs Carter's toes.'

'As long as you don't encroach on the dairy work you'll be fine.' Eve laughed. 'She's not one for getting her hands mucky.'

'Which brings me back to what I meant. How on earth do you stay looking so glamorous?'

'Kind of you to say so, love. It's just a bit of extra trouble morning and night. That's all. I've no patience with these young girls who take hours in front of a mirror. I use face cream at night and curl my hair in rags and then, in the morning, I have the same make-up routine and it only takes me ten minutes to apply. I'm well practised.'

'Well, you always look lovely.'

'So do you, Beryl, love. You've lovely smooth skin that doesn't need much help, if any, and your hair's so pretty. Is it naturally curly?'

Beryl nodded.

'Then you're lucky. Mine is too but, as I'm a redhead, it can be a bit wild and woolly. It needs taming into these neat curls.'

When Beryl took baskets of food and drink out to the fields, Peter always found time to sit with her and Jamie while he ate.

'You're getting brown,' Beryl murmured, admiring his smooth skin glistening in the summer sun.

'It's good to be out in the open air again. Oh, we do a lot of square-bashing and plenty of cross-country running, but it's not the same as knowing your efforts actually mean something.' He glanced into the pram where Jamie lay beneath a sunshade, sleeping blissfully.

'He's growing, isn't he? He'll be trying to crawl soon, I shouldn't wonder.'

'Mr Frank has said that once harvest is over, he's going to make him a play pen in the corner of the kitchen so that when I'm busy, Jamie'll be safe.'

'What a good idea.' Peter sighed. 'Beryl, I have to leave early tomorrow morning. I'll come to the house to say goodbye before I go home tonight.'

Beryl nodded, unable to speak for the lump building in her throat.

By the middle of September, when all Frank's harvest had been gathered in and those of the other local farmers too, a Harvest Festival service was held at the church in the town.

'All the produce given to make a grand display is afterwards distributed to those most in need in the area,' Frank told her. 'Sadly, there are quite a lot now with the war taking menfolk away from their families. You will come with us, won't you?'

Beryl stared at him in horror. 'Oh Mr Frank, please don't ask me. I don't want to disappoint you, but I – I can't. I really can't face all the stares and the whispering.'

'You'll be with us. With the family.'

'I know, but not even you can stop the gossip.' She bit her tongue to stop herself adding, 'Not while Phyllis Carter is around.'

'You'll have to brave it sometime, lass. You ought to have the little chap christened before too long, you know.'

'That doesn't have to be public though, does it? Wouldn't the rector do that in private, if we asked him?'

'Yes, he might if I ask him. But Jamie's nearly six months old already. You ought to be thinking about it very soon.'

'I will, I promise I will, but please – don't make me go to the Harvest Festival.' Beryl's face was screwed up with anxiety. 'I'd do anything for you, Mr Frank, you know that, and if you're adamant, then I – I'll do it, but . . .'

'Don't look so worried, love.' Frank smiled at her. 'I'm not going to try to make you go. But give Jamie's christening some thought, will you? Just for me, eh? That'd be a start, wouldn't it? And like you say, we could probably get it done privately.'

Beryl relaxed. 'Yes, I will. I promise I'll do that.'

He was disappointed, but Frank was wise enough

not to push her. She was doing very well. She not only did the housework and cooked him some lovely meals but she was also working around the farm now and again. He was surprised that a city girl like her had taken so well to rural life. She seemed happy enough and he didn't want her to take flight if he tried to force her to do something she really didn't want to do. Frank was a great believer in the notion that time would sort things out. So, that was what he would give her. Maybe something would happen that would bring her back into the fold, so to speak. Frank had a deep faith and he would leave the matter in the hands of the Almighty.

Forty-Five

During the final months of 1943, the feeling of cautious optimism remained.

'I believe the tide began to turn in our favour with Monty's victory at El Alamein about this time last year,' Eddie remarked to his brother-in-law, Harold, as they came out of church one Sunday morning at the end of November.

'I think you're right,' Harold agreed thoughtfully. 'And now Italy has capitulated to the Allies . . .'

'And actually declared war on Germany.'

'It's alleged that the Germans are treating them appallingly. There are reports of some dreadful reprisals against the Italians, if the papers are to be believed.'

'There'll be some truth in them, I've no doubt. But it's war, Harold. I've always said – and Lilian will back me up on this – that it's not the ordinary German folk who wanted this war, nor, I'm guessing, the Italians, any more than we did.'

'I agree with you. You know old man Fairbrother, who farms the other side of Spilsby?'

Eddie nodded.

'Well, I meet up with him at market sometimes and he says he's got two Italian POWs working on his farm and they're fine fellows. Hard workers, honest and polite and, just as our chaps must be, they're missing their families and desperately worried about them. They haven't got a good word to say for Hitler. Or Mussolini, if it comes to that.'

With the news at the end of November of the first meeting in Tehran of the Big Three – Churchill, Roosevelt and Stalin – hopes really began to rise that a concerted effort against the enemy would bring about the invasion of France by Britain and America the following year, with Russia playing its part from the east.

Neither Carolyn nor Peter would be able to get home for Christmas, but Carolyn managed a forty-eight-hour pass at the beginning of December.

'Things are a lot better at Beaumanor now,' she told Beryl when they could snatch a few moments alone. 'The ATS girls we're getting now are so much better trained than we were and we're beginning to outnumber the EWAs. We're able to man over a hundred and thirty sets, twenty-four hours a day now. And I think, at last, we've been accepted.' She laughed. 'Though that's possibly because we out-number the civilians now. And because so many of us have become adept at recognizing certain operators on particular frequencies, they're letting us handle our own stations. It's much better.' She sighed and then lowered her voice. It had been instilled in them all that secrets must be kept and even telling Beryl now felt a little wrong. 'You won't say anything to anyone the things I tell you, will you?'

'Of course not. I'm still bound by the Official

Secrets Act.' Beryl pulled a face. 'Actually, I expect we will be for the rest of our lives. Go on.'

'Now things are going badly for the Germans we're getting more and more messages in plain language. Usually when they're in a panic about an air raid or something. Bill picked up one recently saying that fires were raging. He knows a bit of German.'

'And how is Bill?' Beryl asked archly.

'Same as always. He's taking me to the Annual Christmas Party at the end of the month.'

'He's a nice man. I know he's a bit older than you but—'

'There's nothing doing there, Beryl. Look, I'll tell you, but he doesn't want it to get around Beaumanor.'

Beryl laughed. 'I'm hardly likely to spread gossip, am I? I'm not even there and the only person I have contact with now is you.'

'Bill is married.'

Beryl blinked and then frowned. 'So why is that a dark secret?'

'His wife – she's a bit younger than him – is in the Wrens and she doesn't want anyone to know she is married.'

'She wouldn't get discharged though, not just for being married, would she?'

'I'm not sure. I do know that if she got pregnant she'd have to leave.'

Beryl grimaced. 'Don't I know it.'

'Sorry,' Carolyn said contritely, but Beryl only shrugged.

'It happened.' She paused and then added, a little wistfully, 'I do miss it, you know. Even the long night hours when nothing much was happening, but we couldn't leave our sets in case we missed something. Oh don't get me wrong, Carolyn. I wouldn't be without Jamie now for the world and your family have been so wonderfully kind, but just now and again I miss my time at Beaumanor.'

'I bet you don't miss the awful static and interference, or the jamming the enemy sends out deliberately to try to stop us listening to their messages, or when they change frequency suddenly and we have to try to follow them so as not to miss the message.'

'Even all that sometimes. We were all in it together and we still managed to have some fun, didn't we?'

Carolyn nodded. She didn't want to upset her friend by saying that they still had a lot of fun there despite the gruelling work, the changing shift patterns that played havoc with their sleep, and the cold in the winter. But Beryl was more perceptive than Carolyn gave her credit for. 'I do hope you're still having fun, though I'll be terribly put out if anyone gets as close to you as I was.'

Carolyn laughed. 'No one could ever take your place, Beryl, believe me.'

Now Beryl beamed.

Neither Carolyn nor Peter were home for Christmas and Phyllis refused to sit at the same table as Beryl, so it was a depleted family gathering at the farm.

'I really don't know what's the matter with the woman,' Frank said as he carved the goose. 'Still, it's her loss.'

'It's our fault – mine and Jamie's,' Beryl said apologetically. 'We shouldn't be here . . .'

'Now, you sit right where you are, lass. I'm still in charge in me own house and I say who'll sit at my table.' He cast a quick glance at Lilian. She had condescended to join the rest of the family and she was civil towards Beryl, though she did not make a fuss of Jamie. But Tom and Adam more than made up for it. They kept the little boy amused for the afternoon until Jamie's eyelids drooped and Beryl took him upstairs for an afternoon nap.

'Right, Grandad,' Adam said, 'you sit by the fire. Me and Tom will see to the animals. High time he got some good, fresh air into his lungs,' Adam added, teasing his cousin.

By arrangement with George Fox, Tom had most of the day off, although he would be on duty again at six o'clock that evening for four hours while George then took a break.

Just before the families returned to their own homes, Frank filled everyone's glass and said, 'I'd like to make a toast. I know it's a week early, but here's hoping that 1944 will be a better year for all of us and bring an end to this wretched war.'

'Amen to that,' they all murmured and raised their glasses.

And then, in February, lambing time began again.

'There's always something happening on a farm, isn't there?' Beryl said happily. 'No time to mope.'

Jamie was now crawling and even starting to pull himself up to stand. As he'd promised, Frank

390

had built him a play pen in one corner of the kitchen.

'That'll keep him safe when you're busy, lass. I don't want any accidents with the little chap. Now, can you make me some sandwiches and a flask of strong tea, love. I think I'm going to be up most of tonight. It seems several ewes have decided to drop their lambs all together and there's one who always has a bit of trouble. I don't want to leave her.'

'You shouldn't be sitting up all night in a draughty barn, Mr Frank. Can't Mr Harold or Adam do it? Or even one of the land girls could sit with her and come and fetch you if you were needed.'

'Harold and Adam work hard enough in the day.'

'So do you,' Beryl retorted, greatly daring.

Frank chuckled. 'Now don't you dare say "for a man of your age".'

'I wasn't going to, but now you mention it . . .'

They smiled at each other with the warmth of their mutual growing affection.

'Of course I'll do it, and I'll come out now and again to make sure you're all right.'

'Don't disturb your sleep on account of me.'

But Beryl only laughed. 'And you think I get a full night's sleep with a ten-month-old?'

Carolyn got a forty-eight-hour pass in February and came home with exciting news.

'You'll never guess what?' she said as she sat on the floor playing with Jamie.

'Probably not, so go on, tell me.'

'The Yanks have arrived in our area now.'

Beryl's mouth dropped open as she stared at Carolyn. 'Where? At Beaumanor?'

Carolyn shook her head. 'No, they're camped – in tents mostly – in the grounds of the manor house in Quorn.'

Beryl sat down slowly, her eyes wide with questions. 'And is it true what they say about them?'

Carolyn laughed. 'With some, yes, but mostly they're lovely. They're very smart in their uniforms, very courteous and always handing out chocolates and sweets to the local kids. Especially chewing gum.'

'I bet all the local girls are around them like bees around honey.'

'Well, you can't blame them. A lot of our lads are away. Mind you, those who are at home are so jealous, you wouldn't believe.'

'Are there many fights?'

'A few in the pubs – when they've all had too much to drink, but the American military police soon arrive and break it up. On the whole, they've been made very welcome. A lot of the villagers invite them for a meal or do some washing for them. And, of course, they come to all the local dances.' Carolyn giggled. 'They're teaching us all to jitterbug.'

'To what?'

'It's a dance that's all the rage in America. Very lively, but it's great fun.'

Beryl tried to swallow her envy. 'And have you been out with anyone?'

'We go out as a group, usually. There's one really nice guy I dance with quite a lot, but I don't want it to get serious. They're not likely to be with us for very long. But he's a long way from home and missing his family.'

'They must be here for a reason,' Beryl murmured. 'Do you think an invasion of Europe is being planned?'

'I wouldn't be at all surprised, but we don't *know* anything.'

'No, it'll all be kept very hush-hush.'

They talked for over two hours until Jamie began to whimper.

'He'll be hungry. I must get him his tea and see to Mr Frank's meal too. Sorry, Carolyn. It's been lovely to hear all your news but I must get on now.'

Carolyn kissed her cheek. 'Take care of yourself and keep an eye on Grandad for me, won't you? He's looking very tired.'

'It's the lambing. He insists on doing his share, but he's up half the night sometimes.'

Carolyn shook her head. 'It's too much at his age.'

Beryl laughed wryly. 'Well, you try stopping him.'

'I would, if I thought he'd take any notice.'

'Don't worry. I'll look after him, I promise.'

Back at Beaumanor, life was even more hectic than it ever had been. The social life of the ATS girls soon became one long round of dancing, cycling, walking or just going to the local pubs – all with the GIs. Even Noreen, who had adamantly declared she was being faithful to her English boyfriend, was swept into the arms of a tall, handsome, dark-haired Yank and seemed to walk about in a dream. Only when sitting in front of her set did she concentrate fully and do her job as well as she always had done.

'Noreen, love, I don't want to pry,' Carolyn said carefully, 'but are things serious between you and this Joe?'

To her surprise, Noreen burst into tears. 'Oh Carolyn, it's awful. I so wanted to remain true to Alan, but – but – Joe is just wonderful.'

'You do know they won't be here very long, don't you?'

'Yes,' she whispered. 'Joe told me as much. He thinks they're here in readiness for the build-up to the invasion.'

'I expect he's right.'

'I haven't – I mean – nothing's happened between us. He's a real gentleman, but he – he has said that if he survives the war, he will come back for me.' Her voice rose to a wail. 'He – he's asked me to *marry* him.'

'You don't mean now?'

'No – no, when it's all over.'

'Then don't worry about it. Thing's will work out.'

'But what about Alan? I feel so awful about him.'

'There wasn't anything really definite between you, was there? I mean, you weren't secretly engaged, were you?'

'Oh no, nothing like that. We've just been writing to each other, that's all.'

'Every week?'

'Oh no, only about once a month.'

'Doesn't sound a very hot romance to me.'

'No,' Noreen said, calming down, 'I don't suppose it does.'

'Then carry on as you are. Just enjoy yourself, but don't get pregnant.'

Noreen sighed. 'No, I won't do that. You know,' she added thoughtfully, 'I always tried to be nice to Beryl, though I was a bit – well – disappointed in her, but now I have to admit I can understand how she felt. It's – it's very hard to not get carried away when you believe you're truly in love.'

'Well, mind you don't. He's American and however nice he is, he'll be gone soon and he might not come back for whatever reason. Now, come on, cheer up. We're on duty in twenty minutes and the troop carrier will be waiting.'

Forty-Six

The banging on the back door startled Lilian. 'Oh no, not the police again,' she whispered and hurried to open the door.

It was not the police; it was Beryl. Lilian stared at her and then her glance went beyond the young woman to the pram standing just behind her.

'I'm sorry, Mrs Holmes. I got here as fast as I could. It's Mr Frank . . .'

'Dad? What's happened?'

'He's had some sort of seizure.'

'Oh my! I'll come at once.'

'There's no need. I telephoned for an ambulance. They've taken him to the local hospital.'

'Then I must tell Harold.'

'I think he'll know by now. Aunty Eve will have told him. I went there first.'

'Why? You should have fetched me.'

'Her place is nearer and I thought Mr Harold might be there, but he wasn't. That's why Aunty Eve has gone to look for him.'

At that moment the baby in the pram began to whimper. 'I'd best be getting back,' Beryl said and turned away.

'Wait a minute, I'll come with you. If Harold

decides to go to the hospital, I want to go with him. Can you just hang on a minute until I get my hat and coat? Oh, and I'd better leave a note for Tom and Eddie for when they get home. I've no idea how long I might be.'

Beryl hesitated for a moment but then said, 'If – if you want to leave a message for them both to come to the farm, when they get home, I can cook tea for them. Then you won't have to worry about staying at the hospital as long as you need to.'

Lilian stared at her. 'That's – very thoughtful of you. I won't be a moment.'

As they walked back along the rutted lanes to the farm, Lilian said, 'Tell me exactly what happened.'

'He'd been up all night with a ewe that he told me always has difficulty lambing. I – I tried to tell him he shouldn't be doing that but . . .' She sighed. 'Anyway, this morning, he ate all his breakfast just as usual and then sat down in his chair to put his boots on to go out to the barn again. The ewe had had her lamb in the night and he just wanted to go and make sure she was all right before catching some sleep. And then suddenly he just fell forward out of his chair onto the hearth rug. I put him on his side and put a blanket over him and telephoned for the ambulance. They weren't long in getting to us and they said they thought he'd had what they called apoplexy.'

'I think that's how his own father died,' Lilian murmured. 'Maybe it runs in families. I don't know.'

When they got back to the farm, Harold, Eve and Adam were standing in the yard.

'We thought you'd come back with Beryl,' Harold said. 'Shall you and me take the truck, Lilian, and go to the hospital?'

Lilian nodded.

Harold glanced at Beryl and gave her one of his rare smiles. 'Thanks, lass. I reckon your quick thinking could've saved his life. Good job you was here. If he hadn't been found for hours . . .'

He left the words hanging in the air, but his meaning was clear.

Moments later, as the truck drew out of the yard and headed towards the town, Eve murmured, 'He's right, you know, Beryl. If you hadn't been here, he might not have been found yet.'

'Mrs Carter would have been here by now.'

'Funny you should say that, Beryl, because she isn't.'

'What?'

'Here. She's not arrived yet. Milking's all done. The land girls have done it as usual and the milk's all in the dairy, but there's no sign of Phyllis.'

'Then I'd better see to it,' Beryl said. 'We don't want all his precious milk going to waste, do we?'

'I'll help you, lass, but first I need a good strong cup of tea with plenty of sugar. And so, by the look of you, do you.'

'Thank you, Aunty Eve. That'd be lovely. I'll just see to Jamie and then we'll make a start in the dairy together.'

Frank was in hospital for two weeks and came home during the first week in March.

'Do you think you can manage him, Beryl?' Eve

asked, the day before Frank was due to be discharged. 'He could come to us, but I haven't got the room now with the land army girls staying with us. He could go to Lilian's, but he doesn't want to. I've asked him.'

'Oh we'll be fine,' Beryl said. 'It'll be lovely to have him home. It's so nice his speech has come back, isn't it?' She'd been to see Frank twice during his stay in the hospital. She would have liked to have gone more frequently, but he was only allowed two visitors at a time and, as the visiting times were restricted, there were family who wanted to see him too. But she'd been delighted to see him sitting up in bed and talking almost normally. His speech was clear, but he spoke more slowly than usual, seeming to think about each word before he uttered it. 'How's his walking? Do you know?'

'One arm is a bit weak,' Eve said, 'but he can walk quite well, although the nurse told us that he shuffles a bit and ought to have a stick just at first to help with his balance. We don't want him falling.'

Peter came home on leave the weekend after Frank came home from the hospital. He sat on the opposite side of the hearth to talk to the man he had known and liked for the whole of his life.

'Now then, Mr Frank, how are you?'

'A-one, lad.'

Peter hid his smile. That had always been Mr Frank's response to enquiries after his health. Obviously, it wasn't quite true this time, but he admired the old man's spirit.

'And it's all thanks to young Beryl,' Frank added.

'If she hadn't been here and acted quickly, I daren't think what might have happened. The doc was telling me that the sooner you get into hospital with these things, the better the recovery you make. So, Peter, how are things with you? Like the army life, do you?'

'Not particularly, Mr Frank, but I felt I had to do my duty. I miss working on the farm.'

'Well, there'll always be a job for you here, lad, as long as I'm still in charge.' His eyes twinkled. Peter could see that, despite his illness, he had not lost his sense of fun.

'Thank you. That's good to know.'

'And have you any other plans when all this nonsense is over and you come back home?'

Peter grinned at him. 'I want to ask Beryl to marry me, Mr Frank.'

'Ah, now that is good news. Does she know?'

Peter shook his head. 'Not yet.'

'Then don't let the grass grow under your feet.'

'It's just . . .' Peter hesitated, feeling he was about to be disloyal, and yet Mr Frank was perhaps the only person he could confide in. 'My mother. She hates Beryl with a vengeance. We won't be able to live with her.'

'Aye, I do know a bit about that,' Frank said, but he did not elaborate. He didn't want to add to the lad's troubles, though there was a way he could perhaps help him. 'You can always live here after you're married, Peter. Beryl has self-contained accommodation at the side of the house, as you know. And there are still rooms in my part of the house that I'm not using. We could make it bigger for you, if necessary, though Lilian and Eddie lived there for about three years. You won't remember that, of course. I'm not even sure that Carolyn does.'

Peter stared at him, but now Frank chuckled softly. 'And, of course, I do have an ulterior motive. I've grown fond of both Beryl and her bairn – very fond – and now it seems that I am not safe to be left on my own for very long. So you see, you'd both be doing me a huge favour. I don't want to live with either of my children. I still want to be master in my own house. Well . . .' He laughed aloud now. 'My bit of it anyway.'

'I don't know what to say, Mr Frank.'

'Say "yes" lad, as I hope Beryl will too. And if you take an old man's advice, you'll get married as soon as you can.'

'I'd been thinking about that too,' Peter said slowly. 'You see, if we were married and anything happened to me, I'm pretty sure she'd get some sort of army pension as my widow.' He paused and then added dolefully, 'It'll upset my mother though.'

'I made a will a few years back, just after me wife died. Her going made me think, you see, and I thought I ought to have everything written down so there could be no arguments,' Frank confided. 'It didn't please everybody, of course. I don't think wills ever do. I've left the farm and the farmhouse to Harold and then to young Adam, and Lilian's house and a bit of land around it – about ten acres – to her and her family. The house that Harold lives in at the moment and the house you and your mother live in are both part of the farm, of course, but I have

401

stipulated that your mother should live in her cottage for the rest of her life. I couldn't leave it to you for life, Peter, I hope you understand that, but if you come back to work here, I am sure that Harold would let you rent the house he's living in now, because at that point he'll likely move into this farmhouse.'

Now Peter really was lost for words. It was a few moments before he said hoarsely, 'That's incredibly generous of you, Mr Frank. I really don't know how to thank you, especially where my mother is concerned.'

'She can be a bit difficult, Peter, there's no denying that, but your dad worked on this farm for my dad and for me before he went off to the last war – and more recently, of course, you too – so I won't see yar mam homeless. And also, it leaves you free to do what you want with your own life. I'd be delighted to have you back here after the war, but if you decide you want to spread your wings, I wouldn't blame you.'

'I want to come back here, Mr Frank. It's home. Though . . .' He hesitated.

'Go on,' Frank prompted.

'I'm not sure how Beryl will feel about staying here. She's a city girl, after all.'

'There's one way to find out, lad. Ask her.'

Forty-Seven

At Beaumanor, the hard work continued. Conditions were a little better. The girls were now allowed to wear battle dress to work, which was a lot warmer during the winter, and they still wore as much warm underwear as they could get beneath their outer garments. The fingerless gloves that Carolyn had introduced were a godsend.

'You can't operate with ordinary gloves,' Noreen remarked, 'but these work a treat.'

'Thank my grandad,' Carolyn laughed. 'He's always worn them about the farm in winter.'

Noreen eyed her speculatively. 'I still think there's something going on between you and Bill that you're not telling us.'

'We're just mates, all working together in a common cause.'

'Doesn't stop romances, though, does it? And he was your "knight in shining armour" that time.'

'We're just good friends, that's all.'

Noreen sniffed. 'I don't believe you.'

Carolyn shrugged. 'I've been just friends with a lad before. Peter at home. Our mothers wanted us to get married, but we didn't feel like that about each other.'

Noreen said no more but she eyed her as if she didn't believe a word.

Peter arranged with Beryl that he'd come over the following afternoon and they'd go for a walk, taking Jamie with them. The afternoon was warm and bright for early March. Peter took charge of the pram over the rough ground.

As they walked, Peter summoned up his courage. 'Beryl, are you happy here?'

'Deliriously. I never thought I could be so happy again, not after – you know. I'm just dreading the day when I'll have to leave.'

'Well, there would be a way that you wouldn't have to.'

Beryl glanced at him. 'I don't understand.'

Peter ran his hands through his hair. 'Oh, I'm not putting this very well.' He stopped pushing the pram and turned to face her, taking both her hands in his. 'Beryl, you must know I've fallen in love with you. I don't know how you feel about me, but will you marry me?'

'Oh Peter, I love you too. You're the most wonderful man I've ever met, but I can't possibly marry you. It wouldn't do.' Tears sprang to her eyes as she turned down the only chance of happiness she might ever have. 'Your mother hates me and I wouldn't want to come between a man and his mother. There's a saying that you don't marry your husband's or wife's family, but you do.' She shrugged and added bitterly, 'Of course, you wouldn't have to worry about mine. They've thrown me out and won't have anything more to do with me because of what I did. But your mother's here and – and you're all she's got. You can't – you mustn't – hurt her like that.'

'Darling Beryl, from the day I decided to volunteer for the army, I determined that from that moment on I would live my own life. If – if I tell you something, will you give me your word that you won't ever tell another soul?'

Beryl smiled tremulously through her tears. 'I'm very good at keeping secrets. It's all the training we had.'

Sidetracked for a moment, Peter said, 'Actually, you've never told me what you did. I know you were in the ATS alongside Carolyn, but . . .'

Already Beryl was shaking her head. 'I can't tell you anything, Peter. All I'll say is that Carolyn and I were doing the same job and we both had to sign the Official Secrets Act.' She paused and then, although she was sure she already knew the answer, added, 'Has she told you anything?'

Peter smiled. 'Not a word.'

'There you are, then.'

There was silence between them before Peter took the plunge. 'It was Mr Harold who encouraged me to volunteer.'

'Mr Harold? Now you do surprise me, unless . . .'

'Go on.'

'Well, I just wondered if you were a bit of a threat to his son, Adam.'

'In what way?'

'On the farm. Taking his job.'

'No, I don't think that's the case. There's enough work for the four of us. Three, as Mr Frank steps back a bit and, bless him, he'll have to now.'

Beryl giggled. 'He's itching to get back outside. I have a real job with him sometimes to make him stay put. I nearly have to tie him into his chair. I've threatened to do it once or twice, but only as a joke, of course. But go on. What happened?'

'We were in the pub we used to go to on a Saturday night in town and the group of lads we usually met were in a funny sort of mood. I think it was all to do with the war. The main topic of conversation was should they volunteer or wait to be called up. Most of them weren't in reserved occupations like I was and knew they would have to go eventually. One of the ideas being bandied about was that if they volunteered at the beginning they'd have a chance of getting into whatever service they preferred. You know – army, air force or navy. And then their discussions got a bit – well – personal.' He paused, remembering the banter that had become barbed. 'One of them said directly to me, "Well, you won't be going, will you, Peter? Mummy's boy will be safely at home ploughin' an' sowin' an' reapin' an' hoein'."'

'That's horrible.'

'On the way home, Mr Harold said, "Look, lad, I'm not telling you that you should go. I don't want that on my conscience if you didn't come back. And there's a lot that won't, but don't let yar mam run your life. If she and our Lilian had their way, you'd be married to Carolyn by now and I'm proud of you both that you've stood up to them." And then he went on to say that I should stand up to me mam in other ways too. He said that she'd always have her cottage, but that didn't mean that I had to stay in it with her, nor did I have to follow the life she'd mapped out for me if I didn't want to. "Be a man, Peter," he said. "Plough your own furrow." So that's what I'm doing. I joined up and I don't regret that for a minute. I'm seeing another side of life and it's making me appreciate what I've got here to come back to.' He hesitated a moment, not wanting to add 'if I do come back'. 'And also, I intend to marry the woman I love and that, Beryl darling, is you. And now you've said you love me too, then I won't take "no" for an answer.'

'You really mean it, don't you?' she whispered.

'I do. And before you ask, I love little Jamie too and he will always be treated just as if he were mine. I will never ask you about his biological father, because I don't want to know. From now on, he's mine. After we're married, we'll change his surname to Carter.'

'But – but then everyone will think you *are* his father.'

Peter grinned. 'That is exactly what I want.'

'But – your mother?'

'She'll come round eventually. And if she doesn't . . .' He shrugged his shoulders. 'Then it will be her loss.'

'If you're really sure, then, yes, I would love to marry you.'

Peter took her in his arms and kissed her long and

hard until a whimper from the pram made them reluctantly pull apart.

Peter left it to Beryl to make arrangements so that they could be married as soon as possible. He didn't tell her the whole reason he wanted to tie the knot so quickly; he let her believe it was for her sake and the baby's. In truth, back at camp, there was a feeling in the air that an invasion of Europe couldn't be so very far away now. Rumours were rife that there was a build-up of troops, transport, arms and ammunition and increased activity on the South Coast.

'They'll want to wait until there's the hope of decent weather though,' the soldiers agreed amongst themselves. 'And it'll take some organizing and, of course, we'll have to do it jointly with the Yanks.'

And so Peter wanted a ring safely on Beryl's finger and arrangements made for her to receive the majority of his army pay before he was plunged into actual fighting. He was not being pessimistic or morbid, just practical and facing reality. And he knew too that he would be granted special leave to get married. Several of his pals had already done so.

The night before he was due to go back to camp, when he had said goodbye to Beryl, he sat down with his mother and told her what was going to happen. Phyllis, as he had expected, turned white and then colour flooded her face as anger took over. 'You're not serious, Peter. Tell me you're not.'

'I've never been more serious about anything in my life, Mam.'

'You really expect me to welcome that little slut

as my daughter-in-law and treat her little bastard as my grandson?'

'I would like you to do just that, Mam, but if you feel so strongly . . .'

'I suppose you want to bring them here? Into *my* house?'

'No, we don't. Mr Frank has already offered us a home with him.'

Now Phyllis's mouth fell open. 'Mr – Mr Frank has encouraged you to ruin your life?'

'No.' Peter kept his tone calm, though he was having difficulty in keeping a lid on his own rising temper. 'He's helping us out, that's all. And he's glad to have company in the house, especially after what has just happened.'

'Oh, that little slut has wormed her way in there good and proper, hasn't she? I'll see what Lilian has to say about all this. She'll soon make her father see sense and put a stop to it.'

'Despite his illness, Mr Frank is still his own man. He made the offer and I accepted it.'

'After all I've done for him.' Tears of self-pity rolled down her cheeks now. 'What about me? How will I live? I suppose she'll get all your pay, won't she, and a widow's pension if . . . ?' Even Phyllis shied away from speaking about what could happen.

'Mr Frank has told me that you have this cottage and the little bit of land that goes with it for life. You have my father's war pension and you'll still have your work in the dairy for as long as you can manage it.'

'But what about when I'm old and can't work? What then?'

'Mr Frank would never see you go short and nor would Beryl.'

Phyllis's anger rose again as she shook her fist at him. 'I'd sooner die than accept one penny piece from *her*.'

If his mother had hoped to shake her son's decision, she was disappointed. It only served to harden his resolve.

Forty-Eight

'I'm not putting up with it, Lilian, and I'd like your help.' Phyllis had marched across the fields to Lilian's cottage, still in high dudgeon.

Peter had left that morning, refusing to discuss the matter any further and with the parting shot to his mother, 'We'll be getting married in about a month, so it's up to you whether or not you come to the wedding.'

'We've always been friends, haven't we?' Phyllis went on to Lilian now.

Lilian cast her a quizzical look, but said nothing.

'And our dearest wish was to see my Peter and your Carolyn get wed, wasn't it? Now, I'm asking you to talk to your dad and make him see sense. He's been egging them both on.' She went on at great length about Frank's involvement in what she saw as a plot to thwart her. She fell silent at last, ending, 'Well, will you help me?'

For a moment, Lilian said nothing, as she fiddled nervously with her apron. 'Phyllis,' she said at last, 'you're putting me in a very difficult position.'

'Why?' Phyllis snapped.

'To put it bluntly, if Beryl hadn't been staying at the farm, she wouldn't have been there when Dad was taken ill; it's unlikely he would have survived. Her quick thinking more than likely saved his life. I can't forget that, Phyllis. I owe her a lot.'

'You owe that little slut nothing. He'd have been found. Mr Harold goes across every morning and I'd've been there too, because I'd've still been doing his housework if *she* hadn't been there.'

'But that would have been at least a couple of hours later. The hospital said he's only made such a good recovery because he was taken in very quickly.'

Phyllis glared at Lilian. 'You should have had an old man like him living here with you. I don't know why you haven't insisted on it years ago.'

Lilian gave a wry laugh. 'You don't *insist* on anything with my father. You should know that, Phyllis.'

'So, you're refusing to help me, are you?'

'I – er – yes, I suppose I am.'

Phyllis's face twisted into ugly resentment. 'Can't you understand how I feel about Peter – my Peter – marrying a girl like her?'

'He's a grown man, Phyllis, and a courageous one who's gone to fight for his country. Can't *you* see that you ought to let him lead his own life, but still love him enough to pick up the pieces if it goes wrong? To be honest with you, this war has taught me a lot. I'm trying very hard – even though it is difficult – to let my children make their own decisions. Just like you, I wanted Carolyn and Peter to get married, but I'm coming to the conclusion – reluctantly, I have to admit – that we were wrong. Youngsters should be allowed to decide for themselves. Oh, we can give them advice, of course, but it should be up to them whether or not they take it.'

Phyllis flopped into a chair and tears rolled down her face. 'Nobody understands me. I've worked hard all my life to bring Peter up on my own, to do the very best I can for him. His father was selfish – going off to war to play the hero when he needn't have done. Your father would have kept him on the farm, but no, off he had to go and get himself killed.'

'I know, love, and you've done a grand job. Peter is a fine young man, but now you've got to let him be that man. You've got to let him make his own choices. If you don't, Phyllis, you'll lose him, because – and I'm sorry to say it – he will choose the girl he's fallen in love with over his mother any day of the week.'

'He already *is*,' Phyllis wailed. 'He says Beryl's going to arrange a wedding as soon as possible.'

'And you'll go.'

It was a statement rather than a question, but Phyllis answered, 'No. I can't.'

'No, Phyllis, you misunderstand me. You *will* go to their wedding because I am going to make sure you do. If you don't, you'll regret it for the rest of your life that you didn't see your only son – your only child – get married.'

'But why her? Why does he have to pick a whore?'

'That's a little unfair, Phyllis. The lass made one mistake . . .'

'How do you know that?' Phyllis snapped back, regaining some of her vigour. 'You don't know how many men she went with besides the one who got her pregnant.'

'Maybe she thought she was in a long-term romance . . .'

'Like you did, you mean?' Phyllis said vindictively.

Lilian winced, but all she said was, 'Times are so different now with all the young men going off to war. They want to feel there's someone at home waiting for them when they come back.'

'And if – if they don't come back?'

'I'm guessing that Peter wants to be sure that Beryl has some security.'

'What about *my* security, if all his money goes to her? What about *me?*'

Her words hung in the air between them and even to both women they sounded selfish and self-centred. At last Lilian said quietly, 'My family would always see you right, Phyllis. You should know that.'

'So,' Frank said, 'there's going to be a wedding, is there? That'll be two celebrations, won't it?'

Beryl gaped at him.

'The little chap's first birthday. I do hope you haven't forgotten that, because I haven't.'

Beryl blushed a little. 'No, no, of course I haven't and I've to arrange the wedding as soon as I can, Peter said.'

'Good idea. Now, you go and see the rector in town and tell him I sent you. Be sure to tell him Frank Atkinson sent you. But be honest with him. Tell him you have a babby.'

'He'll refuse to marry us – me – won't he?'

'I doubt it. Even men of the cloth have to understand what unusual times we're living in. He might
want you to go and see him a few times before the
service, but if he does, you go. Do whatever he asks
you to.'

That afternoon, leaving the baby with Eve, Beryl
went into town and knocked hesitantly on the door
of the rectory near the church. The door was opened
by a silver-haired man with bright, kindly eyes and
a welcoming smile. 'Come in, my dear. Frank's just
been on the telephone to me, so I knew to expect
you.'

Beryl stepped nervously inside and followed the
rector to his study. 'Do sit down. Now, I understand
from Frank – we are old friends, by the way – that
you want to be married fairly quickly before your
husband-to-be is likely to be sent abroad.'

'Yes, sir,' Beryl whispered, awed by her surroundings and the elderly gentleman sitting in front of her.

'We might have to get you a special licence, but
that shouldn't present a problem. Have you both
been christened?'

'I don't know about Peter, but I haven't.'

The man's smile broadened. 'I happen to know
that Peter was christened in this church because I
performed the ceremony myself. It would be a good
idea for you to be christened, too, before your
marriage. Is there someone who would stand as a
godparent for you? We only need one, as you're an
adult.'

'Perhaps Aunty Eve – I mean, Mrs Atkinson –
would.' Beryl drew in a deep breath. 'There – there's

something I should tell you. You might not want to marry us. I – I have a baby and it's not Peter's.'

The rector regarded her kindly as he asked softly, 'And Peter knows this?'

'Oh yes. You see, I was in the ATS and working – well, I can't tell you where I was, it's top secret – and I met this man there. I – I fell for him and I thought he loved me, but when I fell pregnant, he told me he was already married.' Tears filled Beryl's eyes at the memory of that awful time.

'And you didn't know that before?'

'Heavens, no. Oh sorry, I shouldn't say that, should I?'

Reverend Jennings chuckled. 'Don't worry, my dear. I have been known to say it myself on a regular basis.' He paused and then asked, 'Have you been churched since you had the baby?'

Beryl looked blank. 'Er – I don't know what that means.'

'It's just a short ceremony that a woman undertakes after she's given birth. It would be just between the two of us, my dear. No cause for alarm, but, again, it would be nice to do it before you're married.'

'I'll do whatever you say,' Beryl murmured trustingly.

They talked for another half an hour, the rector wanting to reassure himself that Beryl now truly loved Peter and that he, in turn, was willing to accept her baby as his own.

As she got up to leave, Mr Jennings said, 'Leave everything to me, my dear. I'll ring the farm with some dates and times for everything we have to do.

We will have enough time to call the banns and do everything properly. I'm thinking of a date early in April. How does that sound? It would give Peter plenty of time to apply for special leave. And Carolyn too. I'm sure she'll want to be here.'

Beryl walked back home in a trance. She was so lucky. She couldn't believe her life was turning out to be so wonderful, after the terrible mistake she'd made. Now, when she looked at little Jamie, her love for him overflowed and she wouldn't wish it any other way, although, deep down, she wished he had been Peter's child. She smiled as she thought that, one day, she and Peter would have children of their own too. There was only one cloud in her otherwise sunny world: Peter's mother.

'We'll have a little celebration for Jamie's first birthday,' Frank said. 'But I think you'll have to resign yourself to the fact that Peter might not be able to get home for it, because the wedding's only a few days later, isn't it? And I don't think Carolyn will get home for it either. She's applying for special leave for your wedding too, isn't she?'

Beryl nodded and then said shyly, 'I – um – I've been to see the rector a few times, as you know, and we – we thought it would be a good idea to have Jamie christened on the same day as our wedding.'

Beryl's own christening had taken place in a private ceremony the previous week, with just Eve standing in as her godmother.

'Now that *is* a good idea because all our family will be there already,' Frank said. 'Is there anyone you'd like to invite? I'm sure we can put them up.'

Beryl shook her head. 'No, no one. I did ask Noreen – a girl who worked with me and Carolyn – but she can't get leave. But as long as Carolyn's there, I don't mind.'

The wedding, three days after Jamie's first birthday, and followed by his christening, went off very well. It was a relatively quiet affair, with only the Atkinson and Holmes families there and one or two old friends of Peter's. No one came from Beryl's family, even though she had written to tell her mother that she was getting married. She didn't even receive an answer. Carolyn got special leave to support Beryl's side and also because she was to be Jamie's godmother. Luckily, Frank was well enough to escort the bride down the aisle, looking as proud as if she was his own daughter. Eve took charge of Jamie during the service. Outside the church, Eddie's father, Norman, took a few photographs with his prize possession; a box Brownie camera. The guests all went back to the farm where Eve and Beryl had been busy all morning before the service preparing sandwiches and cakes for a buffet wedding breakfast.

'Beryl insisted on helping,' Eve told them as the guests helped themselves, 'even though she should have been pampering herself.' She glanced at the blushing girl. 'But she still looks pretty as a picture, doesn't she?'

It was a merry gathering and everyone present genuinely wished the couple every happiness. There had been only one notable absence from both the service and the wedding breakfast: Phyllis. Despite her best efforts, Lilian had been unable to follow through with her declaration that Peter's mother would be at the wedding.

After the exciting day, Peter moved into the farmhouse to share the rooms which Beryl occupied. He made sure, however, that he visited his mother each day and didn't make a point of moving all his belongings from her house straight away.

'I have to go back, darling,' he whispered as he and Beryl lay in bed together. 'I daren't risk being on a charge, but I can hardly bear to leave you and little Jamie. I'm so glad you arranged to have him christened at the same time. I feel as if he's really mine now.'

They'd only had two nights together, but duty called.

'I know, but you'll come home again whenever you can, won't you?'

'Of course. You know I will.' He didn't want to tell her – because he didn't know for sure yet – that there was a strong possibility that things were building up for an invasion of Europe, probably within the next few weeks, and if there was one, he knew he'd more than likely be going. There was a feeling of tension in the air – of excitement too.

'Summat's up,' as one of his fellow soldiers had said. 'You mark my words, we'll be off soon now. I'll bet you a month's pay we'll be getting our feet back in France very soon now, and not before time.'

*

After Peter had gone, Beryl and Frank fell back into the routine they'd had before. The only difference was that now Beryl proudly sported a shiny wedding ring on her finger. Phyllis carried on with her work in the dairy and rarely came near the house, though gradually she started to cross the yard to sit in the kitchen to drink her morning cup of tea. Few words passed between the two women, though Beryl was aware of Phyllis's eyes watching her all the time. It was unnerving, but the young woman tried to ignore it.

'What are you making?' Phyllis asked one morning as Beryl weighed white pudding rice.

'A rice pudding for tonight's tea.'

'Mr Frank doesn't like rice pudding,' Phyllis said, and then could have bitten off her own tongue. Let the silly girl make it and have Frank refuse it. That would make her look foolish and be a waste of good food too, which Frank wouldn't like.

But Beryl answered smoothly, 'I know, and nor does Jamie. He spits it out if I try to give it to him, but I make it for myself once a week. It's my favourite pudding with a nice thick skin on the top. It cooks lovely in the range oven.'

Phyllis finished her tea, stood up, and nodded to Beryl. Out in the yard, she stood a moment, thinking, then, slowly, she made her way into the barn before returning to the dairy.

Forty-Nine

'Mr Frank, I've got the most awful stomach cramps and I have to keep running out to the privy.'

Frank eyed her carefully. 'You've got red blotches on your face, lass. If it doesn't go away, I'll take you to see the doctor.'

'You're not allowed to drive at the moment, are you?' Beryl winced as another spasm of pain gripped her.

'Then I'll get Harold to take you. We can ring for an appointment first.'

But the unpleasant symptoms lessened over the next few days and Beryl put it out of her mind, at least until the following week when the same thing happened. This time, the diarrhoea was much worse and she suffered two bouts of debilitating vomiting, leaving her weak and shaky. It was as much as she could do to tend Jamie.

'Never mind about getting meals ready, love,' Frank said. 'We won't starve for a day or so and you don't look as if you want to eat anything anyway. Nice bit of ham'll do me.'

'There's some rice pudding left.'

Frank pulled a face. 'I'll give that a miss, if you don't mind. I'd have to be starving to eat that.'

Beryl lay back in the chair and closed her eyes. She could snatch a few minutes; Jamie was asleep in his pram. 'I'll eat it up later when I feel a bit better,' she murmured.

During the night, Beryl felt really ill. She was sick into a bucket at the side of her bed and had to stagger outside in the cold night to the privy. She hardly slept and the following morning looked so ill that Frank was truly alarmed. This was more than just a mild bilious attack now.

'I've got cramps everywhere, not just my stomach,' she said. 'In my legs, my hands, even my feet. The pain is awful.'

'I'm ringing the doctor's surgery and I'll get Harold to take you. You can't go on like this, Beryl. It's happening too often now.'

'But the baby . . .'

'Eve will come across and look after him while Harold takes you. I won't take no for an answer, lass. There's summat wrong.'

Frank hobbled out into the yard with the walking stick he was obliged to use now. He hated it and had threatened to burn it once he could walk unaided again.

Phyllis was just arriving through the gate. She was surprised to see Frank in the yard.

'What is it, Mr Frank?'

'Before you start the dairy work, can you find Mr Harold for me and can you also go to his place and ask Eve to come over.'

'Of course, if you want me to, but can I help? It seems a shame to fetch Mrs Eve across when I'm here.' She came towards Frank with a smile on her face. 'Is it the girl? Is she ill again? Do you want me to look after the baby?'

For a moment, Frank stared at her. Some inner sixth sense was screaming at him not to let Phyllis anywhere near Beryl or the child, though he could not have said exactly why. He was about to ask her to find Harold first, but instead he said, 'Just go and fetch Eve here, please. She'll know where Harold is this morning.'

Without another word, Phyllis turned away, went out of the gate again, and took the lane towards Harold's house. She hurried until she knew Frank could no longer see her, then she slowed her pace. She was thinking quickly. She would allow herself enough time to have gone to Harold's cottage, then to return to tell Frank that she couldn't find either of them.

Once Phyllis had gone, Frank went back into the farmhouse. Beryl was trying valiantly to give Jamie his breakfast, but she kept having to leave him to hurry to the privy. She had strapped him safely in his high chair and the child looked up at Frank with such trust in his blue eyes that the old man's heart turned over. He had become very fond of both the baby and his mother and he was worried out of his mind as to what was wrong with Beryl.

'Now then, little man,' he said, sitting down. 'I'm not a dab hand at this, but let's see if I can help you eat your breakfast, eh?'

Jamie grinned at him and opened his mouth in readiness for the next spoonful. 'There's one thing,

Jamie, I'm pleased to see your mam has made you summat nice and not that awful rice pudding stuff she eats.'

He chatted to the baby until Beryl arrived back looking white-faced and shaking. 'Phyllis has gone to fetch Eve across and find Harold. He'll take you to the doctor's. I'm going to telephone the surgery now and make sure he'll be able to see you this morning.'

Frank hobbled across the kitchen to where the telephone sat on the dresser to make the call, while Beryl tried to help Jamie finish his breakfast. A few moments later, Frank put the receiver down and said, 'He can see you as long as we get there before eleven. He goes out on his rounds then. I asked him if he could come here but he said he couldn't get to us before late afternoon. I want you to be seen sooner than that, lass.'

By the time Beryl had managed to change Jamie and strap him into his pram, she was exhausted and sat down in the chair near the range. She was shivering and every muscle in her body seemed to be aching. At that moment the back door rattled and Phyllis came in.

'I've looked everywhere, Mr Frank, but Mrs Eve isn't in and I've no idea where Mr Harold or Adam are. I didn't even see either of the land girls. I expect they're out in the fields by now, but goodness knows where. It's a huge area to cover.'

Frank couldn't argue with that, but it did help him come to a decision. 'Right, Beryl, get your coat on and bring Jamie. I'll take you in the truck.'

'You're not allowed to drive, Mr Frank,' Phyllis said swiftly, even before Beryl could protest.

'I'm quite capable,' Frank snapped at her.

'Then leave the baby with me.'

'We'll be fine. You've got work in the dairy to do.' He nodded curtly and Phyllis knew herself dismissed. 'Come on, Beryl. We'd best get going.'

Frank was, as he had said, quite capable of driving. It was only his left leg that was still a little weak after his illness, but even that had enough strength to operate the clutch pedal. With Beryl sitting beside him holding Jamie on her lap, he drove out of the yard and took the lane that eventually led them towards the town.

Sitting in the doctor's waiting room, Beryl began to feel waves of nausea attacking her again.

'Mr Frank,' she whispered, 'I feel sick.'

'Just hang on a minute, lass, if you can.' Frank struggled to his feet and went out into the corridor. In a small room near the front door where they had come in he found the doctor's wife sitting behind a desk. She acted as the receptionist for the practice.

'Mrs Johnson, I'm sorry to bother you, but Beryl feels sick. Can you help us?'

'Oh my goodness, of course.' The woman almost leapt to her feet, took a large bowl out of a cupboard, and hurried into the waiting room.

'Here you are, love,' she said, thrusting the bowl towards Beryl and sweeping the baby into her arms in what seemed like one deft movement. Now Beryl gave way thankfully and vomited into the bowl. Thankfully, saving Beryl's embarrassment – she was the last of the doctor's morning patients – there was no one else left in the waiting room.

'I'll show you in now,' Mrs Johnson said.

Leaving the baby with Frank and clutching the bowl, Beryl followed the doctor's wife.

Dr Johnson examined Beryl thoroughly and asked her lots of questions.

He sat down at his desk to write a few notes, while Beryl got dressed again behind a screen. When she emerged, still holding the bowl, he said, kindly, 'Come and sit down. Now, you live on Mr Atkinson's farm, I understand.'

'That's right.'

'Hmm.' He was thoughtful for a moment. 'And do you help around the farm?'

'Sometimes, but mainly I'm in the house. I do all the housework and the cooking.'

'Has anyone else in the household been ill like this?'

Beryl shook her head. 'Only me. There's only me and Mr Frank and my baby, Jamie, at home at the moment. My husband . . .' She paused over the word, feeling pride in being able to say it and also thinking of Peter at the same time. '. . . is in the army.'

'And have you eaten any different food to Mr Atkinson?'

Beryl frowned. 'Only rice pudding. It's my favourite, but Mr Frank doesn't like it and Jamie spits it out.'

'So, does Mr Atkinson keep arsenic on the farm? A lot of farmers do use it to keep down vermin.'

'Yes, there's a container on a shelf in the barn, clearly marked. But I've never touched it.'

'Hmm,' the doctor said again. 'I'm going to send a sample of your vomit for analysis, but all your symptoms lead me to think it could be arsenic poisoning.'

Beryl stared at him. 'But how . . . ?'

'That's why I asked if you help around the farm. It's a powder, so it's possible that you could have got some on your hands or even your clothes. And then if you'd been cooking – making a rice pudding perhaps . . .' He spread his hands. It didn't seem likely. She was a neat young woman, who, he had no doubt, would wash her hands thoroughly before she touched food, but then it was the only explanation he could think of.

But as she left the surgery, Beryl's thoughts were in a whirl.

'What did he say?' Frank demanded.

'Some sort of bilious attack,' she said vaguely. She'd already decided she would tell no one what the doctor had actually said. 'He's given me some medicine he says will settle my stomach and I've not to eat for forty-eight hours. I must just drink plenty of water.'

Eve met them at the back door. 'I just came across to see you, but Phyllis said you'd gone to the doctor's. You shouldn't be driving yet, Dad. You should have got Harold to take her and I'd have looked after little 'un.' It was Eve's pet name for Jamie.

'I sent Phyllis across to your place,' Frank said, 'but you were out and she had no idea where to look for Harold. Like she said, the farm's a big place.'

Eve stared at him. 'I wasn't out, Dad. I've been at home all morning until I came here, that is. And Harold was pottering about the yard until gone eleven.'

Frank stared at her and though both Eve and Beryl saw his mouth tighten, he said nothing.

'Come along in, both of you,' Eve said. 'I'll get you a cup of tea.'

'I've only to drink water for the next forty-eight hours,' Beryl said as she shifted Jamie's weight against her shoulder. 'And I'd better get this one into his pram. He's fast asleep.'

'I'll do it.' Eve was already reaching for the baby. 'You sit down, Beryl love. You look as white as a sheet. Get some rest, at least while I'm here.'

A little over a week after her visit to the doctor's, Beryl was almost back to her old self, though her stomach still felt a little delicate occasionally. She received a letter from the doctor marked *Private and Confidential*. It contained confirmation of what she already half expected:

The analysis by the laboratory concludes that there was a small amount of arsenic present in your vomit. It was enough to make you ill but luckily not sufficient to cause you any lasting damage.

Beryl mulled over the mystery as to why she had been the only one to be ill and not Frank or Jamie. What was it that she had eaten that neither of them had? It had to be the rice pudding. Now she thought about it more, her worse bouts of sickness had been when she had made and eaten it. But how . . . ? She'd had an awful thought as she'd left the doctor's surgery, and it came back to her now with even more intensity. But how could she find out if her suspicion was true? She went into the pantry and was in the process of reaching up to remove the offending bag of rice when an idea began to form in her mind. Instead, she left the bag of rice where it was. In the same post that the letter from the surgery had arrived had been a letter from Peter.

I'll be home at the weekend. It'll only be a flying visit, I'm afraid, but it'll be worth it just to see you and Jamie . . .

Later that morning, Beryl took a cup of tea and two biscuits across the yard to the dairy. She set the cup down and said cheerfully, 'Peter's coming home at the weekend, but I expect you'll get a letter too.'

Phyllis sniffed and carried on with the churning. 'Post doesn't get to my place until later.'

'I'll have to think of something special to make for him. I was thinking of a nice rice pudding.'

Phyllis stopped churning and stared at her. 'He doesn't like rice pudding.'

'Oh, he'll like mine, served with raspberry jam,' Beryl said airily as she turned and left the dairy, smiling to herself. She didn't see Phyllis standing watching her go with fear in her eyes and her hand to her chest as if she had a sudden pain there.

The following morning, Beryl took tea and biscuits to Phyllis in the dairy as usual. The woman looked dreadful, as if she hadn't slept at all the previous night.

'Mr Frank's asleep by the fire,' Beryl told her. 'So I'm just going to take Jamie out for a walk in the pram. I think he's teething. He won't settle to his nap for some reason this morning. I won't be long . . .'

As soon as she'd seen Beryl leave the yard and walk some distance along the lane, Phyllis quietly let herself into the house by the back door. She crept to the kitchen door and saw that Frank was indeed fast asleep, his head against the back of his chair. His mouth open, he was snoring quite loudly. Phyllis tiptoed into the pantry and took down the bag of pudding rice from the shelf. Then she hurried outside again and to the privy where she poured the last of the contents of the bag into the huge pail set below the wooden seat. She hoped the night soil men would be visiting the farm soon. She stood a moment with the blue paper bag in her hands. There might still be traces left in it, so she tore it into shreds and dropped it in after the rice. She replaced the wooden lid on the seat, went back into the scullery to wash her hands in the deep white sink, then returned to the dairy to continue her morning's work. Only then did she breathe easily again.

About two hundred yards from the farm gate,

Beryl had parked the pram and herself behind a tree. She could see the farmyard clearly from here but no one could see her. Only a couple of minutes later, she saw Phyllis come out of the dairy to stand looking down the lane towards her. Beryl kept perfectly still and watched as the woman hurried towards the back door. She emerged only seconds later, carrying something in her hands, though from this distance Beryl could not see what it was. She continued to watch Phyllis go into the privy and close the door behind her. A few minutes elapsed before she re-emerged, went back into the house for a few moments and then back to the dairy.

'Now I wonder what you've been up to, Mrs?' Beryl murmured to herself. 'As if I didn't know.'

Beryl continued her walk a little further and then turned and retraced her steps to the farm. Leaving the pram in the sunshine near the back door, she went inside and into the pantry.

The bag of rice, which she had used to make puddings for herself, was no longer sitting on the shelf where she had left it.

Fifty

Beryl and Peter spent a tender and poignant two days and nights together.

'You know I can't tell you much, darling, but you understand secrets, don't you?' he whispered as they lay in the darkness, their arms wrapped tightly around each other. 'But there's a feeling amongst the lads that something's going to happen very soon now. This – this is probably what they call an embarkation leave. You know what that means, don't you?'

Beryl buried her head against his chest and her muffled voice was husky as she murmured, 'Yes, I do.'

He stroked her hair and kissed the top of her head. 'Keep writing to me every week, just as you have been doing. The letters'll get to me eventually.'

'So – so you think you'll be going abroad? To France?'

'It's likely. It's high time we got a foothold back in Europe. If I've got to go anywhere, I'm glad it's there. We've got to get our own back for Dunkirk and I never fancied Africa. But please don't say a word to anyone. Not even to Frank and especially not to my mother.'

'Of course I won't.'

'And now,' he said, finding her mouth with his eager lips, 'let's forget all about the war . . .'

Carolyn came home two days after Peter had left. She too was on a short visit and, just like him, she could say nothing to her family, though she did confide in Beryl. 'We're going to be kept even busier very soon now. Things are hotting up, so the rumours are saying, and there's a feeling in the air too.'

'That's just what Peter said. He – he . . .' Beryl hesitated only a moment. They were both still bound by the Official Secrets Act so they thought they could speak to each other – just a little bit – but even then Beryl was wary of saying too much. 'He thinks they'll be going overseas.'

'Yes, back to mainland Europe.'

They were out in the fields on a warm day in May. They'd brought a picnic and were sitting beneath the shade of a huge tree. Jamie was lying on a rug kicking his bare legs and chuckling happily.

'He's a gorgeous little boy. Peter loves him dearly. It was written all over his face when he held him at the christening. No father could have been prouder. And when he heard you'd already changed his name to "Carter", his face positively shone.'

'I wanted to do it before – before . . .' Beryl fell silent as they were both thinking what might be going to happen very soon.

'Does Phyllis know?'

'I haven't told her. I expect she'll find out eventually.'

'Are things still difficult between you?'

433

'That's the understatement of the year.' Beryl paused for a moment before saying, 'Carolyn, I need to confide in someone. It can't be Mr Frank and certainly not Peter, so can I ask you to treat this as if it's part of that document we both signed?'

'Of course, Beryl. Anything you say to me will go no further. You have my word.'

Taking a deep breath, Beryl told her everything about her baffling illness that, in the end, had not been so mysterious after all.

'And please don't suggest I go to the police, Carolyn,' Beryl ended her tale. 'This is Peter's mother we're talking about.'

'No, you can't. She'd go to prison for something like that.'

'Except that I probably couldn't prove it anyway.' She explained to Carolyn what she had already done to frighten Phyllis by suggesting she was going to make a rice pudding for Peter. 'That threw her into a right old panic, I can tell you. I took Jamie for a little walk but watched her from behind a tree hurrying between the house and the privy and when I got back, the rice had disappeared from the pantry shelf, though I'd been clever enough to take a small sample out of the bag. I've got it hidden safely away in my bedroom in a small box together with the doctor's letter.'

'Mm.' Carolyn was thinking. 'D'you know what I'd do, if I was you?'

'What?'

'Give her an even bigger fright. Let her know that you've guessed what she did.'

'How?'

'Does she still come into the kitchen for a morning cuppa?'

'Sometimes, but normally I take it across to the dairy for her along with two biscuits.'

Carolyn chuckled. 'Then do that and, as you put it down, say something like, "You're quite safe, there's no arsenic in it," and walk straight out without looking at her.'

Beryl stared at her for a moment and then a smile spread across her face. 'That's a brilliant idea. I'll do that.'

She carried out Carolyn's suggestion the next day, turning and leaving the dairy before Phyllis could say a word. She would have dearly loved to have watched the woman's reaction, but knew she should trust her best friend's instinct.

The matter was never spoken about between them, though Phyllis spent many a sleepless night imagining what would happen when her son found out, as she believed he surely must. But what Phyllis didn't understand – and never would – was Beryl's deep love for her husband. She would never hurt Peter in such a way and although his mother would never realize it, her appalling secret was safe. Only Carolyn would ever know and she would never break her friend's confidence.

'Captain Delaney. How nice,' Lilian greeted her visitor. 'Do come in. The kettle's on the hob as always.'

The officer, carrying a bulky parcel under his arm, removed his cap and stepped into the cottage.

'I've brought a uniform for Tom. It's the same as

the soldiers at the Point wear, though he won't be expected to take part in drill or PT or, in fact, become involved in anything that's going on there.' He smiled. 'He's doing a grand job here, but we thought wearing a uniform might save him any embarrassment – or even trouble – in town.'

'He doesn't often go into the town,' Lilian said. 'He's a good lad. But thank you. I appreciate your thoughtfulness – and so will Tom.'

'So, how are things with you?' Captain Delaney asked conversationally, as he sat drinking the tea Lilian handed him.

'Much the same, really. The war doesn't affect us out here. There were some bombings in the town early in the war, but that seems to have stopped now. They even opened the beach up last summer during the day.'

'And are you all keeping well?'

'Yes, except my father. He had some sort of seizure in February, but he's made a good recovery, I'm glad to say.'

'I'm sorry to hear that.'

'Silly old fool thinks he can carry on just the same as he did when he was forty,' Lilian confided, but the words were said fondly.

'It must be hard to give up doing what you've always done.'

'It might have been a lot worse if it hadn't been for Beryl living there.'

'Oh? Who's Beryl?'

'A friend of Carolyn's. An ATS girl who was daft enough to get herself pregnant.'

436

Captain Delaney was thoughtful for a moment. He had to be careful how he phrased the next question. He remembered now how, on a previous visit here, Major Jefferson had been very interested in the Holmes's daughter. 'Did they work together?'

'I don't know where they were or what they were doing, but I do know they were together.'

'Mm.' He set down his cup. 'Thank you, Mrs Holmes. That was most welcome. And now, I'll just have a word with Tom before I leave. He's in the usual place, I take it.'

Captain Delaney sat patiently, until there was a break in the transmission and Tom removed his headphones and turned to face him. When he had explained the reason for his visit, Captain Delaney asked, 'This Beryl, who's living with your grandfather – d'you know if she knows Morse?'

Tom stared at him, not quite sure how to answer. Was this a trap to find out just how confidential Tom kept his work? But he was able to answer truthfully. 'I really don't know. All I know is that when you visited that time with Major Jefferson, he seemed very interested in them both, but what happened after that, I couldn't say. Carolyn never says a word about where she is or what she's doing when she comes home on leave. She never has and neither has Beryl.'

'Right. Thanks, Tom.' He stood up and shook the young man's hand.

'I hope the uniform helps you to deal with any problems you might get from the locals. Your work has been most valuable, always remember that, but you do understand, don't you, that it must never be spoken about, not even after the war is over? Probably never.'

Solemnly, Tom nodded. 'I do, sir, yes.'

'One more thing. When this is all over, I will personally see that you get your transmitter back.'

'Thank you.'

'By the way, what are your plans for after the war?'

'I shall apply for a university place.'

'Then I wish you good luck.'

The captain smiled, gave a brief nod and left the room. In the kitchen he bade his farewell to Lilian and left the house. Outside in the lane, he sat for a few moments in his car debating what he ought to do. He would have liked to have had a conversation with the major, but that would all take time – valuable time – and he was here now. If what he had in mind was going to work, he had to act now.

He started the car and found the lane that led to the farm. Minutes later, he was sitting in the farmhouse drinking yet more tea and showing Beryl his ID. All credit due to her, he thought, the girl seemed doubtful until Frank, from his chair by the fire, said mildly, 'I've heard of Captain Delaney. He's something to do with what Tom's doing.' He glanced at the captain. 'It's all right, young feller. The family all know about it *and* we know to keep quiet. And now, I expect you'd like to talk to Beryl on yar own.'

He began to lever himself up out of his chair, but Captain Delaney said swiftly, 'Please don't go, sir, because what I am about to ask Beryl will concern you as well, but all this must remain top secret, even if nothing comes of it.'

Frank sat down again and prepared to listen as the captain turned back to Beryl. 'If I'm not mistaken, you were in the ATS and you went to Trowbridge with Miss Holmes.'

Beryl blinked but remained silent.

'After that,' he went on, 'I don't know where you both went, but I can make a shrewd guess. All I need to ask you is: at what speed can you take down Morse?'

Beryl glanced at Frank and, when he nodded, said, 'I could do twenty words a minute. I might be a bit rusty now, though I expect I could soon get back to that speed, but – but why? I have a baby to look after and Mr Frank to care for. I'm not leaving either of them.'

Captain Delaney smiled. 'I wouldn't dream of asking you to, but I think, if Mr Frank is agreeable, you could be very useful working from here whenever you can. It needn't be at any set time and it wouldn't even matter if you duplicated Tom's work or . . .' He hesitated, realizing that he should not, perhaps, mention Mr Fox. 'Messages are often distorted or difficult to read and if monitored by two or more listeners, it can help to fill in any blanks.'

Beryl nodded. She knew about that all too well.

'Anything you pick up will be useful, I can assure you. I'm sure you both will have guessed from the news that things are starting to hot up and over the next few weeks and months we will need all the voluntary interceptors we can get.'

'How do we get a set for her, then?' Frank put in.

'That will all be taken care of. Everything will be delivered here under cover of darkness. The fewer people who know about this the better, and engineers will set the whole thing up for you. I'll arrange for the soldier from the Point who picks up Tom's messages to call here each evening too. So, will you help us?'

'Of course she will,' Frank said before Beryl could even open her mouth. 'There's just one other person we'd need to tell. My daughter-in-law, Eve. She'll help look after the bairn if needed.'

'She'd have to sign the Official Secrets Act.'

'Oh, she already has done,' Frank said airily. 'The whole family have, because of Tom.'

Captain Delaney smiled broadly.

Fifty-One

Matters moved swiftly. Engineers arrived late one evening and set up the wireless set in the second bedroom in Beryl's side of the house, with an aerial concealed in the tree just outside the back door. No one else, except Eve, knew what was going on at the farm now, how Beryl listened in whenever she could, soon picking up her Morse speed again. Not even Harold or Adam, and certainly not Phyllis Carter, knew anything about it. They never even knew about the soldier who came on his motorbike each evening to pick up a sheaf of papers from Beryl. Not even Tom was informed, though Mr Fox did know.

The arrangement worked well. Eve was delighted to do her bit to help and neither Jamie nor Frank ever felt neglected. Best of all, Beryl no longer felt that all her training had been wasted. The only thing troubling her was that if 'something big' was going to happen, then, instinctively, she knew that Peter would be a part of it.

There was a definite tension in the air throughout Beaumanor. All leave was suddenly cancelled and Carolyn and her colleagues guessed something was indeed about to happen. They all knew that they would not be able to visit their families for some time. They didn't even have the time or the energy to write home very often either, though Carolyn did make time to write to Peter. She had to be careful what she wrote, but she hoped that he would read between the lines and know that she was wishing him luck. And then one day at the end of May, they all saw hundreds of gliders being towed southwards.

'He's gone,' Noreen whispered to Carolyn as they came out to watch and stood side by side gazing skywards. 'Joe will be up there, I just know it. It must be the invasion.'

'Come on. We'd better get some sleep. We're going to be busy.'

Carolyn had been right and so had Noreen. The invasion had started and the American Airborne Division based at Quorn was heavily involved. They'd disappeared without even being able to say goodbye to their newfound friends in the village.

The following days were frenzied at Beaumanor and the stress on the operators heightened. Carolyn coped very well, even though she was permanently tired. The enemy repeatedly changed their frequencies and this put extra pressure on the listeners trying to keep pace with them.

'It's happened then,' Eddie said as he threw the newspaper onto the table. 'Allied troops have landed in Normandy. There have been heavy losses, but they've got a foothold now. This is the beginning of the end, Lilian.'

Lilian's eyes widened. 'That's good news. But what about Peter? Where is he?'

Husband and wife regarded each other solemnly. Lilian reached out and grasped Eddie's hand. 'Thank the good Lord that Tom didn't have to go.'

Eddie nodded. 'Yes, we should be very grateful for that. I believe he has done his bit right here, though you do understand, don't you, love, that we'll never be able to tell anyone about it? Not ever.'

Solemnly, Lilian nodded. 'But at least it's kept him safe.'

'Lilian! *Lilian!*'

Two weeks after the news of the Normandy landings, Phyllis burst in the back door of the Holmes's cottage without even knocking.

'Oh whatever's the matter, Phyllis?'

'He's missing. She's had a telegram. It went to *her* and not me.' Tears streaked her face. 'Why would they do that, Lilian? Why would they let her know and not me? I'm his mother.'

'Oh Phyllis, no. Sit down, love.' Lilian pushed her gently into a chair. 'Because she's his wife. I know it's hard' – she rushed on before Phyllis could say any more – 'but that's the way they do things. How did you get to know?'

'She brought the telegram across to the dairy to show me. She – she was in floods of tears. I – I think she really does love him.'

'Oh I'm sure of that. Carolyn said so. And . . .' Lilian hesitated for a brief moment but then decided to press on. 'She also said that Peter really loves Beryl and the baby.'

Phyllis was silent, wiping away the tears only for fresh ones to form.

'It's such a shame,' Lilian said softly, 'that the two of you can't get along. You could be such a comfort to one another and – and she doesn't see her own family now, does she? She – she must miss having a mother.'

Phyllis said nothing. She was sorely tempted to confess to Lilian, but then some inner sense told her to keep silent. If Beryl told anyone – and it was obvious that she'd guessed what Phyllis had done – then it would all come out. If Beryl reported it, Phyllis could face arrest and, if she was found guilty, perhaps she would be sent to prison or – or worse. Phyllis shuddered. But now there was something even worse to face: the loss of her beloved son. If he was gone, she didn't care one way or the other what happened to her, but Lilian's voice penetrated her thoughts.

'Did you say that the telegram said "missing"?'

Phyllis nodded.

'Well, there's still hope, then. From what they're saying in the papers, it must be a melee out there.'

'Yes, I suppose so. We shouldn't give up hope until – until . . .' Phyllis couldn't bring herself to say the words aloud.

Over an hour later, Phyllis returned to the farm and went to the back door. She knocked hesitantly and then, when no one came to answer, she walked in. Beryl was sitting at the kitchen table, her face red and swollen with crying, the telegram still lying open in front of her. Frank was sitting in his chair, rocking the pram with one hand. Even Jamie seemed to have picked up the tension in the room. He was whimpering.

'Can't get him to settle,' Frank said. 'Reckon he feels summat's wrong. Mek us a cuppa, Phyllis, will yer? Poor Beryl's not up to it at the moment.'

Beryl didn't move, not even when Phyllis put a strong, hot cup of tea in front of her. She didn't even look up at her mother-in-law.

'Drink it up, lass,' Frank urged gently.

Obediently, Beryl picked up the cup with only the slightest hesitation before she put it to her lips.

'Can we make any sort of enquiries, do you think, Mr Frank?' Phyllis said.

'I doubt it. It'll be chaos out there. They'll let you know any more news as soon as they know it themselves. It's the waiting that's so hard. The not knowing for definite. I understand that. But try to keep busy, that's my motto.' He glanced at Beryl still sitting like a statue locked in her anxiety and misery.

'It's not the same as last time,' Phyllis murmured. 'Last time when – when Raymond was killed, they – and we – knew straight away. I don't know which is worse – to have hope or not to have any at all.'

Slowly Beryl lifted her head and looked straight at her mother-in-law. 'That must have been the worst. Not to have any hope at all. At least we – we can cling to that until . . .'

'That's right, lass. Keep the faith,' Frank said.

'We'll all be praying for him. Now, Beryl lass, this little man isn't going to settle. I think he wants a cuddle from his mummy.'

The whole neighbourhood was cast in gloom at the news that Peter was missing in action and when the families attended church on the following Sunday, there were sympathetic handshakes all round and prayers were said.

'News travels fast and bad news even faster,' Lilian remarked sagely as she walked away from the church with Phyllis clinging to her arm. Beryl was standing by the truck with the baby in her arms. 'Mrs Carter – er – do you want a lift? Mr Frank says he can squeeze us in.'

'You go with 'em, duck,' Lilian said quickly. 'We're cycling back home,' she added, referring to herself, Eddie and Tom. 'Did you walk here?'

Phyllis nodded.

'It's a long way. You should come with my dad, like you always have done.'

Phyllis sighed as she murmured, 'I didn't think I'd be welcome.'

'Phyllis, it's high time you put all this nonsense aside. They're married and that's an end to it. Now, go and get in the truck.'

The only things that kept Beryl going through the tough days that followed were Jamie, Mr Frank and the useful work she was now doing as a voluntary interceptor. She wrote to Carolyn, who she knew would be devastated to hear about Peter too, but she had to be told.

Carolyn received Beryl's letter on the same day that Noreen, too, had news. She found her sitting on the bed in the room they now shared, an open letter in her hands and tears flooding down her face. Carolyn sat beside her and put her arm around her shoulder.

'What is it?'

'It's – it's Alan. He's – he's been killed. On the Normandy beach as they landed, his mother says. He never even got properly ashore.'

'I'm so sorry, Noreen.'

'It's all my fault,' she burst out, almost hysterical now. 'If I hadn't taken up with Joe, Alan would have been safe.'

'Now you're being silly,' Carolyn said firmly. 'Whatever has happened is nothing to do with you or with you being friendly with Joe.'

'But I can't forgive myself. If – if Joe does come back, I'll – I'll have to send him away.'

'You'll do no such thing. You weren't engaged to Alan, not even officially promised to him.'

'But his mother will blame me.'

'Don't tell me about mothers,' Carolyn muttered bitterly. 'My name will be mud back home right now.'

Noreen's crying stopped briefly as she stared at Carolyn, though she continued to hiccup miserably. 'What – what do you mean?'

'I've just had a letter too. Peter's missing.'

'And his mother will blame you for not marrying him, you mean?'

'Exactly.'

'But – but that's years ago. He's married to Beryl now.'

447

'True, but his mother is none too pleased about that. She's a very bitter woman and has a long memory.'

They were silent together for a while until Noreen said at last, 'Poor Beryl. She doesn't have a lot of luck with men, does she?'

With a sigh, Carolyn got up and pulled Noreen to her feet too. 'Let's go and get something to eat before we go on duty. We've got to keep our strength up. It's going to be another busy night.'

Both girls were thankful to be so busy; it kept their minds off their own sadness. On the farm, Beryl also kept herself busy, even though she felt as if her heart was breaking.

By the end of July, the Allies had driven the enemy out of Normandy and were pushing on through France, but still there was no news of Peter. But for Noreen there was happier news. After a month or so of fighting, the Americans had returned to Quorn, mourning their heavy losses and yet regrouping and preparing to go into battle again. Amongst their number was Joe. He came to the billet in person to see Noreen. Despite her misgivings, she couldn't stop herself flinging herself into his arms and weeping with relief.

'We need to talk, honey,' he said softly. They found a quiet corner in a local pub while Noreen, haltingly at first, explained about Alan.

'I understand,' he said, when at last Noreen fell silent. 'I was seeing a girl back home before I came over here, but, just like you, it wasn't serious. She's written to tell me that she's met someone else, so I've written back to tell her that I, too, have fallen in love with an English girl and I intend to marry her, if she'll have me. But you must realize, darlin', that this isn't over yet. We've got a lot more fighting to do. Rumours are flying around the camp that we'll be parachuting into Holland very soon. All I can ask, Noreen, is that you'll wait for me.'

'Oh Joe, you know I will. But please, come back safe, won't you?'

He gave her a lopsided grin that melted her heart. 'I'll do my very best, honey.'

Fifty-Two

'Mrs Carter. *Mrs Carter!*' Beryl was running across the yard waving a letter. She paused breathless at the door of the dairy. Phyllis looked up at her, fear in her eyes.

'It's all right. He's alive.' She waved the letter again. 'He's safe. He's wounded, but he's safe. Oh, Mrs Carter . . .' Beryl rushed across the space between them and threw her arms around the startled woman. 'He's alive.'

Phyllis, with tears running down her face too now, couldn't stop herself hugging Beryl in return. Their mutual overwhelming relief pushed all other thoughts and feelings aside.

After a few moments, when they had both calmed down a little, Phyllis asked, 'You said "wounded". Do they say how – how badly?'

Now Beryl stood back and showed Phyllis the piece of paper she held. 'It's not from *them*, it's from Peter. He's in hospital, but he's been able to write to both of us. I bet there's a letter waiting at home for you too.'

'Oh Beryl . . .' Now Phyllis wept again. 'I'm so sorry – so very sorry. Can you ever forgive me?'

There was no need to ask what she meant, both women knew full well. Beryl put her arms around

Phyllis and held her close, whispering into her ear, even though there was no one else to hear. 'Of course I can and we'll never – ever – speak of it again.'

Now Phyllis's arms were tightly around Beryl again. 'Do you mean it? But – you'll tell Peter.'

'No, he'll never know. I promise you.'

They loosened their hold on each other and stood back a little. Beryl smiled through her tears. 'I do understand what you think of me and I'm sorry I'm not the sort of girl you wanted for your son but – but do you think we might try to get along a little better, even if it's only for his sake?'

'I've been so wrong, Beryl, and – and very wicked. I thought Peter being posted missing was my punishment. But now he's alive, I feel as if I've been given a second chance. *You're* giving me a second chance too. I've spent years being bitter and twisted about how life has treated me. As if I was the only woman left a war widow when, in fact, there were thousands. Some lost fathers, husbands and even sons. In some cases, more than one son. How they carried on, I can't imagine. From now on, Beryl, we'll get along, I promise, and not just for Peter's sake but for our own too.'

They hugged again, sealing Phyllis's promise.

'Now, let's go and find Mr Frank and tell him the wonderful news.'

'Doesn't he know?'

'No, I came to find you first, but he must have wondered why I flew out of the kitchen as if a swarm of bees was after me. And I left him with Jamie sitting on his lap.'

The two women entered the back door together.

451

'Sorry I rushed off like that, Mr Frank, but we've had some marvellous news. Peter is alive. He's wounded and in hospital, but he's written to me – to us both, I expect.'

There were tears in Frank's eyes. 'Aw lass, that is good news indeed. How badly is he wounded and where is he?'

'He's got an injury in his left leg. It's – it's quite a bad one, he says.' Beryl's smile faded. After the euphoria of knowing he was alive, she was now anxious about the seriousness of his wound. 'He says they've operated on it.'

'Where is he?'

Beryl consulted the letter. 'The Haslar Royal Naval Hospital. He says it's at Gosport.'

Frank nodded. 'That'll be where they're taking all the casualties from Normandy. Maybe when he's improved a bit, they'll transfer him further north.' He glanced at the two women. 'But if you want to go down to see him, just say the word and we'll get it arranged.'

Beryl and Phyllis looked at each other. 'We'll go.' They said in unison and then laughed together. The new understanding between them did not go unnoticed by Frank.

When Phyllis had gone home, Frank said, 'There's just one thing you ought to do, love, before you go. Ring Captain Delaney on that number he gave you and tell him what's happened. I'm sure there'll be no problem, but you ought to tell him.'

'I will, Mr Frank, I'll do it now.'

*

'Captain Delaney was very nice,' Beryl said. 'He said how pleased he was to hear that Peter is alive. I'm to take whatever time I need off and I'm to let him know if I want to give up the work altogether when Peter gets home.'

'But it's been a godsend, hasn't it, while you've been so worried about him?'

'Yes,' Beryl agreed quietly, 'it has. Maybe I could carry on. Peter would understand.'

'Of course he would, but there's just one thing.'

'What's that?'

Frank chuckled. 'He'd have to sign the Official Secrets Act.'

Word soon travelled that Peter was alive, though injured.

'I'll look after Jamie – and Frank – while you and Phyllis go,' Eve offered. She too had spotted the difference in the attitude of the two women towards each other. 'He'll be fine with me.'

'If you don't mind, Eve, that'd be great. It's a long way to take him. We'll have to stay overnight, I expect, and the travelling won't be easy.'

As Beryl had guessed, there had been a letter by the same post waiting for Phyllis at home. Both women wrote back to Peter at once, telling him they were going to travel down together to see him and, only three days later, they were able to set off. Beryl was a little anxious at leaving Jamie, but, with his arms round Eve's neck, he smiled and waved her off happily.

'He'll get spoiled rotten,' Phyllis said as they sat together on the train journey south.

'I really don't mind. I just want to see Peter for myself. Make sure he's not hiding just how bad he is. I haven't had a reply since we both wrote to tell him we're going.'

'I'm sure if he had been really bad, the hospital would have been in touch,' Phyllis said reasonably.

'I expect you're right,' Beryl murmured, 'but I still need to see him for myself.'

'I feel exactly the same.'

The two women sat side by side as the train rattled southwards. They didn't speak much, each was busy with her own thoughts.

Phyllis was feeling smug. She believed she had convinced Beryl that her contrition was genuine. She now realized she'd been foolish in playing a very dangerous game that could have resulted in ridding herself of Beryl as she had wanted, but at the same time bringing dreadful trouble to her own door. Somehow, Beryl had guessed at what she had done and in a moment of sheer panic, Phyllis had confirmed that suspicion by removing the bag of rice. Now, she knew she was at the mercy of her daughter-in-law, though there was now no evidence for the girl to bring against her. All she had to do was to act a part. It wouldn't be easy, but then Phyllis had always been a bit of a drama queen. She would revel in playing the biggest deception of her life and if, at some point in the future, an opportunity presented itself to eliminate Beryl, then she would do so. But, next time, she would be more careful. A lot more careful.

Beside her, Beryl, too, was thoughtful. She was

no fool. Not for one moment had she believed Phyllis's apology was sincere. She had, as Carolyn had suggested, frightened the woman by revealing just enough to let her know that she had worked out for herself what Phyllis had done. She smiled inwardly. Phyllis had proved her guilt by removing the rice. What her mother-in-law didn't know was that, locked away in a small box to which only Beryl had the key, was the doctor's letter and a small sample of rice taken from the bag before Phyllis had had a chance to remove it. These two items were Beryl's insurance policy. She guessed that Phyllis was now acting out a part that would convince her son that all was well between his mother and his wife. Well, two could play at that game, Beryl thought.

As they alighted from the train, the two women linked arms as if they were bosom pals. Without the other realizing it, there was an unspoken mutual wish that they would present a united front to Peter.

They got a taxi to the hospital.

'Oh my,' Beryl said as they stood looking up at the huge building. 'We'll never find him in there.'

'Of course we will,' Phyllis said, taking her arm again as they began to walk up the tree-lined driveway to the main entrance. 'There should be some sort of reception.'

It took some time for them to find the ward where Peter was and they had to ask for special permission to see him, because it was not visiting time.

'We've come all the way from Lincolnshire,' Phyllis explained in her haughtiest voice. 'It's taken nearly the whole day to get here. We're going to have to stay overnight as it is.'

At last they were standing beside Peter's bed. He lay with his eyes closed. Beads of sweat stood out on his forehead. He was muttering unintelligible words and moving restlessly. A cage, holding up the bedclothes, protected his leg.

'What's the matter with him?' Beryl whispered. Suddenly she was fearful. The joy of hearing he was alive, which had buoyed her up thus far, died quickly. Even to her inexperienced eyes, he was very ill.

'It looks like he's got a fever,' Phyllis muttered. 'We should ask someone.'

They sat beside Peter for a while, but he neither opened his eyes nor spoke to them. He kept mumbling and thrashing about. It seemed to them that he didn't even know they were there. A ward sister came to the end of the bed. 'I'm sorry, ladies, but I will have to ask you to leave now. The doctor is about to do his rounds and—'

'May we have a word with him, sister?' Phyllis asked. 'I – we – want to know the truth.'

The sister bowed her head. 'Of course. If you come with me, he might have time to have a word with you now. Or, if you prefer, you can wait until he has seen Corporal Carter and then you'll have the latest information.'

'We'll do that, if we may, please,' Beryl said politely.

'Then if you would sit in the visitors' waiting room, I will fetch you when he's ready.'

With one last glance at Peter, though neither of them dared to bend to kiss him, they followed her.

There were only the two of them in the room.

'Corporal Carter? I didn't know he was a corporal, did you?'

Beryl shook her head and smiled weakly. 'He's not one to boast though, is he?'

'That's true.'

They waited for over an hour before the doctor himself appeared in the doorway.

'Mrs Carter?'

Phyllis and Beryl both said 'Yes?' together and the doctor smiled briefly, guessing correctly that they were both 'Mrs Carter'. He came into the room and sat down in front of them.

'Corporal Carter is your son and your husband?' he said, glancing first at Phyllis and then at Beryl. When they nodded, he went on, 'There's no point in me lying to you. He is still very ill. His leg was badly injured, the wound is infected and, sadly, there is still the chance we might have to amputate it to save his life. But we have recently taken delivery of what everyone is hailing as a new wonder drug: penicillin. Corporal Carter is being given regular doses and I am hopeful.'

'Thank you, doctor,' Beryl said huskily. 'We've travelled from Lincolnshire and are due to return tomorrow. May we be permitted to see him again tomorrow morning before we go?'

'I'll arrange it with Sister.' He smiled as he got up to leave. 'Keep the faith.'

Beryl almost shed tears. It was what Mr Frank had said when they'd first heard that Peter was missing.

Stiffly, Phyllis got to her feet. 'Come on, there's

nothing more we can do here tonight. We'd better go and find this bed-and-breakfast place we're booked into.'

They shared a twin room, each lying wide awake in the darkness but not speaking. Both were praying for Peter, but Phyllis's prayers had a slightly different note to Beryl's. Beryl just prayed for Peter's recovery, promising to look after him always. As for Phyllis, she prayed for her act of reconciliation towards Beryl to be sincere, to become a reality.

'Forgive all my bitterness and resentment over the years, my nastiness towards others and my greatest sin, my wickedness towards Beryl. Please let Peter live and I promise I will be good and kind to her. I will accept her as his wife and – and her little boy as part of my family, if only, dear Lord, you will let him live.'

She could do no more and though no one would ever know it, she truly meant the silent vows she was making and she would reiterate them every Sunday in church for the rest of her life – if only Peter lived. And if anyone remarked upon the change in her, she would tell them quite openly, and truthfully, that almost losing Peter had made her see everything with new eyes and a new understanding.

She fell asleep at last with the words on her lips: *If only he lives.*

Beryl slept fitfully, tossing and turning in the hard bed. Her overriding worry was, of course, Peter, but she also wondered if little Jamie was all right. Was he fretful and missing her? She hoped he wasn't too much of a handful for Eve, who had promised to sleep at the farm so that Jamie's surroundings were not strange. Eve had been such a wonderful friend to her. Almost as much of a friend as Carolyn, but not quite. But for Carolyn, God alone knew where Beryl would be by now. Cast out by her own family, suffering the indignity of a mother-and-baby home, losing her child who had now become so precious to her. It was all because of her dear friend that she had been cared for, had been able to keep her son and even, though indirectly, that she was now happily married to a man who truly loved her and Jamie. In the darkness of the strange room, she wondered how Phyllis was going to be in the future, how long she would keep up the friendliness towards her, for Beryl was sure it was an act. She fell asleep at last, longing for morning to come so that she could see Peter again and with the words on her lips too: *If only he lives.*

Fifty-Three

They went to the hospital as soon as they could the following morning, anxious to see how he was.

'I knew you were coming in early today,' the same sister who had been on duty the day before greeted them. 'Doctor told me he'd given permission for you to see Corporal Carter before you have to travel back to Lincolnshire. Come with me.'

She led them into the ward and gestured towards the first bed, a broad smile on her face. 'Your visit must have done him good. Just look at him this morning.'

Peter was still lying against the pillows, but he was no longer sweating and moving restlessly. His eyes were focused and he smiled when he saw them.

Beryl rushed to his side and took his hand. 'Oh darling, you look so much better this morning. We were so worried last night. How – how do you feel?'

'Still got a bit of pain, but better than I was. Mam – how are you?'

Phyllis stood at the end of the bed, tears of thankfulness running down her face. Her prayers had been answered. Now all she had to do was to keep her solemn vow. She stood drinking in the sight of him looking so much better but she knew deep down that the image she would always hold was the way she had seen him the previous day, fighting for his life. That was what would make her keep her silent promise.

'All the better for seeing you looking so much better,' she said, managing to inject a little lightness into her tone.

'You've come a long way,' he said, 'but once I'm well enough, they'll move me further north. They need the beds here anyway for more casualties coming. I'll try for Lincoln or Boston, or even Grantham, if I can. That'd be so much easier for you. Now, we haven't got long. Tell me, how's my boy?'

'Thank goodness we saw him again this morning, Mrs Carter,' Beryl said as they left the hospital on their way to the railway station. 'I was worried sick after we saw him yesterday. That new drug the doctor spoke about must certainly be a miracle worker.'

'You're right. Thank goodness for it.' Phyllis paused and added hesitantly, 'I think, if you agree, we should try to find a name for you to call me other than "Mrs Carter", don't you?'

Beryl glanced sideways at her. How she wanted to believe that the woman's change of attitude was genuine and permanent. Perhaps seeing her son so desperately ill that first day had had some effect on Phyllis, but Beryl could still not be sure. However, she was willing to meet her mother-in-law halfway, even if only for Peter's sake.

'Have you any ideas?'

'Well, I don't want it to sound as if I'm trying to take your mother's place . . .'

Beryl shrugged. 'Wouldn't matter if you did. It's a place my mother doesn't seem to want any more.'

'And "Mother-in-law" is a bit of a mouthful, so what about Granny? Jamie will then grow up calling me that too.'

Beryl wondered if the surprise showed on her face. She swallowed hard and said, 'That's a lovely idea, if you're sure . . .'

'Oh, I am,' Phyllis said firmly.

'Have you heard how Peter is?' Carolyn asked as soon as she stepped through the back door when she was home on leave.

The recent intensity of the work had left her feeling drained and her supervisor had insisted that she should take a few days' sick leave. 'Go home. Get some of that good sea air into your lungs. Stay for a week, if you need it. I'll square it for you. You've done sterling work, Holmes, but you're no use to us if you're working under par and making mistakes. Mistakes which could cost lives.'

Carolyn had nodded, knowing the supervisor was right and so here she was, arriving home on a few days' unexpected leave.

'A lot better than when they first arrived at the hospital,' Lilian said. 'The sight of him that first day frightened them both witless, but the next day, he was much better.'

'Thank goodness for that,' Carolyn said, dropping her kitbag on the floor and sitting down. She slipped off her shoes and rubbed her feet. 'The train was crowded. I've had to stand all the way from . . .' She paused and grinned. 'Well, I'd better not tell you exactly where from.' She sniffed the air. 'Is it my favourite for tea, Mam? Roast pork and all the trimmings? It's not Sunday, is it?'

'Your grandad killed a pig last week – with a licence, of course – and we've got our usual allowance.' Lilian's smile broadened. 'And I've got a nice surprise for you. Steve will be here for tea. He's got the weekend off and he's been working with your dad at the workshop. I always ask him to come for his tea when he does a day's work there.'

'So, who collects Tom's notes when Steve is on leave?'

'Oh, the other one. Gordon.'

Carolyn chuckled to herself, but didn't let her mother see her amusement. 'So, he doesn't get an invite to tea, then?'

Lilian wriggled her shoulders. 'He's a nice enough lad, but we haven't known him as long as Steve and, besides, poor Steve needs friends more than ever just now.'

'Yes,' Carolyn said quietly, 'that's true. How does he seem to be coping?'

'Not bad, considering. He says it's easier not to go back to Hull at all. He says he wants to move on – make a new life – and he feels he couldn't do that back in Hull with all the memories. And your dad says he's a very good carpenter. He fits in nicely at the workshop. Grandpa and your granny too have really taken to him, so I think he'd stay round here after the war if there was a job for him.'

463

'Well, things do seem to be looking up after the success of D-Day.'

Lilian eyed her daughter. 'I expect you know far more than you're letting on.'

'I'm only repeating what's in the papers, Mam. That's all I can say. Now, I'll go and freshen up ready for tea.' She planted a quick kiss on her mother's cheek and disappeared upstairs. When she reappeared, Lilian noticed that Carolyn had changed into a pretty dress and had applied lipstick. Her eyes were bright and her cheeks suspiciously pink as they awaited the arrival home of the menfolk. They heard their voices before the two men entered the back door.

'I'll dish up,' Lilian said. 'Call Tom, will you, love? If he's too busy to leave the set, tell him I'll plate his up as usual.' She sighed. 'He often doesn't eat until nine. It's not good for him to be eating so late, but then, there's nowt I can do about it. He wants to do his bit, as everyone keeps saying.'

'He's certainly doing that, Mam, so just let him carry on.'

After washing their hands at the sink in the scullery, the two men came into the kitchen.

'Hello, love,' Eddie greeted her, while Steve smiled a greeting. 'I didn't know you were coming home this weekend.'

'I was given leave at short notice.' Carolyn did not elaborate; she didn't want her mother to fuss. 'A nice long one this time – four or five days – so I'll be able to see everyone. I'm hoping if I smile nicely at Uncle Harold, he will take me to the station when I have to go back.'

'I can take you on my motorbike,' Steve said. 'Your kit will fit in the panniers.'

'Are you allowed to use it when you're not on duty?'

Steve grinned. 'It's my own bike. I have an arrangement with the powers that be. I use my bike for them so they provide the petrol for me, so it all works very well. I'm glad I brought it with me now,' he added softly, as his tone sobered. He said no more but they guessed his meaning; he had lost all his other personal possessions in the bombing of his home.

'Right, sit down before it all gets cold,' Lilian urged.

Tom appeared just after eight o'clock, his eyes bleary with concentration.

'Hello, Caro. How're things?'

'Fine, thanks. You?'

Tom nodded and began to eat hungrily. 'All good. Lots of radio traffic now, as you'd expect.' Then he fell silent, unable to say more. The brown envelope containing his notes for the evening sat beside him on the table. As if on cue, there was a knock at the door.

'That'll be Gordon,' Lilian said, hurrying to answer it and a few moments later, the young soldier followed her into the room.

'Hello, mate,' he greeted Steve. 'When are you back? Can't say I like this trip to Waddington every night, 'specially when it's throwing it down.'

Steve frowned at him. 'Watch what you're saying,' he snapped.

Gordon raised his eyebrows. 'Oh sorry, I thought they were in the know.'

'No,' Steve said shortly. 'The less they know the better it is for them.'

Gordon seemed nonplussed by the reprimand. He shrugged. 'I don't really know what it's all about anyway, mate. I just pick up three envelopes from here and – the other places – and take 'em to – wherever. Mind you,' he grinned cheekily now, 'that aerial poking up out of that tree in the back garden's a bit of a giveaway, I would have thought.'

'It's not for you to think, soldier. You just do what you're told and keep quiet about it.'

'Getting a bit big for your boots now you've been made up to corporal.' Gordon feigned a mock salute, but he was still grinning. It seems nothing could offend him. 'Right, I'd better be off, then.'

'Oh, do have a cup of tea before you go,' Lilian insisted.

'You're all right tonight, Mrs. I'll be on me way. Maybe next time, eh?' He shot a quick look at Steve as if to say it was his fault he wouldn't stay any longer, but even so, there was no animosity in the glance.

Steve didn't leave until late and Carolyn walked to the gate with him. 'I wish I'd known you were coming today,' he said. 'We could have gone into town this evening.'

'That's nice of you, Steve, and I would've liked that. But to be honest, I've been sent home on sick leave, but please don't tell my mam. She'll fuss. I'm so tired I wouldn't have enjoyed it tonight. Maybe . . .'

She hesitated, suddenly a little shy. 'Maybe later in the week, if you're free.'

She held her breath, wondering if she'd been too forward. Perhaps it was too soon after his awful loss. But then she sighed inwardly; she couldn't go through life treading on eggshells. It was better to speak truthfully and naturally, rather than trying to tailor what she said. What had happened to Steve was unbearably tragic but he wasn't the only one who, after this war, would have to try to build a new life for one reason or another. At least, she thought, there was perhaps a way her family could help him to do that.

As if reading her thoughts, Steve said, 'I do enjoy working with your dad and your grandpa. They've got a thriving little business there. Will Tom go into it too, d'you think?'

Carolyn chuckled. 'No, I don't, or rather, I hope he doesn't. He's cack-handed with anything practical. He's more academic. I think Mam's got her sights on him going to university.'

'Your dad's hinted that there might be a job for me after the war, if – if I wanted it.'

'And do you?'

'That rather depends on you.'

'*Me?* Why would I have anything to do with it?'

'Because I'm falling in love with you, Carolyn, that's why, but if you didn't feel the same way, then I wouldn't want to stay around here. And before you say it's too soon after losing my wife, I do know it's a bit quick but I just know that it's not – what do they call it? – on the rebound. I know what I feel for you is genuine. It's not the same sort of love as I felt for Sal. We were teenagers when we met and it was young love, without a doubt. Oh I'm not putting this very well, but I just know that, this time, what I'm beginning to feel for you is different. And besides' – his tone hardened – 'what she did to me while I was away in the forces, well, I'll never forgive her for that. It's – it's tainted what we had.'

Carolyn put her hand on his arm. 'I understand exactly what you mean. I met someone when I first went away. The same time that Beryl met the father of her baby. We went out as a foursome to start with and then we paired off. I fell so hard for him, it's untrue, but he wasn't the man I thought he was and he let me down badly – very badly. I need time to learn to trust again, Steve, and you need time to come to terms with your terrible loss. So, let's just take things slowly, eh? Be good friends first and see what happens?'

Steve nodded. 'That sounds like a very good idea and a sensible one. So are you up for a date sometime this week before you have to go back?'

Carolyn smiled. 'You're on.'

They saw a lot of each other for the rest of that week, and Carolyn wondered how and why he was able to take quite so much time off. By the end of the week, she knew.

'Look, I didn't want to tell you before. I didn't want to spoil this time we've had together, but I've been posted abroad.'

'Oh, I'm sorry to hear that. I thought, after all this time, you wouldn't be going now.'

'I thought so too, but I'm guessing that there's one last big push coming. So many of the lads who have been out there for months, some of them probably since D-Day, must be exhausted.' He grimaced. 'They want fresh blood.'

Carolyn shivered as a wave of cold apprehension ran through her. Huskily, she said, 'Take care, won't you?'

But Steve only grinned with his old sense of humour. It was good to see.

'I'll do my best,' was all he said.

Fifty-Four

Once Paris had been liberated in August and the Allies had chased the Germans from Belgium in September, the feeling of optimism grew. The British Government lifted some of the blackout restrictions in certain areas of the country, and young children saw street lighting for the first time in their lives, though in coastal areas the blackout restrictions remained in place. Victory in Europe seemed assured, but the war with Japan was far from over.

Peter was coming home and both Beryl and Phyllis were overjoyed. He had been moved to a hospital further north and visiting for Beryl and Phyllis had been easier, but at last he was coming home.

'Obviously, he'll come here to the farm,' Phyllis said to Beryl, 'but please let me help you in any way I can to look after him. You'll have your hands full with keeping house for Mr Frank, the little one and then Peter on top of everything else.'

Beryl felt a twinge of doubt, but did her best to quell it. Give the woman a chance, a little voice inside her insisted. 'Oh that would be wonderful, Granny, if you could. I was feeling a bit daunted by everything I'll have to do.'

Phyllis knew nothing of Beryl's intercept work.

When the news had first come through that Peter could come home, Beryl had said, 'What shall I do, Mr Frank? Ought I to tell Captain Delaney so they can take all the equipment away?'

'Do you still want to do it?'

'Well, yes. I don't think Peter will mind. What about you? Are you happy for me to carry on?'

'Of course, but I think we'd better move everything into the spare bedroom on my side of the landing.'

'Could we do that? You wouldn't mind?'

'Not a bit. Phyllis never normally goes into my side of the house upstairs but she'll want to go up to see Peter, so I'll put a lock on my spare bedroom door in case she decides to have a nosey. I wouldn't put anything past her if she thought she'd been given the run of the house. There you are. Problem solved.'

'How would you like us to organize it?' Beryl asked Phyllis now. Again she was being crafty in putting the onus on the other woman as to what she could do.

'What I thought is this: I'll still come and do the dairy work every morning as normal and then I could sit with Peter and do anything he needs done, while you take Jamie out for a walk. You'll both need to get a bit of exercise and fresh air. And I'll be on hand, too, if Mr Frank needs any help.'

The tension between Frank and Phyllis had lessened recently. He had observed her change of attitude and though he wasn't quite ready to believe the woman totally, he too was prepared to give her a chance. She now came back into the farmhouse kitchen each morning for her elevenses and chatted with Frank as he sat by the range. He knew she was trying to get back into his good books as well as Beryl's, but he had watched the interaction between the two women closely and had decided that if Beryl was prepared to bury the hatchet – as long as it wasn't in each other's heads – then so was he. But for the moment, he couldn't help still being a little wary.

One morning, when Beryl was attending to Jamie in her bedroom and Frank and Phyllis were alone over their morning cup of coffee, Frank said casually, 'You seem a lot happier than you used to be, Phyllis, and I don't think it's just because Peter is back home, injured, I grant you, but it's likely that he won't be fit enough to return to the fighting. That must give you cause to be thankful.'

It was at that moment that Beryl came down the stairs, her slippered feet making no sound. She was about to reach out to open the door into the kitchen, when she heard Frank's words. She hesitated and bent a little closer to the door . . .

In the kitchen, Phyllis was silent for a few moments and Frank thought she wasn't going to reply. Then he heard her give a deep sigh as she raised her head and met his gaze. 'I've been a stupid, ungrateful and bitter woman ever since my Raymond was killed. I railed against what I saw as the unfairness of it all. I never stopped to think that there were thousands of women in just the same circumstances as me, many of them in a far worse situation. At least I had a home, employment and my little boy. You've been so good to me and my family, Mr Frank, and I am grateful to you, even though over the years I haven't shown it. And then there was my Peter and Carolyn.' She paused a moment before going on. 'It had always been my dearest wish – and Lilian's – that they should marry and, for a long time, I blamed Carolyn for refusing him – which, I believed, had made him join up.' She sighed. 'I realize now that I was wrong. So wrong.'

'You can't arrange other people's lives for them,' Frank put in gently. 'Not in this day and age. It's a sad fact of life that you have to let the young ones make their own mistakes.'

'I just hope Peter hasn't made a big mistake.'

'I'm sure he hasn't. I think him and Beryl will be very happy together. She's a good lass, I'm sure of it. Aye, she made a mistake, I grant you, but surely we're allowed to be forgiven for one mistake in our lives, aren't we?'

'Oh I hope so, Mr Frank, I truly hope so.' There was no mistaking the fervency in Phyllis's tone. 'I realize now that my bitterness and – and, yes, possessiveness – have made me say and do things I should never have done. I hope, too, that I can be forgiven.'

On the other side of the door Beryl tiptoed back up the stairs.

Peter was brought home by ambulance and put straight to bed. He was weary after the journey, but happy to be home. Beryl and Phyllis fussed over him and, being honest with himself, he quite enjoyed it for a while, though he hoped it wouldn't last. He knew he'd soon get irritated if it went on too long. He lay back against the pillows, amused to see Jamie standing up in his cot on the far side of the bedroom, watching with wide blue eyes as to who this strange man was who had arrived in their lives.

'How he's grown. I hope he's going to take to me.'

'Of course he will,' Beryl said. 'He's a placid little chap and friendly. He'll soon get used to you being around.'

Everyone who knew him came to visit over the next week or so, even Carolyn was able to wangle a compassionate forty-eight-hour leave.

'Wasn't easy.' She grinned as she sat at the foot of his bed. 'It's not that long since I had almost a week at home. But I played a blinder, said you'd been like another brother to me.'

'Talking of brothers, how's Tom doing?'

'He's fine,' Carolyn said guardedly.

'Still listening in, is he?'

Carolyn's eyes widened. 'You know about that?'

Peter grinned. 'Well, I do now. I haven't actually had to sign the Official Secrets Act because of what Beryl is doing, because, as a member of the armed forces, I'm already bound by it.'

Carolyn frowned. 'What is Beryl doing?'

'Oh heck. Didn't you know? Oh Lor'. Me an' my big mouth. Don't say a word to Beryl. She'll kill me.'

Carolyn chuckled. 'I very much doubt that, but no, don't tell me any more. Though, actually, I think I can probably guess.'

Later, in the kitchen, she caught up on all the local news from both Beryl and Phyllis.

'And how is Grandad – really?' she asked while Frank was out in the yard, talking to Harold.

'Doing very well,' Phyllis told her. 'He was very lucky. It was a good job Beryl was here and acted so quickly. Everyone says so. She probably saved his life, or at least saved him from suffering far more serious after-effects. As it is, he's recovering nicely. I noticed yesterday that he's begun to walk without a stick again.'

'I don't think it'll be long before Peter's up and about too. Thank goodness he didn't lose his leg.'

Beryl and Phyllis exchanged a glance.

'We think he might have a permanent limp though,' Beryl said.

'But he's determined to get back working on the farm eventually,' Phyllis added.

'Well, if I know my grandad, he won't push him. And I'm sure Peter will still be able to drive a tractor. Harold and Adam will see that he is given the jobs he can do.'

'Everyone's been so – so good,' Phyllis said with a crack in her voice.

'Well, I'd better be off,' Carolyn said, 'I've to go back tonight. This was just a flying visit on compassionate grounds and I probably won't get back for several weeks now.'

She hugged them both, surprised at herself for hugging Phyllis, but even she could see the change in the woman. Out in the yard she exchanged a few words with her grandfather and her uncle before bidding them a cheery farewell.

'Might be a while before I get back, so behave yourselves.'

As they said their goodbyes, Harold said, 'I'll come across after tea and take you to the station, lass.'

Carolyn smiled her thanks and, as she left the farm, she glanced up at the tree standing at the corner of the house and was sure she could see a thin aerial poking out the top of it. So, she was right, she thought. Beryl was still doing her bit. Good for her. But as she walked back home, her smile faded. She had not confided her worries in anyone. She had not had word from Steve since he had been posted abroad. It must be chaos out there, she tried to tell herself – the last thing they'll be able to think about is writing home – but it didn't stop her worrying. When she arrived back at the cottage, her mother did nothing to help lift her mood.

'Have you heard from Steve, Carolyn? We haven't, and Gordon doesn't seem to know anything either. Oh I do hope nothing has happened to him,' Lilian fretted. 'It'd be just too, too sad.'

She wouldn't let the subject drop all through tea and Carolyn was thankful to hear the farm truck draw up outside.

'So, lass,' Harold said as they trundled along the lane towards the town's station. 'How much longer do you reckon this lot's going to go on, then? The newspapers do seem more hopeful now.'

'I think the end of the war in Europe is in sight, Uncle, but not the one with Japan.'

'Aye, that's a nasty business. But the Americans are the main foe for them, aren't they?'

'In a way, but our lads are out there too. It won't be truly over until the Japs are defeated as well.'

'I'm just thankful Adam didn't have to go. He got a bit twitchy when he reached eighteen, thinking he ought to volunteer, but I must admit, I persuaded him not to. He wouldn't have been called up, of course, being in a reserved occupation.'

'I don't blame you, Uncle,' Carolyn said swiftly. 'I'm glad you did. We've got too many people we're fond of already involved.'

Once again, her thoughts turned to Steve.

Fifty-Five

Christmas 1944 came and went and although there was now real hope that the war would end in victory for the Allies, there were still many ups and downs along the way. It wasn't until March, when they crossed the Rhine in a massive operation and captured Cologne, that everyone began to believe that the end was really in sight.

But as the weeks went by, there was still no word from Steve.

And then, almost when they weren't expecting it, the war was over.

'I'm so sorry that I can't let all of you go out celebrating,' the commander told all the ATS girls under her charge on the day that victory in Europe was announced. 'We still have valuable work to do.'

Although they were disappointed, all the operators understood what a difficult position their superior officer was in.

'But,' she went on, 'what I can do is draw up a rota for you all to have some leave in turn over the next few weeks.' She smiled, more in hope than with confidence, 'Your supervisor has said that we can manage with a slightly reduced staff and I'm sure the celebrations in your homes will go on for some time.

No doubt, your families will put on something special for you. I'll do my best to give you advance notice of when each of you can go home so that you can let them know.'

'Any idea when we'll get demobbed, ma'am?' Noreen asked.

Miss Everatt smiled. 'Are you arranging a wedding, Hunter?'

'Not exactly, ma'am, but I have heard from my fiancé that he is coming back here as soon as he can.'

'Is that the American?'

Nothing, it appeared, escaped the commander's notice.

Noreen blushed, but said, 'Yes, ma'am. He's alive and well and coming back for me.'

'Then you have my congratulations.' She raised her voice and now addressed everyone in the room. 'For anyone who's arranging a wedding for when their other half gets home, let me know. I can try to arrange an earlier demob.'

It was towards the end of June by the time Carolyn's name came up on what had become known as the 'leave rota'.

'I'm sorry I can't make it longer than seventy-two hours,' the commander said apologetically, 'But I have to be as fair as I can and give everyone a chance to go home even if it's only for a comparatively short time.'

'That's fine,' Carolyn said. 'I'm on earlies the day before my leave starts, so if I could go home that night, it'd give me a bit longer.'

'Yes, I can approve that, Holmes. Have a good

time. By the way, I haven't asked you recently, how's Beryl?'

Carolyn smiled. 'In the pink. She's married now.'

Miss Everatt's eyebrows rose. 'Married? Really? To the father of her . . .' She fell silent as Carolyn shook her head quickly.

'No, no. Someone she's met where I live.' She chuckled. 'It was the young man who my mother and his mother were determined I should marry.'

For a moment, the officer looked unsure how to respond, but Carolyn put her at her ease swiftly. 'But we didn't want to marry each other. He's a dear friend – my oldest friend – but there was never any romance between us. It was our fond mothers trying to run our lives. At least the war helped to put a stop to that.'

'Well, there's a saying, isn't there? "It's an ill wind that blows nobody any good." But what about you, Holmes? Have you got a sweetheart?'

Now Carolyn's face clouded as she said hesitantly, 'There is someone I'm fond of, but he was sent abroad and I haven't heard from him since.'

'I'm sorry to hear that, but surely you would have heard if something had happened to him. His family would have let you know, wouldn't they?'

Carolyn shook her head. 'He hasn't any family left. He was brought up in an orphanage in Hull and then – and then . . .' Her voice faltered for a moment. She took a deep breath. 'His wife and mother-in-law were killed in an air raid in the city.' She said no more about the distressing circumstances of Sally's death, but she felt the commander was owed a little more explanation. 'It was early days after such a tragedy, but we'd become good friends and were taking it very slowly. But – but I did think he would have kept in touch.' She shrugged and added bravely, 'Oh well, time will tell, I suppose.'

Miss Everatt touched her arm and said gently, 'Go home and have a couple of days with your family. I'm sure that will help.'

Carolyn smiled weakly as she thanked her. Her superior couldn't know that Lilian would only add salt to the wound. She would undoubtedly talk non-stop about Steve and what might have happened to him. Still, Carolyn comforted herself, she had other family members she could visit who would take her mind off her worries.

Carolyn was walking back home from the farm. She didn't know whether to laugh or cry. She was thrilled to see Peter and Beryl so happy and her grandfather had recovered more than they could have hoped for and yet . . . She was heartbroken that she'd still heard nothing from Steve. Since he had gone away to war, there had not been a single letter and now that the war was finally over, she had expected to hear some-thing – anything. She hadn't been able to stop hoping that there would be a letter waiting for her when she arrived home. She realized now that she was in love with him, but she wasn't sure about his feelings for her. Although he'd said the words 'I'm falling in love with you', and even though he'd said it wasn't on the rebound, she couldn't help feeling it might be exactly that. To be hurt in such a way by the girl he'd loved since they'd both been little more than children must have affected him far more than perhaps even he realized. It was a wound that went far deeper than anything Michael had done to her. She sighed. If only she could hear something from him – or even about him.

Tom was no longer required to do his 'listening in', as he called it, so there were no more visits from Gordon or anyone else collecting his notes each evening – although, of course, his keenness as a radio ham was still as sharp as ever. He was now applying to go to university. Things were returning to normal steadily, though rationing was expected to go on for some while, possibly even years. The whole country would take some time to recover. She expected to be demobbed soon, but wasn't quite sure when that would be. Any girl getting married might be demobbed before the rest, as the commander had implied, but the authorities might want to keep a single girl like herself on for a while longer. And when that did happen, she had no idea what she wanted to do then. Settling back to life at home and working in the town would be very hard after all the excitement of doing such a worthwhile wartime job. But for now, Carolyn had a blissful three days at home.

It was dusk as she reached the lane and turned towards the cottage. In the distance she heard the sound of a motorbike coming closer and closer from the direction of the town. One of the soldiers from the Point, she guessed. There were still a few there, though not as many as there had been. The noise grew louder and she stepped onto the grass verge out of its way, but the machine drew to a halt beside her. The rider dismounted and took off his helmet.

'Steve!' Carolyn shrieked as she ran towards him, her arms outstretched. He caught her about the waist and picked her up, swinging her round as they both laughed aloud. When he set her on the ground, he bent and kissed her hard on the mouth. Then they stood back and looked at each other. With a semi-playful punch on the shoulder, she said, 'You never wrote. I've been worried sick about you.'

His face clouded. 'But I did write. Several times, but you never replied and I thought . . .'

'Oh Steve,' her voice broke. 'I never got them.'

They stared at each other, both realizing that in the chaos of the last weeks of the war his letters had got lost.

'So,' Steve said softly, 'when are you going to marry me?'

'Tomorrow,' she said promptly. 'Then I'll get demobbed quicker.'

They laughed, but then his expression sobered. 'Carolyn – darling Carolyn – I'm serious. Will you please marry me?'

'Of course I will.'

Their arms tightly around each other, he bent his head again to kiss her and that was how Lilian saw them when she opened the front door of the cottage to look for Carolyn. Smiling happily to herself, she closed it quietly and went to find Eddie to tell him the good news.

*

In the kitchen of the farmhouse, Beryl stood over the fire in the range, the little box she had kept hidden in the back of a drawer in her bedroom in her hand. She opened it and took out the doctor's letter and the bag containing the small amount of rice. She paused a moment and then threw them both into the flames. The rice spat for a moment and the letter curled and crumpled as it burned. Peter came into the room behind her, put his arms around her waist and nuzzled her neck.

'What's that you're burning?' he murmured.

'Nothing important,' she said as she turned to face him. She put her arms around his neck and lifted her face for his kiss. 'Just something I no longer need.'